WHERE IS MY HOME?

To Tim and Sheena
'Over the hills'.

With best wishes,
Martin Gillard.

December 2017.

Copyright © Martin Gillard 2017

First Edition
Published by Oswald Badger

ISBN number 978-1544706726

All rights reserved

Martin Gillard has asserted his right under the Copyright, Designs and Patents Act 1988 to be identified as the author of this work. This book is sold subject to the condition that it shall not, by way of trade or otherwise be resold, hired out, or circulated, in any other way without the author's prior consent.

Cover artwork by Eunice Gillard
Cover design by John Gillard

WHERE IS MY HOME?

MARTIN GILLARD

Oswald Badger

For Eunice

Where is my home, where is my home,
Water roars across the meadows,
Pinewoods rustle among crags,
The garden is glorious with spring blossom,
Paradise on earth it is to see.
And this is that beautiful land,
The Czech land, my home,
The Czech land, my home!

National Anthem of Czechoslovakia

Chapter One

October 22nd – 25th, 1938

It was the priest who broke the silence.

"Do you wish to confess your sins, my son?"

"I don't know, Father. I'm not sure what brought me here."

"Penitents are guided here by our Lord, my son. You must know that."

"I'm not a Catholic, Father. I have hardly ever set foot in a church."

"Have you been baptised?"

"My mother had me baptised just before my first birthday."

"Then you have a life in Christ, my son. In which church were you baptised?"

"The Church of Saint Wenceslas."

"Then you are doubtless a Lutheran. Did you know Lutheran pastors also take confession?"

"No, Father. I didn't know."

The priest turned his head and looked through the wooden grill which separated them. "I cannot grant you absolution, my son, but if you wish to talk, I can offer you the confidence of the confessional."

"Thankyou, Father, but I think I may have made a mistake coming here."

"Don't go, my son. Something clearly troubles you. You are staying with Monsieur Musil and his family at the château, aren't you?"

"Well no... not staying. I work for him. My wife and I have one of the houses in the grounds."

"Monsieur Musil is highly regarded in the village. He is a good man."

"I know."

"He has been a great benefactor to this church. He takes communion here, you know, whenever his affairs bring him to Castiran."

"I thought he... No, it's not my business."

"You thought Monsieur Musil was an Israelite, a descendant of Jacob."

"Yes, I did."

"Your employer converted to his wife's religion some years ago. I had the honour of conducting his first communion here. You and your wife are also very welcome here, Monsieur Kovařík."

"You know my name?"

"I knew a Czech couple had arrived with the Musil family. Your French is excellent, monsieur, but I had detected a slight accent. Besides, in a village like this I'm afraid everyone knows the other's business."

"I see."

"But the people of Languedoc are known for the welcome they afford strangers, monsieur, and for the refuge they offer the displaced. None more so than the Castiranais."

"I've noticed you have many Spanish people here."

"Refugees from Franco. They still come. Alone mostly. Fortunately we have plenty of work in the vineyards for them."

"I know. I work with some of them."

"Have you left family behind in Czechoslovakia, monsieur?"

"I wish I could say I had, Father."

"What do you mean by that, my son?"

Tomáš Kovařík stared down at the hat he had been turning over in his hands since he first sat down. At last he held it still in his lap.

"One month ago my grandfather was murdered by the Nazis. My grandmother died from the shock of it. This morning I learned that both my parents are gone too. That is what brought me to your church, Father. My grandmother used to love going to the church in Cheb." He smiled to himself. "'Prayers bring roses, Tomášek,' she used to say. My mother went less often. I think only when she was afraid something bad was about to happen to one of us. My father never went. I think he had seen so much evil in his life that he thought we had to fight it ourselves, and not rely on anyone or anything else. And that's how he died... a hero, trying to destroy the evil that had befallen his country."

Tomáš sat back. Through the wooden grill he glimpsed the priest's face in profile for the first time. He was older than Tomáš had expected. His face was heavily lined and what remained of his hair was white. He was looking up at the cross above the curtain of the confessional box.

"And now you feel you abandoned them, I suppose?" the priest said.

"More than that. I feel the manner of my father's death reproaches me. I feel I abandoned what he fought and died for."

"Was your father against you coming here to Castiran?"

"No, it was he who insisted on it."

"He thought you might be in danger if you stayed in Bohemia?"

"Yes."

"And clearly you honoured your father?"

"Very much."

"One day, God willing, you will have children, my son, and you will be a good father. Everything you ask them to do will be for their benefit, not yours. You find yourself in our village because it was your father's wish. Now he is gone you will have to make your own decisions, guided by his example. Do not let his death be a burden to you, my son. Take strength from his life. Let it help you."

"Yes, Father. Thankyou."

Tomáš stood up and drew back the curtain.

"Live happily, my son, and bring your wife to our church. You will both be welcome here."

Tomáš shielded his eyes as he stepped from the dark interior of the Church of Saint Julien into the bright October sun. He raised his cap in greeting to the workers finishing their lunch outside the Bar de la Poste in a shaded corner of the square. Soon they would be returning to the vineyards, an ocean of green at this time of year, which surrounded Castiran and every other village in this part of Languedoc.

He set off across the square and turned down the Rue Jean Jaurès towards the Château de Monteux. There he would rejoin the Musil picking crews. They had been out every day since early September gathering in the ripe fruit by hand. Only the late-ripening grapes now remained on the vines and, before the week was out, they too would be on their way to the winery to be crushed.

When Tomáš, Anna and the Musils first arrived from Prague a week before, Monsieur Musil had offered Tomáš the job of assistant manager in his bottling plant, but Tomáš had turned the offer down. He insisted he first had to learn every part of the work for himself, before he could manage others. And so for the last six days he had been sharing the men's back-breaking labour in the vineyards. When Anna received her father's letter that morning with the news of Tomáš' father's death and of his mother's suicide, she had gone to the château to explain to Monsieur Musil Tomáš' absence from work.

"Tell the dear boy to take as long as he needs," Viktor Musil told her. But Tomáš insisted he would return to work that afternoon.

He opened the side gate and followed the shaded path beside the driveway up to the château. Carts laden with grapes had worn deep tracks into the earth, and two men, one with a shovel, the other with a sack, were collecting the manure left by the horses. Tomáš reached the open courtyard in front of the château where the drivers of the carts held their horses steady in an orderly queue, as they shouted good-humoured exchanges to one another. Two carts at the front were being backed up towards open trap doors where the pyramids of grapes they carried were tipped into the cellars of the winery, guided by men with long-pronged forks. As an unlikely backdrop to all the noise and industry stood the elegant Château de Monteux, its light sandstone reflecting the afternoon sun.

He passed in front of the château and made his way towards a row of five houses which faced the winery and formed the other side of the courtyard. He approached the house nearest the château. Its outside walls were rendered and painted ochre like the rest. Each house had two openings on the ground floor. One was vaulted and large enough for the carts from the vineyards to pass through to be stored there. The other was much smaller and guarded by a weathered oak door, which opened onto a staircase leading up to the first floor and the house's living quarters.

Tomas climbed the stairs and opened the door to the main room. Anna turned and stood up as he entered, leaving the letter she was writing lying on the small desk by the window.

"Tomáš, my darling, how are you?" she said. She put her arms around him and kissed him. Tomáš held on to her.

"I'll be alright, Anna. As long as you're here, I know everything will be alright."

She kissed him again. "Don't worry, darling. I'll always be here." She went over to the desk and picked up the letter. "I was just replying to my father. Is there anything you want me to say from you?"

"Please thank him for all he did for my parents. Tell him I'm sorry I cannot return to make all the arrangements, and that I would like roses to mark where they rest. And tell him to stay safe for all our sakes."

"I've already told him that. I'll add the rest later."

"I must get back to work, my love."

"No, Tomáš. Stay here and lie down with me. I want to help make things better for you."

Tomas cupped her face in his hands and felt her press herself against him.

"I could stay for a while," he said.

He stroked Anna's back as she lay across him with her head on his chest. He looked down the length of her naked body. Her hair rested on her white shoulders. Her skin was perfect. She was perfect. The sounds from the winery seemed far off in the distance, but the scent from the grapes being crushed filled their bedroom, even with the window closed. He wondered how he could be so happy on a day which had brought such misery into his life. He had no answer. Perhaps one day he would understand.

"Pani Musilová came over whilst you were out, darling," said Anna drowsily. "She invited us to eat with them tonight. I think she wants to help somehow. I thought it might be too much for you, so I said tomorrow. Is that alright?"

"Yes, my love. Tomorrow will be better."

Tomáš was pleased when dinner at the château proved to be so informal. The Musil's German butler at their home in Bohemia had declined the invitation to follow his employer to France, insisting that all Germans now had a far greater duty to serve the new Reich. Dinner was served by the housekeeper, Madame Fournier, who lived in the château with her husband, Auguste, the Musils' chauffeur and gardener.

"I hope you find the French cuisine to your liking, pani Kovaříková," said Nataša Musil, as Madame Fournier placed a plate of cooked Bouzigues oysters on the table. "The oysters are prepared in garlic and parsley with a little Gruyère cheese grilled over the top."

"They smell delicious. I would love to try one."

"They are a speciality of the region," said Viktor Musil. "The best oysters in the world, in my opinion. Madame Lenoir, our cook from the village, does them especially for Milan whenever he comes here."

All eyes turned to Milan, who was seated at one end of the table, opposite his father, in a wheelchair designed to match the dining chairs. His left side, which remained permanently paralysed as a result of his injury in the Great War, was supported by a bank of cushions. He nodded and smiled, and lifted one of the oysters to his lips.

"Be careful not to burn yourself, Milan," said his mother.

He glared at her. "Do... not... fuss..., Máma."

"I'm sorry you all have to speak Czech because of me," said Anna. "Tomáš is teaching me French as fast as he can, but I don't find it an easy language."

"Try to use what you are able to, pani Kovaříková. The people here will appreciate it," said Viktor.

"They seem to understand the little I can say, but I never understand their replies."

"That's because they are speaking Occitan," laughed Viktor. "No wonder you're confused. It's the language of Languedoc. They're very proud of it."

"That explains why I've struggled so much then."

"Next time just say, *'parlez français, s'il vous plaît,'* and smile. They will want to help. They are wonderful people here."

"I must say, sir, all the people I've met have been very friendly," said Tomáš.

"I hope you will both come to love France and its people as much as we do," said Viktor. "I know some Czechs blame them for deserting us at Munich, but I happen to know that Premier Daladier was ready to stand up to Hitler if only…"

"Please, Viktor, not tonight, my love," said Nataša.

"I'm sorry. I wasn't thinking. I just want to reassure our young guests that France will always welcome them. It is a veritable *'terre d'asile'*. It always has been."

He turned to Anna. "A land of asylum, my dear. A place of refuge."

"Thankyou, pan Musil. I understood."

"I think France should prepare herself for a lot more refugees, pan Musil," said Tomáš, "surrounded as it is by Fascists in Germany and Italy, and in Spain too very soon."

"Let them come. They will be safe here. France has by far the most powerful army in Europe, and *la ligne Maginot*. There will always be a refuge here."

"The local priest said the same thing to me today," said Tomáš.

"You met *monsieur le curé*? Father Benoît? He is a very good man. Did he try to persuade you to come to his church?"

"Yes, he did."

"You should both go. It's a very good idea to join in the life of the village."

"I can't go," said Anna.

"Father Benoît is an exceptional man, my dear. He welcomes everyone to his church."

"But you must know, pan Musil, that I am Jewish. My brother is a rabbi."

"Yes, I do know, my dear, but that needn't make a difference."

"It does to me."

"If that is the way you feel, pani Kovaříková, then I can assure you no one would expect you to act against your beliefs. Least of all me."

There was a crash and Milan cursed. Nataša started to get up to clear the oysters he had spilled on to the table.

"I'll do it, pani Musilová," said Anna. She smiled at Milan and placed the oysters back on his plate. She dabbed the tablecloth with her napkin.

"May I?" she asked him. He looked back at her and nodded. She wiped his hand and the front of his jacket.

"Well, I'm blessed. I have never known Milan allow that before," said Nataša beaming at her. "It seems you have the magic touch, my dear."

"My father needed help sometimes. I always liked helping him."

"Yes, I remember your father. He came to our home in Karlovy Vary many years ago, soon after Milan came back from Russia. I met him only that once, but I liked him very much."

"Thankyou."

"I believe my parents were frequent visitors to your home in Karlovy Vary, pani Musilová," said Tomáš.

"Yes, they were. They both cared about Milan so much. And they were very dear to him. They were very dear to us all..."

"I... am... sorry..., Tomáš," said Milan. "Your mother... your father..." He reached out his hand and Anna held it.

"I know, Milan," said Tomáš. "Thankyou."

"We are all sorry, dear boy," said Viktor. "This is such a dreadful business. Anything we can do..."

"Thankyou, sir. You are all very kind. I know my parents were very grateful to you for bringing us here to France with you."

"And I know they loved going to visit you in Karlovy Vary, Milan," said Anna. "They were very proud of your success."

Milan smiled and squeezed her hand.

The housekeeper came in to clear the plates. She placed a large earthenware dish in the middle of the table.

"Ah, Madame Lenoir is making all my favourites for our young guests this evening," said Viktor. "Cassoulet. Thankyou, Madame Fournier. We shall serve ourselves."

Viktor ladled the cassoulet onto five plates and then sat down again at the head of the table.

"It's delicious, pan Musil," said Anna. "I think I might come to love France as much as you do."

"I am sure you will, my dear. I'm sure you will."

At the end of the meal Viktor asked Tomáš to remain with him at the table, while Anna and Nataša retired with Milan to the drawing room.

"There are a few things I need to discuss with pan Kovařík regarding work," he explained to his wife.

"Well, don't take too long," said Nataša. "I am sure pan Kovařík can do without such things at the moment."

The two men sat down at the table when the others had left the room. Viktor poured them both more wine.

"My wife is right. I shouldn't bother you with anything after your tragic news, but there is one matter that really cannot wait."

"I accept that work does not stop because of my problems, Monsieur Musil. Please tell me how I can help."

"The work can wait, dear boy. I am amazed how quickly you are learning. Amazed and impressed. I see a big role for you here in the future, if you want it. I am an old man. Milan cannot play the role I had planned for him. One day I will tell you all about my business interests, but not tonight. There is something else I need to discuss with you."

"Yes, monsieur."

"It concerns the status of you and your wife here in France."

"Our status?"

"Yes. You obviously would like a permit for you both to reside permanently here in France, but I am afraid you will not get one. Don't be alarmed, but you will both soon be issued with an expulsion notice."

"What?"

"Don't worry, it's not as serious as it sounds, and it doesn't just affect you. France has been inundated with refugees from Austria, Germany and Spain, and now from Czechoslovakia. So the authorities are issuing all foreign nationals with expulsion notices, which are suspended in exchange for temporary permits which have to be renewed each week."

"How do we do that?"

"You must present yourselves every Tuesday at the *Mairie* next to the church."

"Yes, I know where it is."

"Up to now Monsieur le Maire has allowed me to vouch for you and your wife, but from now on you have to get your temporary permits stamped in person each week. There won't be a problem, Tomáš. I can tell you, you have impressed people here in the very short time you have been in the village."

"May I ask if you and Madame Musilová have to do this, sir?"

"Officially, yes, but they exercise a little discretion in my case. My mother was French, you see, Tomáš, and my wife and I do all we can to integrate into the life of the village. And of course I provide a lot of employment here. We are able to arrange things a little differently for ourselves."

"I see."

"The important thing is that you and Anna do the same. She needs to learn French quickly."

"She will, monsieur. She is very enthusiastic."

"And it would be very helpful if she would agree to come to church. She needs to join in."

"I don't think she will do that, monsieur. Anna had a Jewish mother who died when Anna was very young. It has become very important to my wife to hold on to that legacy from her mother."

"Well, she can still hold on to it, of course. In private."

"But surely, monsieur, the French are known for their tolerance. They were the first country in Europe to give equal rights to the Jews. After the Revolution."

"Yes, of course the French are tolerant, but anti-Semitism exists everywhere in some form or other, Tomáš. And remember, we are the foreigners here. It is up to us to blend in and conform. It is only fair. Try to explain to your wife."

"I will try, Monsieur Musil. I will try."

Tomáš and Anna walked up the rue Jean Jaurès towards the mayor's office in the square. When Anna tried to hold Tomáš's hand he offered her his arm to link instead.

"What's the matter?" she asked him.

"Nothing, I just feel we shouldn't draw too much attention to ourselves, that's all."

"We're only walking together, Tomáš. That's no great scandal."

"I know, it's just that you don't see people in the village holding hands. Let's just do as they do."

"Oh, don't be so stuffy," she said, and she held her arms tight to her body as she walked, with her nose in the air and a serious look on her face.

Tomáš knew she was only teasing him, but for once in his life he wished Anna did not always look so pretty, and that she had not chosen the dress with the floral print which accentuated her figure so much. The cobbled streets narrowed as they reached the medieval heart of the village where the sun could not penetrate below the roofs of the small terraced dwellings. He felt relieved when they stepped out into the sunlight of the Place du Peyrou, and Anna was no longer so out of place amidst the greyness.

They crossed the square linking arms and entered the office of the mayor. A middle-aged woman stood up from behind a desk and greeted them at the counter.

"Bonjour, monsieur, 'dame. How can I help you?"

"We have come to register as foreign nationals, madame. My wife and I are from Czechoslovakia."

"You are Monsieur and Madame Kovařík? Monsieur Musil told the mayor you would be along this morning. Unfortunately Monsieur le Maire is out at the moment."

"Can we register without him being here?"

"Of course, but the mayor would like to meet you at some time. He will want to welcome you to Castiran."

"Thankyou. My wife and I would be delighted."

"We must fill in these forms for you and your wife, monsieur, and I will need to see your marriage and birth certificates."

Tomáš passed the certificates over the counter. Anna tried to follow what was being said, and nodded and smiled when she thought it was appropriate.

"But you will have to translate these documents for me, monsieur Kovařík."

"Of course, madame."

Tomáš translated the marriage certificate from the Czech and thanked the mayor's secretary for her congratulations on their recent wedding. He explained why their birth certificates were written in German, and why they both had an Austrian imperial crest stamped on them. He confirmed that, in spite of the crest, both his parents were Czechoslovaks, and they would not be joining him in France.

When it came to Anna's certificate he explained that, in spite of her father's German name, he was also a Czechoslovak, and that her mother's Polish maiden name did not mean that she had not been a Czechoslovak too. The mayor's secretary shook her head at the complexity of it all, looked over at Anna and smiled sympathetically. She continued filling in all the details on their registration forms.

"Your religion, monsieur?" she asked.

"Lutheran," replied Tomáš.

"And the religion of Madame Kovařík is also Lutheran?"

Tomáš looked at Anna to see if she had understood the question.

"*Non, madame,*" Anna said. "*Je suis Juive.*"

Chapter Two

March 15th, 1939

"Tomáš!"

The voice carried through the thin, cold air and made Tomáš glance over his shoulder. He saw a figure at the bottom of the slope, but could not make out who it was.

"Tomáš!" the figure called again.

"*Arrête-toi, arrête-toi,*" Tomáš commanded, and the small plough came to a halt between the vines, as the donkey obeyed. Tomáš turned, shaded his eyes against the low sun in the east, and peered down the slope. He still could not make out who was approaching. He stood and looked with satisfaction at the long, dark strips of newly aerated soil between the bare vines. It felt good to be working outside again after nearly two months in the winery, grafting vines onto rootstock and repairing machinery.

The figure had now stopped shouting and was saving his breath to climb the slope. Tomáš at last recognised the short, stocky frame of Marek Kral, whose blond hair was hidden beneath a French peasant's broad cap. Kral was a fellow refugee, who had fled his home when the Hungarians took southern Slovakia a month after Hitler took the Sudetenland. He was wearing only a woollen shirt and corduroy trousers against the cold March morning, but when he reached Tomáš sweat was running off his forehead. He rested, bent over with his hands on his knees.

"Tomáš," he panted. "It's just been announced... on the radio. The Nazis are in Prague."

Tomáš turned away from his friend. "Did we fight?" he asked.

"I don't think so... There are no reports."

"So we just let them walk over us again, did we?"

"I don't see you had any choice this time."

"There's always a choice, Marek."

Kral stood up, placed his hands on the small of his back and stretched.

"The time to fight was last October, Tomáš. After Munich."

"Do you think I don't know that?"

Tomáš held out the reins. "Take these for a minute, will you please, Marek?"

Tomáš walked a few paces down the slope. He stopped and looked out over the plain which stretched from the Montagnes Noires down to the sea to the south.

"There's something else you won't like, Tomáš," said Kral. "Slovakia has declared its independence from Czechoslovakia."

"My God." Tomáš stood motionless, saying nothing, then lowered his head. "All that struggle, all that suffering and sacrifice. For nothing. Our country just ceases to exist and we do nothing about it. It's beyond belief."

"I've told you before, Tomáš. Nation states only create nationalism and Fascism. It's internationalism we should all be striving for."

"Oh, for God's sake, Marek, don't give me any of your Communist rubbish now." Tomáš looked over his shoulder at Kral. "Don't you understand what our country stood for? No, of course you don't. That was part of our problem. Too many Slovaks who never really believed in Czechoslovakia."

"Now be careful with your opinions, Tomáš. I know you're angry, but you have no right to say that to me. It's that Fascist priest Tiso who's tied Slovakia to Hitler. You know I had to run for my life from those bastards."

Tomáš turned to face his friend.

"I realise that, Marek. But you know there were a lot like you who never believed in President Masaryk and Beneš and what they were trying to achieve."

"Beneš was a fool, Tomáš, and a clever man like you ought to see that. He chose the wrong allies and now we're all suffering because of it, Czechs and Slovaks alike."

"You mean he should have gone with the Russians?"

"Of course he should. They offered him help before Munich, and Beneš turned them down."

"But he had to, Marek. Without France and Britain with us we'd have Russian Communists in Prague and Bratislava now instead of Hitler. But of course, I suppose you'd like that."

"Of course I'd like it. There'll come a time, Tomáš, when you realise Communism is the only answer to these Fascist bastards, and to the likes of France and Britain who make deals with them."

Tomáš walked towards Kral and took the reins back from him. "You are a hypocrite, Marek. You stand here now as a refugee, safe in this beautiful country, and you criticise it."

"This beautiful country can kiss…"

"I can't argue with you any more, Marek. Not today. I'm grateful for you coming up here to tell me what's happened, but I've got to finish this and get back to Anna. Her father's in Prague. She'll be worried."

"That's why I came up here, you fool. To take over, so you could go to Anna."

"You'd do that for me?"

"Of course. I'll probably hear more sense coming from the donkey anyway."

"Thanks, Marek." said Tomáš, and he started down the slope.

"But I've heard you say it often enough yourself, Tomáš," Marek called after him.

"What?"

"If it weren't for the French and British we wouldn't be refugees. If they had stood their ground…"

"I know I say that," Tomáš shouted back, "and I know they betrayed us. But I still wouldn't wish Communism on them. They still have the best of what Czechoslovakia had for twenty years."

"What do you mean by that?"

"I mean freedom, Marek. Democracy."

Tomáš ignored the curses coming from the top of the slope and carried on walking back to the village.

When Tomáš arrived home, Anna was not there. He went out into the courtyard and saw Viktor Musil coming from the winery. As soon as he saw Tomáš, Viktor waved and hurried towards him.

"There you are, Tomáš. Have you heard the news?"

"Yes, monsieur. I've come down to see Anna. Kral is doing the ploughing."

"But Anna has taken Milan to Clermont L'Hérault to sell his paintings. It's Wednesday. Market day."

"Of course. I forgot. I'm not thinking."

"I understand, Tomáš. It's a terrible blow. A terrible blow."

"But surely, monsieur, we've all been expecting it."

"Even so, my boy. Even so. It still comes as a shock."

"My father predicted it would take three months for Hitler to find an excuse to take the rest of our country. He was wrong. It took five."

Viktor drove his fist into the palm of his left hand.

"President Hácha should never have tried to hang on to Slovakia. That was the mistake."

"Hitler would always have found some excuse or other, monsieur. It was always his plan. Poland will be next, and then who knows?"

"It's been on the radio, Tomáš. The British have guaranteed Poland. Daladier is expected to follow later today."

"But British guarantees won't stop Hitler, monsieur. Surely everyone realises that by now."

"He won't challenge the might of France again, Tomáš. He knows he will not get away with another Munich."

"Maybe you're right, monsieur. But anyway, it's too late for us. Our country is wiped off the map."

"They have a new name for it. It was on the radio. They are calling it the Reich Protectorate of Bohemia-Moravia."

"My God, it gets worse. But it doesn't really matter what they call it now, does it? The truth is, we let it go."

"That's a bit harsh, my boy. We were only ever a small country."

"We were a bit more than that, Monsieur Musil."

"Of course. I understand how it is for you, Tomáš, but remember it's different for me, being half French. I am as much at home here as I was in Czechoslovakia. Come inside, my boy. Let me get you a drink."

"No. Thankyou, Monsieur Musil. I'll wait here for Anna, if you don't mind. She'll be home for lunch soon."

"As you wish."

"Before you go, monsieur. What has happened to President Hácha and General Syrový?"

"The Germans have kept Hácha as President. Syrový has been dismissed. I got a call through to my office in Prague this morning. Apparently the people are out on the streets in the snow, jeering the German columns as they drive in. There's talk of a general strike. Not everyone is taking it lying down. But the main station is packed again apparently with people trying to get away. Jews and leftists mostly, I should think."

"So we can expect a lot more refugees here then?"

"I'm sure of it. Thank God for the might of France, I say."

"I thank God you gave my Anna a way out, monsieur. I'll always be grateful to you for that."

"Your father saved my boy's life in Russia, Tomáš. This is the least I can do."

The two men turned, as they heard the sound of the main gates whining on their hinges. A car appeared and drew up beside them. Tomáš saw Anna's smiling face looking out from the back seat.

"There you both are," said Viktor clasping his hands together.

Monsieur Fournier, in chauffeur's uniform, came around and took down a wheelchair from a space next to the driver's seat. With Tomáš's help he manoeuvred Milan into it from the back of the car.

"What are you doing here, Tomáš?" said Anna. "I wasn't expecting you down for another hour."

"I'll tell you in a minute, my love, once we're in our own place."

"It's just terrible, Tomáš, but I'm more worried about you than I am about my father. Vati has never really been political, and he's a war hero, so I don't see why the Nazis should do him any harm. And didn't he get a German passport just before we left?"

"Yes, I'm sure he did. The night he brought my mother home to Cheb."

"That's right. He told me in one of his letters. He had to get a Sudeten passport to re-enter the occupied zone."

"Your father will be alright then, darling. He'll just immerse himself in his work, as he always does."

"I just hope he'll still be able to write to me. Will they still let letters through?"

"I don't see why not. Germany and France aren't at war. Sometimes I wish they were."

"Don't say that, Tomáš."

Anna got up from the table and stood by the small window overlooking the courtyard.

"Why shouldn't I say it, Anna? A war with Germany is the only way we'll ever get our country back. We have to fight one day."

"I don't want you to fight, Tomáš. Ever."

Tomáš went over to her and put his arm around her shoulders.

"I don't understand you, Anna. What about last year back home when I was called up. You wanted me to go. You even said you wish you could come and fight with me."

"I know I did, but that was then."

"A couple of the Czechs here are going to Agde to join the Foreign Legion. There's talk of forming a Czech Legion again."

Tomáš went back to the table and slumped down onto a chair.

"What's the matter, Tomáš?"

Tomáš put his elbows on the table and held his head in his hands. "I can't go on watching my family and my country being destroyed, Anna. I have to do something. I have to fight back."

"You have to stay here with me, Tomáš."

Anna stood behind him and put her arms around his neck. "The most important thing now is that we stay here together."

"I want to, Anna, but I don't think I can."

"You have to, my love."

She kissed the top of his head.

"I left Milan with Monsieur Fournier this morning when I was in Clermont. I went to see Docteur Moreau. You have to stay, Tomáš. For the sake of our child."

Chapter Three

August 31st – September 1st, 1939

Tomáš closed his book and put his pen down on the table. Through the open window the noise of the cicadas in the linden trees grew louder as the evening heat warmed them.

"What are you doing in there?" he called out to Anna in the bedroom.

"Nothing."

Tomáš went to the bedroom door and saw Anna at the top of the step ladders.

"Anna, are you mad? Get down from there."

He closed the bedroom window and took the measuring stick from her hand.

"I can't believe you would be so silly. Taking a risk like that."

He placed his hands on her hips and gently coaxed her backwards down the steps.

"You could so easily have fallen."

She turned around and slowly raised her eyes to look at him. Her smile was more mischievous than apologetic.

"I'm sorry, Tomáš, but I just wanted to help with the blackout."

He placed his hand on her hard, swollen stomach and stroked it.

"You wouldn't be helping him if you fell."

He felt their baby kick.

"There, you see. Even little Luc is annoyed with his máma."

"I still think little Luc could be little Eva," said Anna, and she kissed Tomáš on the lips.

"Come and sit down in the other room, Anna. I'll make you some coffee."

Tomáš filled the coffee press and took the pan of water from the range which burned constantly in their living room. The range made their house unbearably stuffy in this hottest part of the year, and Tomáš could see how uncomfortable Anna was. He went to the scullery to prepare a cold compress for her. He primed the small pump which sat over their stone sink, and wrung out a towel in the water drawn up from the aquifer beneath the courtyard. He stood behind her and placed the towel on the back of her neck. She sighed with relief.

"It gets impossible in the evenings," she said. "And that material Madame

Musil has given us for the blackout is going to make it even worse."

"Why's that?"

"It's black velvet. It's so heavy. We shall have no fresh air coming into the house at all. Couldn't we just make do with the lights out and the shutters closed?"

"I don't think so, darling. You know it's the law. I told you I would fix it in the morning."

"But it's ridiculous to think the Germans will ever bomb a little place like this in the middle of nowhere."

"But lights here could guide them to somewhere important, Anna, like Toulouse or Bordeaux."

"Trust Madame Musil to give us something so expensive. I'd much rather make a dress out of it, or clothes for the baby."

"I'm sure you would." Tomáš shook the towel, refolded it and put it on Anna's forehead.

"I hope you understand, Anna, why I didn't want us to move into the château."

"It was nice of them to ask though."

"It was, but it would have made it very difficult in the village if we seemed favoured in any way."

"If you say so, Tomáš. It would be nice in this heat though."

"We have to fit in, Anna. It's very important. That's why I'm so proud of you for learning French so quickly."

"Milan and I use nothing else now. When he's out painting we go a whole day speaking only French. *Je parle très bien le français.*"

"I'm really pleased."

Anna picked up the book from the table and looked at his latest writing. "This one's about me," she said.

"A lot of them are about you. Can you understand it?"

"You read it for me, Tomáš."

Anna passed Tomáš the book and he read the poem as he stood behind her:

Mes lèvres touchent ton nom
Ils dansent, An-na
An-na, ces deux syllabes
Ma vie, ma joie

Le son aimé joue bien aisé
Simple sur ma langue

Anna, Anna
Mon âme écoute

"It sounds wonderful, but I'm afraid I don't understand every word."
"I have a translation."
"Read it to me," she said.

My lips touch your name
The syllables dance
An-na, An-na
My life, my joy

The sound I love plays happily,
At home upon my tongue
Anna, Anna
My soul is listening

"It's beautiful, darling. I'm so lucky."
"I only write the truth."
Anna smiled and rubbed her stomach. "When do you think you'll get your poems published?" she said.
"When we get home, I hope. When all this is over."
"A lot of people in the village don't seem to think there will be a war. They think Hitler's only bluffing."
"But we Czechs know he's not. We know what he really wants."
"I suppose so, but I find it difficult to imagine war from here. Back home we were right in the middle of it. But it's so peaceful here. It all seems so far away."
Tomas knelt down in front of her and took her hand.
"That's how I want you to feel, Anna. I want you and little Luc to feel safe."
"I know you'll keep us safe, Tomáš."
She stroked his head.
"I can do it if we stay here, Anna, and lie very low."
Anna slid down in the chair and covered her face with her hands.
"Is this low enough?" she said.
Tomas smiled and stood up.
"You are very silly, Anna Kovaříková."
"And you are very serious, Tomáš Kovařík."
"Maybe."

Tomáš brought the coffee press to the table and filled two cups.

"You were convinced Hitler was going into Poland five days ago and he didn't," said Anna.

"He will attack any day now, and I pray the Poles will fight and that the French and British keep their word this time."

"You still think war is the only way?"

"It's the only way to rid the world of Hitler and get him out of our country."

"It still seems wrong to wish for it, but in the end I know you're right."

"It's so frustrating, Anna. A year ago it would all have been so much easier. If France and Britain had kept their word, Russia would have backed us, and our army was much stronger than Poland's is now."

"I find it unbelievable that Russia has done a deal with Hitler over Poland."

"It's treacherous. My father never trusted Russia. I see why now."

Anna saw a familiar shadow pass over Tomáš's face. "Why don't you leave your coffee and go to the Poste for a drink with the others?" she said.

"I'm not leaving you here on your own. You're already restless enough."

"I'll be fine. You work so hard, Tomáš. I worry about you. Besides, I want to know what the men in the village are saying."

"I'll disturb you when I come in."

"It's so hot I won't sleep. I'll be awake anyway."

"If you're sure then, and you promise not to go near those ladders."

"I promise. You go."

Tomáš kissed her and took his cap from the peg. He stopped at the door and looked back at her. She was slouched down with her legs stretched out and feet apart. Her hair and face were damp with sweat and her whole body seemed weighed down by the bulk of their child. She gave him one of her smiles. He smiled back. He had never loved her more.

The air was no cooler outside. Tomáš fanned his face with his cap, but the evening was so sultry that even the gentle stroll along the rue Jean Jaurès caused his clothes to cling to his skin. Locals had assured him that after Assumption Day in mid August the air was always refreshed by thunderstorms, once the moisture collecting over the sea during the summer was driven inland towards the cool slopes of the Montagnes Noires. But no storm had come and the heat still sat unmoved on the plain between the mountains and the sea.

Monsieur Musil was delighted. It meant the harvest of 1939 had been treated to the most perfect conditions: a wet winter, a fine spring with only gentle rainfall, followed by a warm, dry summer and a very hot summer's end. It mattered less to the bulk of Castiran's vignerons, who cared about quantity rather than quality, and whose small family vineyards produced vin de table from the dark, sharp Carignan grape. Without Castiran's cooperative winery it is doubtful how much of the wine from their grapes would have found a market, but since it opened in 1936 the cooperative took all they produced, regardless of quality or damage caused by rain or hail.

Tomáš counted himself fortunate to have learned so much working for a conscientious producer like Viktor Musil. When the first picking crews went out in the next few days, he would have completed a full year's cycle in the vineyards and winery, and Monsieur Musil was clearly anxious to give him more responsibility. The Château de Monteux grew no Carignan vines, but produced instead its own *appellation* using Syrah and Grenache grapes of character. The only choice of vine the Château shared with other producers in the village was Clairette, but whereas most of theirs went to the cooperative, the de Monteux Clairette was turned into delicate, dry wine in its own winery, before being sent to the Monteux factory on the coast where it was made into the finest vermouth.

Tomáš turned into a narrow cobbled street leading up to the square. He stopped at one of Castiran's many drinking troughs, which were constantly replenished by springs, regardless of any lack of rain in the village. He cupped his hands and threw the water over his head and neck. He stood and dried his hands on his shirt and heard raised voices coming from the window at the back of the Bar de la Poste. For once the talk was not of the state of the vines and the possible earnings from the coming harvest, but of the possibility of war.

He climbed the steps which led to the bar over the village post office. The door and all the windows back and front were open, but the smell of smoke, sweat and alcohol, trapped by the sultry air, only became noticeable when he stepped inside. It seemed most of the men of the village had gathered there tonight. A few raised their hands in a gesture of recognition to him and others nodded.

"*Bonsoir, tout le monde,*" he replied.

"*Une grande pression, Thomas?*" asked Gaston Daguenet, the patron.

"*Oui, s'il vous plaît, Gaston.*"

Tomáš sat down at a table next to Marek Kral, who was the only other person in the room drinking beer rather than red wine, and the only person who did not pronounce Tomáš's name as if it were French.

"Bonsoir, Monsieur Kovařík. How is your wife?" said a voice to their right.

"Ah, Father Benoît. Forgive me. I did not see you there."

Tomáš stood up and went over to shake the priest's hand.

"Anna is very well, Father, thankyou. But she doesn't enjoy this heat in her condition."

"I expect not. I have been disappointed not to see Madame Kovařík in the church, monsieur. You have both been amongst us for nearly a year now. Does she have no wish to join us?"

"I'm afraid Anna is not one for the church, Father."

"That saddens me. Please convey to your wife how welcome she would be."

"I shall, Father." Tomáš turned to survey the room. "I'm surprised to see so many people here tonight," he said.

"It is men's excitement at the prospect of war. When their excitement turns to fear, I have no doubt they will flock to my church as readily as they now flock here."

"I'm sure you're right, Father. Will you permit me to buy you another Ricard?"

"You are very kind, monsieur, but thankyou. This will suffice. Please feel free to rejoin Monsieur Kral. I am very happy to sit here and observe."

"I shall then, Father. Good evening."

"I'm telling you all," said someone from the far end of the bar. "Hitler's bluffing. They'll be no war."

"He wouldn't dare. We've put six million men in the field in the past week. He'd have no chance."

"We don't even need the army to fight. With our navy and the British we could starve them out in weeks. Even an idiot like Hitler can work that out."

A low mumble of approval spread through the bar.

"I am not as certain as you all are," said Fabian Vega, a Spanish refugee. "These Fascists are brutal... determined. They love war. I know it, because I have seen how they are in my country."

"I don't see why we don't just give them what they want," ventured a man on a stool at the bar. "It's only what they lost at the end of the last lot. They've got the Rhineland already, then Austria and that Sudetenland. Why not let them have Danzig, if it's German anyway? I don't see how one town can be worth a war."

"Then what in God's name did we fight for last time?" shouted an older man who had long abandoned his game of cards. "If we just give it all back to those German *salauds*... excuse me, Father... it means all my mates died for damn all. Sorry, Father..."

"I don't see what it has to do with France anyway," said the man on the stool. "All the trouble seems to be between Hitler and the English. I can't see it has anything to do with us."

"You're a bloody fool, Roudier," someone called out, and those around him muttered their agreement. "You're a bloody defeatist."

An old man sitting on his own rapped his stick on the wooden floor and everyone fell silent. Tomáš had often seen him sitting in the square and had heard somewhere that he had once been the mayor of Castiran.

"This is not about Hitler or the Fascists," said the old man. He leaned forward with both hands resting on the top of his walking stick. "This is about our struggle with Germany which remains unresolved to this day. I fought them in 1870 when they took Paris. My sons fought at the Marne with some of you or your fathers in 1914 to keep them out of Paris. France is the land of liberty and decency and honour, and Germany is still the land of the Hun. If we do not fight them over Poland, we can no longer call ourselves a Great Power. I say, this is the third and last time. *Il faut en finir.*" *We must finish it.*

The men in the bar all banged their hands on the tables, rattling their tumblers of wine and sending at least one to the floor.

"Well said, Monsieur Tousselier."

"He's right. It's about honour."

"Someone speaking some sense at last."

"Well spoken, monsieur."

"Well, I think it's all bloody nonsense," said Arnaud Bousquet, an office worker from Clermont L'Hérault, who sat at a table on his own. "All this crap about…"

"Watch your language, Arnaud," interrupted the patron, nodding quickly in the direction of Father Benoît. The priest raised his hand and shook his head to show his willingness to let it pass.

"It's bloody ridiculous to want war with Hitler. What France needs is its own Hitler."

"Shut your mouth, man. You're talking shit."

"You're a damn Fascist yourself, Bousquet."

Bousquet stood up. "Some land of freedom this is," he shouted.

"Sit down, salaud."

Father Benoît rapped his glass on the table. The bar fell silent again. "Let Monsieur Bousquet speak. We may think we know what he will say, but he deserves his chance."

"Thankyou, Monsieur le Curé," said Bousquet, and he bowed his head towards the priest. "I only want to say again that France needs strong leadership. Look at the mess our politicians have made. Daladier doesn't even know what side of the bed to get out of in the morning. Parliament is full of Jews and Socialists who want to destroy France..."

"Here he goes."

"Sit down, Bousquet."

"No, I won't sit down and you won't shout me down. How can you close your eyes to what is happening to our country? We are overrun with refugees. There are a million foreign Jews in our country already. In twenty years they will have become twenty million. All these foreigners are taking our jobs and our houses. How much of the real France will be left?"

Apart from some shuffling of feet and a few low groans no one protested.

"France needs its own Hitler or Mussolini to put an end to it. To keep French blood pure from dirty Jews and Arabs."

The men seemed relieved that Bousquet had overstepped the mark and dissent could be shown again. "Sit down, you Fascist arsehole," someone shouted, and the abuse and laughter went on for some time before Gaston Daguenet restored calm.

"I won't stop any man expressing his opinion," he insisted, "but I won't have cursing in front of our priest. My father never allowed it, and neither will I."

"Monsieur Bousquet does not have it correct anyway," said Fabian Vega. "Spanish refugees do not take houses and jobs. Now the war in my country is over, all new refugees are being placed immediately in camps."

"Never!"

"Yes," insisted Vega. "One has been constructed in Agde. *Centres Recepteur* you call them."

"He's right," someone said. "I passed it the other day. I've heard conditions are pretty bad in there."

"Such things shame the name of France," said Father Benoît from his corner table. "No one needs to be locked away. There is enough work here for everyone."

"Only because so many of our young men have been called up, Father."

"Ask yourself then how many of you are homeless or out of work because of refugees in our village," asked the priest.

"That's only because Monsieur Musil employs more than he really needs."

"He can afford to," someone called out from a corner table.

"That is his business then," said Father Benoît. "I take the view that everyone is welcome in my house as long as they do not break the china. I suggest you all try to follow the church's example."

"Well said, Father," said Gaston Daguenet. "I think I'm going to start charging for broken china in here, the way you all treat my glasses."

Everyone laughed.

"Perhaps we should ask two of our own refugees what they think of how France treats them," said Father Benoît. He looked across at Tomáš and Marek.

"Not me, thankyou, Father," whispered Marek, who had remained unusually silent over the past week, since Russia had made her pact with Hitler.

"How about you, Monsieur Kovařík? How do you find it here?"

"I can only say that I was brought up to admire France and all that it stands for," said Tomáš. "And everyone I have met in this village has shown my wife and me only kindness and hospitality. I thank you all, even Monsieur Bousquet."

"I didn't mean you anyway, Thomas," said Bousquet. "It's nothing personal."

"I'm sure it's not. But there is something I would like to say about the threat of war that hangs over us all."

Tomáš stood up.

"Before coming here I lived amongst Germans in Bohemia all my life. Most are the same as people everywhere. They are decent and only want to be left in peace. But trust me when I tell you that these Nazis are different. They believe in the same thing the Hapsburgs once believed in. They see us Slavs as people inferior to themselves. They want what many Germans have wanted for hundreds of years. They want Slav land, and they want Slavs to be their underlings. That is what Hitler is really after."

He turned to the old man who had spoken earlier.

"With respect, Monsieur Tousselier, I believe you are mistaken when you say Hitler wants war with France. I do not think the Germans wanted war with France or the British in 1914 and neither do they now. They want war with the Czechs, the Serbs, the Poles, and most of all with the Russians. Stalin is a fool to think he can do deals with them. France has only one question to answer. When Hitler attacks Poland in the next few hours or days, will France do what it failed to do for my country? Will it fight for the freedom of Slavs?"

Tomáš sat down and remained oblivious to the uncomfortable silence that filled the bar.

Six hours later Hitler's troops crossed the border into Poland. Prime Minister Chamberlain and Premier Daladier delayed two days before they honoured their guarantees, and finally declared war on Germany.

Chapter Four

June 11th – June 18th, 1940

The transport plane circled the airfield before making its final approach. Major-General Spears looked up at the protective Hawker Hurricanes darting and swirling above it. He counted nine, nearly a full squadron. They circled in pairs at each point of the compass, while a single fighter shadowed the lumbering Flamingo as it came in to land.

The plane taxied to a halt next to his staff car. The steps were lowered and a short, stout figure in a pin-striped suit climbed down, holding a stick in one hand and a large cigar in the other. He strode towards Spears and raised his bowler hat as he passed him.

"Come with me, General, the others can catch us up," he barked above the noise of the plane's twin engines.

Spears climbed into the backseat of the Humber and took his place next to the newly-appointed Prime Minister.

"How long do we have before we arrive at the château?" asked Churchill.

"About ten minutes, sir. It's on the other side of the Loire."

"Time enough for you to brief me. Who's going to be there?"

"Premier Reynaud, of course, and General Weygand, but also Deputy Premier Maréchal Pétain and Admiral Darlan."

"Good. So all those who can make decisions?"

"Yes, sir, and in addition I'm led to believe the Minister of the Interior, Monsieur Mandel, will be present, and possibly de Gaulle, the new Under-Secretary of State for War."

"And in what mood do you suppose I shall find them?"

"A rather dire one, I'm afraid, Prime Minister. Having to leave Paris yesterday has left them demoralised, and the Italian declaration of war hasn't helped."

"I believe the day we become demoralised by the Italians is the day we should all retire to our rose gardens, General."

"Quite so, sir."

"You're not telling me they're all ready to give up the ghost?"

"No, sir. Premier Reynaud remains steadfast, and Mandel and de Gaulle are determined to fight on. Weygand and Pétain are the ones ready to pack it all in."

"And Admiral Darlan still sits on the fence?"

"As always, sir."

"You were close to Pétain in the last war, General. Can you understand how a man of such vim and vigour can become so defeatist?"

"It could be his age, sir. I think Reynaud made a mistake bringing in a man of eighty-four. He wanted a national hero..."

"And has recruited a liability?"

"Exactly so, sir. And Weygand is even worse."

"No stomach for a fight?"

"No idea how to fight, sir. If I may offer a frank opinion..."

"You may, General. We are engaged in a struggle to save the civilised world. No less. There is no room now for anything other than complete candour between us."

"Then I venture to say, sir, that Premier Reynaud may be a brave and tireless man, but his recent appointments of Pétain and Weygand are proving disastrous. Pétain, I believe, thinks it's 1916 again. He sees himself as the only man who can save France."

"As we all hope he can be."

"Yes, sir, but at Verdun he stiffened France's resolve to fight, now he talks of saving France by seeking an armistice."

"But he must know the battle for France is not yet lost."

"I'm afraid, sir, Pétain represents those who believe France's weakness and military disasters are the result of years of corrupt government. He sees himself as the only man able to lead the French out of their moral torpor."

"You make him sound like another Hitler or Mussolini, General."

"As we know, Prime Minister, Pétain is a far greater national hero than Hitler or Mussolini ever were."

"I can only hope, General, that your assessment of the Maréchal is overly pessimistic."

"I fear it is not, sir. I fear he might even see France's defeat as a lesson the country has to learn."

"And do you have the same doubts about Weygand?"

"General Weygand is Maréchal Pétain's puppet, and a man completely out of his depth with the present military situation."

"You paint a desperate picture, General."

The car turned onto a gravel drive.

"Are we there already?" asked Churchill.

"Yes, sir. Weygand's new headquarters. The Château du Muguet."

"Come along, General Spears. Let us not allow ourselves to be too downcast," said Churchill as the car doors were opened for them. "I believe there is still much that can be done."

The fourth meeting of the Anglo-French Supreme War Council was due to begin at three o'clock that afternoon. After lunch Edward Spears went for a stroll alone in the château grounds. He loved the Loire valley, the greenness of it and the great river which wound through it, where nature had been enhanced by some of man's most beautiful creations.

Spears loved all of France. He was born in Paris and grew up there. And, as one of the few high-ranking British officers able to speak fluent French, he met most of France's military and political leaders in the Great War, and still counted many as his friends. This made him the natural choice in the present crisis to be Churchill's personal representative to the French Premier, a role which had provided him with a front seat as the catastrophic events of the past month had unfolded.

He had watched first the panic and then the paralysis of the French High Command, as they realised the main German thrust was not coming through Belgium, where they had committed the best allied troops, but rather through the weakly defended Ardennes. He had witnessed the encirclement of the armies stranded in Belgium, and the desperate defence of Dunkirk, as beaten men were plucked to safety from the beaches. Then had come the second phase begun only in the past week: the German push south towards Paris, and the flight of the French government and High Command here to the Loire.

Spears lit a cigarette and turned to walk back to the château. It was an appropriate place, he thought, to act as Weygand and Reynaud's temporary home. It was a beautiful structure, showing all the best Italianate features popular in the reign of Louis XIII in the first half of the seventeenth century. Only it was a sham, a recently-built copy of the Palais du Luxembourg, constructed not for a strong French dynasty, but for a Parisian speculator whose descendants had been bankrupted in the economic collapse of the thirties.

Spears sat on Churchill's left. To his left sat General Sir John Dill, Chief of the Imperial General Staff. On the Prime Minister's right sat Anthony Eden, the Minister for War, and next to him General Hastings Ismay, Churchill's chief military adviser. Facing them across the table were Premier Reynaud, flanked by his deputy, Pétain, and the Chief of the French Army, General Maxime Weygand. Admiral Darlan sat to Weygand's right.

Georges Mandel and General Charles de Gaulle occupied seats slightly away from the table to the side.

No one was speaking, and Pétain and Weygand stared straight ahead showing no emotion. To Spears it resembled less a gathering of allies and more a reckoning between adversaries. Finally at three o'clock Reynaud cleared his throat as if calling for order.

"It is time to commence our discussions, gentlemen," he said. "I call on General Weygand to outline the current military position."

Weygand picked up a single sheet of paper from the table and read slowly from it, almost with indifference. His thin voice complemented his slight frame and small pinched features.

"Of the 103 allied divisions in the line at the start of the renewed German attack on 5th June," he began, "thirty-five have been lost in their entirety. Other divisions have been reduced to two battalions and a few guns. The existing line, such as it is, is being held by a light screen of weak and weary divisions."

He placed the single sheet on the table to signal he had no more to say.

"And your reserves, General?" asked Churchill.

"There are no reserves."

Churchill looked at Weygand over his black-rimmed spectacles.

"What we desperately need, Prime Minister," said Reynaud, grey-faced, "is more air cover from the RAF."

"I can send no more planes," said Churchill. "But tomorrow fresh British and Canadian troops will arrive in Brest, and they will deploy around Le Mans, as General Weygand has requested. I urge you all to take heart."

Reynaud turned to Weygand with a faint look of hope.

"It will not be enough," said Weygand. "We need more air support."

"General Weygand, one hundred bombers from our bases in Britain are attacking German lines of communication every day, targeting specific objectives given to us by you. In addition to this, you have seventy British fighters and fifty bombers operating from bases here in France."

"We need at least ten more fighter squadrons," said Weygand.

"General, if France were to fall, I am advised that a minimum of thirty-nine fighter squadrons will be needed to defend our island. We now have fewer than thirty. We cannot commit more."

"Then we must be allowed to seek a separate peace," said Pétain.

"But the Maréchal knows that our agreement of March 28th does not allow for France or Britain to act separately in this matter."

"Then we must be released from it."

Churchill looked at Pétain, but the old man continued to stare ahead, refusing to engage him.

"Maréchal, I do not believe the Hero of Verdun and the Saviour of France would surrender until all possibilities are exhausted. You overcame far greater odds in 1916."

"I do not propose surrender, Prime Minster Churchill. I propose an armistice."

"Maréchal, France still has enormous fighting strength. Your army is still in the field. Your navy stands untested, and the fighting power of your empire remains untapped. You have time to prepare. The Germans can be held for weeks outside Paris."

"We shall declare Paris an open city," said Pétain.

Churchill looked at Reynaud.

"It is true. We are all agreed," said the French Premier.

"Not all," said de Gaulle.

"No. It is right to record that General de Gaulle and Monsieur Mandel are in favour of defending Paris."

"And they are right," said Churchill. "A great city, stubbornly defended, can absorb immense attacking armies."

"To make Paris a city of ruins will not affect the issue," said Pétain.

"There are other strategies we have yet to consider, Deputy Premier," said de Gaulle. "We have not explored the possibility of turning the Breton peninsular into a redoubt, protected and supplied by our navy."

Pétain turned to de Gaulle. The old man's benign, grandfatherly appearance, which so reassured the French people, changed into a look of contempt as he glared at the young general. "One victory against German tanks does not make you a supreme strategist, de Gaulle," he said. De Gaulle glared back.

"Perhaps we should adjourn our discussions until the morning," suggested Reynaud.

"Before we do," said Churchill, "I have one word of warning to every man here. If we do not fight on, we shall be reduced to the status of slaves. There will be no such thing as an honourable peace with the Nazis. I repeat to you the words of your great countryman, Clemenceau, when the Germans threatened Paris in the summer of 1914. 'We shall fight outside Paris, inside Paris, behind Paris.' That, gentlemen, is the spirit we all need now."

The next morning the Council met again. Reynaud announced that orders had been given to declare Paris an open city. Pétain continued to argue that an armistice was inevitable, as Britain clearly intended to leave France to fight alone. Churchill continued to protest.

"No," he insisted. "You will never be left alone. The British will fight on, we must fight on, and that is why we must ask our friends to fight on with us."

In the afternoon Churchill returned to London. His intention, he said, was to contact President Roosevelt to urge him to give the French and British all the help he could. Within an hour of Churchill leaving the Château du Muguet, the French government and Army High Command left too. They fled further to the south-west, to the town of Tours.

Edward Spears followed them in his own car, accompanied by the British Ambassador. The 120-kilometre journey took seven hours. At first the roads were clogged by cars abandoned by fleeing citizens when their petrol ran out. A few kilometres further on lay the suitcases and personal items thrown down by their owners when they could no longer carry them. And finally came the people themselves, shuffling along, heading away from danger in the same direction as the leaders they no longer trusted to keep them safe.

The following day Churchill flew back to France to try once more to stiffen the French resolve.

"I have good news," he told them. "I spoke to President Roosevelt yesterday evening and he is dispatching 900 field guns, 80,000 machine guns and half a million rifles to France immediately. And furthermore he assures me that two hundred fighter planes will follow in eight weeks."

"Then he will openly declare his support for us?" asked Reynaud, in a tone more animated than Spears had heard for days.

"I regret not at this stage, Premier Reynaud," said Churchill. "All shipments will be sent via Canada."

"There you are, you see," said Pétain. "It is clear that neither you British nor the Americans will commit yourselves fully, and yet you expect total commitment from the French."

"My countrymen and yours are fighting side by side as we speak, Maréchal," said Churchill. "What they and the American President both need is a clear sign that France's military leaders believe in their cause."

He turned to Reynaud.

"Premier Reynaud, I urge you to allow no more talk of an armistice from your Deputy Premier, and to make a clear declaration that France will fight on. Reinvigorate your fighting men, reassure the American President, and give him a reason to declare his open support for your cause."

"I would like to, but the situation is very complicated."

"I understand that. But you could begin by instigating General de Gaulle's plan for a Breton Redoubt."

"It is too late. The roads are no longer open to us," said Reynaud.

"Then we should carry on the fight from North Africa, Monsieur Premier," said Georges Mandel, the Interior Minister.

"Oh, so now we have civilians who think they understand military strategy," mocked Pétain.

"It seems to me, Maréchal Pétain," growled Churchill, "that you regard all those with any fighting spirit as the real enemies of France."

Pétain looked at Churchill with cold, clear eyes. "Prime Minister," he said slowly, "an armistice guaranteeing the sovereignty and honour of France is not the worst fate that could befall my country."

"For my own country I would fear few things more."

"A far greater fear for those of us who truly love France is the thought of civil and military breakdown, and the risk of a Communist uprising in Paris."

"I hasten to reassure you, Prime Minister," stuttered Reynaud, "that this is not the official view of the French government."

"Hear, hear," said Mandel and de Gaulle.

"I find it disgraceful," countered Pétain, "that men who declare themselves patriots should support France's suffering in this way. Prime Minister Churchill. I demand that you release my country from its agreement and allow us to make a separate peace."

"The British government will not release you."

"Then we must act alone."

"If you do, Maréchal, whilst British forces fight alongside you, and British pilots struggle for your freedom in your skies, we shall blockade your country and bomb any of your ports already in enemy hands. And then we shall fight on alone."

"Gentlemen, gentlemen, please," pleaded Reynaud. Sweat was running down his face, which had drained of colour. He took a handkerchief and wiped his forehead. "France is not asking to be released from her agreement at this time, Prime Minister Churchill, but I regret it may have to do so very soon if the situation deteriorates any further."

"Then I have a suggestion, Premier Reynaud. You and I will together send a telegram to President Roosevelt. We shall make a direct appeal in the strongest terms for American participation in our cause. We shall ask him to throw the weight of American power on the scales in order to save France, the advance guard of democracy."

Churchill stood up and reached his hand across the table. "Are we agreed?" he said.

Reynaud rose wearily and took it. "I fear this may be our last chance, Prime Minister Churchill."

Later that day Churchill returned to London and the French government moved on again, this time to Bordeaux. Major-General Spears followed in Reynaud's footsteps, and refugees in their thousands moved south with them. Progress was again slow and, for the first time in all his years in France, Spears sensed hostility from those he passed at the sight of his British army uniform.

All the next day Reynaud and his cabinet waited in Bordeaux for a response from President Roosevelt. None came. Instead he heard the Germans had entered Paris and two million French citizens were fleeing the city. The following day, June 15th, news reached Reynaud that Verdun, the fortress town whose defence in 1916 had made Pétain a national hero, had also fallen.

Finally the answer from Roosevelt arrived. America would supply arms to France secretly, but could make no open declaration of support. Spears watched Reynaud descend into despair.

"I cannot hold out against Pétain and Weygand any longer," he told Spears. "If only Churchill could have remained here for a few more days."

"It was not possible, Premier."

"Then I fear Pétain has triumphed. You must ask your Prime Minister to release France from her agreement not to seek a separate peace."

An answer was promised from London the next day. When it arrived the French members of the Supreme War Council assembled to hear Spears give the British Government's reply. When Spears was called in and took his seat, it appeared to Reynaud that the Englishman was trying to suppress a smile.

"I am able to inform the French government," Spears said, "that its request to be released from the 28th March agreement is approved on one condition: that in order to ensure the French fleet does not fall into enemy hands, it should sail in its entirety to a British port before any armistice is sought."

Everyone looked to Admiral Darlan who shrugged his shoulders, unable on the spot to decide whether any personal advantage lay with his fleet in German or British hands. He was saved from a decision by Spears, who at last allowed the smile to spread across his face.

"I do, however, have a separate proposal from Prime Minister Churchill, which also has the approval of the British Government," he said. "I have here a document for your government to consider, Premier Reynaud."

He passed a folder across the table. Reynaud opened it, took out a sheet of paper and passed copies to his left and right.

"What is this 'Declaration of Union'?" he asked.

"It is the idea of Prime Minister Churchill. It proposes no less than the union of our two countries," said Spears. "France and Great Britain will no longer be two great nations, but one Franco-British Union. Every French citizen becomes a citizen of Great Britain, and every Briton becomes a citizen of France."

"And what is the point of such nonsense?" asked Pétain.

"It means, Maréchal, that even if Metropolitan France is occupied, the country is not defeated and need not surrender, because part of the country will still be free. The British part. The French part of Franco-Britain can wage war from North Africa and the rest of its empire around the world. Franco-Britain will have the greatest empire and strongest navy in the world. It cannot be beaten."

"This is wonderful news," said an exultant Reynaud. "It is an inspired idea. France will be saved."

De Gaulle and Mandel vigorously nodded their approval. Spears saw the anger in the faces of Pétain and Weygand.

"So France must now become a dominion of Great Britain?"

"No, Maréchal, an equal partner," said Reynaud.

"Is there to be no discussion about this?" asked Weygand.

"Of course, Général," said Reynaud. He stood up. "Please excuse us, Major-General Spears, while I call a full meeting of the Cabinet. And thankyou very much. We shall have an answer for you very soon, I hope."

The answer did not come soon. Spears waited for four hours before being summoned in again. The sight that greeted him caused his heart to sink. Reynaud was sitting at the side next to de Gaulle and Mandel. In his former place sat Maréchal Pétain. Spears was not invited to sit down.

"We shall not detain you long, Major-General," said Pétain. "Monsieur Reynaud has resigned. I have taken his place as Premier and will form a new government. This British proposal is rejected. Tomorrow we shall seek an armistice with Germany, with or without your government's agreement. From today politicians will no longer be permitted to meddle in military matters, and the honour of France can be saved. That is all. You are dismissed."

Spears turned and left the room. He offered no salute.

At noon the next day Pétain broadcast to the French people, informing them that negotiations for an armistice had begun. An hour later Spears drove with the British Ambassador to Bordeaux airport. Georges Mandel and General de Gaulle were allowed to accompany them to see them off.

"This is the saddest day of my life," Spears said to them. "I have known the Maréchal since I was his liaison officer before Verdun. I always counted him a friend. To hear him now and to see where he is leading France breaks my heart."

"Not all Frenchmen feel a part of this defeat, General Spears," said de Gaulle. "Many of us have spoken out for years against appeasement, just as your Prime Minister did. We too were ignored."

"The mistake was made nearly two years ago at Munich," said Georges Mandel. "Some of us pressed for an offensive war to stop Hitler then, but it was not popular. And can I tell you a terrible irony? The decisive point of this war has been the concentrated thrusts by German tanks. But how many people know where the Germans gained the idea for such tactics?"

"I know the answer to that only too well," said Spears. "From General de Gaulle's own book on tank warfare."

"Yes, and no one in our high command would listen to him. Instead they poured billions of francs into the Maginot Line."

"I'll share another irony with you, Monsieur Mandel," said de Gaulle. "A large proportion of the German armour we have been facing here in France was not German at all. It was plundered from the Czechs. The Germans have used French tactics and Škoda armour to defeat us."

"We're here," said the ambassador.

The four men climbed out of the car and stood next to Churchill's personal transport plane.

"You must board at the very last minute, General," Spears said to de Gaulle, "in case we have been followed. I'll shake your hand in farewell in case we are being watched."

"Are you sure you will not come with us, Monsieur Mandel? I'm afraid they will arrest you."

"Yes, General Spears, I am sure."

Spears and the ambassador climbed the steps of the plane.

"Come with us, Georges," said de Gaulle.

"No, Charles. I know you fear for me, because I am a Jew. But it is just because I am a Jew that I will not go. It would look as if I am afraid, as if I am running away."

"I'm sorry I have to leave you."

"Go, Charles. Carry on the fight from London. Give us hope. My fight will be here."

Chapter Five

August 6th, 1940

The tramontane had been blowing for four days. The cool, dry air came from the northwest above the Atlantic and gathered speed as it was funnelled between the Pyrenees and the Massif-Central over the plains of Languedoc. Here it was at its most destructive, as it powered its way towards the Golfe du Lion.

Anna enjoyed the relief it gave from the summer heat, but Tomáš shared the concern of all the village's vignerons that a strong tramontane could damage the vines at one of the most crucial times of the year. The grapes had stopped growing, and the time of coloration and ripening had begun. They needed the heat of the sun. Only hail was a more unwelcome visitor to the softening grapes than a strong, cooling wind.

Tomáš was anxious to get to the vineyards, but it was a Tuesday, and for nearly two years now his first priority on that day had been to call at the mairie to get the temporary residence permits renewed.

Even at seven thirty in the morning the whole village was up and about. The anxiety and despair of May and June had begun to lift over the past month, but people were still sombre, trying to come to terms with the armistice and their new circumstances. Most were placing their faith in their new leader, and hoping somehow the nation's disgrace was part of a greater plan, which would soon be revealed by their omniscient and omnipotent Maréchal.

All the Castiranais agreed how fortunate they were not to have to live under German occupation. The people of northern France and along the entire western seaboard down to the Pyrenees were now subject to occupation and German military law. But the Maréchal had managed to secure self-government and neutrality for the remaining two-fifths of France south of Bourges, including the whole of the Mediterranean coastline as far as Nice.

Pétain had chosen the small spa town of Vichy as his new capital. There in the town's casino the last parliament of the Third Republic met on the 10th July to vote itself out of existence. On the same day Pétain proclaimed himself the new leader of Vichy France with full powers vested in himself. He took the title '*Chef d'Etat*', and resolved to lead France on a crusade towards national recovery.

Most householders in Castiran proudly displayed a picture of the Maréchal in their front windows. Walking through the village to the mairie, Tomáš noticed one in particular seemed very popular: the Maréchal wearing his képi, symbol of the commander-in-chief, his white moustache and kindly face showing his fatherly concern, and his piercing blue eyes looking to the right into a brighter future.

In many houses the Maréchal shared a window with a photograph of a French serviceman. A few had a band of black ribbon over one corner in memory of a son, brother or husband, one of the 100,000 killed in the six weeks of fighting. The majority had no ribbon, and reminded fellow villagers of the nearly two million Frenchmen still held in German prisoner-of-war camps.

Tomáš reached the town hall in the Place du Peyrou. It was closed. He looked in the window at the small plaster busts of Pétain on sale. He allowed himself a smile and let out another sigh of relief.

To Tomáš the armistice had come as the answer to a prayer. His initial dismay and disbelief at the feebleness of the French army had turned to fear for Anna when the Germans crossed the Loire and the government fled to Bordeaux.

It was then he approached Viktor Musil to help arrange his family's escape. He did not tell Anna the real reason for his three trips to the coast. A crossing from Sète to North Africa for both men's families was finally secured at great cost, only for a reprieve to arrive when the terms of Pétain's armistice were broadcast. The French would remain in control in Languedoc, and the lives of the two families could continue as before.

Tomáš heard footsteps behind him and the sound of Madame Fauchery, the mayor's secretary, turning her key in the lock.

"You're always the first, aren't you, Monsieur Kovařík?" she said. "Come in."

In the anteroom to the mayor's office a larger version of the picture of Pétain hung on the back wall. Above it were the words which were to replace *Liberté, Egalité, Fraternité* under the new regime. *Travail, Famille, Patrie.*

"Here you are, monsieur," said Madame Fauchery, and she passed Tomáš's permit back across the counter. "And Madame Kovařík's. And here is the little one's."

"Merçi, madame."

"How is your little girl?"

"Our Eva is thriving. She's cutting her first teeth."

"How old is she now?"
"Nearly ten months."
"Oh, so you'll be having her baptised soon."
"Yes, I expect so."
"That's wonderful. Something to look forward to. It must be a great relief to you and your wife now the war is over."
"We're relieved the fighting never got this far south. But, of course, the hardship isn't over for everyone, Madame Fauchery."
"I know. Those poor people in the Occupied Zone. I feel so grateful to the Maréchal." She turned to Pétain's picture. "Thank the Lord," she said, and made the sign of the cross. "*La pauvre France*. But the Maréchal shares our suffering."
"Yes, we all have a lot to be grateful for here. Thankyou, madame. Give my regards to Monsieur Fauchery and Henri."
"I will, Monsieur Kovařík. *Au revoir*. Until next week."

Tomáš always felt happier when he left the mairie with his family's permits freshly stamped, their legal status in the village reconfirmed for another week. His hard work for six days of every week cemented his position with the other men in the village, but it was the stamp which he had come to value most.

He turned up his collar against the wind blowing into his back, and walked out of the village along the road to Paulhan. The last building before reaching the vast sea of vineyards beyond the village was the *Cave Coopérative*. Tomáš slowed down, expecting to exchange banter with some of the men there, but it seemed everyone was inside preparing machinery for the harvest. Above the cream limestone building he saw the personal flag of Maréchal Pétain flying in place of the tricolore of the old republic. The colours of the vertical stripes remained the same, but dominating the middle was the *francisque*, a double-headed axe once used in battle by the ancient Gauls. Tomáš continued down the road, the new standard of France flapping angrily in the wind behind him.

Ten minutes outside the village he reached the blue wooden posts which marked the vineyards belonging to the Château de Monteux. Here, as elsewhere on the plain, there were men bent double, clearing the ground of weeds in a constant battle to save the soil's precious nutrients for the vines. But there were far more of these stooped figures in the Musil vineyards. And only in the Musil vineyards were men to be seen swaying from side to side between the vines with large metal cylinders strapped to their backs. Castiran's smaller producers saw no gain in spraying expensive weed killer over the ground to nurture grapes which would only form part of an inferior, anonymous blend, while Victor spared no expense in maintaining the prestige of the de Monteux label.

A few of the Musil men had stopped work, and were standing around talking and smoking. As soon as they saw Tomáš, they put their cigarettes in their mouths and returned to the weeding. Tomáš was not a strict foreman, but he believed in giving Monsieur Musil value for the money he was laying out for all this labour, to far more men than he needed. Most of the refugees he employed had no experience in the work and not much enthusiasm for it, but all of them recognised that Monsieur Musil provided food and a roof over their heads, and wages enough for them to contribute to the life of the village.

Tomáš joined in the work for the next two hours, bent double and pausing only to direct teams to adjacent vineyards, as they all worked their way off the plain and up the south-facing slopes, where the vines flourished best. At ten o'clock he called a halt, and the men sat down in small groups on the leeward side of the vines to enjoy their second breakfast.

Marek Kral loosened the straps around his shoulders and waist, and lowered his metal cylinder to the ground. He sat down next to it and lit a cigarette. He never bothered bringing food out for himself. He had long become used to sharing whatever Anna had prepared for Tomáš.

"So what has your lovely wife put in there for us today?" he asked, as Tomáš approached.

Tomáš opened the canvas bag he had slung over his shoulder. "*Bramborak*. Your favourite."

Marek laid his cigarette on a flat stone and reached out his hands, palms upwards. Tomáš took one of the pancakes Anna had made from rough-grated potatoes and spicy sausage, and placed it on Marek's makeshift plate.

"She's a wonderful girl, your Anna. What else is in there?"

"Fruit dumplings."

"I love her," said Marek, filling his mouth with pancake. Tomáš passed him a bottle of beer. "If only she could find some Slovakian beer, she would be perfect. Even Czech would do."

"You know, I've never met anyone as ungrateful as you, Marek."

"I'm grateful, Tomáš. You know that." He examined the beer bottle. "But you must admit this French stuff is terrible."

"It's Belgian."

"You know what I mean. The French are bloody useless. They make a mess of everything they do. Beer, war, peace. You have to admit it."

"I'm just grateful to be here."

"Are you telling me you're not even a bit pleased to see the Germans doing to France what they did to Czechoslovakia?"

"I try not to be, Marek."

"But you were pleased when the British sank the French fleet a few weeks ago."

"I think the British did the right thing. It stopped the Germans getting their hands on it."

"So you've changed your mind about the English now, have you?"

"No, I haven't changed my mind. I'll always blame them for deserting my country. More than I blame the French. But at the moment I'll support anyone who fights Hitler."

"Oh, so after all you said about the English at Munich, you now support them?"

"Listen, Marek. You're a single man. You have no close family here or back in Slovakia. When you have a wife and a child to worry about, you start to see things a bit differently. All I want is for them to be safe here in this village. And I'll support anything that keeps the Germans away from them."

"So you're pleased about the armistice then?"

"I was relieved it stopped the Germans coming here. But only one thing would really please me, and that's to see Hitler and every other Nazi dead in the ground. Then I could take my family home. I know Pétain's armistice won't make that happen, but if it protects Anna and Eva from Hitler's thugs, then I'll settle for it."

"Tomáš, I think you have a lot to learn about Pétain and his National Revolution." Marek took a last draw on his cigarette before grinding the stub into the ground with his heel. "Has Anna put in one of those fruit dumplings for me?"

"She's put in two. I'm not sure one of them is for you, though."

Tomáš smiled and passed one to his friend. "Don't think for a minute I agree with Pétain abolishing the Republic, and with all this hero-worship nonsense, Marek, but the French here are in shock. They need something to believe in."

"The man's a damned dictator, for Christ's sake, Tomáš. I thought you were all for democracy? They've already put all the German and Austrian refugees into camps."

"But every country interns enemy nationals in wartime, Marek."

"The war was over here weeks ago. I'll tell you why they're keeping them locked up, shall I? Because most of them are Communists, and they're holding on to them as a little present for Hitler."

"You're paranoid, Marek. Unless it's Russia, you suspect anything any country does as anti-Communist."

"Why shouldn't I? Everyone is anti-Communist."

"Vichy France is neutral now, Marek, the same as your precious Russia. Of course I don't approve of the Vichy government, but like I say, as long as the Nazis aren't allowed here, that's good enough for me."

"You've changed, Tomáš."

"My principles haven't. My priorities have."

"You've given up the fight."

"You have no right to say that to me, Marek. I fight every day to keep my family safe."

"And in the meantime you'll put up with what's happening here?"

"Nothing is happening here. That's what I like about it."

"So you don't mind they've stopped all entry visas for foreigners? That refugees like you and me can't travel anywhere now without a permit?"

"Of course I mind, but I expect things will ease gradually."

"Ease? Ease? I knew you were naïve, Tomáš, but I think you've got your damned eyes shut. What about all the foreigners who had French citizenship before Vichy? They've all been stripped of it…"

"Not all. Pan Musil hasn't."

"Just because Musil and his money can get round it, doesn't mean most people can. The plain truth is, Tomáš, this new government doesn't like foreigners being here. The likes of you and me have to watch ourselves."

"For God's sake, don't you think I already watch what I do every damn day? The real truth is, Marek, that if we treat people right and show some gratitude, we'll be tolerated. Try it. You might even find some of the people here liking you."

"Bah. They like you because you sound French and could even be French. They like Musil for the same reason, and because he gives the village so much money."

"They like him because he's a good man."

"He's a capitalist reactionary."

"Who gives people work."

"And takes profit from their labour."

"People here respect him."

"Maybe, but you'll find his biggest problem with people here is the way he looks."

"What do you mean by that?"

"I mean he looks like a typical Jew."

"What difference does that make?"

"It makes no difference to me. Marx was Jewish, so was Lenin. We Communists aren't against Jews. But I'm damned sure Pétain is, and his National Revolution."

"You get anti-Semitism everywhere. It's no bigger problem here."

"Oh, no? Try talking to Musil about it. He's not stupid. He's got his front seat in the church. Always first there on a Sunday."

"You see the worst in everyone, don't you, Marek?"

"I'm a realist, Tomáš. That's all. The Germans are clearing out thousands of foreign Jews from the north and sending them here. How welcome do you think they're going to be? And how long do you think the likes of you and me and your family are going to be tolerated?"

Marek lit another cigarette. Tomáš packed the remains of Anna's meal into the canvas bag. A piece of the greaseproof paper she had wrapped around the food was plucked from his hand by the wind and swept down the slope. He watched the wind toying with it. For a moment he wondered if he could retrieve it, but another gust took it, and it was gone. He heard Marek talking.

"Come on. We can't have you slacking, *Monsieur Chef d'Équipe.*"

He felt Marek's hand on his shoulder.

"Come on, Tomáš. You've given us ten minutes over. Makes no difference to me but..."

"Yes, alright. Sorry, Marek." Tomáš stood up and brushed the crumbs from his clothes. "I was miles away."

Tomáš hurried home at lunchtime. He had hardly seen Anna and Eva before he left for work, and he wanted to spend a few minutes with Eva before she went for her midday sleep. He could be home in ten minutes if he ran, and he knew Anna would try to keep Eva awake for him.

Eva laid her head on his shoulder and he nuzzled her neck. "*Ma petite mignonne. T'es si belle,*" he whispered.

Tomáš never imagined he could love anyone as much as he loved Anna. But he found he had no choice. Whenever he saw or even thought of Eva, his love for her flooded out of him too. He could sit endlessly watching her absorbed in a new discovery, or simply kicking her legs and clapping her hands at the joy of her own existence.

"Don't get her over-excited, darling, she needs to have her sleep," said Anna. "You put her in her cot and I'll put out our lunch."

They ate the dill soup Anna had prepared. Her grandmother had taught her how to make it from soured milk, and it had always been one of Tomáš's favourites.

"Do you think Eva's first word will be in French or Czech, darling," Anna asked.

"It depends how long we stay here, I suppose."

"It won't matter if she ends up speaking both. It could be useful for her later."

"I see she's wearing more new clothes."

"Nataša keeps getting them from the *Galeries Lafayette* in Béziers. I tell her not to, but she gets so much pleasure from seeing Eva in them. She keeps saying it's years since she's been able to fuss over a baby."

"I wish she wouldn't."

"But Eva looks beautiful in them."

"I know she does."

"Well then, what's the matter with it?"

"People are having a hard time here, Anna. Lots of their menfolk are still prisoners of war. Families are grieving. Food and clothes are rationed. It's the wrong time to be spending money on fancy dresses for our daughter."

"I don't know what's the matter with you, Tomáš. You said yourself the worst is over. Why do you have to be so serious all the time?"

"I've told you before, Anna. We're foreigners here. Guests. We have to be sensitive to what people are going through."

"What about what we've been going through? Your parents and grandparents. My father in Prague and Otto in Palestine, who I may never see again. Doesn't that count?"

"Yes, darling, of course."

Tomáš put down his spoon and took Anna's hand.

"The soup's delicious, darling, but I can't eat much at the moment."

"I've done some pork with dumplings and cabbage."

"Do you mind if I have it later? I need to talk to you about things."

"What things?"

"The war, Anna. We don't know how long it will last. The Germans will probably invade Britain in the next month or two..."

"Is that what it is? You want to fight with the Czechs in England?"

"No. Well, yes, I suppose I would... No, I want to stay with you and Eva and keep you safe."

"We are safe now. You said so yourself. Even the Americans have recognised the Vichy government."

"I know they have, and I know Hitler has no say in Vichy, but even so

45

I think the situation could get quite strained here."

"It doesn't seem that strained to me."

"But it might not stay like that. Pressure on people is building, Anna. There are too many refugees entering the southern zone. Marek was saying the Germans are sending all the foreign Jews from the Occupied Zone down here. I read in the *Figaro* yesterday that another 22,000 will be arriving from Alsace soon."

"But what can we do about that?"

"We must become part of things here. People look for scapegoats when times are hard. Your father always said that. We mustn't stand out in any way."

Anna squeezed Tomáš's hand and smiled at him.

"Alright. I won't dress Eva up in such nice clothes, and I'll speak French to her when we're out. Will that make you take that serious look off your face?"

Anna stood up and cleared the soup bowls.

"Now, will you have some of this lovely pork?"

"Not now, Anna. Sit down, will you? Please."

"What's the matter now, Tomáš?" Anna pulled her chair back, sat down and sighed. "I thought we were over all this worrying in June."

"Anna, I think we should have Eva baptised."

"But you know I can't do that. I would have to attend church myself first."

"Then I think you should."

"But we've talked about this. I thought we were agreed. We let Eva choose herself whether she wishes to be Christian or Jewish."

"That's what I would like, Anna, but circumstances have changed. We must be pragmatic. Would it hurt you to go to church? It's not as if you ever go to the synagogue."

"I can't believe you would ask me such a thing. It's you who keeps telling me Vichy France has no anti-Jewish laws."

"It doesn't, but what if that changes? My father told me all my life that France was such a 'wonderful guarantee of our country's freedom'. But look how all that has changed. Our own country is under the Nazis, and now most of France is too. We can't take chances."

"I won't do it, Tomáš, and you have no right to ask me."

"No right? You expect me to keep you both safe, but you won't help me do it."

"I'd rather go to Palestine than deny my heritage."

"I've told you, Anna. It's too late for Palestine. The British quota for the next five years has already been filled."

"Then people here will just have to dislike me, if that's their choice."

"Why must you always be so stubborn, Anna?"

"I prefer to think I'm standing up for myself, instead of doing what people tell me to all the time."

"That's not fair."

"Yes, it is. You're always so worried about what people think of us. We could be living in the château now, if you weren't so anxious to keep in with everyone. I wouldn't have to carry Eva out here at night so you're not disturbed, because she's so hot she can't sleep. I wouldn't have to wrap her in damp towels to keep her cool for hours on end."

"I didn't know you did that."

"Well, I do."

"Do you really think, Anna, that I would ever put other people before you and Eva?"

"No, but I don't understand why you need to hide things about me. Do you know what I say when people ask me why we left Czechoslovakia?"

"No."

"I say, because the Nazis were coming and I'm Jewish."

"I wish you wouldn't say that."

"What do you say then?"

"I say we left because I'm a socialist."

"Why do you say that, when it's not true? Are you ashamed of me?"

"Anna, that's a stupid thing to say."

"Then what is it? Are you too cowardly to tell the truth?"

Tomáš gripped the edge of the table.

"Is that what you think of me, Anna? That I conform because I'm a coward?"

He looked at Anna and waited. When she did not answer or look back at him, he stood up, grabbed his coat, and left.

Through the door Anna could hear Tomáš telling Eva a bedtime story in French. Although Eva was too young to understand a story in any language, the sound of Tomáš's voice calmed her. Even when the story was finished and Eva was settled, Tomáš chose to stay in the bedroom with her. The table was laid and dinner was past its best, but Anna did not call him.

When Tomáš eventually appeared, Anna brought the food from the range to the table. She served it on to their plates and they both sat down to eat.

"It's the pork you didn't want at lunchtime. I couldn't waste it."

"It's good. Thankyou."

"Did Eva go off alright?"

"Yes. She was a bit restless, but you know how she loves being talked to. It did the trick."

"She's been restless all afternoon. She senses something's wrong."

"Bless her."

"We shouldn't argue, Tomáš. It's so pointless."

Tomáš put down his knife and fork. "I only need the answer to one question, Anna," he said.

"What's that?"

"Do you really think I'm a coward?"

Anna placed her hand on the table next to his.

"No, Tomáš. I know you're not. And I don't want you ever to have to act like one because of me. That's the point."

"I'd do anything to protect you and Eva. Anything."

"We know you would, my darling." Anna got up and put her arms around his neck. He turned in his chair, held her around her hips, and rested his head on her breasts.

"I love you, Anna."

"And I love you, darling."

"I did a lot of thinking whilst I was out working this afternoon. I try all the time to do what I think is best for you, but it's pointless if it means you're not living the life you want."

"I don't think either of us has been doing that for a long time, darling. We both know we really belong in Prague, not in this place. You should be teaching at the university and doing your writing, and I'd love to be working with Vati again in the theatre."

"And we could bring up Eva as a little Czech girl."

"I don't mind that so much." Anna sat down on Tomáš's lap and kissed his cheek.

"She will be happy as long as you and I are happy."

"I am happy, Anna. You are all I've ever wanted my whole life. And now we have Eva. I don't care where I am, as long as I'm with both of you."

He eased Anna up from his lap. "Which is why I made a decision this afternoon."

"What decision?"

"Let's eat our dinner and I'll tell you."

"What decision?"

"I think we should move into the château," he said, smiling at her. "As soon as possible."

"Oh, Tomáš, that's wonderful." She reached out her hand and held his. "What made you change your mind?"

"You've been through so much, Anna, and I never hear you complain. I just want your life to be easier."

"Thankyou, darling. It will be wonderful for Eva too. She'll have her own room, and can you imagine having proper running water again?"

"I just want you to be happy."

"I've made a decision too. I think we should leave this awful dry dinner."

"To be honest, Anna, I'm not that hungry."

"Good." She stood up and took Tomáš by the hand. "I have a much better idea. Let's go to bed."

They started to laugh at the same time. They had been trying so hard to make no noise for Eva's sake, and now both of them realised their lovemaking was mimicking the rhythm of the shutters squeaking and rattling in the wind outside the window.

"Don't laugh. You'll wake her up."

"Me? It's you."

They laughed silently and embraced. They looked at each other and kissed, and within moments they were lost again to anything beyond each other.

Anna flopped down onto her back and lay still. "I don't care where we live or what happens, as long as we always have that," she said.

"Come here," said Tomáš. Anna laid her head on his chest and felt his arm around her shoulders.

"That was wonderful, Tomáš. I love the way you make me feel."

He kissed her. "You're so beautiful, Anna. You've always been beautiful."

"How far back can you remember me?"

"I remember you in a high chair at our grandparents' chata. That was very early. You were wearing a white smock and your mouth was full of cake."

"It wasn't."

"Yes, honestly, it was."

"We must have been about two or three."

"I remember I loved you. Not like cousins. I actually remember the feeling of loving you. Even before I knew what it was. I've always felt that about you."

"I have about you too, darling." She kissed his chest. "Do you think it's possible to remember as far back as two?"

"I don't know. Three maybe."

"It's strange, because I know my mother died a few days before I was two, and yet I'm sure I remember her."

"It could be possible, I suppose."

"It can't have been my stepmother, because she didn't live with us until I was five. And the person I remember was very warm and loving. She was different from Mutti. It must have been my mother, but I often wonder how I could have a memory from such a young age."

"If it's what you remember, then you hold on to it."

"Mutti tried to be a good mother, but I never got that feeling of comfort and complete security I felt from my real mother. And when it was my father's wish for Otto and me to share her religion... and Otto embraced it so completely... I feel I can't deny any of them."

"I understand. I was wrong to ask you to."

"No, you weren't wrong, darling. You want what is best for us all. I know that. But I just can't do it."

"It's alright, my darling. I understand. I won't ask again."

"I love you, Tomáš."

"I know, Anna. And all the love you and I have from one another and from our parents will always stay with us. And it will always live on in our Eva."

"I'm tired now, darling. I think I want to sleep."

"Goodnight, darling Anna." Tomáš kissed her. "I'll close the window so the wind won't disturb you."

Chapter Six

August 31st, 1940

"So what's it like being a member of the upper classes?" asked Marek.

Tomáš stopped walking, spread his arms like a scarecrow and looked down at his filthy clothes. "Upper class. Me?" he laughed.

They carried on walking with the setting sun still hot on their backs. The vineyards all around them had emptied of men.

"You're a strange one, Tomáš. You live in luxury with the bosses, but you still insist on doing what the rest of us have to."

"You're disappointed I don't exploit the proletariat a bit more, are you, Marek? I'll have to try harder."

"No, not you, Tomáš." Marek slapped his friend on the back. "I just think it must be strange going home from this every night and having servants waiting on you."

"You know I don't have servants. The Musil's have a cook and Monsieur and Madame Fournier, that's all."

"They cook and clean for you too though, don't they?"

"Yes, we eat with the Musils but..."

"There you are then. Servants."

"You know why I moved in, Marek. Stop making such a big thing of it."

"I'm only saying, it must be strange for you. A tramp going home every night to a château."

"Say what you like, Marek. I know you're only goading me."

"I'm not goading. I'm just trying to work out which side you're on."

"You know which side I'm on. I'm on Eva's side. Tonight she'll have an electric fan to keep her cool, and in the morning a bath with hot water from a tap. And she and Anna will have good company all day."

"Good company?"

"You know how close Anna is to Milan."

"Musil's son?"

"Yes. He's got an exhibition in Clermont. You should see it."

"I have."

"Really? You surprise me. It's good. Don't you think?"

"Paintings of workers at their labour from the son of a millionaire don't appeal much to me, Tomáš. However skilful they may be."

"You can't judge Milan by what his father is. If you knew what he'd overcome to get this far..."

"They belong to the same class, Tomáš. You'll understand one day."

"I'll never understand why you..."

"Hold on, Tomáš. Isn't that your Anna?"

"What's she doing out here?"

Anna was waving at them. When Tomáš waved back she started to run along the road towards them.

"What's wrong?" he called out, as she came closer.

"Nothing's wrong, Tomáš."

When she reached him, she flung her arms around his neck.

"I've had a letter from Vati. It arrived this morning. He's alright. They've just allowed letters through... because of the armistice."

"Slow down, darling."

Anna refused to release him.

"He's alright, Tomáš. Vati's alright."

Tomáš looked over Anna's shoulder at Marek, and smiled.

"I'll get back to the village. I'll leave you two alone."

"No, Marek," said Anna. "I'm just happy, that's all. And I've been waiting all day to tell Tomáš, but you're both so late. Let's walk together."

They started down the road. Tomáš put his arm around Anna's shoulders, and she held him tightly around the waist.

"This is such a good day," she said.

"I'm really pleased for you, darling. It's the best news," said Tomáš, and he kissed the side of her head.

"Is your father still in Prague, Anna?" asked Marek.

"Yes, I've written back to him already. He'll be so thrilled about Eva."

"Didn't he know about her?"

"He knew I was expecting, but when the post stopped last September I was only seven months. He'll be so proud."

"What does he say about things in Prague?" asked Tomáš.

"Not much. I think letters must be censored, because it's all about personal things. His health is good. He still has some work in the theatre. He hasn't heard from Otto, though. Otto is my brother, Marek."

"And where is he?"

"In Palestine."

"He's a Zionist?"

"Yes, he is. He's a rabbi."

"Doesn't your father say anything about life in Prague, Anna?" Tomáš asked again.

"You can read it when we get home, darling. He says there was a film in all the cinemas last year showing Hitler sitting at Benes's desk in the castle. And people are still leaving apparently, but it's impossible to get to France now. People are going to Romania and Hungary instead."

"From the frying pan into the fire," said Marek. "Why didn't your father come here with you after Munich?"

"I wish he had. I miss him so much. But he didn't want to be a burden, and he had friends there and his work in the theatre… But it doesn't matter any more, now I know he's safe."

She pulled Tomáš towards her. "I'm so relieved, Tomáš."

They stopped at the top of the former rue Jean Jaurès, now renamed rue Philippe Henriot after a member of the Vichy government.

"Will you come and have dinner with us, Marek?" asked Anna. "Nataša always says we can invite guests. We could all celebrate together."

"Thankyou, Anna. It's very kind of you. But I don't think the Musils would find me very good company."

"Of course they would, once you've both got cleaned up and changed."

"Thankyou, but I like the Poste on a Saturday. Pan Musil gives us one day off a week, and I intend to start enjoying it right now with as much French beer as I can stomach."

"If you're sure."

"I'm sure, Anna. I'm very pleased about your good news. I'll see you on Monday, Tomáš."

"Until Monday, Marek."

Marek entered the Place du Peyrou. The light was fading. He hated these still, sultry nights when there was not a lungful of cool air to be had. He stopped at the fountain and let the cold spring water run over his head. He turned his face towards the flow and took several mouthfuls from one of the spouts. "Damn," he said, cursing his own impatience at not saving his thirst for Gaston Daguenet's beer, weak and inferior though it might be.

He made his way up the steps. The bar was full as usual on a Saturday night and the place smelled of cigarettes and sweat. Marek's arrival was greeted with indifference by most people, although a few groaned at the sight of the *refugié rouge* from somewhere in the east. Gaston Daguenet placed a large beer on the zinc counter. Marek gulped it down while Daguenet pulled another. Marek took the second and sat down next to Fabian Vega, a Spanish republican who shared his politics, and who was one of the few willing to share his company.

"I thought your mate Kovařík was coming tonight?" said Vega.

"He's busy."

"We never see him in here now."

"Tomáš is thinking of other things."

"He's too friendly with the bosses in my opinion. People are weak. They let the bourgeoisie suck them in too easily."

"Tomáš was always bourgeois, Fabian. But he is not weak. He has his own reasons for what he does. I worry more about those people over there."

Marek nodded towards a crowded table where Arnaud Bousquet, the office worker from Clermont, was holding court.

"A year ago he sat there alone without one friend in the world. Now look at him."

"They're all Fascist pigs," said Vega.

Bousquet noticed the two men looking at him and shouted over to them.

"So, what do you Reds think then? Should we round them all up and ship them off to Madagascar?"

"What crap are you talking now, Bousquet?"

"Oh, the Reds think our government's proposals are crap, lads."

"Get rid of the Yids *and* the Reds," shouted someone from behind Bousquet.

"Reds and Yids are the same thing, aren't they?" said someone at the bar, and the men at Bousquet's table laughed and rattled their tumblers of wine in approval.

"What rubbish are you speaking, you idiot?" demanded Marek.

"Haven't you read today's papers?" said Bousquet. "At last Vichy's got a plan to deal with all the Jews who come here polluting our country. They're sending them all to Madagascar. Every last one of them."

His men laughed and rattled their tumblers again. A few of the men playing cards and dominoes at the other tables joined in, without looking up from their games. Marek looked at Vega, who shrugged his shoulders in reply.

"You see, lads," said Bousquet, "our Communist refugees don't even know where or what Madagascar is." He stood up to address his audience. "And that's the problem we French have. Jews and Communists, often the same thing mark you, who have no interest in our country and no loyalty to it." He took a step towards Marek's table and leered at him. "Madagascar is an island off the coast of East Africa and is part of our

French Empire. And that is where all parasites who suck the lifeblood from France are going to end up."

"Well said, Arnaud."

"You tell 'em, Arnaud."

"About time."

Marek drank some beer and waited for the noise to die down.

"That is going to leave you with a big problem then, isn't it?" he said.

"And what would that be?"

"There are going to be no poor bastards left who France can blame for all the shit it lies in."

The men at Bousquet's table stood up and jeered at Marek.

"Sit down, all of you," ordered Gaston Daguenet. "If there's any trouble, I'll close the bar."

Knowing the patron to be a man of his word, the men sat down, mumbling insults. Madame Daguenet brought two more unlabelled bottles of red wine to their table. Each man filled his glass.

"May I ask you a question, Gaston?" said Bousquet, who had retaken his seat with the rest of them.

"If you must."

"How easy is it nowadays to get food for your customers and petrol for your van?"

"You know the answer to that, Arnaud. I'm rationed like the rest of you. And if I bought food on the black market, you'd all be too tight to pay the prices anyway."

"It's a good job the wine's still cheap then, eh?" Bousquet said, looking around him. He raised his glass and drank. Everyone followed him. "But I have often wondered, Gaston, why you never offer us any of Monsieur Musil's wine."

"You know well enough, Arnaud. You lot couldn't afford it."

"Why haven't you tried to negotiate a discount with him, so his fellow villagers could afford it?"

"Why should he do that? He can sell it easily enough as it is."

"And that just supports what I've been telling you all along, lads," said Bousquet. "Jews like Musil only care about money. Ask yourselves why he's never joined the coopérative?"

"Because he wants all the profits for himself," suggested Roudier at the bar.

"That's right, Paul, and because Jews have no loyalty as citizens. Musil never really lived here before, did he? But as soon as things got bad in his own country, he comes here and lives off us. Just like all the red Jews from the east and all the German Jews, who are no more than fifth columnists anyway. And I ask you all a simple question. How long are we Frenchmen going to put up with all these Jews coming here?"

"We're not."

"We should get rid of them, I say."

"You're right."

"No wonder we lost the war."

"I'll tell you all something," said a voice from behind Bousquet. "That girl who lives with Musil is a Jew. And she's German."

They all fell silent.

"Who is?"

"The one who's always with the cripple in the wheelchair."

"The girl with Musil's son?"

"Yes, her."

"That's Thomas Kovařík's wife. She's not Jewish."

"She is, I tell you. And her real name's not Kovařík. It's Neumann."

Marek looked hard at the young man who was speaking, and recognised Henri Fauchery, the son of the mayor's secretary.

"Kovařík's wife's too pretty to be Jewish."

"I'm telling you. She's a Yid. I've heard her speaking it. *'Oy. Oy veh.'*"

Marek stood up. "*Vy bastardi*, that is enough," he shouted through the laughter. "One more word from a man over there about Madame Kovařík and I hit his teeth out of his mouth."

The men at Bousquet's table got up as one and shouted back at him across the room. Then as one they looked towards the door and stopped. Marek looked behind him and saw Father Benoît standing in the doorway. Next to him, bent over his stick, was Monsieur Tousselier, the former mayor.

Father Benoît glared at Bousquet's men as Monsieur Tousselier slowly crossed the room and sat down at the small table which was always left vacant for him. Madame Daguenet brought Tousselier his glass of wine, then went over to Father Benoît's table by the door, and put his Ricard and a carafe of water gently down on the marble surface.

The priest stood at the end of the bar, his hands clasped in front of him, and looked down the length of the room. He was a slight figure with his wispy, white hair and black cassock, but all activity in the bar had stopped for him. There was complete silence, but he waited as if it were still not silent enough. He spoke softly.

"Monsieur Tousselier and I could hardly believe our ears when we came from mass a few moments ago. I cannot imagine what the ladies with us must have thought, listening to the insults coming from here, directed towards poor Monsieur Musil.

"Do I really need to remind anyone here that Monsieur Musil is a member of the Church of Rome? This most worthy of men recognised long ago that the Roman Catholic Church is the only path to salvation, and he is therefore forgiven for his people's crimes. I will not hear one more word said against him."

He waited for a contradiction which he knew would not come.

"If all of you here were as conscientious in your devotions as he, you would not need to be reminded of the Church's teachings on the subject of Jews. Yes, God did cancel His Covenants with the Jewish people, when Jesus came amongst them and they rejected Him. But the Church has kept its doors open to Jews for the past 2,000 years, and still keeps its doors open to them. Only those Jews who pass by shall be condemned. Now let that be an end to the matter."

Father Benoît made the sign of the cross, turned and sat down. No one moved, as Monsieur Tousselier brought his stick down hard on the wooden floor.

"I demand to know which man here said that France had lost the war."

He leaned forward with both hands resting on the silver top of his stick and waited, but no one spoke or risked catching his eye.

"Let me remind you all that France has not surrendered. Maréchal Pétain has confronted the Germans, and his prestige alone has brought their armies to a halt."

He paused to sip his wine. No one filled the silence. He put his glass down and looked to left and right.

"Am I the only one here who understands what the Maréchal is doing? Do none of you realise why he has chosen to raise his flag at Vichy in the Auvergne, where our forbears resisted Caesar? I'll tell you why. Because the Maréchal is only waiting for the right time to strike again at the Boches."

There was some tentative mumbling, and most men were relieved when Bousquet spoke up for them.

"There is not one Frenchman who does not agree with what you say about the Maréchal, Monsieur Tousselier. But the men here and throughout France are still struggling to understand our army's collapse."

"It was not the army's collapse, Monsieur Bousquet, which has led to our nation's agony," insisted Tousselier, "but the moral collapse of our people."

Bousquet nodded his understanding.

"And must I remind you this is not the first time our nation has suffered such a moral collapse? It happened also in 1870. Then it was the Jews alone who had sapped our nation's spirit. Too many with divided loyalties who put their needs above the needs of the nation. We all know that. But I must tell you, Monsieur Bousquet, that I fought alongside many brave Jews defending Paris, and I agree with Father Benoît. It is possible to find a worthy Jew, even if most still remain a dire threat to our national revival."

"Hear, hear, Monsieur Tousselier."

"But do not blind yourselves, my friends. Our nation stands in greater peril now than ever before, and it is not only the Jews who threaten us."

Tousselier turned slowly in his chair and looked towards Marek and Vega.

"With respect to the two gentlemen sitting over there, France has been too generous to the flotsam of Europe for too long. We Frenchmen are rightly proud of our country as a land of refuge, and as the birthplace of the rights of man, but our generosity has been shamefully abused, and we are paying a heavy price for it."

"Well said, Monsieur Tousselier."

"We now have too many foreign Communists and foreign Jews here who do not share our moral values, and these people, together with the French Jews, have once again undermined our national fabric."

"That's right."

"Republicanism and democracy have also made us weak. We now need strong leadership and a return to the old values of order, discipline and respect for authority."

Men stamped their feet and rattled their tumblers.

"And that is what the Maréchal is creating for us. A bastion of men of pure French descent who will lead France to greatness again."

"Hear, hear, monsieur."

"Have faith in the Maréchal, Castiranais," said Tousselier, and he banged his stick as hard as he could on the floor.

"Well spoken, Monsieur le Maire," shouted Bousquet, who took a step towards him and started to applaud. Within seconds every Frenchman in the bar was on their feet, applauding.

Someone started to sing the new anthem, which in recent weeks had become more popular than the Marseillaise.

"Maréchal, nous voilà,
devant Toi, le Sauveur de la France.."

Tousselier waved his appreciation as if the song were in his honour.

Bousquet went over to the old man and levered him to his feet, in order that he might join in. Tousselier tottered on his stick, while Bousquet sang with the rest of them at the top of his voice.

Marek and Vega sat watching, drinking their beer.

"There is something we say at home, Fabian," said Marek. '*Hněv je špatný rádce.* Anger gives bad advice.' I've had enough of this. I'm going home."

At the door the two men passed Father Benoît, who had also remained seated and was pouring water into his Ricard. He looked up and nodded formally to them as they left.

In the château Tomáš lay in bed with Anna in his arms. "It sounds like a good night at the Poste," he said, as the sound of the singing drifted over the village.

"Good," said Anna. "It means Marek will be having fun too."

Chapter Seven

October 4th, 1940

Viktor Musil was in shock. Tomáš found him in the orangery, staring out over the vineyards behind the château. Viktor looked over his shoulder when Tomáš entered, then turned away. He raised the folded newspaper he was holding in his right hand.

"Have you seen it?"

"Yes, monsieur, but I find it hard to believe. Do you think the Germans are behind it?"

"No, Tomáš. The Nazis have no jurisdiction here. This is all Vichy's work."

He turned and faced Tomáš.

"Has Anna seen it?"

"No, not yet. I wanted to speak to you first, monsieur."

"Does she qualify?"

"I don't think so. *Le Figaro* says you have to have three Jewish grandparents to qualify. Only her mother's parents were Jews. I'm sure her father's people were Catholics, from Linz. I know they weren't Jewish. Will it affect you, Monsieur Musil?"

"Oh, yes. I'm solid Jewish stock, I'm afraid. My father was a Czech Jew from Karlovy Vary."

He gazed once more out of the window.

"That's how he met my mother, Sophie. She was from the champagne house, de Monteux, as you probably realise. Good Jewish family. Not Orthodox, of course. She was taking a cure there. They married and stayed in Karlovy Vary. It was very fashionable then, you know. When my mother inherited, they decided my father could run the business from there. As I once did, of course."

He put his hand to his face and looked down, shaking his head.

"This is a dreadful affair. I don't know how far they intend to go with it."

"Will Milan be affected, monsieur?"

"No. He's in the same position as Anna, thank God. Only two Jewish grandparents. Nataša's people are Catholic. Family name is Schiffer. Good Austrian Czech stock."

"That must be a relief to you, monsieur."

Viktor walked over to Tomáš and put the newspaper down on a low wicker table.

"Indeed it is. Milan's been through enough, poor boy. At least he isn't burdened with this." He laughed weakly. "Not that the dear chap would care very much. He's tougher than any of us, I think."

"Why don't you sit down, Monsieur Musil?"

"Yes, I will shortly. Take a seat yourself, Tomáš. I'll ask Madame Fournier to bring us some coffee. I'll only be a minute."

Tomáš sat down and picked up the Vichy copy of Paris-Soir from the table. *'New Statute Addresses Jewish Problem'* said the headline. Half-way down the page was a list of the professions from which all Jews were now excluded - government, the armed forces, the law, education, the media, and the management of businesses. A separate law allowed for any foreign or stateless Jew to be interned. Tomáš started to read the editorial on the inside page. *'These measures to remove Jewish influence from the national economy and indeed from national life are seen by many to be long overdue...'*

"Our coffee will be along in a moment," said Viktor. He sat down opposite.

"This is unbelievable," said Tomáš. "Were you expecting any of this, monsieur?"

"Nothing of this magnitude, no. We all knew public opinion against immigration was getting a bit out of hand. But for the government to react like this..."

"Do you think it's Pétain?"

"No. I see the hand of Prime Minister Laval in all of this. And Alibert, the Justice Minister. They're the extremists. We should have suspected in June, when the only ministers arrested from Reynaud's government were the Jews. Blum, Mandel, Mendès-France and the rest."

"How will it affect us all here do you think, monsieur?"

"It won't affect anyone directly, except me."

Viktor shook his head and sighed. Tomáš studied him and remembered seeing his grandfather suddenly aged by events.

"That's the nonsense in all of this," said Viktor. "Vichy is treating Jews as a racial type, and they're not. Judaism is a religion one chooses to follow like any other. Anyone can be a Jew, in the same way anyone can be a Catholic. And I chose Catholicism long ago. I was baptised by our own Father Benoît in Saint Julien's in 1923."

"So, in terms of religion, the only real Jew amongst us is my Anna."

"Yes, but don't look so worried, my boy." Viktor held up his hand as if to halt Tomáš's anxiety. "Even if Anna were classified as Jewish, this isn't Germany or Poland or Russia. The French aren't anti-Semitic fanatics like they are. There's no history of pogroms here."

"This is all new to me, monsieur. At Charles University we only learned about France's literature and philosophers. My father told me about her political tradition, but what he described was nothing like this. He always held France up as the shining example of democracy and republicanism. Masaryk modelled our own country's constitution on it, for God's sake. My poor father would be horrified."

"Don't upset yourself, Tomáš. Every country has its share of anti-Semitism. Czechoslovakia had it."

"It did amongst the German population."

"And amongst some Czechs too, if we're honest."

"I can't accept that, monsieur."

The door opened and Madame Fournier came in with a tray, which she placed on the wicker table.

"Thankyou, Madame Fournier," said Viktor.

She turned and walked out without speaking. Tomáš poured the coffee.

"A lot of people misunderstand France, Tomáš. They fail to realise that democracy and republicanism have never been popular with everyone here."

"I see that now."

"The army, the church and civil service have always contained an élite who favour the monarchy. That's why an authoritarian figure like Pétain can be accepted so readily. And in times of crisis like this it's always easy to blame democracy and republicanism for France's failings."

"But why turn on the Jews?"

"Because they've always been great supporters of the Republic. It emancipated them, you see. And many Jews have succeeded in the law, education and business, all middle class professions which lead some into politics. After this year's disasters the élite are encouraging people to do what they always do, unite around their anti-Semitism. The Jews learn to deal with it."

"How do you deal with it?"

"My father taught me long ago. He told me never to be provoked and overreact. 'Soak up their hatred,' he used to say. 'Don't fuss. Show respect for the established order and don't give them more reason to hate you'."

"But this Statute nonsense goes beyond anything that's happened here before, doesn't it, monsieur?"

OCTOBER 4TH, 1940

"Its severity has come as a shock, I must say. I think the government is panicking because of the large number of new arrivals. People always reserve a special hatred for the wandering Jew, driven from one place and forced to seek refuge in another."

"Like my Anna."

"Remember, Tomáš, she's not regarded officially as a Jew. That's all that matters."

"So you don't think we need to consider leaving again?"

"I don't. But even if I did, where would we go? North Africa is subject to Vichy laws now, and there is nowhere else. Besides, we were facing the prospect of living under the Nazis four months ago. At least that danger is past."

"So we stay and do what, monsieur?"

"Keep our worries from our wives. It has been difficult for Nataša acclimatising to life in a small village, and she was very worried for Milan's sake back in June. It must have been the same for your Anna."

"She doesn't worry about anything except Eva having what she needs."

"That's natural enough. But I urge you again to persuade her to attend church and get your daughter baptised."

"Anna won't do it."

"Well, make her do it. You must."

"I have tried."

Viktor placed his coffee cup on the table.

"Do you know the only way I shall escape internment, Tomáš, if they decide I am a Czechoslovak rather than a Frenchman?"

"No, monsieur."

"Through the support of Father Benoît and through my friendship with the mayor here in Castiran. They will plead my case with the subprefect in Béziers, who also happens to be a frequent guest in my house. That's the way it works, Tomáš. Anna must join in with the people here. You're the head of the family. You tell your wife what she must do."

"I'll try again, monsieur."

"Do more than try, my boy. Make her listen to you."

Tomáš put down his cup and stood up.

"Please don't go yet, Tomáš. I need to ask you something."

"Of course."

Tomáš retook his seat.

"Six days ago the German authorities in the Occupied Zone decided to attribute my father's nationality to me rather than my mother's. They have confiscated our vineyards in the north and the family champagne house in Epernay. Aryanisation of business they call it, but it's just legalised theft."

"I'm very sorry, monsieur."

"It's the worst possible thing that could have happened. The de Monteux house was in my mother's family for over a hundred years. It was entrusted to me, and I have lost it."

He turned his head to the side, brought his hand to his mouth and cleared his throat.

"But there you are. Who could have foreseen all this?"

"None of us, monsieur."

"The thing is, Tomáš, Vichy may try to do the same thing here. If I am interned... at my age... Excuse me, Tomáš..."

Viktor got up and stood by the window with his back to Tomáš. "I apologise. This has obviously been more of a strain than I realised."

He turned and placed his hands on the back of a tall rattan chair.

"If I have to leave, Nataša and Milan will be left here alone. My French manager is not up to the job of running this place without my direction. You have learned everything so thoroughly and so quickly, Tomáš. I need you to help him. The business here will now provide my family's only income, so it must keep going."

"I'll do all I can, monsieur."

"And, Tomáš, one more thing. Please tell me, if I am forced to leave, that you will take care of Nataša and Milan, as if they were part of your own family."

"I already regard them as part of my family, Monsieur Musil. I give you my word, sir. I will look after them."

Chapter Eight

November 9th, 1940

"Anna, may I come in? It's Nataša."

"Yes, come in. I'm just getting Eva ready."

Eva was sitting on her parents' bed, holding up an arm ready for her mother to ease it through the sleeve of her dress.

"I knew that dress would suit her," said Nataša. "As soon as I saw it, I thought, 'that is perfect for Eva's birthday party'."

Anna sat down on the bed, put Eva on her knee, and looked up at Nataša.

"Pani Musilová," she gasped. "You look beautiful."

Nataša was wearing a sweeping, black silk cocktail dress with padded shoulders, which had just come into fashion before the war. Her greying hair was swept up with combs into neat curls on the back of her head.

"I know it is a little too much," she said, "but I always try to look my best when Viktor seems a little dispirited. And I have something here for you too, my dear."

"Nylons! My goodness. Where did you get those?"

"From the Galeries Lafayette some months ago. I bought several pairs, but I never dared wear them before. It seemed so frivolous. But the last few weeks have been so awful, I just thought..."

"They're wonderful. May I put them on?"

Anna put Eva down on the floor with her toys. She stood to the side, lifted her dress and unfastened her cotton lisle stockings.

"You are very lucky, my dear, to have such shapely legs," said Nataša. "Nature has certainly been very kind to you."

"Thankyou, pani Musilová. My father always told me I look like my mother. I have her to thank for any good fortune like that."

"What was she like, your mother? Did she have your colouring?"

"There's a picture of her over there on the dresser, when she was a maid of honour."

Nataša picked up the photograph in the silver frame. "Yes, I can see the likeness. She is beautiful. What a lovely scene under the cherry blossom. Who are the couple getting married?"

"My aunt and uncle. Tomáš's parents."

"Oh yes, I recognise them now. But I didn't know you and Tomáš were cousins."

"We're not related by blood. It's quite complicated. Auntie Karolina in the picture and my step-mother were sisters."

"So you and Tomáš have known one another a long time?"

"All our lives. We've hardly ever been apart."

Anna raised her dress to her knees and looked at herself in the cheval-glass. "Thankyou, pani Musilová. I'm so delighted with these. I've never had nylons."

"You are very welcome, my dear. We all need to raise our spirits at the moment. And I am sure Tomáš is going to like them."

Anna looked over her shoulder and smiled at her.

"Something tells me that young man needs cheering up. He works too hard," said Nataša.

"He does."

"Both our husbands take their responsibilities very seriously. We should be grateful for that."

"Oh, I am. I just wish Tomáš wouldn't worry about everything so much."

"Perhaps he feels he has to. I find men like to take a broader view of the world than we do, Anna."

"I think I take a broad view."

"I'm sure you do, my dear. But I find we women tend to make our children and our homes our first priority. Men have a greater need to feel in control of their place in the world. It must be very difficult for them in uncertain times like these."

"But Tomáš worries about things which may never happen. I keep telling him that whatever happens we'll get through it together."

Eva crawled over to her mother, chatting all the time to herself, and handed her one of the wooden animals Tomáš had made for her.

"Thankyou, darling. What a lovely horse for Mámi."

Eva found this very satisfying and went off to fetch another. The two women sat on the edge of the bed and watched her play.

"Tomáš is obviously concerned for you, my dear," said Nataša.

"Because of this new law?"

"I expect so."

"But in their eyes I'm not even Jewish."

"It must still be a worry for him."

"Well, I see no point in worrying about things that might never happen. When we had to leave Czechoslovakia we both thought it was the worst thing imaginable, but we coped. And now we have our Eva, it's turned into the best time of our lives."

"She would make anyone happy, bless her. I understand Tomáš wants to have her baptised."

"How do you know that?"

"Viktor told me. He and Tomáš have been talking about it."

"I had hoped Tomáš had dropped that subject. But since this Jewish Statute he's been keeping on about it again."

"They do a good baptism here. The whole village turns out. They have tables and wine and food in the village square."

"I'm sorry, pani Musilová, but I insist Eva will decide for herself which faith she chooses to adopt. When she is old enough. Her religion isn't a gift for the Castiranais or for Father Benoît. It's for her alone."

"Please forgive me, my dear. I understand how you feel." She patted Anna's hand. "I feel just as strongly over matters concerning Milan."

Eva reached out to give Nataša a wooden sheep, but then decided against it and kept it for herself, chuckling over her new power. The two women laughed and watched Eva studying every detail of her toy.

"Has Tomáš told you about Viktor's vineyards in the Occupied Zone?" said Nataša.

"No. I didn't even know you had vineyards in the Occupied Zone."

"Oh, yes. Champagne is where the main part of the business has always been."

"What's happened?"

"The Germans have confiscated them. I'm surprised Tomáš hasn't told you about it. He's known for nearly three weeks."

Anna stood up from the bed. "This is so like him. My father was the same, always keeping unpleasant things from me. Why don't they understand I don't need protecting like this?"

"They've probably never wanted to burden you, my dear. Because they love you so much."

"But I always told Vati, and I say the same to Tomáš, I need to know. I just have to be allowed to have my own opinion'."

"My dear, I have been trying for years to make Viktor understand that."

"So why has it happened? Is it something to do with the new law?"

"Yes. The Germans say Viktor is a Jew and not allowed to own property or run a business, so everything in the north has gone. That's the reason he hasn't quite been himself over the past weeks. It's not even about the money. He feels he has betrayed the faith his parents placed in him. That's hurting him more than anything."

"Oh, poor pan Musil. I do understand how he feels."

"And now it seems Vichy may take control of his holdings here."

"Do they have the right?"

"I'm afraid so. The new Statute says Jewish businesses here have to be run by non-Jewish administrators. Viktor had to appear before a special commission last week. He tries to keep it from me, but I have my ways of finding out. Denaturalisation they call it. I believe they may have already taken away his French citizenship."

"Oh, pani Musilová, I'm so sorry..." Anna sat down and took Nataša's hand.

"No, Anna, We shall be alright. Viktor is a very resourceful man. He will find a way around it. That is when he will tell me about it. When he has found a solution."

"You're both very brave."

"No. This is not brave. Seeing my Milan after he came back from the last war was the time I was brave. These stupid laws and rules are nothing compared to that."

Nataša squeezed Anna's hand and stood up.

"And that is why I have put on my best dress and my pearls for our Eva's first birthday party. To celebrate the things that really matter."

She went over to Eva and picked her up.

"My, what a big girl you are now. Auntie Nataša can hardly lift you. Go to your máma."

Anna took Eva and kissed her.

"When I look at you and Eva, my dear," said Nataša, "I wish I had not left Milan with a nanny at this age. I wish I had shared this time with him."

"You have him now. He's a wonderful man."

"Thankyou, my dear. You are very thoughtful. I cannot wait for you all to see the present he has for Eva."

"Really? That's very kind of him. It's wonderful that Eva is surrounded by people who love her so much."

"We are all grateful to you and Tomáš for bringing her into our lives, my dear."

"Tomáš wrote a little poem for her birthday. Would you like to read it? There's a copy over there on the dresser."

"I would love to." Nataša fetched the single sheet of paper. She stood by the bed as she read it.

For Eva

Sit on your horse, I'll rock you
Turn the page, I'll read to you
Come to me, I'll comfort you
Your Papa will be there

Hand me the spoon, I'll feed you
Point the way, I'll carry you
Take my hand, I'll walk you
Together we'll know where

"It's lovely, Anna." Nataša went over to Eva and kissed her. "You are such a lucky girl." She placed her hand on Anna's arm. "I shall see you both downstairs, my dear, when Tomáš comes home."

Dinner was brought forward to six o'clock to allow Eva to eat with the adults in the dining room. Only Viktor and Milan took their usual positions at either end of the polished walnut table. Everyone else moved, in order that Eva could sit on Milan's right in her high chair to be fed by him, an arrangement which made both of them happy. Anna sat on Milan's left opposite Eva, and Tomáš sat next to his daughter to retrieve the spoon she liked to drop onto the floor during mealtimes. Having given up her usual place next to Milan, Nataša sat with her husband at the far end of the table. She insisted no covering need be laid to protect the rare Turkish carpet. She had, she said, learned long ago not to worry about such things.

Eva had two spoons. One she insisted on having to feed herself, and a second used by Milan to ensure that some of the food found its way into her mouth. Anna had suggested Eva should have the same dinner as the adults, and Nataša had sent Monsieur Fournier to collect a black-market chicken from a smallholder Viktor knew in Pézenas.

Eva was always fascinated by Milan whenever he fed her. Not once did she bar the food from her mouth, something she often did with anyone else, including her father. They talked and smiled to one another, Eva studying Milan as he brought food to his own mouth, and then opening her mouth as soon as she saw him loading her spoon.

"You ladies will both go hungry if you keep watching them, instead of eating what's on your own plate," said Viktor.

"It's the same when we're out and I sit Eva on Milan's lap," said Anna.

"She doesn't wriggle or complain. She sits absolutely still for him. You have a magic touch with her, Milan."

Milan smiled. Nataša only picked at her food. She seemed unable to look away from Milan and Eva, and Tomáš saw her more than once dab her eye with her napkin, when she thought Viktor would not notice.

The cake was brought in by Madame Fournier who, to everyone's surprise and pleasure, joined in the singing of *'Bon Anniversaire'*. Eva was fascinated by the candle burning just out of her reach, and a little bemused by the unusual behaviour of the adults. When the singing was over, everyone applauded, and she clapped her hands too and beamed at everyone, showing off her four teeth.

"Presents," said Milan, and everyone made their way into the drawing room, where several packages were laid out on the floor in front of the fire.

It took Eva some time to realise that far from being stopped from touching these brightly coloured objects, she was instead being encouraged to rip the paper and do almost anything she wanted with them. Books, a rocking horse, a large ring to hold with a bell on it, which no one prevented her from putting into her mouth, and a single sheet of paper. And then finally a large object standing against the wall, covered in paper which she was only allowed to remove very carefully with Máma's help. And when the paper did come off, it seemed to make Máma very happy.

"Oh, my goodness," said Anna, "it's beautiful, Milan."

Milan's painting of Eva showed her reaching out to give something to someone standing next to the viewer. Her whole face smiled at the person receiving whatever she held in her left hand beyond the picture frame. And every feature, the uncombed hair, the emerging teeth, and the child's chin, almost submerged by baby neck and cheeks, were all described by the finest touches of oil paint.

Since his return from Russia the brutality and pessimism of Milan's painting had decreased very gradually. Only in the last two years had it diminished to a background mood in his painting, rather than the dominant theme. The village square, the people, the men and machinery in the vineyards, had all been painted in less violent colours, with more harmony, and even at times with humour. But the painting of Eva was altogether different. It showed the delight the little girl felt at the people and the world around her, and it showed the artist understood her and felt it too.

The impact of the painting on the adults was apparent immediately. They stared at it and said nothing. Viktor went over to Milan.

"It's magnificent, my boy," he said, and shook his hand.

"It's beautiful, Milan," said Anna, and she went to him and embraced him. Tomáš also went over and shook his hand. "Thankyou, Milan. I know Eva will always treasure it."

Nataša did not speak. She kissed her son, and pulled up a chair and sat next to him. Amidst all the distraction Eva crawled to the picture and banged the ivory teething ring she was holding against the frame.

"No!" shouted Anna and Tomáš together, and Eva was so taken aback she started to cry. Tomáš picked her up and soothed her.

"I think it's time for her bed," said Anna. "I'll take her."

Everyone wished Eva a final 'happy birthday' and waved her goodnight. Over her mother's shoulder Eva waved only at Milan. He smiled broadly and waved back.

Madame Fournier entered the room. "Monsieur Musil, one of the workmen is here to see you. It's one of the Spaniards. I think his name's Molina."

"What does Monsieur Molina want?"

"He won't say. He'll only speak to you."

"Alright, I'll come out and see him."

When Viktor returned ten minutes later, he looked drawn.

"Is there a problem, monsieur?" asked Tomáš.

"You know Marek Kral, don't you?"

"Yes, he's a good friend."

"Well, he's been arrested. Together with Fabian Vega."

"Why? What have they done?"

"They haven't done anything, according to Molina. They reported to the mairie tonight to renew their weekly permits and two gendarmes were there from Clermont. They just took them away."

"For no reason?"

"I cannot think of one. They're not Jewish."

"No, monsieur, but I think I know why. Vichy is arresting the Communists."

Chapter Nine

November 18th, 1940

"What time are you expecting him, Monsieur Musil?"
"Ten minutes ago. He's late."
"But he's only coming from Clermont."
"I think they're trying to tell me how little I matter to them, Tomáš."
"Do you know who it will be?"
"I know exactly who it will be. Here's the letter. Look."
"Bousquet? Not Arnaud Bousquet?"
"Yes. Do you know him?"
"Only from the Poste. He's often in there spouting off."
"About foreigners, Yids, and Reds, I suppose."
"Usually. He is not a very likeable man."
"Well, he's going to decide the future of my business, whether I like him or not."
"How can they let a man like that work in a government department? The world has gone mad."
"If he hates foreigners, Jews and Communists, Tomáš, I imagine they regard him as ideally suited."

Viktor shifted from one foot to the other. He looked around the courtyard before focussing again on the winery.

"You've done a good job getting this ready, Tomáš. So, everything is as it should be in there, is it?"
"Yes, monsieur. Everything's looking at its best. And most of the men are out spreading the mash on the vines. It's composted nicely."
"You're doing a very good job, Tomáš. I'm sorry to have to ask you to bow and scrape to a little weasel like Bousquet."
"Do you know him too then, monsieur?"
"Oh, yes. I know him. His father was the schoolmaster here for years. We let little Arnaud help with the harvest every year, as a favour to his father. He never much liked hard work."
"That will make him the perfect local bureaucrat then, monsieur."

Viktor stamped his feet and looked at his watch.

"Where is the little so-and-so? Did you leave the gates open, as I said?"
"Yes, monsieur."

"Where is he, then?"

"I think I can hear a car now, monsieur."

"You can. This is him. Remember, Tomáš, however difficult we may find it, we must defer to him in all this."

A small black Renault appeared on the driveway and drove past the two men, before stopping in front of the main doors of the château. Arnaud Bousquet emerged, carrying a brown briefcase. In spite of the clear blue sky, he was wearing a grey raincoat with the belt tightly fastened, and a black beret, which to Tomáš seemed incongruous to the point of comic. Pétain had set the trend when he demanded a return to the old values of rural France, for which he earned himself the sobriquet *Maréchal-paysan*. Now it seemed every minor government official regarded the wearing of a black beret with their dark-grey suits and light-grey raincoats as an obligation.

Bousquet stood by his car and waited for Viktor and Tomáš to join him.

"Bonjour, Monsieur Bousquet," said Viktor holding out his hand.

"I believe you know Monsieur Kovařík, one of my managers."

Bousquet's hand remained limp when Tomáš gripped it.

"I have arranged a tour of the facilities, Monsieur Bousquet," said Viktor. "I thought we could begin with the winery."

"That will not be necessary," said Bousquet, making his way towards the front entrance of the château. "All I need is somewhere quiet, where I can sit at a desk and where we shall not be disturbed."

"Oh, I see. Well, in that case may I suggest my study? I'll lead the way."

Bousquet took his place at Viktor's desk, while Tomáš and Viktor sat in straight-backed chairs in front of it.

"Let me make the procedure clear to you, Monsieur Musil," said Bousquet, as he took papers from his briefcase and laid them on the desk. "As a Jew you are not permitted under French law to run a business in metropolitan France, or in any of France's overseas possessions. I trust that is clear to you."

He looked up and waited for a reply.

"Yes. That is clear to me."

"Good. Then my first task is to determine whether the companies known as Château de Monteux Wines, De Monteux Production, and De Monteux Distribution, contribute in a positive way to the economy of France."

"If you mean, monsieur, whether our payment of taxes is up to date, I can assure you they are."

"Please do not interrupt, Monsieur Musil. I would hardly arrive here without that information, would I?"

"No, monsieur. Of course. I apologise."

"If in my judgement this business contributes positively to the economy of France, a trustee of French nationality will be appointed to run it. If I judge that it does not, it will be liquidated and sold."

"Liquidated? But my business is still making good profits, monsieur."

"I'm sure it is, otherwise I have no doubt someone like you would have washed your hands of it long ago. But the question to answer is whether it can continue to make profits given likely future circumstances."

"Why shouldn't it, monsieur?"

"Your business is only viable, Monsieur Musil, because you rely so heavily on the labour of foreign refugees. It is the actions of people like you which have encouraged these people to come here and make themselves such a burden to France."

"But I employ them in order that they do not become a burden to France, monsieur."

"Are you going to sit there and contradict me on every point I raise? Perhaps I should examine your business without the risk of your interruptions, and merely inform you later of my findings."

"I do apologise, Monsieur Bousquet. But, as you must be aware, it is very difficult to find French labour. Many of my former employees have not returned from the war, and most Castiranais, as you know, are employed in their own vineyards."

"And do you ever feel any shame, Monsieur Musil, that your foreign labour enables your profits to continue to flow, while your former French employees languish in German camps?"

"I still pay their wages to their families, monsieur."

"That may well be, but it must be small comfort to them. Now, let us stop all this idle chit-chat and look at the clear facts of your business. You have thirty hectares of land under cultivation in the environs of Castiran. Is that correct?"

"It is, monsieur."

"Last year your entire harvest of Clairette grapes was used in the production of 465,000 bottles of vermouth at your plant in Bessan."

"Yes, monsieur."

"All of which found a market."

"Yes, monsieur. But may I please make a point, Monsieur Bousquet? Due to shipping problems our export market, especially to America, will contract substantially in the future, and I had therefore planned to decrease production over the next twelve months."

"But are not most of your employees in Bessan Frenchmen?"

"The majority yes, but I was not going to..."

"So you were planning to deprive Frenchmen of their employment, whilst continuing to employ all these foreigners here in Castiran who owe no allegiance to France?"

"No, you misunderstand, monsieur..."

"I understand well enough, Monsieur Musil. The Bessan plant will continue in full production."

"But how, monsieur?"

"In pursuit of the policy of collaboration recently announced by our Maréchal, I am pleased to be able to inform you that the Department of Industrial Production in Vichy has agreed a contract with the German forces in the Occupied Zone which will more than make up for any lost markets, and be advantageous to both sides."

"I see, but the unit cost..."

"The decision has been taken, Monsieur Musil."

Bousquet placed the paper he was holding face down on the desk, and picked up another.

"Now, I see the number of bottles produced under the Château de Monteux label last year was slightly over 553,000."

"Yes, monsieur, but that number can change significantly from year to year depending..."

"That no longer matters, Monsieur Musil. The production of wine under the De Monteux label will cease."

"But... but that cannot be, Monsieur Bousquet. Wine has been produced under the De Monteux label in Castiran since 1836."

"That is not relevant in today's world. It will cease, and your work force will be cut by half."

"But the grapes we cultivate are so labour intensive. The quality..."

"I am growing tired of your constant interruptions, Monsieur Musil. This is not a debate. Your work force will be cut by fifty percent and your grapes will go to the coopérative like everyone else's. Our country is striving to renew itself, and this is not a time for us to concentrate on the production of luxury items such as de Monteux wine. Every Frenchman must play his part."

"I regret my French citizenship has been taken from me, monsieur."

Bousquet smiled. "Of course. I had quite forgotten."

"And it is becoming very clear to me, Monsieur Bousquet, about the part you now intend me to play."

"What else do you expect, Monsieur Musil? You are a foreign Jew who has sought refuge in our country. You impose yourself on our country and expect us to welcome you?"

"Perhaps France should be proud that people from all over Europe have sought her out, believing her to be a land of tolerance and refuge," said Tomáš.

"Ah, so Monsieur Kovařík also has a voice. Well, let me remind you, monsieur, that like your employer you are from a country which no longer exists, and that as a stateless refugee you can be interned at any time the Préfecture decides you should be. Perhaps in the circumstances you should both continue to be grateful to France for her tolerance and generosity."

"I am, but you…"

"Please, Tomáš, let me deal with this," said Viktor. He looked up at Bousquet. "Monsieur Bousquet, in the past six weeks all my possessions in the Occupied Zone have been confiscated by the Germans. My personal bank accounts in Vichy have been frozen, allowing me no access to my own money. Now you tell me that the business bequeathed to me by my French family in Castiran will also pass out of my control. You call me a foreigner, but did you know, Monsieur Bousquet, that my great-grandfather fought with Napoleon at Austerlitz? That my grandfather who founded this business was once the mayor of this village? You have known me…"

"Monsieur Musil, Monsieur Musil, I implore you, you must stop this. It is all irrelevant. You were born and brought up in Bohemia and you are a Jew. The economy of France will not be run by foreigners or Jews or Germans. It will be run by Frenchmen. It is the law, monsieur. You should not take it all so personally. Now I insist you listen while I tell you of the arrangements."

Viktor breathed out heavily and shook his head.

"You will be allowed to continue to oversee the day-to-day running of this business, but any decisions regarding expenditure or the hiring of employees must be approved by my office. I shall act as the trustee for the business and will control all the accounts. You will be allowed a salary of 5,000 francs a month."

"5,000 francs? But that is ridiculous. That is less than I pay my managers. How will my family live?"

"Many French families live on much less."

"But the cost of running the château? I shall have to dismiss the staff.

They are all French."

"I know your staff, Monsieur Musil. As you are no doubt aware, women are no longer permitted to work in government offices, and their employment elsewhere is to be discouraged. Their place is in the home. *Their* home, Monsieur Musil, not yours."

"But wait. My son's nurse. I ask you with great respect, Monsieur Bousquet. Please allow me sufficient funds to pay for my son's nurse."

Bousquet stood up and put his papers into his briefcase.

"Very few French families can afford nurses, Monsieur Musil. Even those whose men were injured making France a safe place to which you and Monsieur Kovařík could bring your families."

He put on his raincoat and his beret, and smiled.

"I shall put all these arrangements in writing to you, Monsieur Musil. I bid you both a good day. I shall see myself out."

"No, Monsieur Bousquet," said Viktor, levering himself to his feet. "I believe I am still capable of seeing visitors from my property."

When he came back, Viktor slumped into an armchair by the bookcase. Both men sat in silence.

"I'm sorry I let him speak to you like that, monsieur," said Tomáš at last. "I feel I should have supported you more."

"No, my boy. I am pleased you stayed silent. Anger would have made no difference anyway."

Tomáš moved his chair to face Viktor.

"Monsieur Musil, the situation here is getting steadily more intolerable. I really believe it is time to leave."

"And where would we go, Tomáš?"

"England. Or Switzerland."

"It's not practical, my boy. Even if we were successful, the Swiss would certainly intern us, and English cities are being bombed every night. Hitler might even invade Britain in the spring. We are much safer here."

"At least the British are fighting back. I'd like to play my part."

"But how could you get there with a wife and a baby? And how could I with Milan? This is the time to be practical, Tomáš. We must make the best of what we have here."

"What do you propose then, monsieur?"

"Well, at least we know they have done their worst. There is nothing more they can do to us."

"But he threatened internment."

"No. Bousquet wants us to run this for him. What use are we to him locked up? It would cost them money, and they would be left with the problem of looking after our wives and children."

"But a few weeks ago you thought you might be interned?"

"I did, but not now. I see what they're after. What we must do now, Tomáš, is work out how to make the best of our new circumstances, and then present it to Nataša and Anna. I am blessed with a wife whose true strength comes to the fore in hard times such as these. And I believe your Anna is the same."

"She is, monsieur, she is..."

Chapter Ten

November, 1940 – June 3rd, 1941

Everything changed at the château after Arnaud Bousquet's visit.

Monsieur and Madame Fournier, and Madame Lenoir, the cook, were all given notice with as much compensation for their long years of service as Viktor could afford. Anna took over the cooking, and all agreed that whatever the meals might now lack in French delicacy was more than compensated for by Anna's use of her grandmother's tested recipes.

Anna and Nataša shared all the other household duties, which were considerably lightened by their decision to close most of the rooms of the château. Viktor and Nataša gave up their separate bedrooms, personal dressing rooms and bathrooms, and shared a room for the first time in many years. Tomáš removed the leaves from the oval dining table, and with Anna's help found a place for the now small, round table in the drawing room, where all meals were taken.

In the harsh winter of 1940 into 1941 only four bedrooms, one bathroom, and the drawing room and kitchen remained open in the château, and the two families spent more time together than ever before.

"If Bousquet thought he was impoverishing us by all this," said Viktor one evening, as wood from his vines crackled in the fire, "he could not have been more wrong. I feel enriched."

Only one matter remained unresolved with Bousquet as spring arrived - the continued employment of Milan's nurse. Bousquet reminded Viktor the employment of French women in private households, especially foreign Jewish households, was contrary to French government policy and an insult to the French people. He also took the view that he was paying Musil too high a wage if he could still afford such luxuries. Or was it the case, he wondered, that Musil was earning money illegally through dealings on the black market?

The truth was that each month Nataša was selling pieces of her jewellery at low prices in Béziers in order to retain the nurse, and that soon she would have no more left to sell. It was only with the help of Father Benoît that Milan had received his medicine since Christmas, and the need to find a solution to the problem was becoming urgent. It was Anna who provided one. She had spoken to the nurse, and they both agreed that Anna would be capable of administering Milan's medicine and taking care of his personal needs. The nurse was keen to take up the offer of employment at the hospital in Clermont, and Milan, who had always objected strongly to his mother involving herself in such things, seemed happy enough for Anna to take over the role of caring for him.

Tomáš spent most of his time, as he had always done, caring for Victor's vineyards. It had been impossible for him to decide at the end of November which of the foreign workers should be laid off, and which should remain. He had been thankful when they all agreed to draw lots from a barrel. He wrote the word 'stay' on twenty-six pieces of paper and 'go' on twenty-six more. Those who had to leave were given one week's pay. Many made their way to the coast or inland to the plateau of Lozère in the hope of finding work. It had surprised Tomáš how many, at least a dozen, had been taken in by the Castiranais, with or without the offer of work. Perhaps Father Benoît was right, he thought, and Castiran really was a place of refuge, even if so much of France had ceased to be.

When the first buds appeared on the vines in April, Arnaud Bousquet became a more frequent visitor to the Château de Monteux, and it was usually Tomáš he wanted to see. Bousquet sought constant reassurance that the Musil vines would yield enough Clairette wine to fulfil the contract he had made with the German occupiers in the north. Anna hated the way Bousquet spoke to Tomáš, and wondered what damage could be done to the man by sabotaging his precious harvest. "A lot," Tomáš told her, "but even more to the Musils and to ourselves."

Having been taught so well how to care for the Musil vines, Tomáš found it hard to follow Bousquet's orders and leave the finest neglected. Vines which had been nurtured for a hundred years were left untended, the ground around them impoverished by weeds. Viktor could no longer bear to walk out to see them, and asked Tomáš less and less about the state of his family's business. He withdrew to life inside the château and seemed content with it. He took pleasure in watching his son work, and in spending time with Nataša. In February it was he who helped Eva take her first steps.

Everything settled into place. Anna at last heard news from her father about Otto. He remained safe in Palestine and was doing all he could to help Jewish immigrants from Europe find ways around the British quota. He sent his sister his love.

Tomáš heard too from Marek Kral. In early May he received a grey envelope stamped by the Red Cross in Geneva. Inside was a form allowing Marek to write twenty-five words. He was in the internment camp at

Agde, only twenty kilometres from Castiran. He was in fair health but had lost weight. He told Tomáš he did not need a visit from him, and added in block capitals, 'Stay away from this place'.

The reassuring routine of life at the château was strengthened by the warmth of May. Tomáš grew more relaxed, as it became clear no late frost would damage the vines and affect the crop. While he worked from early morning until early evening in the vineyards beyond the village, the others spent their days under the shade of the linden trees in the courtyard or by the orangery behind the château, depending on the light favoured by Milan for his work.

Milan's painting focussed increasingly on portraits; of Anna and Eva for the most part, but recently of his mother and father too. One painting in particular pleased Viktor. It showed him and Nataša in typical pose, sitting in rattan chairs taken from the orangery, both reading and content. Viktor insisted the painting should not be one of those taken to the market in Clermont L'Hérault to be bartered or sold, but instead should take pride of place in his study, which had been opened up once again for the summer.

Anna and Milan continued to make their weekly trip to the market in Clermont, even in the absence of Monsieur Fournier and the Musil's ten-litre Hispano-Sousa limousine. The car had become a liability once Arnaud Bousquet claimed the petrol allowance for the De Monteux business, and it was sold. Viktor hid any disappointment he felt and insisted that, at the rate the car gulped petrol, journeys in it would have become impractical anyway, regardless of anything Bousquet had done.

So now every Wednesday Anna, Milan and Eva went to market in an open donkey carriage. Milan sat on one bench seat propped up with cushions and held Eva, while Anna sat opposite and took the reins. Between them lay the folded wheelchair and up to a dozen of Milan's smaller paintings. The eight-kilometre journey took over an hour, instead of the ten minutes by car. But Anna and Milan both agreed it was far more fun, and they reassured Nataša there were always more than enough helping hands at the market to ease Milan safely down into his wheelchair. But no assurances were ever enough to calm Nataša's anxiety, which lasted all day until the carriage reappeared on the driveway around four o'clock. Nataša never waited in the courtyard for them, but she always appeared by chance from around a corner as soon as they returned, and she remained until Milan was safely inside.

When one day the carriage had not appeared by five o'clock, she dropped all pretence, walked down the driveway, and waited by the road outside the main gate. A bus from Clermont approached and, as it passed, Nataša noticed people looking out at her and pointing to her. The bus stopped halfway up the rue Philippe Henriot and Nataša hurried after it. When the bus drove off she saw two women, latecomers from the market with their bags at their feet, waiting for her to reach them.

"What is it? What has happened?" she called out to them.

"It's your son, Madame Musil," said one. "He's been taken ill. He had a bit of a turn."

Nataša stopped a short distance from them. "Where is he?" she asked.

"They took him to the hospital in Clermont."

"When?"

"About two hours ago. Monsieur Kovařík's wife was with him."

Nataša turned and strode back to the château, pausing only to call out more questions over her shoulder.

"Was my son conscious?"

"I don't think so, madame."

"Was he breathing?"

"I think he was, but he did look bad."

Viktor and Nataša arrived at the hospital by taxi. They found Anna in the small waiting room, Eva asleep on her lap. Nataša sat down next to them and took Anna's hand.

"Oh, pani Musilová, I'm so sorry. It was awful. There was nothing I could do."

"It's alright, Anna. We've spoken to a doctor. It was a fit. A grand mal seizure. I told you it could happen."

"Is Milan alright? They wouldn't let me see him. I tried to telephone you."

"We were outside in the garden. Milan is unconscious. He will be in a deep sleep for a while."

"Did something out of the ordinary happen to Milan, Anna?" asked Viktor. "He hasn't had a seizure for over five years."

"I gave him his medicine, I promise you. We were laughing. We'd just sold three paintings. He had Eva on his lap. He was happy. He just stopped and stared at me, and held Eva out to me. Then one of his arms went rigid and he made this terrible noise as if… It was just so awful. His lips went blue and I thought…"

"It's alright, my dear. I know how upsetting it can be the first time."

"Someone came and helped me. I did what the nurse said. Put the cushions around him. Reassured him. But some people were terrible. Some were annoyed with me, as if we were doing something wrong. Some were even laughing."

"People are easily scared by things they don't understand, my dear."

"What will happen now?" asked Anna.

"When Milan wakes up, we will know if there has been any permanent damage. There never has been before. Then we will speak to the doctors about his medication and take him home."

"They told me he might be taken to Montpellier."

"To Montpellier? Why?"

"They didn't say."

"Viktor. Can you find out why they would want to do that? As quickly as you can, please."

When Viktor came back, his face was ashen.

"Oh, my God, Viktor. What has happened?"

"Nothing, my love. Milan is still asleep, but he's alright."

"What then?"

"Anna's right. They intend to take him to the *Asile d'Aliénés* in Montpellier. To the insane asylum."

"But they cannot do that. They must know Milan's not mad. It's just a fit."

"They say it's not epilepsy. They say he's feeble-minded and needs special supervision."

"That's nonsense. I will speak to them."

"I've tried. They say Milan is now a ward of the state and we have no say in the matter."

No pleas from Nataša would change the minds of the doctors at Clermont. Only their assurances that she would be permitted to visit Milan in Montpellier during the following days persuaded her to return home without him. But every attempt she made to see Milan was blocked. In the end it was only the credit Viktor still held with the sub-prefect in Béziers which secured their right to visit Milan, almost three weeks after his transfer to the Hôpital Psychiatrique in Montpellier.

The hospital stood in its own parkland in the suburb of La Colombière. The taxi from Montpellier station dropped Viktor and Nataša at the main gates. From the end of the long driveway they agreed the hospital resembled a fine country house in its beautiful setting, but as they drew closer they were able to make out the prison bars behind every window.

Viktor rang the doorbell and, after a long wait, a tall, stocky young man in white trousers and white shirt with a mandarin collar came to the door.

"Yes?" he asked through the glass.

"We have come to see our son," said Viktor.

"We don't allow visitors here."

Nataša approached the glass.

"Our son is Milan Musil. He was brought here without our permission, because three weeks ago he suffered a grand mal seizure in a public place. The sub-prefect from Béziers arranged this visit and, if you do not allow us inside at once, I shall contact the Préfecture and return here with the police."

She glared at the young man. "I won't be a minute," he mumbled.

An older man in a white coat appeared and opened the door. "Good morning. I am Doctor Cassel, the Deputy-Director here. I apologise for the confusion. You must be Monsieur and Madame Musil. Please come in."

Viktor and Nataša stepped into the large entrance hall. The marble floor and the dark, wood panelling confirmed that this had once been a stylish private residence. Now the smell of disinfectant pervaded everything. From the corridors leading to the left and right, and from above the grand staircase in front of them, they could hear a mixture of muffled cries, protests and laughter.

"Please follow me to my office. We can discuss your son there," said the doctor, smiling at them.

"Please take a seat."

"I am very anxious to see my son and arrange his removal to our home as soon as possible," said Nataša. "I trust Milan is now well."

"He is as well as one might expect in his condition, madame. He is bed-ridden and needs constant care, as you know. And his ability to communicate is very limited. I am surprised you talk of his removal in the circumstances."

"You are not describing my son, Doctor Cassel. Milan has a bright mind. He can speak, he can sit up, and the right side of his body is completely functional."

"I regret, madame, your son is feeble-minded and incurably sick. His doctors are surprised he was ever allowed out in public in that state. You allowed him to be a danger to himself and to others."

"How dare you say such a thing," said Nataša. "Milan has a sharper mind than most of his doctors…"

"Please, my dear, please. Don't upset yourself," said Viktor. "Let us try to deal with this calmly. Doctor Cassel, can you please tell my wife and me whether Milan's seizure has impaired his mind in any way?"

"Not significantly. His recovery from that episode was satisfactory, but the damage was done a long time ago. You must know that, monsieur."

"Yes, yes, we know. Our son was injured in the last war. Fighting the Germans, I might add. He was decorated for his bravery. My wife and I are very aware of our son's limitations, Monsieur le Docteur, but we can assure you that major parts of his brain work to full capacity. One might even say that his injuries have awoken gifts and insights in our son which are quite unique to him."

Nataša turned to Viktor and took his hand. "Thank you, my love," she said.

Doctor Cassel stood up. "This is all very interesting, but I think it best if you come with me to see your son for yourself. We don't usually allow visits to our inmates but, due to the personal request of your influential friends, it appears we must make an exception in your case."

Viktor and Nataša were led up the stairs and along a corridor on the first floor. A thick metal bar ran along the walls on each side and hanging from them at three metre intervals were heavy leather straps. Viktor put his arm around Nataša. She looked at him showing no emotion. "I am alright," she said. From behind heavy wooden doors to their left and right came the sporadic sound of human activity.

Finally Doctor Cassel stopped in front of one of the doors. "Your son is in here," he said. Nataša took a deep breath, and breathed out as the door was opened. When she next inhaled, she was hit by the smell of carbolic and human waste.

"Oh, my God..."

"Please say nothing to upset the inmates, madame," said Cassel.

There were six metal-framed beds in the room, three on each side. In each bed lay a lifeless figure. One of the shutters outside the window had been left closed, leaving half the room in shadow. In the middle bed on that side lay Milan. His eyes were open and he was moaning gently and rhythmically. Nataša went to his side and sat on his bed. She took his hand and kissed it, and then stroked his stubbled cheek.

"Hello, Milan darling. We are here. Máma and Táta are here."

Milan's breathing quickened, but he did not speak or move.

"Have you drugged him?" Nataša asked.

"Your son is sedated for his own safety and for the safety of others."

"And what terrible thing do you think he is going to do, doctor? If you would let him wake up and talk, you would find he is the gentlest of men."

"It's hospital policy, madame. In everyone's best interest."

Nataša stood up.

"Do you not wish to stay longer, madame? I thought…"

"No. I have seen enough. I know what has to be done here."

She walked to the door.

"I shall see you in your office, doctor."

Viktor bent down and kissed Milan on the forehead. "Be brave, my dear boy," he said. "We'll come back for you."

Nataša was sitting in Cassel's office when he returned from the ward. Viktor arrived soon after.

"I want my son released into my care immediately," she said. "I will arrange for an ambulance to pick him up today."

"You cannot do that. You have no legal authority."

"I am his mother. That is my authority."

"Your son is incapable of playing a role in society, madame. It is the policy of our government that such people are kept separate from the fit and healthy, in order to ensure a healthy race and social stability."

"You talk as if Milan has a contagious disease."

"It can be passed on in other ways, madame. You forget the moral question here. You should be pleased I have not given instructions for your son to be sterilised."

"Sterilised? Milan is never going to father a child."

"Who was the woman who accompanied him to the hospital? I believe there was a young child involved."

"That is the wife of our manager. She is a friend."

"And what does this manager think of his wife in the company of someone who is feeble-minded and subject to violent seizures?"

"You are mistaken about all of this, Monsieur le Docteur," said Viktor. "Our son is no threat to anyone, and neither is he feeble-minded. He is a well-known painter. He and our friend were selling his paintings at Clermont market. If you let us take Milan now, we promise you we will keep him at home with us. He will cost the state nothing. We will take full responsibility for him."

"I regret it is not possible, monsieur. These are general measures set down by our government. Someone with your son's mental disability must be kept in a secure environment."

"The law contains the madness, Monsieur le Docteur. It is the lawmakers who should be put in places like this."

"You should be careful what you say, Monsieur Musil. Such opinions will not help you."

"If you take our son from us, what do you suppose my wife and I have to lose?"

"In the new circumstances I should think you would thank me for keeping your son here."

"What new circumstances? Why would we possibly thank you?"

"You are Jewish, are you not, monsieur?"

"Not by religious observance. Only according to last October's statute."

"But you have not been interned?"

"No. I run a profitable business. It is not in the state's interest to intern me."

"But the same cannot be said of your son."

"Milan is not classified as Jewish."

"How many Jewish grandparents does he have?"

"Only two. My mother and father."

"And was your son baptised before June 25th last year?"

"No, he has never been baptised."

"Then your son is a Jew under Vichy law. Would you rather him stay here or be interned at Agde?"

"But the law says he must have three Jewish grandparents."

"Have you not read the newspaper today, Monsieur Musil?"

"Not yet. We left before it arrived."

"A new Jewish statute came into effect today. All people with two Jewish grandparents are now counted as Jews under the law. And they will need a good reason not to be interned. Especially if they are foreigners, like your son."

Chapter Eleven

August 22nd, 1941

"Goodnight, Nataša. Is there anything I can get you before we go up?"

"No, my dear. You are so thoughtful. I shall sit with Viktor a while. It's such a beautiful night."

Anna went over to Viktor, who was sitting stock-still in his tall rattan chair, his eyes fixed on something in the middle distance. She kissed him on the cheek.

"Goodnight, Viktor. I'm pleased you enjoyed your talk with Father Benoît today."

"Viktor. Anna and Tomáš are wishing you goodnight."

"What? Oh, yes. Goodnight, both of you. Lovely meal. Thankyou."

"Goodnight, monsieur," said Tomáš. "Goodnight, madame. I won't see you in the morning. I have an early meeting with Monsieur Bousquet."

"I won't have that man on my property," said Viktor, turning suddenly in his chair. "I won't have him here."

"No, monsieur. I'm seeing him on the Adissan slope." Tomáš looked at Nataša. "I'm sorry, madame. I shouldn't have mentioned it."

"It was probably best not," she whispered. "But never mind. Goodnight to you both."

Anna and Tomáš went into Eva's room and stood by her cot under the ceiling fan. She was lying on her front with her head turned to the side and her legs tucked up as if she were kneeling. Anna and Tomáš looked at one another and smiled. Tomáš put his arm around Anna, and they stayed there watching her. Tomáš breathed out heavily, kissed the tips of his fingers and touched Eva's head. Anna nudged him and pushed him gently towards the connecting door to their room. She closed it quietly behind them.

"She is so beautiful," Tomáš said. "I still can't take it in sometimes."

"It makes you realise what they must be going through."

"I think Viktor is getting worse, Anna. I thought it would be Nataša who suffered most from all of this."

"She's still putting all her energy into finding out where Milan is. I worry what will happen to her if she ever runs out of ideas."

"She's a remarkable woman. And so are you, Anna. I can't believe how brave both of you are about all this."

"I refuse to be despondent. I'm determined we'll bring Milan home."

Tomáš sat on the bed and took off his shoes. "I find it unbelievable that they can take someone and do what they like with him," he said. "Without even having to inform his family."

"It's happening all over. I was reading your paper today. It was full of reports of new round-ups. They say 50,000 have been arrested as saboteurs."

"I wish you wouldn't read all that, Anna."

"Remember I'm a Jew, my love. I'm forbidden from listening to the radio."

"Don't joke. You know what I'm saying. I don't want you to have to worry about it."

"I worry about it far less than you. I keep telling you, Tomáš. I'm not a child who needs protecting from the truth."

"It's mostly Communists they're arresting anyway. Once Hitler attacked Russia they were bound to turn on the Communists again."

"Oh, come on, Tomáš. You know as well as I do they make no distinction between Jews and Communists. They're the same thing to these people."

"Please, Anna. Can we not talk about it?"

"I don't mind, if you'd rather not. But I know you still blame me for not getting baptised."

"It wasn't you I thought should be baptised. It was Eva."

"Well, we're going to now. So you can stop worrying about it."

"I'm really relieved, Anna. I know what it means to you, and I'm grateful."

Anna stood in front of him in her slip and nylons as he sat on the bed.

"Do you blame me for not going to church before? I might have managed not to be classed as a Jew, if I had."

Tomáš placed his hands on her hips and looked up at her.

"You know better than that. You're very stubborn. But you hold to your principles. How can I object to that in my wife?"

"Do you think Nataša and Viktor blame me for what has happened to Milan?"

"No. We both know they don't. They've seen how much you have been affected by it. They know how you feel about Milan."

"I think Viktor blames me."

"He doesn't. I've talked with Viktor. He's not angry with you. He's angry because he finds himself powerless. First the business with

Bousquet, and now he can do nothing about Milan. He's angry with the world, Anna."

"Poor Viktor."

"I know how he feels. The world grows madder by the day. All I want is to have you and Eva safe with me."

"Well that's alright then." She rested her hands on his shoulders and brushed her legs against his. "Because Eva is asleep next door, and you have me here."

"So when will you start the harvest, Kovařík?"

"In about three weeks, Monsieur Bousquet, if the weather stays fine."

"Three weeks? The grapes look ready now."

"They will get much bigger, monsieur. They still have a high acid content. They need two or three more weeks of sun."

"As long as you know what you're doing. I can't afford any mistakes."

"You will get your harvest, monsieur."

"I better had."

"But you do realise, Monsieur Bousquet, that this year's harvest will not produce vermouth for another two years?"

"Do you take me for a bloody fool, Kovařík? Of course I know that. I'm looking at a long-term investment here. I've known from the start the Germans were going to win this war. The British are as good as finished and the Germans will be in Moscow in a matter of weeks. My contract with the Wehrmacht is for the next five years."

"Five years?"

"Yes, and so far I've been very pleased with you, Kovařík. If you do this right, I'll keep you on to manage all this for the length of the contract."

"Thankyou, monsieur."

"We can do without Musil though. I can't see he's worth a sou of what I'm paying him."

"Oh, no, you're mistaken there, Monsieur Bousquet. Monsieur Musil oversees everything. He gives me advice all the time."

"I've heard he hardly speaks nowadays after what happened to his son. I haven't seen him for weeks."

"He's very upset about Milan of course, but his mind is still sharp. We need his expertise."

"My job is to remove all Jewish influence from the economy, Kovařík, and there's a lot of pressure on me to get it done. Are you really telling me you can't do this without the help of a useless old Jew?"

"Monsieur Musil's expertise would be invaluable if there were ever any problems, monsieur. He's just distracted at the moment."

"Doesn't he realise his son must be dead by now?"

"His son isn't dead. We've been told his records have been lost in the system because of all the upheaval."

"Oh, really?"

"He's been transferred from Montpellier, and we're trying to find out where they've taken him."

"He's dead, Kovařík. In times like this how much time and money do you think France is spending keeping a cretinous foreign Jew alive?"

"The France I admired would have spent as much as was necessary."

"You disappoint me, Kovařík. I thought you understood what's at stake here. France is now part of a crusade against Communism and the Jews. You need to get your priorities right."

"I have been working hard to help you with your contract, Monsieur Bousquet. You must know that."

"I do, Kovařík. And I think it's very sensible of you. But France cannot spend money where it is not needed, and I don't think you need Musil any more."

"I do, monsieur. We both do."

"Oh well, in that case I must trust your judgement."

"Thankyou, monsieur."

"I understand French law now regards your wife as a Jew, Kovařík. Is that right?"

"Yes, monsieur. It is."

"But I'm informed by Henri Fauchery at the mairie that she doesn't report with you to get her residence permit stamped each week."

"I get the stamps for my wife and my child. I have done for three years."

"France's priorities and laws have changed in those three years, Kovařík. You should make sure your wife and child obey the law and appear in person."

"I shall do, monsieur. I'm sorry."

"Good, because Monsieur Musil respects the law. He manages to appear every week in person."

"I'll put it right, monsieur."

"Good, because I expect you rely on your Jewish wife's support in your work as much as you do on Monsieur Musil."

"I do, monsieur. Totally."

"Yes, I can understand a man needing the support of his wife, when he has as much responsibility as you do. It's just a pity you can't do without the 'expertise' of old Musil. It's asking a lot of France to support him *and* your wife."

"I would be grateful if it could be done, monsieur."

"I hope you understand, Kovařík, I'm offering you an official position here, working under me for a government department for the next five years."

"I am very grateful for the opportunity, Monsieur Bousquet. I won't let you down."

"As long as you produce what I need, your position is safe, Kovařík. Enough Clairette for my contract, and 300 tons of anything else for the coopérative to keep the villagers happy."

"I can do that, monsieur. I assure you."

"But you need to assure me you can manage this business without anyone else's expertise, Kovařík. Can you do it?"

"But Monsieur Musil will soon be back to his normal self."

"Can you do it without him?"

"Please, Monsieur Bousquet..."

"It's a simple question, Kovařík. With just the continued support of your wife, can you do it?"

"I understand you, monsieur Bousquet. Yes, as long as I have the support of my wife, I can do it."

Chapter Twelve

August 22nd – 23rd, 1941

"If I have received nothing by the end of next week, I intend writing to Pétain himself."

"Who did you send the last letter to, Nataša?" asked Anna.

"The Minister of Public Health. And it's the third time I've written to him. I'm now considering going to Vichy in person and refusing to leave his office without an answer. Someone must know something."

"What do you think, Tomáš? Would it help if Nataša went to Vichy?"

"I don't know, Anna. It can do no harm, I suppose."

"Are you alright, darling? You've hardly touched your dinner."

"I'm sorry. I'm a bit preoccupied. I'm afraid I can't eat any more."

"Did Bousquet upset you this morning?"

Viktor looked up at the mention of the name and listened for Tomáš's reply.

"Bousquet always upsets me. It upsets me that people like him have so much power over our lives, and there's nothing we can do about it."

"Don't raise your voice, darling."

"We should raise our voices, Anna. Madame Musil, you should go to Vichy and you should make as much trouble as you can for these people."

Tomáš bowed his head and spoke more softly.

"But, of course, it won't make trouble for them, if you do go. It will only make more trouble for you, because you're not French and your husband and son are Jews."

"Tomáš!"

"And that means they can do whatever they want to you, Madame Musil. And ignoring your letters isn't the worst."

"Tomáš, how dare you speak to Nataša like that," said Anna. "I can't believe you would say such things."

"It's alright, Anna. Tomáš feels the strain of our circumstances, as we all do. I understand very well. There are times when I feel I could scream with frustration, but I know it will not benefit me or anyone else, and therefore I choose not to."

Tomáš put his napkin on the table.

"I apologise, madame. I have no right to speak like that. I'm sorry,

Anna. Please accept my apologies, Monsieur Musil."

Viktor continued moving the food around his plate. Anna reached across the table for Tomáš's hand. Nataša looked at him and smiled.

"I think at times like this, when we find ourselves at the mercy of other people's prejudice," she said, "our strength must come from patience and forbearance. I know it is harder for you men, Tomáš. I know your instinct is to strike out when your path is blocked."

"Usually I try not to, madame. What I said sounded very disrespectful. I did not mean it in that way."

"I know."

"I think you should persevere with your letters, madame, until you find out what has happened to Milan."

"I think I already know what has happened to Milan."

Tomáš and Anna looked at her, but she did not speak. She waited until Viktor looked up at her too.

"It has been almost three months since you and I last saw Milan, Viktor. It is time I told you what I believe has happened to him."

Viktor dropped his hands to his lap. His face was drawn, his eyes liquid and staring. Nataša looked only at him as she spoke.

"I believe Doctor Cassel continued to keep Milan in that state until he died, Viktor, probably from pneumonia or heart failure. You see, in the letters I have written recently I have been asking only for Milan's death certificate. I want them to return him to us, my love, so that he can be with us again here at the château."

Viktor nodded. Tears ran down his cheeks.

"I am not sad, Viktor. I thought we had lost our son in Russia twenty years ago. But your dear father sent him back to us, Tomáš. It was a miracle. We had all that time with him, denied to so many other parents. And the best time was here with you, Anna, and with darling Eva. I never thought I would ever see Milan so happy again, just as he was as a boy at the villa. I am not sad. But I will not let them keep him from me."

Anna held her hand to her mouth in an attempt to stifle her sobs. Tomáš sat with his head bowed. Nataša and Viktor looked across at one another, and she smiled at him.

Victor looked down. "We were just getting to know one another," he said. "I have so much regret. That is the hardest thing for me to bear. Because he came home so damaged, I thought a large part of him was missing. So much I had planned for us to do together was no longer possible. I thought half a body and half a mind needed half my attention. Only since we have been here have I understood how complete my boy was, how gifted he was. Those doctors have no idea..."

He put his hands to his face. Tomáš looked over to him.

"On the day they went to market, monsieur Musil, Milan told Anna how pleased he was that you had hung his picture in your study. Isn't that right, Anna?"

"Yes. He kept saying how happy it made him."

"I appreciate your telling me that," said Viktor. "I have sought forgiveness from our Lord for my shortcomings. And I thank you all for what you have said." Viktor pushed back his chair. "I hope you will excuse me if I take a few minutes in the evening air. Please don't disturb yourselves. I will be back shortly."

They watched him close the door behind him.

"Will he be alright, Nataša?" said Anna.

"Yes, my dear. This is good. I have been praying Viktor would find a way to say these things. I'm sure it will be the start of his returning to his old self. We have you to thank for this, Tomáš. Your willingness to speak so honestly has helped us all to do the same."

"I don't think you should thank me for anything, madame."

"Do not judge yourself too harshly, Tomáš. You have worked so hard for us all, it is no wonder it gets a little too much at times."

Nataša got up and kissed him on the cheek. "I am going out to join Viktor. Look after our dear Anna for us, Tomáš. Everything will seem much better tomorrow."

Even at seven-thirty in the morning the Languedoc sun was too hot for Nataša. Tomáš and Anna found her taking breakfast by the orangery under a trellis of vines.

"Where is Viktor?" asked Anna.

"He has gone to mass, my dear."

"Is he alright?"

"Viktor is feeling much better. Now he can accept what has happened, I'm sure his old strength will return. And talking to Father Benoît will help him too. Come, sit down, both of you. I have put out enough for all of us."

Tomáš and Anna took their places around the cast-iron table. Tomáš checked the condition of the vines above his head.

"And how are you this morning, my dear?" Nataša asked Anna.

Tomáš answered for her. "Anna still blames herself for what happened that day, madame."

"Is that true, Anna?"

"Yes." She looked down. "I hoped to be able to make it up to Milan when he left hospital, but Tomáš has explained to me that what you said last night is almost certainly true."

"You did all you could for Milan when he had his seizure, Anna," said Nataša. "And before that you did more for him than anyone. I cosseted him too much. I know that. And I know how much he hated it, but I could not stop myself. But you ignored Milan's disabilities, my dear, and treated him as you treat everyone else. I am very grateful to you for that."

"Thankyou."

"The only people responsible for what befell Milan are the French authorities, and I fully intend to hold them to account for it."

"You can't, madame," said Tomáš.

"And why not, may I ask?" said Nataša, turning to him.

"Because the authorities here can do whatever they like. To you, to me, or to anyone else. And they don't need to give you any explanation."

"Tomáš, please don't start talking like that again," said Anna, looking up at him. "It's so unlike you."

"I have to, Anna. I'm sick of France."

"But we can manage here. You said so yourself."

"I know I did, Anna, but now I think it's time we left. I thought it two years ago when the Germans invaded. I thought it last October when Vichy started with their anti-Jewish laws, and I think it again now."

"Is it because of this new law? Because now I qualify as Jewish too?"

"Yes, mainly. And because at every stage we find ways of persuading ourselves we can make the best of everything here. We can't. These people will go on demanding things from us, until finally we have no more to give. Then they will cast us aside."

"You are talking about Bousquet, aren't you?" said Viktor from behind them.

They all turned to look at him.

"Yes, monsieur. Bousquet. Milan's doctors. The people who won't answer your wife's letters."

"But mostly Bousquet?"

"Yes."

Viktor came over and sat down at the table. Nataša poured him a glass of water.

"I know you have been worried about Bousquet, Tomáš. And I know well enough what Bousquet wants. I've known for months. He wants us all out of the way, so he can run the business and take over the château."

"No, monsieur. He wants me to run the business for him. It's only you he wants out of the way."

"Tomáš!"

"What do you want me to say, Anna? Do you want me to lie about it?"

"It's alright, Anna," said Viktor. "Tomáš did not have to say anything to us about any of this. I am grateful to him for his candour. I want to know what Bousquet has said to you, Tomáš."

"He thinks I can run everything here without you, monsieur. I told him I cannot, but he didn't believe me. He offered me the job of manager for five years, but only if I agreed... The details aren't important."

"It's alright, Tomáš. I understand."

"I don't," said Anna. "If you agreed what?"

"It does not matter, Anna," said Viktor.

"It matters to me. I want to know."

"Bousquet gave me a choice, Anna. I could agree to do the work without Viktor, or I would lose my job too."

"So you sacrificed Viktor."

"I was afraid you would think that, if I told you about all of this, Anna. What would you rather I had done? Make a grand gesture of defiance? Or try to keep us safe?"

"I wouldn't expect you to sacrifice Victor just to keep your job."

"We must not argue," said Viktor. "Tomáš hasn't sacrificed anyone, Anna."

"I was trying to gain us some time," said Tomáš. "So we could all decide together what to do."

"I know, my boy, and that is what we shall do now."

"What will happen if we do nothing, my love?" asked Nataša.

"I shall be interned, I expect. Do you think so, Tomáš?"

"Yes, monsieur. Bousquet made that quite clear."

"We can't allow that," said Anna. "We'll all have to leave."

"Tomáš and I have talked about this many times," said Viktor. "Where would we go?"

"We should take our chances with Spain," said Tomáš. "And then on to England. It is the only option now."

"No. I believe there is another," said Viktor. He looked over at Nataša. She held his gaze and he read from her face what he needed to know. "We are agreed then," he said to her. He turned to Anna.

"There is something Tomáš does not want to tell to you, Anna. It is this. If he had refused to work without me, Bousquet threatened to have you interned as a foreign Jew instead of me. Isn't that right, Tomáš?"

Tomáš nodded his head. Viktor continued.

"And if that happened, you would be left with a terrible choice, Anna. You would either have to take Eva with you into the camp, or allow yourself to be separated from her."

He put his water glass on the table.

"Nataša and I have made our decision. Tomáš must continue to do as Bousquet asks of him, and keep you all secure here. It will allow Nataša the time she needs to find Milan, which is the main priority for both of us now. And it will allow Eva to grow up here with you in peace. As for me, internment is not such a terrible thing. There are countless thousands of people who are going through the same thing all over Europe. It may even be possible for you all to visit me. I'm sure the regulations will not be too strict, and Agde is a beautiful place."

He stood up.

"Now, in spite of the hour, I am going to treat myself to an armagnac," he said. "Will anyone join me?"

"We all will, my love," said Nataša.

"I'm sorry, Tomáš," Anna whispered across the table. "I'm so stupid. I didn't realise."

Viktor came from the kitchen carrying a tray with four crystal brandy glasses on it.

"Here we are. One for each of us. You know, I have been blessed this morning. I am so thankful that in my old age I have been given the chance to do something of such benefit for the people I love."

He raised his glass.

"I drink to you all. I am very happy."

Chapter Thirteen

September 15th – 16th, 1941

Tomáš could not sleep. He was pleased the picking crews were going out in the morning. He took his father's fob watch, his parting gift, from the bedside table and struck a match. Ten past two. Less than five hours. That should keep Bousquet quiet. All week he had complained to Tomáš as the other growers started their harvest. "Be patient," Tomáš told him, "one more week of sun and the grapes will be perfect." And now they were. Ripe, with taut skins, perfect colour, and the optimum blend of sugar and acidity.

His hatred of Bousquet knew no bounds. The way he had toyed with Viktor. Only three days after learning of Bousquet's plan to get rid of him, Viktor said all his goodbyes and set off to the mairie to renew his stamp, fully accepting his fate. He knew that was when people were taken. Two gendarmes would be there, and after a nod from Henri Fauchery, whoever they wanted would be arrested. It did not happen often in Castiran but, according to rumours, in Béziers and Montpellier it had become a daily occurrence.

But Bousquet delighted in playing his little games. He waited until Viktor's second visit to have him arrested; a week later, when Viktor was less prepared for it. He was allowed to return home to pack a small bag, which made it even harder for Nataša. She had been determined to show no feelings other than confidence and reassurance, and she succeeded until Viktor waved to her from the bus as it pulled away. Then she sobbed with such violence that Anna had called for Father Benoît.

It was as if Bousquet had deliberately chosen the moment for Viktor's arrest, just days before Milan was returned in a sealed coffin. His body arrived in an SNCF delivery van from the station in Clermont L'Hérault. There was an envelope attached with the address of the château on it, and inside was Milan's death certificate. He had died in an asylum in Toulon, more than 300 kilometres away. There were three causes of death, listed one under the other: 'Pneumonia, epilepsy, imbecility'.

Nataša decided not to bury Milan at the château, for fear that one day the property might fall into the hands of strangers and his grave might not be tended. Father Benoît held a service for him in St. Julien's and, ignoring the fact that Milan was officially a Jew, arranged for him to be interred in the village cemetery, a short distance from the church.

Anna stirred in her sleep and pulled the thin sheet over her shoulders. Tomáš realised for the first time how cold it was, and wondered if it was that which had woken him. Or was it the sound of the wind rattling the shutters, which had grown louder as he had been lying there? He got up, went to the wardrobe and took a blanket from the top shelf. He laid it over the bed and tucked it in around Anna. He got under it himself and pressed his body against hers. Her presence and her warmth stilled his thoughts, and he fell back to sleep.

Above them the warm, moisture-laden air, which for days had been blowing in from the sea, had risen high into the atmosphere. There each droplet of water froze and waited, suspended above the plains of Languedoc in huge, anvil-shaped clouds. Finally, the weight of the ice became so great that the clouds could hold no more, and the tiny crystals began to fall. They fell through the freezing air, fusing together to form small balls offering less resistance, and they gathered speed. The pebbles of ice hurtled on, until they reached the warmer air only a few thousand metres above the earth. Passing through the warmer layer, they would usually be transformed once more into droplets of moisture to fall as rain, but on this night that did not happen. They passed instead unchanged through cold air blown down overnight from the Montagnes Noires, and continued on their way to the ground as solid, stinging balls of ice.

For several minutes Tomáš wove the noise coming from outside the window into his dream. The staccato tap, tap, tap, tap of ice on the shutters was the sound of a machine gun. Anna and Eva were crouching in the open, exposed to the bullets. He was behind a wall watching, trying to shout a warning, but no sound would come from his mouth. He cowered behind the wall, his mind unable to direct his body, powerless to help them. He opened his eyes. The bullets were hitting the shutters in their thousands. Panic gripped him, and he sprang out of bed.

"What is it? What's the matter?" said Anna.

"Hail, Anna. My God. It's hail."

He pulled on trousers, shirt and shoes. Rushed downstairs and opened the front door. The ground was white. White lines streaked through the black sky. Balls of ice bounced off the ground in front of him. The loudest sound was the hail hitting the slate roofs of the château, the winery and the cottages. The worst was the sound of it slicing through the leaves of the linden trees.

From behind the château Tomáš heard glass shattering in the orangery.

He turned and walked through the hallway, across the dining room and into the kitchen. He opened the back door and stepped out into the storm. He put his hands in front of his face to protect his eyes and ran to the trellis of vines. He looked up. The leaves were shredded, and through them flowed the juice of the punctured grapes. And the hail kept coming, in stronger and stronger waves. Tomáš eased himself slowly on to one of the cast-iron chairs and put his head in his hands.

Anna watched Tomáš hurrying up the driveway. She heard the front door slam, and then he appeared in the doorway of the drawing room. His face was pale but streaked with sweat.

"How bad is it?" she asked.

"A disaster, Anna. We've lost at least half the crop. Maybe more if they start to rot."

He paced from one side of the drawing room to the other.

"I've ruined everything for us, Anna. Everything."

"Can't you make up what you've lost from the other growers?"

"That's what Bousquet intends to do. But he says it's going to cost him millions."

"Cost *him* millions. That man is unashamed."

"I've lost the job, Anna. We were safe. My God, how could I be so stupid?"

Tomáš went over to the window and looked out towards the winery. He rubbed his forehead with the tips of his fingers.

"What have I done to you, Anna? What have I done?"

Anna went to him and placed her hand on his back.

"You haven't done anything to me."

"I've been so stupid."

"You're not to say that. You did what you thought was right. No one predicted that storm. Nataša says it's the worst anyone here can remember."

"Viktor would have known. I told Bousquet that. That made him even madder."

"Good."

"I shouldn't have waited, Anna. Bousquet didn't want quality. I'm such a fool."

"You're not. And you are to stop saying such things. If Viktor had been here, he would have told you not to harvest too early. Even I know that much about it."

Tomáš turned to face her.

"You do know what all this means, don't you?"

"I think so. Come here and sit down. We'll talk about it."

"Where's Eva?"

"She's upstairs with Nataša. She's alright."

They sat down on the couch facing one another. Anna took Tomáš's hands in hers.

"Is there any chance Bousquet might keep you on as manager once he has calmed down?" she asked.

"None at all. He was so angry I was pleased to get home before he had me arrested there and then. I've left the men saving what they can."

"Tomáš, my darling, the harvest doesn't matter any more. One good thing about this is that you don't have to bow and scrape to Bousquet for the next five years."

"I'd welcome the chance."

"No, this is better. Let's take control of our own lives again. I need you to forget about last night, Tomáš, and think about what we must do now."

"We can't stay here. Bousquet will have you interned now for certain. My God, Anna, what have I done to you?"

"Stop that, Tomáš. Listen to me. You have been so strong since we arrived here. Eva and I need you to stay strong now."

"We have to get to Spain, Anna. It's the only way out. North Africa is more Vichy than here. The occupied zone is out of the question."

"That's better, darling. What about Switzerland?"

"It's too far, and even if we did get across the border, there's nowhere else to go on to. At least in Spain we can get to Gibraltar and England. England should be safe now with Hitler tied up in Russia."

Anna leaned forward and kissed him.

"This is much better than staying, Tomáš. Perhaps the storm was a blessing."

"Do you think Nataša will come with us?"

"No. She will want to stay here to be close to Milan and Viktor."

"We'll have to leave her, Anna. You do know that?"

"Yes, I know."

"And there is another problem."

"What?"

"Our permits need renewing tomorrow. We can't travel without a fresh stamp. We'd be stopped at the first checkpoint."

"But we can't risk going to the mairie, can we?"

"Bousquet waited a week before he had Viktor arrested. I think he'll do the same with us. I'm sure he'll want to come here first to rub my nose in it."

"That's good then."

"We have to take the chance, Anna. We'll go to the mairie first thing in the morning, as soon as it opens."

"Why don't you pick Eva up, Tomáš? We'll be late if you let her walk all the way," said Anna.

"It will be worse to be too early. The last thing we want to do is wait around outside in front of the whole village."

Eva walked over to another water trough and splashed her hands in it. She turned to Tomáš and started to laugh. "You little monkey," he said, and he picked her up and held her close to him. "We don't want you to get all wet, do we?"

"We're nearly there, Tomáš," said Nataša, as they approached the back of the post office. From the open window of the bar on the first floor they could hear Gaston Daguenet taking the chairs down from the tables. Before they could reach the corner, he appeared at the window.

"Bonjour, Thomas," he called out. "Ah, you have the whole family with you. Bonjour, mesdames. And the little one. I've forgotten her name."

"Eva."

"Ah, bonjour, ma petite Eva. Are you all coming up for breakfast? My wife has the coffee on, and she'll have a pain au chocolat for you, ma belle Eva."

"I'm sorry, Gaston, but we're just on our way to the mairie to get our permits stamped."

"Oh, I see... oh, well... perhaps another time then." And he disappeared inside.

They went around the corner and stopped. "I didn't like the way he reacted to that," whispered Tomáš.

"You will be alright as long as you stick to our plan," said Nataša. "You wait here while I go in first. If I do not come out in ten minutes, you get to the train station as quickly as you can. If there are gendarmes in the mairie but they do not want me, I shall be able to warn you about them when I come out."

"Thankyou for doing this, madame," said Tomáš.

"I have already told you, I have nothing to lose. They can either leave me alone or take me to where Viktor is. They can do nothing to hurt me. But just in case, I embrace you all."

Nataša kissed Anna and Tomáš, and then took Eva's hand. "My

darling child," she said, "you have been such a precious gift to me." She kissed Eva and set off across the square.

Tomáš and Anna waited in silence, their eyes fixed on the door of the mairie. After only a minute Nataša reappeared and came back across the square towards them. "It's alright," she said. "The young man was very polite and just stamped my permit. There was no one else there. I even asked if the mayor was available, but was told he is not coming in until later. I think you should go now while it's so quiet."

"Thankyou, madame. We will. Come on, Anna."

"We'll see you at the château, Nataša," said Anna, as she stepped out into the Place du Peyrou. "Just to get Eva's things."

"I'll have them ready at the gate, my dear."

Tomáš opened the door of the mairie. He stepped back to allow Anna in first, and then entered the anteroom to the mayor's office with Eva in his arms. She struggled to get down.

"Alright, darling, but don't touch anything," he said.

Henri Fauchery was standing behind the counter waiting for them. Tomáš placed the three permits on the counter and smiled at him. Fauchery did not react. Without taking his eyes off Tomáš, he reached out his right hand, picked up a small bell with his thumb and forefinger, and shook it. Tomáš scooped up Eva as the door of the mayor's office opened.

"Kovařík, you are so predictable," said Arnaud Bousquet. Behind him stood two gendarmes in dark-blue uniforms and black képis. "You are our first catch of the day."

He turned to the gendarmes. "Take the adults. The child can stay with the Musil woman for now."

"No, please," begged Anna. "Don't take our little girl. She can come with us." Anna went to Tomáš and held on to him with Eva pressed between them. "You must let her come with us."

"It makes no difference to me," said Bousquet. "I thought you might prefer to leave her here, that's all." He took hold of Tomáš's arm and pulled him away from Anna.

"I hope you understand how lenient I'm being with you, Kovařík. I could have you shot as a Communist saboteur for what you've done to me. I hope you realise that. Take them out."

Tomáš held Eva in his arms as he and Anna walked together across the square, flanked by the two gendarmes. Tomáš looked back over his right shoulder at the Poste. He knew Gaston Daguenet was watching, but he was staying out of sight. They reached the top of the rue Philippe Henriot where the buses turned. A yellow municipal bus was waiting for them with the door open and the engine running. The driver did not acknowledge them, but Tomáš recognised him as one of the regulars on the run to Clermont L'Hérault.

"Where are you taking us?" he asked him.

"The camp at Agde, but we won't be there for hours yet. I've got ten more stops to do before I'm finished."

Tomáš and Anna sat together facing forward with Eva on her father's knee. Normally she would be chatting with excitement at being on a bus, but she sensed something was not right and sucked her thumb instead.

"I'm sorry, Anna."

"I don't care, Tomáš. I just don't care as long as the three of us are together."

The doors closed, the driver put the bus noisily into gear and they started down the rue Philippe Henriot. Anna rested her head against Tomáš's arm, and he felt her take his hand.

"Look, look," shouted Eva excitedly. "It's Auntie Nataša."

Tomáš looked back as they passed the château. He caught only a glimpse of a figure with hands outstretched, holding a small suitcase.

Chapter Fourteen

September 16th, 1941

For the first hour Eva enjoyed the bus ride. She liked her mother and father giving her even more attention than usual, pointing out every car and horse and dog they passed. Even cats. The bus driver kept stopping to let people on, but none of them smiled at her like people on buses normally did, and no one was talking. Some were even crying.

After five stops Eva became hungry and thirsty and increasingly restless.

"You'll have to say something, Tomáš. Some of the children are even younger than Eva."

"Monsieur," Tomáš called out to one of the gendarmes. "Our little girl is thirsty. Can we please get her something to drink at the next stop?"

"It's your own damn fault if you didn't bring anything with you," he shouted back. "I wouldn't treat my kids like that."

"We didn't know this was going to happen, monsieur."

"Didn't know?" He laughed to his colleague. "Didn't know it was going to happen. What's the matter with these people?"

The bus pulled into the bus station in Pézenas and the gendarme got out. He went over to a group of five people, and shook hands with the two gendarmes guarding them. Tomáš watched the three policemen through the window. They were laughing and joking, while the small group stood with their arms around one another.

"What does your little girl need?" someone asked him.

He turned to see the gendarme who had stayed on the bus. "Tell me quickly. I'll say I'm going for some cigarettes."

"Milk," said Anna, leaning across Tomáš. "And some biscuits or bread or something. Oh, thankyou."

"I have some money," said Tomáš, reaching into his pocket.

"It doesn't matter, monsieur," said the gendarme. "There's no need."

Their eyes followed him as he got off the bus and approached his colleague, who did not seem pleased to have to return to the bus so soon with his new passengers. The two adults and three children filed aboard; Tomáš recognised a few words of Polish as they passed him. Everyone sat in silence, until a few minutes later the second gendarme reappeared carrying a bag. As he climbed aboard, the driver pointed to his watch and shook his head, before putting the bus into gear and setting off again.

Eva started to cry. The gendarme with the bag said something to his colleague, who was clearly amused by it, and then made his way down the bus and handed Anna a litre bottle of milk and some *madeleines*.

"It's all I could get, madame," he whispered.

"Oh, thankyou, monsieur. You are so kind."

"I have nieces and nephews of my own," he said, and returned to his seat.

Anna unwrapped a madeleine and dipped it in the milk. Eva took it from her and stopped crying.

"What a kind man. I can't believe it," said Anna.

"It restores your faith a little, doesn't it?" said Tomáš.

He looked down the bus and saw their benefactor offering a cigarette to his fellow gendarme and to the driver. The man turned and looked back at Anna and Eva. He noticed Tomáš was watching him and smiled. They nodded to one another.

They had been on the bus for more than five hours by the time they crossed the Hérault River and turned off towards Agde. At a fork in the road the driver ignored the '*Centre Ville*' sign and took a narrow road leading into open countryside, signposted to '*Mont Saint Loup*'. The land was flat and covered in coarse, dry grass with a scattering of Kermes oak and Aleppo pine trees. Through the window to his left Tomáš saw the 'mountain' of Saint Loup. Its gentle slopes suggested it had once been a volcano. Even now, with the top of its cone worn away, it dominated the dull, arid landscape.

The bus slowed, and Tomáš looked to his right. They were passing a high wire fence, supported by white concrete stanchions and topped along its entire length with coils of barbed wire. Behind it he saw row upon row of long, single-storey wooden huts. Anna squeezed his hand. He looked at her and she attempted a smile, but her brow was furrowed and her eyes betrayed her anxiety. They looked down together at Eva asleep on Anna's lap, and they stroked her forehead. As soon as the bus stopped, Eva opened her eyes and, on being greeted by her parents' faces, she smiled. She rubbed her eyes and yawned, and then fought to sit up and see for herself where she was.

The bus had stopped in front of an art-deco-styled gateway, which could have graced the entrance to a Japanese garden, had it not been constructed of unadorned concrete. The bus driver waited until the heavy iron gates were swung open. As they passed through the gateway, Tomáš read the inscription in white lettering beneath the lintel, *'Camp Récepteur D'Agde'*.

The bus stopped again twenty-five metres beyond the gate in front of a large building built of sandstone blocks with a roof of terracotta tiles.

"Right. Everyone out," said the first gendarme.

They filed out and stood apart in family groups, anxious to preserve their separateness. The size of the camp shocked Tomáš. It stood on thirty acres or so of bare, dusty scrubland and was split into two compounds by high barbed-wire fences. The two halves were mirror images of one other, each with three rows of identical wooden huts disappearing into the distance. Tomáš could see people standing outside the huts and a few ambling from one place to another, but he heard no voices.

The door of the large building opened, and men came out carrying tables and chairs. They were dressed in the same uniforms as the gendarmes, but with their steel helmets and knee-length leather boots they resembled soldiers rather than policemen. Each carried a rifle over his shoulder.

They placed four small tables a metre apart adjacent to the bus, and a soldier stood to the side of each one. Four gendarmes appeared from the building carrying sheets of paper, and each took a seat at a table.

"Men form a line here. Women there. Children aged thirteen or under stay with their mothers."

Tomáš passed Eva to Anna, and they looked at one another, each struggling to betray no emotion. The surly gendarme from the bus approached the line of men.

"Jews form a separate line here."

Ten of the sixteen men moved to the next table.

"Same with you women. Jews here."

Tomáš watched Anna move across. She was holding Eva close to her and stroking her back.

Tomáš reached the head of his line.

"Identity card on the table. Name?"

"Kovařík. Tomáš."

"Nationality?"

"Czechoslovak."

"Date of birth?"

"21st November, 1916."

"Barrack 8. Keep this new card with you at all times. Next."

Tomáš joined one of the four lines now facing the huts. He looked around for Anna and saw her at the head of the queue, being registered.

He was pleased to see a Red Cross nurse talking to her, together with the friendly gendarme.

"Is everything alright?" he mouthed to Anna, as she joined the line of Jewish women and children.

She nodded her head. "What number are you?" he asked her.

"Eighty-six. You?"

"Eight."

He saw the disappointment in her face at the difference in the numbers, and the brief moment of reassurance was swept away by a wave of helplessness.

"I'm sorry," he mouthed. There was no time to see her reply.

"Move forward. Non-Jews first," ordered the gendarme. The soldier on guard outside the men's compound opened the gate, and Tomáš's line passed through. As he went round the corner of the first hut, he looked to his left to try and catch a glimpse of Anna and Eva through the barbed wire, but he could not see them. He looked back. There they were, Anna in her best dress and Eva standing next to her holding her hand, still in the line, waiting.

"Kovařík, whoever you are, this is yours," said the soldier at the head of the column. Tomáš dropped out, and the remaining men continued without breaking step. The soldier bringing up the rear pushed him aside as he passed.

"Where are you from?" asked one of the three men sitting on the steps of Barrack 8.

"Castiran, not far..."

"No. What country are you from?"

"Czechoslovakia."

"Jiří," the man called out to a small group sitting on the ground nearby. "One for you."

A middle-aged man got up and walked slowly towards him. He wore a crumpled dark suit and a white shirt unbuttoned at the neck. The suit was a size too big for him and far too formal for his surroundings. He held out his hand when he reached Tomáš.

"Welcome, friend," he said in Czech. "I'm Jiří Zeman from Brno. Where do you call home?"

"Cheb. My name is Tomáš Kovařík." Tomáš took his hand. "Can I ask you something, pan Zeman? I have a wife and daughter here. Will I get a chance to see them?"

"You get half an hour every two days. We went over this morning, so the next time will be Thursday."

"Thank God for that. I was afraid they wouldn't allow it."

"Yes, they allow it, unless you do something to upset them. But you don't get any privacy. You have to stand around outside. I'm told it's not much fun in the winter. Which hut is your wife in?"

"Eighty-six."

"She's Jewish then?"

"Yes."

"But you can't be."

"Why do you say that?"

"Because they put all the Jews together. Jewish men in Barracks 31 to 45, and the women in 76 to 90. The Jews have thirty huts in total."

"They're not treated any differently, are they?"

"A bit. But most of the guards are bastards to everyone, so it makes no difference. Just stay out of the way of the GMR."

"Who are they?"

"*Groupes Mobiles de Réserves*. The ones with the rifles. Nasty bastards. A few of the ordinary gendarmes can be alright. But generally they all hate foreigners as much as they hate the Jews."

"I'm worried about my little girl. She's not even two yet."

"That can be a good age in here, my friend. Young babies and the very old are the ones who don't last long. And older children like my two find it hard. They know enough to understand how bad it is, you see. But children like your little one can stay happy enough, as long as the mother stays strong."

"My Anna will."

"Good. Then they should be alright. Come inside and I'll find you a billet."

It took Tomáš's eyes some time to adjust to the darkness in the hut. The only windows were the two at either end of the building. They were covered with newspaper.

"The windows in the women's huts have glass in them. And they have heat in the winter. Until six o'clock anyway."

Tomáš put his hand over his nose and mouth.

"You get used to that. A few days and you won't even notice it."

The dominant smell was coming from the latrines at either end of the hut, but it was mixed with the sweet smell of rotting straw which covered the dirt floor.

Slowly Tomáš was able to make out more detail in the gloom. The hut was long and narrow. About thirty metres by five, he estimated. Stretching along its length between the two latrines were upper and lower platforms of planks, barely more than a metre wide. The platforms were divided into ten compartments, making forty in all. They too were covered in straw and small piles of grey blankets.

"How many sleep in here?"

"Two hundred. Five in each compartment."

"But they can't be more than a metre wide."

"One metre thirty. When one turns, you all turn."

"But this is bloody barbaric. No one can live like this."

"I told you. You'll get used to it."

"I don't give a damn for myself. Just tell me the women and children don't have to live like it."

"They do, friend. Everyone does."

"My God, what have I done to them?" Tomas muttered, as he walked down the hut. "What have I done?"

Legs, a few with open yellow sores, dangled over the side of the compartments. Fingers moved as he passed.

"The blankets are meant to be disinfected every two weeks," said Jiří Zeman, reading Tomáš's thoughts, "but it doesn't happen very often."

"But it must be crawling with disease in here."

"Everyone has dysentery. It's part of life."

"So my wife and child will be seeing the same as this now?"

"Yes. But most of the women survive it better than the men."

"I can't let them stay here."

"What choice do you have?"

"But there are lice on the blankets. My father was a prisoner of war in Russia in 1916. He said the biggest danger in camps like this came in the winter from typhus."

"You'll find your biggest problem here isn't any disease, friend. It's hunger. And the cold. They're what saps people's spirit. Like the poor devils here now, who can't be bothered getting off their backs. They're the ones who don't last."

"I can't let my family stay here. I've got to get them out."

"What do you mean?"

"I mean, it must be possible to escape."

Jiří grabbed hold of Tomáš's arm and pulled him away from the figures lying on the platforms near them. "Are you mad?" he said into his ear. "How do you know you can trust me with what you just said? Or whether you can trust these people here? Most would sell you out for a bowl of soup, if they could."

"I have to do something."

"We'll talk outside. I need to explain a few things to you."

Tomáš was relieved to rejoin the fresh air and sunshine. "Come with me," said Zeman, and they walked together past the huts towards the open ground beyond.

"What did you say your first name was?"

"Tomáš."

"You can call me Jiří. What work did you do back in Czechoslovakia, Tomáš?"

"I had just left university in Prague in '38. I planned to make my way as a writer."

"For someone who must be intelligent then, that was pretty stupid talking so openly in there."

"I already know how stupid I am, Jiří. Otherwise my family wouldn't be here."

"Coming from Cheb, I assume you understand German. Do you know what *Nacht und Nebel* means?"

"Night and fog."

"But do you know what Germany and Vichy mean by it?"

"No."

"This is a transit camp, Tomáš. People get moved in and out of here all the time. The sensible ones try to stay in the same place because, if they move you, it's usually because they want to lose you in the system. People are here one day, and then get lost in the night and the fog. Understand?"

"Yes, I understand."

"So, do all you can to keep a low profile. Watch what you say. Don't trust anyone. Show willing."

"I've been trying to do that for the past three years, but all it's done is land my wife and child in this place."

"Well, now you're here, try to be inconspicuous, Tomáš. Choose your friends carefully."

"I already have friends here. Do you know Viktor Musil? He's about seventy. He was taken two weeks ago."

"No, I don't know him. You should be able to find him though, if you want to."

"The other one was arrested nearly a year ago. His name is Marek Kral."

Jiří stopped and stood with his hands on his hips. He looked around him.

"You know Marek Kral? The Communist leader? My God, Tomáš.

You live dangerously."

"I only know Marek because we worked together."

"Don't tell me you're a Communist, Tomáš."

"I'm not. I'm a democrat like my father. He supported Masaryk and Beneš, and so do I."

"I'm relieved to hear it. I advise you to stay well away from Kral. He's a bully and a thug."

"He wasn't a thug a year ago when I knew him."

"Russia wasn't fighting Hitler then. Kral and the Communists are all in Barracks 26 and 27. They're the only ones the *gardes mobiles* won't go near. They know if they make a move against any one of them they'll have a battle on their hands. Stay well away, friend."

"I wouldn't mind a battle with these people."

"If you join with Kral, they'll take it out on your wife."

"Don't worry, Jiří, I've learned not to take risks. Not that it's done much good. For years I've only had two priorities. To keep my country free and my family safe. I have failed in both."

"Don't you think it's the same for every Czech in here who has a family, Tomáš? We all thought we were bringing them to safety when we came to France. But we mustn't give up. We still have our government-in-exile in England."

"Anna and I were leaving for England this morning when we were arrested."

"Were you planning to join the Czech Brigade?"

"I had no plan except getting my wife and child to safety. My plans seem to be narrowing as time goes on. Save my country. Save my family."

They stood by the barbed wire looking into the women's camp.

"Which is hut 86?"

"On the far side, the fifth from the end."

Tomáš stared at it through the wire.

"That's how small my world has become, Jiří. The only plan left to me now is to protect my wife and child from hunger and disease in that hut."

Chapter Fifteen

September 18th – October 18th, 1941

"Tomáš. Tomáš darling, we're over here."

The area around the women's huts was packed with women and children greeting their menfolk in a dozen different languages. Most were embracing and talking excitedly, but Tomáš was surprised by the number who, within minutes of meeting, were arguing and shouting reproaches at one another. A few women sat alone with no visitors, and some women and men scuttled about, anxiously inquiring about loved ones who had been expected but had not appeared.

At the entrance to each hut stood a garde mobile, barring the way to anyone who wished to search inside, or to any couple wanting to find some privacy. The couples were the first to drift away towards the open area of scrubland beyond the huts, where even a doubling of the usual garde-mobile patrol was not enough to keep an eye on everyone.

Eva ran towards Tomáš as he approached. He lifted her high into the air, and she squealed with delight. He looked up and fixed an image of her laughing face, before bringing her down to rest her cheek on his shoulder. Anna stood back looking at them and smiling. Tomáš went to her and put an arm round her and pressed her close to him too. He kissed Eva's head and then Anna's.

"My two beautiful girls."

Anna did not speak. She stayed with her head buried against his chest.

"How are you both?" Tomáš asked.

Anna stood back and turned away, so that Eva could not see her tears. "We're alright. Really we are. We just miss you so much, that's all."

"I've missed you too. Come on, let's find somewhere quiet where we can talk."

They made their way towards the open ground and sat down on a spot as far from other people as they could find. Eva sat on Tomáš's lap and clung to him.

"Tell me honestly, Anna, what are conditions like for you over here? Please tell me the truth."

Anna spoke in German, so Eva would not understand.

"It's terrible. I cannot understand why they are making it this bad for us. It's only supposed to be internment, but they seem to want to punish us."

"Do you have to sleep on the boards?"

"No. There are straw mattresses for mothers with young children, but it's so cramped and dirty. I'm worried about Eva catching something."

"But she's alright?"

"Yes, she's being wonderful."

"You've got her some different clothes."

"Some of the mothers lend clothes to people who brought nothing with them. Judita gave us those. We share a bunk with her and her two girls. But others hold on to everything they've got. And some even steal from you, if you don't watch them."

"What about food?"

"Don't talk funny," protested Eva. "I don't like it."

"I'm telling Táta about what we eat, darling," said Anna.

"It's horrible. I don't like it."

"But you like the biscuits."

"Do you have biscuits, Eva?" said Tomáš. "That's nice."

"Do you remember that nice gendarme on the bus, darling? The one who got the milk. He's been so kind. He's called Durand. Émile, I think. He smuggles them in for the children. I'm sure he could get into trouble, if they found out."

"That's good of him."

"But the children are getting no protein. There are no eggs or meat. The women say there never is."

"What do you get?"

"Swede, turnips, lentils..."

"The same as us."

"They even count the chickpeas each person gets in their soup. I'm really worried for her, Tomáš."

"Can this Durand get eggs or meat? It would do more good than biscuits."

"I don't know, Tomáš. It's only three days. I don't like to ask."

"I've been talking to a fellow in our hut. He's a Czech from Brno. He says I can volunteer for work outside the camp, building roads."

"Yes, some of the women were talking about that."

"They only let men with family go, so they won't try to escape. I would get extra rations for it and save them for Eva."

"Yes, darling. And I'll try to speak to the Red Cross nurse and see if she can help in any way."

A whistle blew, followed by many more from all parts of the women's camp, as each guard signalled the end of the thirty-minute visiting time. Tomáš and Anna stood up and brushed the sandy soil from their clothes. Eva still clung to Tomáš with her arms around his neck, and the three of them made their way back to the huts, holding on to one another.

"I knew everything would be alright, darling," said Anna, "once we were together again."

"I'll make sure it stays alright for us, Anna. I promise you. I went to see Viktor yesterday."

"You did? That's wonderful. How is he?"

"He's fine, darling. Viktor's fine."

"Here comes trouble," said Jiří Zeman.

Tomáš looked up at the three figures walking towards the hut. He closed his notebook and put it down on the step next to him.

"There he is. Tomáš Kovařík," said the short, stocky man walking in front of his two companions. "So it is true. You are here."

Tomáš stood up and walked down the path towards his visitor. "Hello, Marek," he said, and the two men embraced.

"I'm disappointed to see you here, Tomáš. I warned you about this place. I hope Anna isn't with you."

"She is, I'm afraid, Marek. And Eva."

"Let's take a stroll, my friend. We'll stay close to the huts, so the Bluebottles don't bother us. I want to know what's been going on." Marek turned to the two men with him. "You can keep your distance. This man is a comrade."

Tomáš and Marek walked slowly up and down between the huts, as Tomáš explained all that had happened over the past few months.

"Don't think for a minute you could have stayed on the right side of that bastard Bousquet for five years," Marek told him. "But you always were naïve, Tomáš. Anyone could see Bousquet intended to have Musil's business for himself. And he was always going to get rid of anyone who stood in his way, including you."

"Believe it or not, Marek, it helps to hear you say that. To know I couldn't have stopped it. Even if it does make me naïve."

"I didn't say Bousquet couldn't be stopped. I just don't think you or Musil were the people to do it. Have you seen Musil since you've been here?"

"I visit him every day. He has a bad heart condition. He's very ill."

"You go to the Jewish barracks every day? That must make you popular with the Bluebottles."

"They don't hide their feelings about it."

"How many do they give you?"

"Three on the way in and three on the way out usually."

"Riding crop or fists?"

"Whatever takes their fancy."

"How long has it been going on?"

"About a month. Since I first went to see Viktor. The day after we arrived."

"Tell me who it is, my friend, and I'll get it stopped."

"No, Marek. You mustn't do anything. I don't want to draw any attention to my family."

"Do it your own way. You always have."

"It's best if I do."

"How are Anna and your little girl coping?"

"Not very well. Anna seems alright, but she worries so much about our Eva. The poor little darling has flea bites that have become infected. She doesn't have the right medicine or the right food. I work to get her some extra, but it's mostly bread and soup. Sometimes some cheese. The Red Cross give out dried milk."

"Oh, yes. They have plenty of that," scoffed Marek.

"What do you mean by that?"

"I mean there's always plenty of dried milk for the kids, because the Bluebottles have no use for it. It's not worth anything on the black market."

"There's a black market here?"

"There's not much of one in the camp. Most people here have nothing to barter. The guards sell most of the food outside."

"What sort of food?"

"Meat, eggs, fruit. It's not the best quality, but it's meant for the people in here. The Bluebottles sell most of it to local shopkeepers, while the poor sods here go hungry. Don't tell me you're surprised."

"The bastards."

"Not everyone goes hungry in here, my friend. My people don't, because we have things to trade with them."

"What do you trade?"

"The guards' safety mostly. We promise to behave, and they leave us alone and give us our rations. Sometimes we trade valuables that come our way. The women have something else to trade, of course. You don't see many pretty girls going hungry. Don't look so shocked, Tomáš."

"I'm not shocked. I'm just sick of learning every day how cruel and corrupt people become, as soon as they find they have power over others. It makes you despair."

"It's the Fascist capitalist system, my friend. I've told you before how ruthless it is. And what you should be learning is how ruthless you have to be to defeat it. You should join us, Tomáš. Only Communism will defeat these bastards."

"I'm not in the mood for arguing with you, Marek. I'll work it out my own way."

"With people like Zeman, I suppose. Did you know he used to be the mayor of Brno?"

"No, I didn't."

"His type are dangerous. Social Democrats. They trick the working classes into copying their own bourgeois ways."

"It's democracy, Marek. We elected our mayors back then."

"Democracy won't defeat Hitler, my friend. Did you hear the latest news from Prague?"

"No."

"That Gestapo bastard Heydrich has been made the new Reich Protector of Bohemia and Moravia. It was in the Vichy press about how he's going to 'germanise the Czech vermin'. They've arrested thousands already. People like Zeman won't stop that."

They arrived at the steps of Marek's hut.

"I told you before, Tomáš, one day you'll have to choose which side you're on. Wait there a minute."

Marek disappeared into the hut. He came back carrying a pair of old shoes.

"When you get back to your hut, take a good look at these, my friend. And remember, if you change your mind..."

When Tomáš got to his hut, he found a quiet corner and looked inside the shoes. In one was a tin of cassoulet, in the other a small bottle of iodine and a note. 'For Eva.'

Anna and Eva were sitting in their usual place on the scrubland beyond the huts. Anna raised her hand in greeting as Tomáš approached. Eva looked up, but did not run to him. She waited until he had kissed them both and taken his place next to them. Then she moved across from her mother and sat on his lap, sucking her thumb.

"She's hasn't done that since she was a baby," said Tomáš.

"It started on the bus. It comforts her, so I'm not going to discourage it."

"I have something here for her bites." Tomáš took the bottle from his pocket.

"Iodine. Oh, Tomáš, I knew you would find something. Where did you get it?"

"Marek. I met him yesterday. It seems he can get his hands on just about anything."

"How?"

"The guards let him have food and medicine as long as he keeps the Communists under control. He gave me this too." Tomáš handed Anna the tin of cassoulet.

"My God. This is wonderful. Well done, darling." Anna knelt up, placed her hands on his cheeks and kissed him on the lips. "We'll put the iodine on now, and have the food ready when she cries. It's going to sting like mad."

Tomáš sang to Eva as he walked up and down with her to halt her screaming. He looked at the brown iodine stains around her wrists and ankles where the bites were worst and the skin raw from her scratching. "My poor little darling. I know it hurts, but I promise it will make it better. My poor darling."

"I've opened it," Anna called out.

"You're going to have a picnic, my darling," said Tomáš. They took their place next to Anna, who held a piece of meat out to Eva. Eva stifled her sobs and put all the meat into her mouth.

"Thank God," said Anna and she held out some more. "All this will do her so much good. Well done, Tomáš."

When Eva had eaten all she could, she fell asleep in Tomáš's arms. He kissed the top of her head, as he unpicked her matted hair and removed pieces of straw.

"It's getting more and more difficult, Tomáš," said Anna. "People fight for the water when the tanker comes, and there's never enough to wash her properly. And her diarrhoea gets so bad she needs to drink much more. You can see how listless she's getting."

"I'll save more of my water. I'll bring some on Sunday."

"I don't see the point of them keeping us here like this. What good can it do to treat children this way?"

"I don't know, Anna. I'll never understand."

"I blame myself. For not going to Father Benoît's church."

"You mustn't say that, Anna. When I blamed myself after the storm you told me not to, and you were right. You haven't caused this and neither have I. It's all Vichy's doing."

"But Eva can't go on like this, Tomáš. Do you think you can get more food from Marek?"

"I think I can get whatever I want from Marek if I join him and his thugs. But it's not that straightforward."

"But if it gets Eva food..."

"Marek trades with the guards, Anna. Jiří Zeman tells me they bully people into handing over their valuables, so they can get what they want. The Communists find an excuse for anything, because of their 'cause'. Just like Hitler and Pétain. How can I join in with that?"

"I don't want you to, darling."

"Even for Eva's sake?"

"I don't know, Tomáš. Please don't ask me."

"Does this Durand character still give you food?"

"Yes, sometimes. Only biscuits and sweets. It doesn't help much."

"Why do you think he does it?"

"Because he likes children, I suppose. Do you think I should ask him for more?"

"No, Anna. You mustn't. Do you hear me? You must not ask him."

"Alright, Tomáš. I won't if you say so."

"Does he act properly towards you?"

"Yes, of course. Émile is a really nice man."

"And he likes you?"

"Yes, I'm sure he does."

"Listen, Anna. We don't need Marek Kral and we don't need Durand. You and I will take care of Eva together."

"Yes, darling. Of course."

"You must trust me, Anna."

"I do, darling. I do." She moved close to him and gripped his arm and put her head on his shoulder. "I miss you so much, Tomáš. I miss you being next to me at night. I love you so much."

"And I love you, Anna. You mustn't worry. I will make everything alright."

Chapter Sixteen

January 20th, 1942

The men in the conference room stood around talking nervously in twos and threes, unsure why they had been selected to be there. They were a distinguished group, fourteen in total. Amongst them were graduates in theology, medicine, and philosophy. Seven had degrees in law, and eight held doctorates. All were highly placed in government or in the military, and each of them was wise enough to be fearful of the man who had summoned them to this elegant villa by the shores of Lake Wannsee in Berlin.

"I have just been informed that Obergruppenführer Heydrich's arrival is imminent, gentlemen," announced Adolf Eichmann. "If you would please make your way into the conference room, the General will join you there."

The men filed through the double doors to an adjoining room and searched the name cards for their designated seat around the large rectangular table. A few spoke quietly to their neighbour as they waited, until they heard the sound of soldiers standing to attention in the anteroom. The double doors opened. Heydrich entered, followed by Eichmann, and everyone stood.

"Heil Hitler," they said as one.

Heydrich returned the Nazi salute and surveyed everyone, knowing the power his presence had on people. He was tall, blond and athletic, and his eyes were so narrow and so close to his prominent Roman nose that his stare threatened menace.

"Heil Hitler," he said sharply, and he took his seat. Eichmann sat to his right.

"I welcome you all," said Heydrich. "You will find a folder in front of you containing documents of interest. These must not be removed from this room. This meeting will last one hour and a half and you may take notes as aides-mémoire, but no notes will leave the room. The only record of this meeting will be the minutes taken by my deputy, Obersturmbahnführer Eichmann, copies of which will be forwarded to you in due course.

"Now, gentlemen, to business. Each of you has been invited here today to find a solution to a problem. It is a problem of storage. In short, what are we to do with our Jews? Within the Greater Reich we have over many years established a basis for a Jew-free economy and a Jew-free society, for which we all owe a debt of thanks to one of our number, Doktor Stuckart, for his expert framing of the Nuremberg Laws."

A middle-aged man with heavy features and thick, wavy hair nodded his appreciation as the rest of the group rapped their knuckles on the table in tribute.

"In Germany we are able to say that the Jew has been removed from our national life," continued Heydrich. "But now the Jew must be eradicated from our living space. As you know, our policy up to this point has been one of emigration, but this has not proved successful; for who would want our Jews? We offered them to America and Britain and, if I recall correctly, twenty-nine other countries who attended the conference in Évian in 1938, but not one would take them. And who can blame them? But in September '39 we acquired 2,500,000 more Jews in Poland and, as we conquer Russia, we shall accumulate another 5,000,000. Colonel Eichmann has more detailed figures."

"Thankyou, Herr Obergruppenführer. If you would all please refer to Sheet One in your folder. Here you will see the extent of the problem facing us. Under List A you will see the number of Jews in countries under direct Reich control or occupation, or in the case of France partially occupied and quiescent. List B shows the Jews in allied or neutral states, and those at war with Germany. The number of Jews under or soon to be under our jurisdiction totals 11 million."

"So, gentlemen," said Heydrich, "it is clear that emigration has failed and that we cannot possibly store that number of Jews. So what to do?" He turned to Eichmann.

"On Sheet Two in your folders you will find a letter from Reichsmarschall Göring."

"As you will see in this directive to me from the Reichsmarschall," said Heydrich, "I am instructed to find a final solution to the Jewish question in areas of German influence. It is in order to implement our new policy that I have invited you here today, as representatives of all the relevant departments and military units which will be involved. Our policy of emigration is now over, gentlemen. Finished. For good. Our new policy will be evacuation, and Reichsmarschall Göring's directive to me is our mandate."

"Evacuation where, Obergruppenführer?" ventured Wilhelm Kritzinger, the chief civil servant in the Reich's Chancellery.

"Jews over the age of sixty-five will be sent to old persons' camps, initially to Theresienstadt in northern Bohemia or to a ghetto elsewhere. The rest will be separated by sex and sent to transit camps. From there they will be sent to the East to build roads and complete other projects. There will inevitably be a high degree of natural wastage."

"But I must protest," said Kritzinger. "Surely the question of the Jews is one which must be determined by my department. It has already been agreed that any policy regarding the Jews must ensure acceptable living conditions and..."

"Herr Kritzinger," said Heydrich. "Let me make this clear. Every department represented here would like to claim some jurisdiction over the Jews. This will stop. From this point on I am the only jurisdiction in this matter. Europe will be cleansed of Jews. From the Arctic to North Africa, from Manchester to Moscow there will be no Jews. Not one. Do I make myself clear?"

Kritzinger looked down at his folder and nodded his head.

"And we shall begin by evacuating all Jews from Germany, Austria, Bohemia and Moravia."

"Obergruppenführer," said Doktor Josef Bühler, second in charge of administering what had once been Poland. "May I please make a case for the Jews in the General Government? The situation in the ghettos there is now urgent. The conditions are a danger to the health of our soldiers and our administrators. Could the evacuation of our Jews possibly take some priority, sir? They live in filth and most are diseased. They are a pestilence."

"Germany first, then Austria, then Bohemia and Moravia. After that we shall deal with your Jews, Doktor Bühler. I promise you."

"Thankyou, sir."

"May I ask something?" said Doktor Wilhelm Stuckart.

"If you think it necessary."

"Will the Nuremberg Laws be used to determine who is a Jew?"

"Colonel Eichmann will answer that."

"The Nuremberg Laws will only apply to German Jews, where half-Jews with two grandparents or quarter-Jews with one will be exempt if married to a non-Jew. But henceforth such people will be sterilised. In addition, mixed-race persons of dubious character will be evacuated."

"But this flouts German law as it stands," protested Stuckart. "And it will be impossible to enshrine such ad hoc measures within a legal framework. I must also ask whether our laws will have any authority in areas administered by Germany."

"In all such areas the SS will be the determining agency," said Heydrich. "They will decide who is a Jew and who is not."

"But this flies in the face…"

"Doktor Stuckart, the Reich is most grateful to you for your legal expertise, and the German people will continue to benefit from the laws you have framed, but elsewhere the SS will make all decisions regarding Jews. I hope that is clear to you. Is it clear, Herr Doktor?"

"Yes, it is clear."

"Good, then let us move on. I wish now to deal with the practicalities in connection with our new policy of evacuation. Herr Luther, your office in the Foreign Ministry will be the crucial link to SS commanders charged with implementing the new policy."

"We are honoured, Herr Obergruppenführer."

"I have a question about evacuation, if I may be allowed," said Doktor Rudolf Lange, an SS Major in charge of operations in Latvia.

"Of course, Sturmbahnführer Lange."

Lange sat forward, his forearms resting on the table. Although only thirty-one years of age his movements were slow and his manner world-weary.

"I am proud to be able to tell you that Latvia is now Jew-free," he said.

There was a loud rapping of knuckles on the table.

"What I would now like to know is this. When my men shot 30,000 Jews in Riga recently, were those Jews being evacuated?"

Everyone turned to Heydrich who showed no reaction to the question.

"Yes, Major Lange. In my opinion your Jews were evacuated."

"But I must protest," said Kritzinger. "You are not talking here about evacuation. You are talking of annihilation. That is quite contrary to what the Reich Chancellery has been told. We have no mandate for such a thing. The Führer himself has assured me personally that such things are not taking place."

Heydrich looked at him and smiled. "Yes, Herr Doktor, and the Führer will continue to assure you. Now, time is moving on and there is still much we have to get through."

"I am sorry, Herr Obergruppenführer," interrupted Stuckart, "but I share Doktor Kritzinger's shock at such a revelation. Surely we must discuss options other than this 'evacuation'; options which might bring us within the framework of the law as it now stands. Surely we should consider the possibility of mass sterilisation as a method of controlling the Jews, rather than…"

Heydrich raised his right hand to stop Stuckart. He looked at him. His voice became harsher as he spoke.

"If you know a more reliable form of sterilisation than death, Herr

Doktor, I would like to know what it is," he said.

There was a moment of silence before everyone except Kritzinger and Stuckart rapped the table louder than ever.

"We will have no more theory," said Heydrich. "To quote Goethe, 'Theory is grey. Real life is green.' Let us be practical here. Policy is decided. It remains only to decide method. Colonel Eichmann."

"If I may refer you to Sheet Three in your folder, I outline measures which have already been tried, with results achieved. As you see, shooting is proving impractical. It is time-consuming and expensive."

"And I might also add that it diverts manpower from greater military necessities," said General Heinrich Müller, Head of the Gestapo.

"And mass shootings create problems of morale amongst the men," added Lange. "Especially when the Jew is of German origin."

"Which is why we are looking at other methods," said Eichmann. "You will see on Sheet Three a breakdown of numbers achieved through our T4 Programme, otherwise referred to as our euthanasia programme. We have used injection as part of this exercise but, as you can see, the numbers achieved are far too low for our purposes. However, we have had far greater success under T4 with gas. We started with lorries specially adapted to allow carbon monoxide gas to enter an enclosed chamber. Forty to sixty Jews an hour can theoretically be processed in this way, achieving a possible 1,440 per day. With our twenty lorries this amounts to 28,800 per day or 10,512,000 each year. It is clear that with gas we can achieve significantly greater numbers."

There was a general murmuring of approval around the table.

"So, gentlemen," said Heydrich, "it seems our method is now defined. Gas it is. Colonel Eichmann."

"Thankyou. Unfortunately the use of gas lorries is not a practical solution. There are frequent breakdowns and the question of disposal has proven insurmountable. We have therefore turned more recently to a more permanent solution. We have three camps, Belzec, Sobibor and Treblinka, where permanent gas chambers will soon be operational. These are made to resemble shower rooms in order not to cause disruption from those awaiting processing..."

"But this is mass murder," exclaimed Kritzinger. "How can we sanction such a thing?"

Heydrich turned on him. "You are the ultimate hypocrite, are you not, Herr Kritzinger? You will imprison the Jew, strip him of home, livelihood and all he possesses, but we must not kill him in case Germany loses her nobility. You shirk from the very thing most crucial to Germany's survival.

I will not countenance it."

He looked around the table.

"Before we go on, I demand from every man here his open support for the course on which we are embarked. I start with you, General Müller."

"You have my wholehearted support, Herr Obergruppenführer."

"Doktor Stuckart?"

"Yes, you have it."

"Herr Luther?"

"Absolutely. No question."

Heydrich gained every man's approval before he returned to Kritzinger. "And you, Herr Doktor Kritzinger. What do you say?"

"I say I shall not oppose it."

"That is not enough."

"Then yes, Herr Obergruppenführer. You have my support."

"Good. Then we can move on. Colonel Eichmann, would you, please?"

"Thankyou. Most recently we have begun a project in Upper Silesia near the town of Auschwitz. This particular place has the dual advantage of being isolated and yet enjoying very favourable rail connections. There we are using Jewish labour to build a camp which will be equipped with gas chambers similar to those at Sobibor, but on a much more ambitious scale. The camp will also benefit from industrial gas ovens which will dispose of waste with hardly any residue. This camp will be able to process 2,500 people each hour for twenty-four hours every day. That makes a total of 60,000 each day."

"Sixty thousand a day," echoed Lange. "Unbelievable."

"Sixty thousand Jews every day. Up in smoke," said Müller. "*Phantastisch.*"

"Yes, gentlemen," said Heydrich. "Twenty-one million, nine hundred thousand Jews every year, if ever there were that many."

Everyone around the table looked at one another. Then Müller began to slap the table with the palm of his hand, and the others quickly joined in. Heydrich looked at Eichmann and smiled. Stuckart and Kritzinger both placed their right hands on the table and moved them across the surface as if smoothing away crumbs.

"Your enthusiasm is a credit to you all, gentlemen," said Heydrich. "I order you now to go from here and do all you must. Work together. Command your ministries, your units; apply your intelligence and your energies to the task. The machinery is waiting, gentlemen. Feed it. Get them on the trains. Keep the trains rolling, and history will honour us for what we are about to do."

Chapter Seventeen

June 2nd – July 12th, 1942

Anna was waiting at the gate between the two camps.

"What's the matter?" asked Tomáš. "Where's Eva?"

Anna walked towards him, her head bowed, and put her arms around him.

"She's so sick, Tomáš. Nurse Zlatin has her in quarantine with the others."

"Take me to her, Anna. Where is she?"

"They're using Barrack 90 for the Jewish children."

They turned and held on to one another, as they walked towards the furthest row of huts.

Suffocating heat and the smell of soiled clothes hit them when they entered the barrack. A low moan came from some of the dozens of children lying on the long rows of bunks. Most were coughing. Very few cried. Anna made straight for a bunk near an open window at the far end of the hut. Sabine Zlatin, the Red Cross nurse, saw Anna and left the child she was tending and walked with her. Tomáš followed closely behind, trying to pick out what they were saying above the noise.

"She's not improving, Madame Kovařík," he heard the nurse say. "I think we shall have to move her."

Anna sat down on the straw mattress next to Eva, who was wearing only a small towel as a makeshift napkin. An older child of about four beside Eva turned to see who it was and he held out his arms and cried. Anna leant across Eva, kissed the child and held his hand. With the other she smoothed Eva's forehead. Tomáš knelt on the floor and put his cheek next to Eva's. He looked down at her child body. Her white skin was covered in a red rash and she was wet with sweat.

"Hello, my precious darling. Táta's here."

When Eva did not respond, he turned to Nurse Zlatin.

"I don't understand, madame. How can measles make her like this? When my wife and I had it as children, it was over in a week."

"I'm sure you were well nourished in the first place, monsieur. Your bodies were able to fight it. These poor things were already weak before they got it."

"Her forehead is burning, nurse," said Anna. "Please let me take her outside."

"You know it isn't allowed, madame. It would be so unfair on the children who aren't infected."

"Did I hear you say to my wife that you want to move Eva somewhere?"

"Yes, monsieur. I have gained permission to move the worst cases to a hospital in Montpellier."

"No," said Anna. "Not unless I can go with her."

"That's impossible, madame. You must realise that."

"She's not going to a French hospital. Tell her, Tomáš. Not after what Nataša went through."

"Madame Kovařík, I think your little girl has pneumonia. If she stays here, I don't think she will be strong enough to survive it."

Anna picked Eva up and cradled her. "No, she's not going. Please, Tomáš. Please do something. Please."

Tomáš stood up and spoke quietly to Nurse Zlatin. "We have a friend whose Jewish son was taken to a hospital in Montpellier, madame. The authorities there just left him to die from neglect. My wife fears the same thing might happen to our Eva."

"No, monsieur, it will not. I would not allow it."

"If our child does go, you must tell them she has only one Jewish grandparent."

Sabine Zlatin sat down on the bunk next to Anna. "I promise you, madame," she said. "I shall account personally for the children I take, and I'll find a way of informing you how Eva is."

"But Émile promised me he would bring some honey and some lemon for her later. That will help her, won't it?"

Tomáš saw the nurse pause and glance up at him before she answered.

"It's not enough, my dear, whatever he brings. Eva needs clean, cool air, and intravenous fluids. She can't get that here. I have ambulances coming later today. There is room for only eighteen children. You must let her go."

"How long would it be for, madame?" asked Tomáš.

"Two or three weeks. Perhaps more."

"No. You can't take her," said Anna. "I m not going to lose her."

"Listen, Madame Kovaříková. I have to tell you that over the last few days we have lost our first children to this epidemic. Fifteen already. We expect to lose a quarter of them before it is over. You will be condemning your child if you keep her here with you." She turned to Tomáš. "You must persuade your wife, monsieur. I have so much work to do. Tell me as soon as you can what you decide."

The mothers and fathers watched from their separate parts of the camp as the children were carried to the ambulances. The women wept and consoled one another. The men stood silent, staring through the wire, each coping alone with their feelings of impotence and failure. Tomáš searched for Eva amongst the bundles being carried out by the gendarmes. He saw Durand holding a tiny figure wrapped in a blanket and knew it would be her. He looked across for Anna but could not see her. He needed to see her. To see her looking for him. He watched Durand disappear with Eva inside the ambulance and fought the urge to call out.

The next day the men's visits to the women's compound were suspended until the epidemic ran its course. Not seeing Anna, not knowing how she was coping, and being unable to do anything to help her, was as painful as the thought of Eva lying alone and stricken in a place he could never find. Then, three days after Eva left in the ambulance, he was summoned to the administration building.

He was told to wait in a small office. There was a desk with a chair on either side, and a telephone, but nothing else. Tomáš could not sit down. He stood in a corner with his arms wrapped tightly across his chest. The door opened and Émile Durand entered the room.

"Monsieur Kovařík," he said, and he offered his hand.

Tomáš did not move. He breathed in deeply, closed his eyes and exhaled the words, "Is my daughter alive?"

"Oh, I'm so sorry. I should have realised. Yes, Eva is being looked after. That's why I sent for you. Anna asked me to tell you that Eva is not yet out of danger, but she is no worse."

Tomáš made it to a chair and sat down with his arms still gripping his body. "I need the address of the hospital," he mumbled, staring at the floor. "I need to know where she is."

"I don't have it here but I'll get it for you. I haven't introduced myself. My name is Durand."

"I know who you are. You were on the bus that brought us here nine months ago. You bought some milk for my Eva. You wouldn't let me pay you."

"There was no need. I was happy to help." Durand sat down in the chair on the other side of the desk. "I'm still happy to help."

"When will they know if Eva will be alright?"

"Two or three more days. She has pneumonia and needs to get over the fever. I asked Nurse Zlatin if there was anything I could do, but she said it was just a case of waiting."

"Why do you take such an interest in my wife and child? Are you doing this for all the children?"

"That would be impossible, monsieur. I help Anna because I met you on the way here. You seemed such a nice family."

"This place is full of nice families. Do they all get help like this?"

"Some of my colleagues are helping other mothers."

"How do you choose who you help?"

"I don't know. These things have a way of working themselves out."

"I just hope the guards' motives in doing such things are honourable, that's all."

"Of course you do, monsieur. I understand that. But are you really in a position to dictate what people do in here, and why?"

Tomáš uncrossed his arms, sat up in his chair and looked at Durand for the first time.

"You may see me only as an internee, Monsieur Durand, but that's not who I am. Even in this camp I am a husband and a father before all else."

"You also need to understand something, monsieur. It is true, some of the guards do take advantage of the women they help. And they certainly have no wish to meet with the husbands they cuckold. But I can meet with you because I know Anna has done nothing to dishonour you. She is a wonderful woman."

Tomáš stood up.

"I don't need another man to tell me anything about my wife. It's your motives that concern me."

Durand stared at Tomáš across the desk.

"You must sit down, monsieur, or this conversation will end now. And it's just as well for you that I do value Anna's friendship so much, because if not, I would do nothing more to help you or her."

"We don't need your help."

"I think you do. Now sit down or leave."

Tomáš retook his seat.

"You need to understand, monsieur," said Durand, "that I am a policeman, not a prison guard. I didn't ask to come here and do this. It sickens me to see how people are treated in this place. To see children like your Eva suffering. I'm helping now for the same reason I helped on the bus. Because everyone has a right to be treated with decency. It used to be what France stood for."

Tomáš sat back and looked at the man across the desk. He spoke more softly. "Are you married, Monsieur Durand?"

"No, I'm not."

"Then it might be difficult for you to understand how a man feels seeing someone doing things for his wife and child that he knows he should be doing himself."

"I do understand, monsieur. I would probably feel the same in your position."

Durand smiled, and Tomáš studied him. Like all the guards his face had a healthy colour and fullness denied to all but the most favoured internees. He was probably in his mid thirties, but he still looked younger than Tomáš, whose handsome features had long become hidden behind the gauntness of hunger and worry. But Durand's face had a benign look absent from the majority of guards, and it was just possible, thought Tomáš, that his motives were benign too.

"If I have misjudged you, monsieur, I will apologise one day. But if not..."

"Please, monsieur, for the sake of Anna and Eva, you must allow me the benefit of the doubt. You and I both want to help them. Nurse Zlatin will have another bulletin on the children the day after tomorrow. Let us meet again then."

"I need to know as soon as you have news."

"You will." Durand stood up. "I have to be on duty at ten o'clock. I must go, but I'll get word to you as soon as I know more."

He went to the door and paused before he opened it. "You are a Czech like Anna, are you not, monsieur?"

"Yes."

"Have you heard the latest news from Prague?"

"No."

"Your people have assassinated Reinhard Heydrich. He was attacked last week on his way to Prague Castle. He died yesterday."

"Are you sure it's not just another rumour? This place is full of them."

"No, it's certain. It was announced officially on Radio Lyon this morning."

"My God. So we are fighting back at last."

Tomáš hung his head.

"It's strange. I know it should mean something to me. But I care about nothing now. Nothing, except my child."

Anna and Tomáš had been waiting since early morning for the ambulance to arrive from Montpellier with the last of the children.

The measles epidemic in the camp lasted for seven weeks. During the first week in July no new cases were reported and most of the hospitalised children were returned. Now only the four children who developed the most severe complications remained in Montpellier, and special permission had been given to their parents to await their arrival together in front of the administration block.

Anna's health declined rapidly in the five weeks she was separated from Eva. While visits to the women's camp were suspended, Tomáš had only been able to see Anna from a distance during shouted conversations through the wire, and now her fragile state came as a shock to him. As they stood with their arms around one another, he could feel her ribs and hip bones beneath her thin dress. The worry about Eva, she told him, had prevented her from eating much at all, even the treats Émile Durand had tried to tempt her with every day.

"I'm so tormented, Tomáš," she said. "I can't wait to see her, but it feels so cruel bringing her back into this awful place. I ask myself over and over whether I should have left her with Nataša. Was I just being selfish?"

"No, my darling, you weren't. Sometimes it's impossible to make a good decision. For all we know Nataša may be sick herself. Then Eva might have been taken anywhere. How would we have felt then?" He kissed the side of her head. "You did the right thing, my darling."

"But, her eyes. What if she can't see well enough to read?"

"Nurse Zlatin said it was a 40 percent loss. When we get home, we'll take her to the best doctors."

"Will we get her home, Tomáš? Will we ever get her home?"

Anna started to cry again and Tomáš held her and stroked her head.

"Yes, my darling. I promise you..."

"They're here!" shouted one of the fathers.

A white Citroën ambulance appeared at the camp's main gates, which were swung open by two gendarmes. Tomáš felt Anna make an involuntary step towards it and he held her gently by the shoulders. "Be patient, darling," he whispered.

The driver decided to perform a lengthy three-point turn, before backing up to the waiting parents and opening the back doors. Nurse Zlatin was inside, getting the children up from the stretchers, fixed one above the other on each side of the ambulance. The children stood at the entrance to the ambulance, blinking and rubbing their eyes against the bright sunlight. For a dreadful moment Tomáš could not see Eva, and then she was there, standing behind the others, unblinking and holding a white cloth in both hands to her chest.

Two gendarmes stood in front of the parents, blocking their path with outstretched arms, while Sabine Zlatin passed the children to Émile Durand. He lifted them down onto the ground until finally he held Eva. He stepped past the other children and the parents, who could be held back no longer, and carried Eva towards Anna and Tomáš.

"There you are, Anna," he said, passing her over. "One healthy little girl, as promised."

"Oh, thankyou, Émile. Oh, my darling Eva. You're so big. Let me look at you."

Eva leaned back in Anna's arms to look at her mother and, realising how much she had missed her, she started to cry. Anna held her close and started to cry too. Tomáš put his arms around them both and Eva reached out to her father. Tomáš had to stop himself from squeezing her thin body too hard. He stood with his eyes closed, holding her and smelling her skin, and experienced peace for the first time since before the night of the storm.

"They're allowing you an hour, before your husband must return to his own barrack, Anna. I can find you a room in the administration block, if you like," Tomáš heard Durand say.

"No, thankyou," he replied. "My family can find its own privacy. Come with me, Anna."

Tomáš put one arm around Anna's shoulders and with the other he carried Eva, who wrapped her arms around his neck as tightly as she could. Behind him he knew Émile Durand was watching them, as they walked together back into the camp.

It was not long before Eva wanted to play. As they passed the last of the Jewish barracks, she wriggled to be allowed to get down. She gave her piece of white cloth to Tomáš and took his hand. With her other hand she reached up to Anna.

"Swing me," she demanded in French.

They crossed the open ground behind the barracks, with Anna and Tomáš counting 'one, two, three' and then swinging Eva between them. Eva chuckled each time and insisted, "*Encore une fois,*" showing no sign of becoming bored with the game. Tomáš looked across at Anna. She attempted a smile and turned away.

They sat down in their old place, as far from the huts and other people as they were allowed. Anna took Eva on her knee and looked at her eyes.

"I can't see anything wrong. There's no sign of ulcers or scarring or anything. You have a look, Tomáš."

"Let's not risk upsetting her, Anna. I'll look when I get the chance."

Anna pulled Eva towards her and held her. She looked at Tomáš over Eva's shoulder, her face full of anxiety and doubt.

"Everything will be alright, Anna," Tomáš said. "Come to Táta, Eva. I want you to do something for me."

Eva walked over to him, confident that her father would have a good idea for a game, or perhaps he would tell one of his stories about his own táta.

"I think we should pick some flowers for Máma. Do you see the purple ones by the fence? I think she would really like those."

Eva looked around her but did not move. "Take my hand, darling. I'll come with you. Point to the flowers you want to pick." Eva looked up at him and reached for her cloth. "Come on then, let's find them together."

Tomáš led Eva to within two metres of the grape hyacinths growing along the fence, before she let out an excited laugh and ran towards them. He walked back to Anna and sat down next to her.

"I know what you're thinking, Anna, but I promise you we will get her eyes treated as soon as all this is over."

"I don't think it will ever be over."

"Don't talk like that, Anna. It's not like you. We mustn't give up."

"I'm not as strong as you, Tomáš. I always thought I was, but I'm not."

"Of course you are."

"No. I never dreamed you could be so strong. The way you have worked for us. Even now. You're so thin your clothes are hanging off you, and I can see how exhausted you are, but you never give up."

"It's simple, Anna. If I have you and Eva, I can do anything."

Anna smoothed out the creases of her dress over her thigh.

"I learned something when Eva was in hospital," she said. "I learned that if I lost her, I would give up. I knew the hopelessness of this place would overcome me."

Tomáš put his hand on hers. "Look, Anna. Eva is there now, picking flowers for you. She's healthy. We are going to keep her healthy."

Anna took her hand away.

"You can't be sure of that, Tomáš. People are getting sick all the time. Death means nothing in here. Look at poor Viktor. One day he was here. Then he was gone. No fuss. No funeral. He was our friend, so important in our lives, but we don't even talk about him any more."

"I know."

"Where has normal life gone, Tomáš? Do you know I watched some of the mothers go mad over the past weeks when they lost their children in the epidemic? You wouldn't believe the things I have seen. The way the guards take advantage of the mothers. The promises they make to get their way with them. I've been lucky."

"What do you mean?"

"I mean I only have to flirt with Émile and infer some promises of my own. That seems to be enough for him."

Tomáš got to his feet.

"I don't want you to infer anything to that bastard, Anna. If he comes anywhere near you..."

"I wouldn't do anything, Tomáš. God knows I'm sick of him hanging around me. But what would you want me to do if Eva got ill again, and the only way to get medicine was..."

"Don't say those things, Anna."

Tomáš knelt down in front of her and took hold of her arms. "That will never happen. Listen to me. I will get whatever you and Eva need. You ask no one else for help from now on. Do you understand? I can look after you. Look at me, Anna. Do you believe me?"

"I know you would do anything for us, darling. But can we risk Eva spending another winter here? You can't stop the cold. You can't stop the lice in her clothes, or the rain soaking her during roll call. You can't stop typhus."

Tomáš let go of her and let his arms fall to his side. "Tell me what you want me to do, Anna, and I'll do it."

"There's only one thing to do, darling. Whatever it takes, get us out of this terrible place."

Chapter Eighteen

July 9th – July 23rd, 1942

"Why don't you ask Jiří Zeman to negotiate a way out for you? Perhaps you could arrange an election together, so it could all be settled democratically?"

"If all you want to do is make fun of me, Marek, go ahead. I'll lie on the ground and kiss your feet, if it means you'll help us."

"You've got a damn cheek, Tomáš. You turn your back on me for months in this place, and then you come here and ask if we're planning an escape. Anyone but you, my friend, and you'd be under one of these huts by now, trying to hold your guts in. Why the hell would I want to share any of my plans with you?"

"Because beneath all your dogma, Marek, you're a decent man. And I know how much you think of Anna."

"My advice to you is, don't take too much for granted, my friend. Neither you or Anna are more important to me than our cause. If you'd joined us at the beginning, you could be part of our plans. But you've left it too late."

"Will you at least tell me if you know of any way I can get them out?"

"I don't. A man could probably find a way on his own, but I know you wouldn't go without them."

"But you must have plans for your people, Marek."

"We'll get out when the time's right, but I can't tell you when, and I won't be able to include any women or children. We'll make our move when it's time to fight."

"Do you think it will be soon?"

"You're asking too much again."

Marek flicked the stub of his cigarette onto the sandy soil under the steps of the hut. "But because I think you'd help me if I needed it, I'll tell you how it is. The tide's turning, Tomáš. Our Russian comrades have already halted Hitler's summer offensive. Soon they'll be pushing him back, and then we'll go."

"But when, Marek? When?"

"I can't give you an exact date. When Vichy turns the screw on the Communists again and the Bluebottles turn on us in here. Then we'll tear this damned place down and go and fight with the Bir Hakeim."

"Who?"

"The local maquis. In a few months, maybe a year, we'll join up with the Soviet armies from the east, and put an end to Fascism for good."

"I need to know when you're going, Marek."

"I can't tell you. It could be weeks. It could be months."

"That's no good."

"This isn't all about you and your family. We're talking here about the Revolution, the future of the whole world."

"My world only has two people in it."

"You're a bourgeois fool, Tomáš. You always were. Look what your bourgeois system has done for you. It's brought you here. And if you refuse to help overturn the system, you have to find a way of surviving on its terms."

"I've done all I could for Anna and Eva. But it's not enough, Marek. What more can I do?"

"I've heard the Red Cross nurse is getting a few Jewish children out and putting them with French families. Why not ask her to take Eva?"

"Eva's not Jewish. Besides, I don't think Anna could bear to be separated from her. Neither could I."

"Well then. There's something else I've heard."

"What?"

"You won't like it."

"Go on."

"I've heard one of the guards is lusting after your Anna."

"Durand. I know about him."

"Well, that's alright then. You don't need to get them out. Let Anna give him what he wants and he'll look after them both. You as well, I expect."

Tomáš sprang to his feet.

"Are you mad, Marek? Do you think I would ever allow something like that?"

"It's the way to keep them safe. It solves your problem."

"Solves my problem? My God, Marek. What sort of world do you want to create? Do you have no principles? Do you think Anna and I have no principles?"

"Principles and morality have to change with circumstances, Tomáš. I've told you already, you're too bourgeois. It's time to be practical, my friend."

"Practical? Damn your world, Marek. Damn the Fascists and the

Communists. I'll find a way myself."

"Understand something, Tomáš. This place isn't so different from the world outside. There are those who survive and those who don't."

Marek cupped his hands around a match as he lit another cigarette. "And I'm not sure any more which one you belong to, my friend," he muttered to himself, as Tomáš walked away.

Tomáš decided to speak to Nurse Zlatin. He knew Anna would never allow Eva to be lodged with an unknown French family, but perhaps he and the nurse together could persuade her to let Eva return to Castiran to be looked after by Nataša. To his surprise Anna agreed, and Nurse Zlatin made the journey to Castiran the next day.

She found Madame Musil living in a cramped cottage in the grounds of the château, she reported. The old lady had suffered a stroke after the death of her husband, and was bed-ridden. Her only visitor was the kindly village priest, who brought her food and provided for her needs as best he could.

Anna's self-recrimination grew worse over the following days. Not only did she blame herself for not attending Father Benoît's church, she now kept reliving the moment nearly four years before when she registered for the first time in Castiran and uttered the word *'Juive'*.

"If I hadn't said it, Tomáš, they would never have found out. None of us would be here. My stupid arrogance..."

Nothing Tomáš said about her mother's Jewish maiden name being on her birth certificate, or the fact that they would have been interned as foreigners anyway, made any difference to Anna. The near-loss of Eva, the damage she was sure she had done to her, and the fear of more illness to come had affected her nerves and her spirit.

Tomáš devised a dozen escape plans every day as he worked on the roads. They all foundered on the need for help from too many other people, and on the necessity of obtaining identity cards, without which no one could get very far in any part of France. He settled on the least flawed plan. He would escape alone from his work party, secure identity cards and money, and break back into the camp to bring Anna and Eva out. It was a plan full of risk, but it had some chance of success, and it relied on no one other than himself. He decided to keep refining it, tell not a single soul, and draw no attention to himself. Then one morning, as his detail left the camp for work, he was ordered to fall out and report again to the administration block.

He was directed to the room where he had his previous meeting with

Émile Durand. Tomáš knocked on the door, a voice invited him in, and he saw Durand sitting behind the desk. The gendarme did not get up.

"I won't offer you my hand, Monsieur Kovařík, because I know you wouldn't accept it. Please sit down."

Durand waited for Tomáš to take his seat, then pushed his képi to the side of the desk and leaned forward as far as he could towards him.

"I have something to tell you, monsieur," he said in a hushed voice, "and I need you to listen to me. Try not to interrupt, but if you do, speak very quietly. If we are overheard, we're both in trouble."

"What do you want from me, monsieur?" Tomáš said wearily.

"I've told you before. I want to help."

"We don't need your help."

"You do. More than ever. Anna is in danger."

"I know that. But I can get her through this."

"No, I mean she's in real danger. From the authorities. Have you heard the rumours about Jews being transported to the east?"

"Of course. They've been around for months."

"Well, I can tell you they're true. The Germans have been arresting Jews in the Occupied Zone since last October. Now they're starting to send them east."

"What for?"

"To work, so they say. But you can be sure conditions won't be as easy in Poland or Russia as they are here."

"I can't imagine much worse. Anyway, how can it affect Anna? She has a child. They can't work."

"I don't know, monsieur. All I do know is there was a big round-up in Paris last week. They expected to net over 22,000 foreign Jews, but they only got half that number. So Vichy has agreed to make up the difference with foreign Jews from internment camps here in the south."

Tomáš shifted in his seat.

"No, that can't be. Even Vichy wouldn't do that. The Germans have no jurisdiction here."

"It shames me to say it, monsieur, but it wasn't the Germans doing the round-up. It was a French operation, using Paris's gendarmes. But the Jews we caught will be handed over to the Germans."

Tomáš stood up. His chair tipped over with a crash. "French gendarmes... rounding up women and children? My God, what's become of you people?"

Durand hurried around the desk to pick up the chair. He looked anxiously at the door.

"Please sit down, monsieur. And keep your voice down."

"Why? Why are you doing this now?" Tomáš lowered himself onto the chair. "The Germans are fighting for their lives. Why is anyone bothering with this?"

"I don't know. But Vichy seems very anxious to show Hitler which side they're on. Prime Minister Laval has now stated publicly that he wants a German victory in this war. I think he wants to buy favour by giving them our Jews."

"But what makes you think they'll come here for Anna?"

"The paperwork arrived yesterday. The men will go first. Then the women and children. They will be taken by bus to Montpellier. Then by train to a transit camp in Paris. A place called Drancy. From there they'll be sent east."

"I'm sorry, monsieur, but I can't hear this and stay in my seat." Tomáš stood up and paced from one side of the room to the other. "This is unbelievable," he muttered. He stopped and leaned with his hands on the back of the chair. "You said you wanted to help her. How can you?"

"I'm going to help you to escape All three of you."

"You'd do that? How?"

"Please sit down, monsieur. Try to stay calm. You must begin by trusting me."

Tomáš stayed where he was.

"Alright. Let's get a few things out into the open, Monsieur Kovařík. I believe you're planning an escape of your own. I know for certain you met with Marek Kral recently. But I must advise you to do nothing with that man. He is marked. He will get you killed."

"And how can you know all that? There are thousands of people in here. How could you gendarmes know everything I do?"

"When people are desperate they will sell anything, monsieur. Information is the easiest thing to buy in here."

"I have nothing planned with Marek Kral."

"Good. And you must do nothing on your own. I have everything worked out for you and Anna and Eva. But you mustn't do anything until I tell you, and you must say nothing to Anna until I tell you. Otherwise I cannot help. Are you agreed?"

"Do I have a choice?" Tomáš retook his seat. "Why are you doing this?"

"I don't think you need me to answer that."

"I want to hear it."

"I won't lie to you, monsieur. I am doing it for Anna... She is such an exceptional woman. And to see her warmth and vitality undermined by what is happening to her... You are a fortunate man, monsieur. Her devotion to you is total. I will not see her sacrificed..."

"Enough. Just tell me your plan."

"I will not tell you the dates of the transports from the camp. I dare not risk the information being leaked. But I can tell you it will all happen in the next two weeks."

"Two weeks?"

"The transports will take place late in the evening. The men first, then the women. They will travel through the night so no one outside sees what is being done. During the afternoon before the transport I shall escort Anna and Eva to the hospital in Montpellier for treatment to Eva's eyes. I shall arrange some reason for you to be brought to this block in the evening."

"Can you do all this?"

"Yes, I have the authority. There will be no problem. You will lie hidden outside the block until it gets dark, and then you will crawl through the drainage gully by the side of the main gates."

"But there are metal grids at each end. I've already checked."

"I was about to say the grids will be loosened."

"And what do I do when I get out?"

"You will meet up with me, Anna and Eva at a time and place I'll arrange. Then you will make your way to a safe house I know. People there will make arrangements for you to get out of France. I don't know those details and I don't want to."

"But we have no identity cards."

"They're already done. Here."

Durand took three new identity cards from the front pocket of his dark-blue tunic and placed them on the desk. Tomáš picked them up. The photographs inside were the originals from the cards confiscated on their arrival ten months before.

"They look completely genuine," he said.

"They are genuine. I issued them myself. But you'll see Anna's religion is now the same as yours. I'll take them back now, but when I return them to you on the day of the transport they will have a month's resident's stamp in them."

Tomáš sat back and stared at him.

"I don't know what to say to you, monsieur. Yes, I do. Perhaps I shouldn't ask this, but how do I know I can trust you?"

"Just ask yourself why I would be saying all this to you, if it wasn't true."

Tomáš kept staring at him.

"Anyway, you'll know it is true when the men's transport takes place. And a word of warning, Monsieur Kovařík. I know you're a decent man, because Anna never tires of telling me. But do not think of making the news of the transports public. You and I will both be arrested and shot, if you do. The disorder you would cause in the camp would result in countless deaths, and the transports will take place anyway, and under much more forceful supervision. You won't stop them. You must be sensible and take this chance to save your family."

Tomáš still did not take his eyes of Durand. "I've already made my decision," he said. "I have no choice. I have to trust you."

"To be frank with you, Monsieur Kovařík, it's not your trust that concerns me. It's Anna's. She hasn't been the same towards me since Eva returned. She used to confide in me and let me help her. Now she seems to have turned against me. To make this work, monsieur, you must persuade Anna to do as I say. She must trust me completely or we could all end up in front of a firing squad. But say nothing to her about any of this for now, however tempted you may be. I shall arrange for you and Anna to meet on the evening before you leave. You can tell her all about the plan then."

Chapter Nineteen

August 3rd – August 5th, 1942

Anna found it impossible to sleep. The heat was unbearable. And the smell. The rough planks of the bunks and the sides of the hut trapped the odorous warmth within them and the thick air clogged her throat.

She lay still, her eyes fixed on the rafters, letting the sweat run off her face and body onto the straw mattress. At least the children were able to sleep. She looked at Eva lying on her back next to her, her flea-bitten arms stretched out above her head. Judita and her two daughters lay at the other end of the bunk, head to toe with them. It was the best way to cope with the heat, lying still with as little physical contact as possible.

A constant shuffle of women passed on their way to the latrines at either end of the hut. The sound and smell of the liquid waste leaving their weakened bodies would continue throughout the night. And Anna knew she would lie awake all night, watching Eva and worrying that her child was drawing the noxious air into her body with every breath she took.

Every now and then a baby cried. At least someone was objecting. It was the sound of normality. Anna thanked God that Eva was no longer a baby. Half the babies born in the camp died. More in the winter. And none of those born as a result of liaisons with the guards seemed to survive. And no one asked why.

Anna had stopped worrying about Tomáš. He seemed to be able to draw on an endless supply of strength. She believed he could do anything. She believed he could even find a way of getting her and Eva out of the camp. He had to. Émile was losing patience with her. She had stopped providing little signs of hope for him. There seemed no point any more. It upset Tomáš, and Émile had been unable to protect Eva when it really mattered. But one question tormented her more than any other. If she had given more to Émile at the beginning, would Eva have been spared all her suffering?

Anna thought she could hear traffic on the road outside the camp. She raised her head to look through the windows at the end of the hut. It was still dark. There was never any traffic during the night, but the noise was growing louder. Car doors opened and closed, and she heard voices. Lots of voices. Then came shouting from the men's camp, and the women in the hut sat up on their bunks and asked one another what was going on outside.

"It must be new arrivals," someone said.

"Not at this time of night."

"It sounds as if there's hundreds of them."

Some of the women got up and went to the windows.

"Can't see a thing."

"What do you think it is, Judita?" asked Anna.

"I don't know."

"Look at this," called out someone from a window which faced away from the men's camp towards open ground. "Look out there on the road. Buses all lined up. Must be more people arriving. Look."

Anna and Judita went to the window.

"But the buses are all empty," said Judita. "They're not bringing new people in, Anna. I think they're here to take people away."

"So, I assume, Monsieur Kovařík, you now realise I was telling the truth when we last met," said Durand.

"I never doubted you were telling the truth. It was the French barbarity which lay behind the truth I found hard to accept. Are you still telling me that France will hand over those Jewish men to the Germans?"

"I'm afraid so." Durand looked down at a sheet of paper on his desk. "They left here two days ago, so yes, they will be in Paris by now."

"And when will the Germans get their hands on them?"

"The Paris police will hold them in Drancy until the trains are ready. Then they will be handed over and sent east. It can be days or weeks, I'm told. Even months sometimes."

"So when will it be the turn of the women?"

"That's why I have called you here, monsieur. The women will be transported during the night tomorrow."

Tomáš put his hand to his face. "Tomorrow night. My God, Durand, Your plan had better work."

"Don't distress yourself, monsieur. It will work."

"This is my wife and child…"

"I know. I understand. But you must promise me, Monsieur Kovařík, that you have said nothing about our plan to Anna."

"How could I? We haven't been allowed to visit the women's camp since the men were taken."

"Because if she did know anything, I don't think she's in a fit state to keep it to herself."

"I realise that. All I can say is, I have not told her. But if the women's transport is tomorrow night, she'll have to know about it soon."

"You can tell her tonight. I shall arrange for you to go to the women's camp at ten o'clock. I'll bring Anna to you at your usual spot on the assembly area. I can let you have one hour. No more."

"And what do I tell her?"

"Tell her above all to trust me and to do as I say. That goes for you too."

"If I didn't trust you, I would have followed my own plan by now."

"I know, and it would have got all three of you killed. That's the main reason I'm doing this. Tell Anna I'll take her out of the camp tomorrow with Eva. Tell her she will meet you later that evening outside the camp. I will take you all to the safe house in Clermont. Then my part is over."

"When will I be called to the administration block?"

"At eight o'clock. After ten minutes you will be told to make your own way back to your barrack, but instead you will hide behind the block. At eight thirty the guard at the main gate will be called away. That's when you will go through the gully. When you are out, make your way left along the road for about 500 metres. My car will be parked off the road on the right-hand side. Then I will take you all to Clermont."

"And are you absolutely sure the other guards will cooperate?"

"I have only involved three others. The one who calls you over to the block. The one guarding the gate to the men's compound, and the other at the main gate. I won't give you their names. But trust only those three."

"And what about our identity cards?"

"I'll give you those in the car."

"I'd rather have them now."

"But if you were caught with them they could be traced back to me. I'd be the first one they'd suspect of helping Anna."

"Then give me mine. To show good faith."

"You insult me, monsieur."

"No, I don't. If I can trust you with my wife and daughter, you can trust me with an identity card."

"Very well. I'll give you yours. But if you're caught with it, I'll deny all knowledge of it, and it will be the end of you and of our plan."

"Tomáš. What's going on?" whispered Anna. "What are you doing here at this time of night?"

"Where's Eva?"

"She's with Judita in the hut. Fast asleep. What's happening?"

"Did Durand tell you anything?"

"Nothing. He said you would explain everything."

She put her arms around him. "I was afraid the buses were coming for us women. I thought I was never going to see you again."

"No, my darling, it's alright. Come over here and sit down. I have some good news for us at last."

Tomáš watched the anxiety lift from Anna's face, as he described the plan for the following day. At first her questions were practical. 'Would they be certain to stay together? Would they be safe? How would they get food for Eva?' But, as Anna realised how well planned their escape was, even down to a safe house and the provision of new identity cards, her excitement grew and, for the first time since Eva's illness, Tomáš saw the old Anna return.

"I can't believe it, Tomáš. It's a miracle. Tell me where we'll go."

"I want to get to England, Anna. I want to join the Czech Brigade and fight these bastards. Please don't try to dissuade me."

Anna leaned back against him and pulled his arms around her.

"I'll say nothing to stop you this time. I want you to fight them. For me and for Eva. So we can go home."

"We'll have a long journey first though, Anna. I've heard the resistance has organised escape lines through Spain, but it may take us months to get through."

"It doesn't matter as long as we're together. And when we get to England we'll find the best doctors to help Eva."

"Yes, we will, darling. The very best."

"I'm so proud of you, Tomáš. I knew you would find a way."

"But I should have got you out earlier. Before things got so bad for you and Eva."

"No, darling, you've done all you could for us. All the extra food you got by working so hard. All the extra water for Eva."

"It wasn't enough."

"Don't say that."

"Can I admit something to you, Anna?"

"What, darling?"

"All the time we've been here, I've asked myself over and over what my father would have done in my place. I know he would have had a way of getting you out, but I could never work out how."

Anna sat up and looked at Tomáš. In the moonlight his face looked more wan than ever.

"Listen, Tomáš. Your father was a wonderful man, but even he wasn't as wonderful as you. Uncle Pavel would never have shown the patience you have. He would have attacked a guard by now and got himself killed. You have been stronger than that. You've put up with so much for us, and you've never complained or reproached me."

"Why should I reproach you?"

"Because you warned me so often about this when we were with Nataša and Viktor and Milan, and I didn't listen."

"But I didn't know I was warning you about this, Anna. No one could have imagined places like this existing in a civilised country."

"I don't think France can call itself civilised any more."

Anna kissed Tomáš and leaned back again in his arms. The sound of the cicadas blotted out all noise from the huts. "But I'm not going to think about that any more," she said. "For the first time in months I feel really happy. The thought of being free of this terrible place... I was afraid I'd forgotten how to be happy."

"There's still a long way to go. There will be risks."

"I know, but we'll be together. I don't care about anything else. When the buses came the other night, I was afraid I was going to be separated from you forever. Now I feel closer to our old lives than I have for years."

Tomáš held Anna tighter and kissed the top of her head.

"It's wonderful to hear you so optimistic again," he said.

"I'll be able to tell Judita that she'll be leaving tomorrow night."

"No, Anna. You mustn't. You mustn't say a word."

"Why not?"

"It could cause panic."

"Panic? Why would it cause panic? Judita will be pleased. None of the women want to be left here without their men. They want to be wherever they are."

"Do they know where their men are?"

"In a camp somewhere in the north, according to the rumours. Or somewhere in the east. Wherever it is, that's where the women want to be. It's only natural."

"Anna, please promise me you'll say nothing to Judita or anyone else. Durand is doing this to keep you off that transport. If he thinks we've talked to anyone about this, he won't help us."

"Alright then, darling. I won't say anything."

"We have to trust Durand, Anna. I've abandoned my own plan because I really believe he's our best chance. I know it goes against everything I said to you before, but you must do whatever he tells you tomorrow night. You understand that, don't you?"

"Yes, of course, darling. Don't worry."

"It all depends on him."

"I understand. But why do you think Émile is helping us?"

"I don't think he is helping us. I think he's helping you."

"Why?"

"Don't you know?"

"I think I do. Does it make you jealous?"

"No. I can understand any man loving you. I have been angry, though, at the thought of you flirting with him to get things for Eva. But I've tried to understand that too."

Anna turned around and kissed him. "Take your jacket off," she whispered in his ear. "And lay it on the ground over there."

Tomáš felt Anna brush against him as he knelt on the ground. She lay down on the jacket and unbuttoned the front of her dress. She took his hand and pulled him down next to her. "You are a wonderful man, Tomáš Kovařík," she said. "And you are the only man I could ever love." They kissed again, and Tomáš felt Anna's body respond to him for the first time in many months. "This is what the rest of our lives will be like," she said.

Chapter Twenty

August 6th – August 8th, 1942

Tomáš could not wait for the night to pass; for the dawn of their last day in the camp to come. He stood at the end of the hut by a window which faced south towards the coast. The newspapers which covered the windows in the winter had been removed, and he was able to smell the sea only a few kilometres away. If he closed his eyes he could imagine the waters of Štasný Lake and the River Ohře. Thoughts of Anna and their intimacy a few hours before filled his head, and for the first time in years he allowed himself to think of a future where they alone would determine the course of their lives.

A guard walked past, and Tomáš drew back from the window. It was not over yet, he realised, and would not be for some time to come. He rehearsed the plan again in his mind. There was no reason why everything should not work out just as Durand said it would. He wished now he had asked Durand how he was going to explain Anna and Eva's absence when he returned alone from the hospital. Mother and child were detained. Yes, that would be it. He looked again out the window, and then at his father's fob watch. Twenty minutes past midnight.

He sat down on his blanket on the floor. On hot summer nights he chose not sleep on the bunk with Jiří Zeman and the other three. Like many of the men he preferred to find a cooler spot on the dirt floor. Only the winter cold would drive the poor wretches he was leaving behind back onto the bunks to seek warmth next to the others. He found his place by the window a mixed blessing. If he stood he had fresh air, but when he sat or lay down he found himself on the same level as the latrines, and only a few steps away from the thin blankets which shielded the sleeping area from the crude wooden platform above the drains.

He checked his pockets again. His identity card was safe. Durand was probably right about keeping the other two. He had the money from Marek, unsolicited and passed to him the day after their last meeting by one of his heavies. Five thousand francs. He always knew Marek would help somehow. The safe house was still a worry. Who would the people be? How sure was Durand they could be trusted? Marek's money would get them to the Spanish border, but how would they get across? He had heard talk of the *'passeurs'* who led people through the mountains. He would probably have to carry Eva. It would be cold. Once on the other side, he would have to rely on the British to help with a passage to England. But how much could he rely on them?

He stood up again. He could not rest. So much could go wrong, and Anna had such faith in him. He heard guards talking outside the administration block. At least Durand had real identity cards and residents' permits for them. They would just be a young family travelling like any other. Someone was opening the main gates. They must make sure they spoke French on the trains and in the street. He should have told Anna to start using only French with Eva tonight. A vehicle was pulling into the camp.

"Here we go again. More damn buses keeping us awake all night," someone complained from the depths of the hut.

'If only you knew,' thought Tomáš. 'It's tomorrow you'll hear the buses, not tonight.' But he too could hear vehicles out on the road.

"They've come for the Jewish women. I told you they would," someone said.

"Why don't you just shut up so we can get some sleep?" said another.

"Clever devils, aren't they? Getting the men out first, so there's no trouble when they come back for the women and kids."

"No you're wrong," Tomáš shouted at the voice coming from the darkness. "The buses aren't coming tonight."

But the sound of vehicles approaching the camp was growing louder. He stumbled to the other end of the hut over bodies that cursed and kicked out at him. "They're not coming tonight," he shouted. "Not tonight! Not tonight!"

He pushed the men at the windows aside and looked out. The other huts blocked a clear view of the road, but in the distance he saw headlights. Many, many headlights in a long line coming towards the camp.

"I hope they're quicker about it this time. Took hours the other night. Bloody Jews. Always causing trouble."

Tomáš levered himself up onto the window frame and scrambled head first through the opening. Someone grabbed his legs.

"Don't be a damn fool, Tomáš," said Jiří Zeman. "It's curfew. They'll shoot you."

Tomáš kicked out at him. "It's Anna, Jiří. It's the wrong night." He kicked again and felt himself falling. He got up, spat blood and sand and ran between the huts past startled guards to the fence separating the two compounds. He could see women and children coming out of the Jewish huts furthest away by the open ground. There were so many he had no hope of picking out Anna and Eva in the weak moonlight. Then he saw Émile Durand standing at the corner of a hut watching.

"Durand," he screamed. "What are you doing, Durand?"

He started to climb the fence. "Stop them, Durand." Tomáš saw Durand turn and look at him as he reached the coils of barbed wire at the top of the fence.

Tomáš pulled at the coils, trying to take hold of enough of them to take the weight of his body. Then once more he felt hands grabbing at his legs. "Anna!" he screamed. "Anna!" Two guards pulled him to the ground, his hands still wrapped around the wire. They stood him up and pushed his face into the fence. Durand had disappeared.

"You know what we've got here, don't you, Laurent?" said one of the guards. "It's the husband of that Jewish slut Émile's been after."

"He's a feisty bastard though, isn't he? Keep still, you cuckold bastard."

Tomáš felt kicks to the back of his legs. "Anna! Anna!" he screamed. More guards arrived and fists pounded his back and his ribs. His face was still pressed against the wire, and he watched the silent procession of women and children walking away from the barracks, as painless blows landed on his body and head. "Anna," he mumbled.

He felt hot breath on the side of his face and heard a low growl. "At least she'll have a real man to fuck her for a while, and not a filthy runt like you."

He felt a final blow to the side of his head and then it was over.

Tomáš woke lying on his back on the floor of a bare, windowless room. A single light bulb hung from the ceiling. His head pounded. He had a sickly metallic taste in his mouth and his body ached so much it was impossible to move. For some reason he could not open his clenched fists. His fingers were glued together. Then he remembered being at the fence. Looking into the women's camp. Buses. Anna. No. No. No. Don't let it be true. Anna and Eva. He moved his head to one side and moaned. Could it be true? He had to think clearly. He closed his eyes and groaned. Yes it was. There was the blood on his hands from the wire. Blood on the floor from his head. It had happened. They had taken them.

He did not know how long he lay there, before he pushed himself towards one side of the room with his feet and sat up against a wall. The physical pain did not matter. Anything that distracted his brain from the truth for one second was a relief. He forced his hands open. His fleshed ripped as congealed blood refused to give up its hold. At last he moved his fingers freely. He felt his head. There was more congealed blood on one side. He tried to stand up. The pain from his ribs knocked him back down against the wall. He tried again, defying the pain. He got to the door and hammered on it as loudly as he could.

The door was opened by the gendarme who had been on the bus with Durand on the day they arrived at the camp.

"Bang on the door like that again, you runt, and you'll get more of what you had last night."

Tomáš recognised the voice that had taunted him at the fence. "Have the buses left?" he asked.

"Hours ago. You might catch one if you run."

Tomáš heard laughter from the corridor.

"Were my wife and daughter on them?"

"Course they were. They'll be on the train to Paris by now. On their way to the Promised Land."

There was more laughter.

"Did Durand go with them?"

The gendarme slapped Tomáš hard across the face. "*Monsieur* Durand to you, you cheeky foreign bastard."

Tomáš took a step back.

"Course he went with them. He wasn't going to let her leave without him, was he?"

"Do you know Durand was going to help my family escape, if the buses hadn't come a day early?"

The laughter from the corridor was louder than ever.

"You're a thick foreign bastard as well as a cheeky one, aren't you?"

"Tell him, Albert," said a voice from the corridor. "Put the poor sod out of his misery."

The gendarme smirked. "The buses didn't come early, Kovařík. They came exactly when they were meant to come. Émile strung you along with that yarn so you and your friend Kral wouldn't get your Jewish slut out before he had a chance to service her."

"He'll have plenty of time for that now," someone laughed.

"Yes, I forgot to tell you, Kovařík," said the gendarme, as he closed the door behind him. "Émile's got himself transferred to Drancy, so he can fuck her as much he wants, before the Germans have her."

Tomáš lunged at the door as it was slammed shut. "We're going to make an example of you, you sad little runt," said the gendarme from the other side. "You're going to Montpellier tomorrow to stand trial for attacking a guard and trying to escape. Don't expect to come back, will you?"

The light was left on in the room. For a long time Tomáš stalked the space, hitting the door with his fist every time it came in range.

He tired and leaned against the wall, catching his breath and holding his ribs. His mind slowly cleared. He was being a fool. Thinking of Durand and the guards and their taunts, instead of concentrating on what really mattered. He took off his jacket, folded it, and laid it down in a corner of the room as a makeshift pillow. They had taken his family away once. They were not going to take them away again. He lay down in the corner with his face turned towards the wall. He closed his eyes and Anna and Eva were there.

He saw Anna pointing out the animals in the fields to Eva as they passed in the train, her only concern to stay as cheerful as possible for the sake of their child. He knew how brave Anna could be. She and Eva would survive. He had faith in her. Durand was on the train with them, but his presence was not a threat, whatever the guards would like him to think. He had sweets for Eva and was doing all he could to ingratiate himself with Anna, who was being pleasant to him, but no more. And however loathsome he found Durand, he knew he would help Anna in the new camp, however bad the conditions were. Tomáš saw it all and stayed calm.

It helped knowing Anna was not worrying about him. She knew he would stay strong for their sakes. The only thing he must do for them now was to stay alive. Stay alive so that one day he could find them again and make everything alright. It was his new resolution and he repeated it to himself. Stay alive, escape, find Anna and Eva...

He was woken by a kick in the small of his back. He sat up. The front of his shirt was covered in blood, which he must have vomited in the night. Stay alive...

"Get up, Kovařík."

Tomáš recognised the voice of the same gendarme.

"What a filthy runt you are. We'll have to get you cleaned up before we let the judge see you."

He pushed Tomáš out into the corridor. The two gendarmes who had dragged him down from the fence were waiting for him. At the end of the corridor was a window overlooking the barracks. It was early morning. The guards were getting ready for the first roll call of the day. He was led to the back of the building and pushed into a shower room.

"Get yourself stripped off. You'll find soap in there. And make sure you get all the blood off you. We don't want the judge thinking we haven't been nice to you, do we? Get another shirt for him from the Jewish store, Laurent. He can't appear wearing that one. My God, what a state you're in, Kovařík."

Tomáš stood naked in front of them, his legs apart, shoulders back and his head up. His hair was matted with blood, his hands swollen and torn, and his thin, pale body covered in bruises.

"No wonder his Jewish slut fancies a real man, eh, lads?"

The gendarmes laughed, and Tomáš stood staring at them, showing no emotion. The laughter tailed off.

"Get in the shower, you bastard. Laurent, do as I say. Get that damn shirt."

Tomáš turned and stepped under the shower. The water was warm, but he did not allow himself to enjoy it.

He got dressed and was led down the stairs to the main entrance of the building. Through the door he saw a black police van with barred windows, waiting with its engine running.

"Right, Laurent, bring out the other two."

The gendarme leaned towards Tomáš. "We've got three of you Communist agitators this morning, Kovařík. But attacking a guard puts you in even deeper shit than the other two."

He put handcuffs around Tomáš's wrists. Two more men in handcuffs appeared next to him. One of them was Fabian Vega, now one of Marek's lieutenants. Vega looked at Tomáš, nodded and winked.

"Right, let's get them out."

As they reached the front door, a garde mobile burst through it.

"Alarm!" he shouted. "They've set fire to the huts!"

The gendarme left Tomáš and pressed a red button on the wall behind the desk. The klaxons around the camp perimeter stayed silent. He pressed it again. Nothing. "Get me the army barracks in Montpellier," he ordered. A gendarme at the desk lifted the phone.

"It's dead, Albert."

"Shit. It can't be." He took the phone, put it to his ear and slammed it down. "The bastards have cut the wire."

From the midst of the huts shots could be heard.

"The Communists. The bastards. Get these prisoners back in their cells quick. Then get a rifle each and assemble back here. At the double."

A young gendarme pressed a revolver into Tomáš's back and forced him to run to his cell. As they passed the window at the end of the corridor, the gendarme stopped to look out over the camp. Tomáš stood next to him, their roles temporarily forgotten. There was smoke coming from at least six huts, and flames were breaking through some of the roofs. Thousands of people were already gathered on the assembly area and many more were hurrying to join them. Directly in front of the window a garde mobile running towards the administration block was shot in the back and fell to the ground in mid stride.

"Holy Mother," said the gendarme. He turned and put his revolver to Tomáš's throat. "You bastards!" he screamed.

"Listen to me," said Tomáš. "I'm not a Communist, but I know their leader. Let me live and I'll see no harm comes to you."

"We won't lose to those bastards out there."

"Maybe you won't. In that case it's the end of me anyway. But if you do lose you'll need me… but make up your mind. Your adjutant's waiting for you."

The gendarme grabbed Tomáš by the back of the neck, marched him along the corridor to the windowless room and pushed him inside. Tomáš heard the door being locked behind him and he slumped to the floor.

The key turned again. He looked up and saw a figure at the door. Tomáš hung his head and thanked God. The man was not in uniform. He was wearing a red band around his right arm and held a rifle at his hip. His eyes darted around the room.

"What is your name?" he demanded in a Polish accent.

"My name is Tomáš Kovařík. I'm a friend of Marek Kral's."

"I know you are friend. It was Comrade Kral send me to find you. My name is Jerzy." He stepped into the room and released Tomáš's handcuffs. "We must be very quick. Comrade Kral wants to leave."

The corridors were full of men with red armbands carrying boxes of papers and filing cards down to the front of the building. Tomáš and Jerzy reached the main entrance, where a dozen or so gendarmes and gardes mobiles were sitting on the floor against one of the walls, their hands tied behind their backs. Two of Marek's men stood over them holding pistols. Tomáš recognised the three gendarmes who had taken such pleasure in goading him, and the younger one who had come so close to shooting him. They were all taking shallow breaths and staring, unable to blink. When the young gendarme saw Tomáš he nodded to him in short, urgent movements, desperate for recognition. Tomáš nodded back.

Tomáš saw Marek outside with Fabian Vega and the two burly men who accompanied him everywhere in the camp. Vega was issuing orders and directing the men with the boxes towards the huts, which were now all ablaze. From beyond the huts came the sound of gunfire, but not the random staccato of a fire fight. It came in volleys. One volley, a long pause and then another. The sound of a firing squad.

Marek Kral bounded up the steps to the administration block and pushed the door open.

"Tomáš, my friend, there you are. I'm pleased to see you safe." He put his arms around Tomáš and slapped his back. "Battered but safe."

"They took Anna and Eva, Marek."

"I know, my friend."

"Two days earlier, Marek, and you could have saved them."

"Not possible, Tomáš. All this wasn't planned for today. We were always ready, but this is much sooner than we wanted. But we had no choice. Once they got rid of the Jews, they started on us."

"This is the last of them, Comrade Kral," said a man passing with a box.

"Good," said Marek. "Make sure it's all burned and then bring the stores out."

He turned again to Tomáš. "You should see what these bastards have stacked up out there. Enough food and medicine for an army. We're taking it all with us."

"How, Marek?"

"We have lorries coming. We can't take all the comrades. Some will have to find their own way. But there's room for you, Tomáš. I don't forget those who helped me in the old days, when I needed it."

"What about the internees?"

"There are twelve thousand of them. They'll have to make their own way. We're burning all the records. That gives them a chance."

The main door opened. "The lorries are here, comrade," said Fabian Vega. "But there's only five."

"Five? Shit. That's not enough. Alright. You use one for arms, food and medicine. Four for the men. In the order we agreed. The rest make their own way to the plateau. Have you finished off the Bluebottles?"

"Yes. Shall I send someone in for these here?"

"No. I'll do it myself."

"What are you going to do, Marek?" said Tomáš.

Marek took a revolver from his belt. "I'm going to shoot the bastards."

"No, Marek. You can't do that. They're tied up. They can't hurt us."

"Don't be a damn fool. They know your name, don't they? They sure as hell know mine. No point burning the records if we leave these bastards to tell their friends who to go looking for."

"Please, Marek. It's not right."

"For fuck's sake, Tomáš These are the bastards who sent your Anna and your little girl to the east. Imagine it was that Durand bastard sitting there. What would you want to do to him?"

"I don't know."

"You don't know? You were begging me two weeks ago to get Anna and your kid out of here. Anna was going mad with worry over the girl, you said. Now you have the bastards who were doing it to her right here in front of you."

"Anna will survive. These men don't need to die for her."

"You make me sick, Tomáš A lot of my men died today to save your skin. I'm not risking any more comrades because of these Fascist bastards or your bourgeois morality."

Marek stepped forward and put his revolver to the temple of the first gendarme in the row. The noise of the gun filled the room and Tomáš looked away. When he looked back the upper part of the man's head was gone and his twitching body was slumped towards his neighbour, who was sliding over the other gendarmes in an attempt to get away from it. Marek grabbed him by the collar, dragged him back to his place and put the gun to his head. The man fainted and Marek fired.

"Marek, that's enough," shouted Tomáš. "You've made your point. Please, no more."

Marek went to the next man. "This one is for Anna and your little girl."

Tomáš lunged for Marek and grabbed his arm. "Don't you dare say that. Don't you dare use my child to justify this. You're not doing this for Anna or Eva or me. It's only for yourself."

Tomáš felt strong hands take him by the shoulders and wrists. Two of Marek's men dragged him away and twisted his arms behind his back. Marek turned and sneered at him.

"You need a lesson, my friend. I'll make a deal with you. Tell me which of these gave you the beating and I'll let the others live."

"I can't, Marek."

"Right then, they all die."

"It was the adjutant and the one to his left," blurted the young gendarme at the end of the row. "The other one's already dead." He started to sob. "Please don't do any more."

"You bastard, Lavisse," spat the adjutant.

Marek went over to him and put the revolver to his temple.

"It was Durand's idea to have Kovařík arrested and shot," said the adjutant, the man from the bus. "He wanted him out of the way, not me. I told him he was mad making such a fuss over one Jew. He could have had any woman he wanted."

Marek looked over his shoulder at Tomáš. "There you are. This man plotted with Durand to take Anna away and have you killed. I'll give you five minutes with him to do what you like."

"I may want to... but I can't."

"I'll leave him until last, in case you change your mind."

Marek went down the line shooting four more men in quick succession, including the young gendarme. He reached back with his right hand, and Fabian Vega passed him another revolver. The remaining men's screams competed with the deafening report of the gun rebounding from the walls and the ceiling. Then there was silence. The adjutant sat hunched, alone, shaking uncontrollably.

"Not so cocky now, are you?" Marek said to him. He turned to Tomáš. "Make your mind up. We're in a hurry. Do you want him or not?"

Tomáš stared open-mouthed at the blood, bone, fluid and tissue and shook his head.

"It's your choice," said Marek, and he shot the man in the temple. He stood back up and put the gun in his belt.

"You're a great disappointment to me, Tomáš. I thought you were a man of passion and ideals, but you're like all bourgeois Czechs. You're too soft. You don't fight when you need to. You might still have a country and a family if you did."

Tomáš looked down, away from the gore, and did not speak. Marek gestured to the men holding him to let him go.

"Look what we've achieved today. All these people are free because of what we've done. And what did you do? Nothing. You have to be brutal, my friend, to get what you want." He stared at Tomáš who looked past him, still not speaking. "Ah, you're useless. I was going to take you with us, but you're no good to me. Do you still have the money?"

Tomáš nodded and pointed to his shoes.

"Good, then I'll say goodbye, my friend, and wish you luck. I hope one day you can find Anna and your little girl. I know it's all you care about."

Marek made for the door with his men.

"Marek," Tomáš called out to him, his voice trembling. "You're wrong about everything. No cause can succeed if it has no humanity, Marek. And you're wrong about me. I am going to fight. And I will get Anna and Eva back. And my country."

Chapter Twenty-One

July 16th, 1943

Tomáš strode out of Hyde Park and stopped on the Bayswater Road to get his bearings. An officer in the Grenadier Guards walking past returned his salute. Tomáš looked up the road and recognised the way he had come on his first visit six months before. He quickened his pace and crossed the road when he saw Porchester Terrace on the other side. He walked along the street of tall Georgian terraces and grand Victorian villas until he reached number 35. The brass plate on one of the whitewashed columns guarding the front door confirmed this was the right place. 'Československý Červený Kříž', it said. And underneath, 'The Czechoslovakian Red Cross'.

Inside the main door a lady in late middle age was posting notices on the wall of the inner porch.

"Good morning, Sergeant," she said in Czech. "How can we help you?"

"Good morning, madam. But how did you know..?"

She pointed to the upper left arm of his British army uniform, to the badge displaying the heraldic lion of Bohemia and the shield of Slovakia. "It's the first thing I look for," she said smiling at him. "Welcome to our small piece of home. Would you like some tea or coffee?"

"Thankyou, madam, perhaps later. My visit is very urgent, you see. I came here six months ago enquiring about my wife and child. They were sent to a transit camp in Paris last August and I'm desperate for news of them."

"I understand, Sergeant."

"The lady I saw previously was unable to help, but she told me to return in six months when there might be more information. I've come back at the first opportunity."

"Have you come far?"

"Only from our training camp in Harwich this morning. But I have three days' leave now before a posting to Scotland. I must find out about my wife and daughter before I go."

The lady took Tomáš's arm. "What is your name, Sergeant?"

"Kovařík, madam."

"And how old is your little girl?"

"Three years and seven months."

"Come with me, Sergeant Kovařík. Let us see if we can get you some help."

She kept hold of his arm while she led him across the hallway to a white door. She knocked gently and walked in. The woman behind the desk stood up when she saw her.

"Miriam, I wonder if you could help our Sergeant Kovařík. He is looking for his wife and child who are being held in a camp in Paris. Perhaps their names are on the new lists from Geneva."

"I shall look, Doctor."

"Good. Pani Nováková will do all she can to help you with your search, Sergeant Kovařík."

"Thankyou, madam."

Tomáš sat down on the chair he was offered, and pani Nováková took a file from one of the wooden cabinets behind her.

"Was your wife sent to Drancy, Sergeant?"

"Yes, in August last year. I came here last December as soon as I reached England, but no one could help me then. I was told to return in six months."

"That's because we had hoped in that time to be allowed to monitor the Drancy camp, but the French authorities still forbid the Red Cross any access. We still have no details of any of the people held there."

"Nothing at all?"

"I'm afraid not. Were your wife and child taken in the big round-up of last July?"

"Indirectly. They were interned in Agde in Languedoc. When the French couldn't find enough Jews in Paris, they took them from the internment camps."

"We know all about that, Sergeant. We have details of most Czechoslovak internees in France, but unfortunately none of those at Agde. There was a fire there and all the records were lost."

"I know. I was there."

"But you weren't taken?"

"No, my wife is Jewish. I'm not."

"And your child went with her mother."

"Yes."

"I'm very sorry, Sergeant. How did you manage to escape?"

"I made my way to the Spanish border and found a guide who took me over the mountains. I managed to reach the British Consulate in Barcelona and they got me into Gibraltar."

"You make it sound very straightforward, Sergeant."

Tomáš allowed himself a smile. He decided to say nothing of the time spent hiding in the crypt of Father Benoît's church while Vichy soldiers searched for Marek's men. The visit to Nataša which nearly proved fatal. The constant fear of betrayal by the Basque guide who made it clear he worked only for the highest bidder. And then frostbite, and the two months in a cell in Gibraltar waiting for the British to verify his story.

"It was straightforward, madam," he said, "compared to what many are going through."

"Yes, indeed."

"Do you have no information at all about Drancy, madam?"

"Not concerning individuals, I'm afraid."

"Do you have any reports about the conditions there? How long people stay. Where they are sent."

Pani Nováková looked down at her papers. "Well, yes, we have some, but I hesitate to go into detail..."

"Please, madam, nothing you can say can be worse than the scenes my mind has created for me over the past nine months. You cannot shock me."

"Very well, Sergeant Kovařík. We do have reports from people who have been in Drancy. You probably know it is the main transit camp for Jews in France, but there are also five sub camps in the city." She took a sheet from her papers. "Drancy is a suburb in the north-east of Paris, and the camp is actually a modern housing development of high towers and low-level apartment blocks. The authorities have simply placed a cordon of barbed-wire fencing around a part of it, and drawn the guards from the Paris gendarmerie. That's it."

"You make it sound so benign, pani Nováková, but you're not helping me." His voice grew more urgent. "I need the truth from people who have seen it. I need to know what my wife and child are dealing with. I must share it with them."

"If you insist, Sergeant Kovařík, I do have some further information." She looked again at the papers on her desk. "The camp is guarded and administered by the French, but the commandant is an SS Captain Dannecker from the Gestapo Office of Jewish Affairs. The buildings which make up the camp were never finished. There are no windows, no heating, no internal walls. People sleep on concrete floors. I'm sorry..."

"Go on."

"The buildings were designed to house 700 people, but there are many more than that held there now."

"How many?"

"Seven thousand. In three separate areas. Men, women and children."

"You mean the men, and then the women and children."

"No. According to the reports we have, the children are held in a separate area."

"Who looks after them?"

"I don't know, Sergeant. I'm sure some adults are kept with them."

Tomáš put his hands on his knees and stared at the floor, before looking up again at pani Nováková. "Where did you get this information from, madam?"

"From a handful of people who have escaped."

"People manage to get out of the camp?"

"No. There are no reports of anyone escaping from Drancy itself, only from the trains taking them east. The last report came from an escapee in March."

"Can you please tell me what it says?"

"If you really insist. It says, *'the children are kept separate from the adults and are made to wear a piece of wood around their necks with their name tapped into it, as many have forgotten what their names are. The only food is cabbage soup which upsets their stomachs'*... Are you sure you want..?"

"Yes. Please carry on."

"*...'which upsets their stomachs so badly that they soil their clothes. There is no soap, so the children wait naked while their clothes are rinsed in cold water and dried. Since the only lavatories are on the ground floor and some children were falling on the stairs in the night, buckets have been placed for them on the landings.'*"

"If their clothes are being washed, it would seem there are some adults helping them," said Tomáš

"I'm sure that is the case, Sergeant. The rest of the report is about the man's escape."

"That's important. Please tell me what it says."

"He says... let me see. *'I was on transport 36. Those to be transported were selected by the French police. We were told we were going to a new Jewish homeland somewhere in the east. The children made up a name for it, 'Pitchipoi'. To calm people's fears, money was changed into Polish zloty and we were shown postcards sent by previous deportees. The gendarmes were being less brutal with us because they wanted our cooperation. We were taken in city buses to Le Bourget station where we were put into railway trucks, sixty people to each truck. The gendarmes accompanied the train to the German border and discouraged local people at every stop from giving us food and water.'*

Then he tells how he escaped by cutting a hole in the wooden floor."

"Did he know what his destination was going to be?"

"No. No one is sure of that yet."

"It's alright, madam. I know what the rumours are. I read the report in the Times when I first arrived here in December."

"There was nothing new in that report, Sergeant. Hitler has been saying for years that he would rid Europe of the Jews. We Czechoslovaks know that. It's probably why you took your family to France in the first place."

"It was. But now there's this new talk about death camps in the east. I was hoping you could tell me my wife and child were still in France."

"I'm sorry, Sergeant. I'm sure they are, but I cannot confirm it. Besides, I'm sure the word 'death' camp is an exaggeration the newspapers choose to employ. People are being mistreated, it's doubtless true, especially in the Polish ghettos, but anything more is rumour and speculation."

"The mass shootings in Russia are not speculation, madam. There are eye-witness accounts."

"That may be, Sergeant, but there is a limit to what the Red Cross can do. We are compiling all the records we can from the Jewish resettlement camps, so that once the war is over we can reunite as many people as possible. I hope one day we can give you good news about your wife and daughter."

When Tomáš did not answer, Pani Nováková stood up. "I am afraid there's nothing more I can tell you, Sergeant." She went to the door and waited for Tomáš to stand up before she opened it. "Good luck," she said as he walked past her.

As Tomáš crossed the entrance hall, he saw the lady who had greeted him on his way in.

"Were we able to help you, Sergeant Kovařík?"

"I'm afraid not, madam. No one has any news."

"And what will you do now?"

"I don't know. I have to think about where I try next."

"You look tired, young man. You have no colour at all. I insist you come into my office and take coffee with me. It's just been made."

She took his arm again and led him to a room at the rear of the building overlooking a large vegetable garden. The room resembled a comfortable study rather than an office. There were two large settees and two armchairs around a well polished coffee table. Tomáš sat down in one of the armchairs and glanced about him. Most of the wall space was given over to bookshelves, but between the two picture windows looking out onto the garden hung a portrait of President Beneš. Above the marble fireplace hung an even grander portrait of Tomáš Masaryk, the first president of Czechoslovakia.

"Thankyou, madam," said Tomáš, as the lady passed him his coffee and a piece of buchty cake. The same as Anna used to make.

"Now, Sergeant, tell me in what way we were not able to help you."

"It seems you have no records for the camp in Paris my wife and child were sent to, and no information about where they might have been sent since. 'Somewhere in the east' is all I ever hear."

"The Red Cross is not allowed into Drancy."

"I know. But pani Nováková seems reluctant to even consider the possibility that Jews are being killed in the east, or that the French camps may be part of a system to deliver them there."

"I think it's too early to talk of a system, Sergeant. She doubtless had no wish to alarm or upset you."

"Upset me? Please listen to me, madam. I spent a year in a French internment camp with my wife and child. People died of disease and maltreatment every day. You would not believe the abuse. Then they were sent to Drancy. Perhaps they're still there, or perhaps they've been taken elsewhere. I don't know. But whatever has happened to them, I don't need protecting from the truth."

The lady looked at him but did not speak.

"May I tell you something, madam?"

She smiled and nodded.

"Before I came to England I spent weeks in hiding and two months in prison. Every day when I woke up I had a split second before I remembered that my Anna and Eva were gone. Then for hour after hour my mind and my body were at the mercy of my imagination. But gradually, mercifully, my mind learned to cope. I claim no credit for it, no strength of character or will. It just happened. I would wake up, my body and brain accepted the truth, and everything became a matter of fact. My life of a sort can go on. Can you understand that, madam?"

"Better than you think, Sergeant. In the last war I too was imprisoned, by the Austrian police. My father's work had taken him abroad and he had left papers with me for safekeeping. They were discovered and I was arrested for possession of seditious material. At one point I was even sentenced to death.

"I often think of my poor mother. She had already lost a most talented son to typhus. Her husband was away and in constant danger. Her daughter was under sentence of death. I think both my parents would say they understood exactly how you feel about Anna and Eva, and I think I do too."

"Sorry, madam, I had no idea."

"I shall tell you all I know, Sergeant Kovařík, but first let me pour you some more coffee."

"Thankyou."

"I am aware of two reports about these so-called death camps. One is from a Czechoslovak officer, Captain Josef Mautner, who escaped from a concentration camp in France, near Natzweiler south of Strasbourg. But don't alarm yourself. It's highly unlikely your wife and child would be sent there. It is for political prisoners mostly, but Captain Mautner does confirm that executions are systematic, making it in some part a 'death camp'. I hate that expression. The other report comes from a Polish officer, Jan Karski. He brought back a report from a Polish camp known as Belzec. His report also mentions systematic killing, this time through the use of gas."

"Gas? What kind of gas?"

"We don't know, and none of this has been confirmed. Most people, including myself, are not inclined to believe it. We think it is most likely to be propaganda inspired by the Russians."

"Gas. My God. That's what they used in the last war."

"We're sure the Karski report is exaggerated."

"But why would the Russians want to exaggerate it?"

"We think it probable that Karski and the Russians are merely trying to force the Americans and British into announcing a second front for this year."

"That's what I've been hoping for more than anything, madam. A chance to get back to France to begin my search."

"We must all be patient, Sergeant. It will come. You will get back to France, and to Czechoslovakia."

"May I ask you, madam, why pani Nováková could not tell me about those reports?"

"The International Red Cross has many responsibilities, Sergeant Kovařík. We are the main conduit for letters and parcels to prisoners of war throughout the world. We cannot make unfounded accusations which might jeopardise all that. Besides, not everyone has access to the Mautner and Karski reports. Sometimes I'm able to take advantage of my connections."

There was a knock at the door and pani Nováková entered.

"Please excuse me, Doctor. I thought Sergeant Kovařík had left."

"No, he kindly accepted my invitation to take morning coffee with me."

"I just wanted to remind you of your meeting with the Polish ambassador in twenty minutes."

"Thankyou, Miriam."

"My apologies for disturbing you, Doctor Masaryková."

Tomáš put his cup and saucer down on the table.

"Doctor... Masaryková?"

"Yes, I am sorry. I should have introduced myself earlier. I am Alice Masaryková, President of the Czechoslovak Red Cross."

She held out her hand. Tomáš stood up and took it. "But you are..." He turned and looked towards the picture over the fireplace.

"Yes. Tomáš Masaryk is my father. Please sit down, Sergeant. We're not in such a hurry."

"But you don't understand, madam. I was named after your father. My own father talked about him all the time. All my life I heard stories about him. My father met President Masaryk in Russia, when he was in the Legion."

"Your father was a legionnaire?"

"Yes, he was at Zborov and Bakhmach Junction."

"You must be very proud of him, as I am of my father."

"Yes, Doctor Masaryková, I am. I do apologise for not realising earlier to whom I was speaking."

"It would have changed nothing. Besides, I was in the wrong for not introducing myself earlier. Now listen to me, Sergeant. You have three days' leave, I believe. Do you have any plans?"

"None as yet."

"Then I insist you join me for dinner tomorrow. It will mean you making your way to Aylesbury in Buckinghamshire. Can you do that?"

"Yes, Doctor Masaryková, of course."

"You get a train from Marylebone Station, and then a bus from Aylesbury to the village of Aston Abbotts. Then you make your way to the Abbey. That is the home of President and Mrs Beneš. There will be a pass waiting for you with the sentries at the gate."

"President Beneš? Will he be there too?"

"Yes, there will be eight of us. The President is always most anxious to meet our fighting men. And you won't be alone. Sergeant Sobotka will also be there. He has been with the Czechoslovak forces since Poland in 1939. A most interesting man. He was in France in 1940. He's just returned from the Middle East."

"But I've done nothing like that."

"Sergeant Sobotka has been a very brave man, Sergeant Kovařík, but I believe no braver than you have been."

"I appreciate your saying that, Doktor Masaryková. I ask only for the same chance our fathers were given. To be allowed to fight for my country and to find my family again."

"My dear Sergeant Kovařík. When I was in prison all those years ago, my father got me back. I believe one day you will do the same for your child. Have faith."

Chapter Twenty-Two

July 17th, 1943

The children playing on the mounds of earth and rubble stopped and waved as the train passed their backyards. Tomáš looked up from his book and watched them, and wished when they were gone that he had waved back. He was beginning to like the English again.

Back in early January he had hated putting on a British Army uniform for the first time. It was the uniform of appeasement, of those who had betrayed and sacrificed his country and its people. But he had no choice but to wear it. It was the only path open to those wanting to join the Czechoslovak Armoured Brigade. And the only things which showed he was a Czechoslovak, and not British, were his cap badge and the heraldic flash on his left sleeve.

But in all the places he had been posted to in England, whether Bridlington, Lowestoft or Harwich, the reaction of people who saw the badge and the flash had been the same. "Well done, you brave Czechs," they said. "God bless the Czechs." Tomáš smiled at the memory of a recent night in a Harwich pub when an elderly man bought a round of beers for him and three other Czechoslovak soldiers. "By way of apologising for leaving you in the lurch," the man said. And then he went on to point out to all who would listen that he, like the present lot, Churchill, Attlee and Eden, had always been against Hitler, Mussolini and Chamberlain's mob.

Tomáš had come to appreciate that the English were not so different from the Czechs. They were fair in the way they took as they found. A smile was readily reciprocated, but so too was a scowl. They complained a lot, but then made the best of whatever came their way. And they were stubborn in a way the Czechs would have been, had they been given the chance. The British would not give in, whatever the Germans threw at them. 'If only...,' Tomáš thought. If only his father had encouraged him to take Anna to England and not to France.

The train passed through the last of a series of tunnels and emerged into open countryside to the north-west of London. Tomáš picked up his book again and tried to read. He could not concentrate. He looked out of the window, lost in familiar thoughts, until the train stopped at Amersham and someone joined him in the carriage. He turned his head, smiled at the middle-aged man wearing a clergyman's collar, and returned his greeting. The train steamed on through the woodland and the rolling hills of the Chilterns. The landscape was so similar to the open countryside which lay between Cheb and the Bavarian border that Tomáš felt discomforting pangs of nostalgia and loss. He picked up his book again and started to read from the page on which it fell open.

"Come live with me and be my love
And we will all the pleasures prove
That hills and valleys, dale and field
And all the craggy mountains yield."

He closed the book and placed it on the seat next to him.

"You appreciate the poetry of Marlowe, I see," said the clergyman.

"Yes, sir, very much."

"It's rare nowadays to find someone who appreciates Marlowe."

"I was fortunate enough to study English poetry at Charles University in Prague. I have neglected it recently. I decided to give it another chance."

"Ah, Prague. You speak such perfect English I had quite missed the shoulder flash. May I say, Sergeant, God bless all you Czechs."

"Excuse me, mate. Is your name Kovařík?"

"Yes. Are you Sobotka by any chance?"

"Miloš."

"I'm Tomáš."

The two men put down their kit bags on the pavement outside the station and shook hands.

"The old girl in London said I had to get a bus to... eh..."

"Leighton Buzzard," suggested Tomáš. "We get off at Aston Abbotts."

"That's it. I wasn't going to bother. I was going to walk it."

"It's five miles, Miloš. The bus is just there. Come on."

The bus dropped them half a mile from the village. The two men lifted their kit bags onto their shoulders and started down the country lane.

"Don't you find it incredible, Miloš, that here we are in the middle of the English countryside, God knows where exactly, and we're on our way to the heart of the Czechoslovak government?"

"I don't really think about it, Tomáš. I just go where they send me."

"Have you been in the army long?"

"I was a regular back in the old country. Joined up in '34. Spent a lot of my time near where you come from."

"In the forts?"

"Yeah. I tell you. That was something you had to see."

"Do you think the forts could have stopped them?"

"Damn right we could have stopped 'em. A whole lot better than the French did, that's for damn sure."

"Doctor Masaryková said you fought alongside the French in 1940."

"I've fought with 'em and against 'em. I've seen the lot, Tomáš. Fought with the Poles in '39. The French in '40. Had to join the damn Foreign Legion to do that. Then with the British for two years in North Africa. Just come back from fighting the French in Lebanon. I tell you, those French bastards fought harder against us and the British than they ever did against the Germans."

"The French fighting in Lebanon and Syria are Vichy French."

"I don't care who they are, mate. All I know is they spoke damn French and they wanted us dead."

"That's where I've been for four years, Miloš. In France."

"Fighting?"

"No, I went to live there with my wife after Munich. Our daughter was born there. But after three years we were all interned. My wife and daughter were moved to another camp, and I escaped to England."

"And where are they now?"

"I don't know."

"That's tough on you, mate."

"It is."

"I've got a wife back in Prague. Saskie. Haven't seen her for nearly five years. I expect we'll meet up again one day."

"Have you heard from her?"

"In the early days. But not for a while. But it's best like that when you're away a lot like me. Ask too much and you learn too much, I say."

They reached the first houses on the edge of the village. Within a minute they were walking past the village green.

"That looks promising over there," said Miloš, pointing to a whitewashed building with black timbers and thatched roof. "The Royal Oak. That'll do for a couple beers before we have to meet these people."

"You're talking about the President of Czechoslovakia and his wife, Miloš. Not just anybody."

"It's people, Tomáš. Just people, like anyone else."

"Ah, here are our guests of honour," said Alice Masaryková. "Ladies and gentlemen, may I please introduce you to Sergeants Kovařík and Sobotka."

She led Tomáš along the line of five people waiting to greet him.

"May I introduce my sister, pani Olga Revilliod."

"Pleased to meet you, madam."

"Likewise, Sergeant."

"My brother, Jan Masaryk. Foreign Minister and Deputy Prime Minister."

"An honour, Foreign Minister."

Masaryk shook Tomáš's hand enthusiastically. He was a tall man, slightly overweight and ungainly.

"Call me Jan, Sergeant," he said with a broad smile. "No need for all these formalities."

"Thankyou, sir."

"This is General Moravec, Head of the Intelligence Service," continued Alice Masaryková. "I have been speaking to the General about the situation regarding your wife and child, Sergeant Kovařík. I wondered if he might be able to advise you."

"I would be grateful for the chance to speak to you about it, General."

"I'm sure we can find some time at the end of the evening, Sergeant."

"Thankyou, sir."

"And our generous hostess. Pani Benešová."

"I hope the presidential guard have found a comfortable billet for you, Sergeant Kovařík."

"Quite comfortable, thankyou, madam. I am very grateful to you for the invitation to your home."

"It is entirely our pleasure."

"And finally, of course, our dear President Beneš."

Tomáš stood in front of the man whose decisions had done more to shape his life than anyone outside his family. His slight frame contradicted the enormity of his influence over his country and its people. His expression was kind and welcoming, but Tomáš saw in his face an underlying look of determination, intelligence and world weariness.

"It is a pleasure to meet you, Mr President," he said, shaking his hand.

"The pleasure is mine, Sergeant Kovařík. Once again the future of our nation depends on our fighting men like you. I am very anxious to hear your opinion of morale in the Brigade."

Alice Masaryková took Tomáš's arm and asked him to accompany her into dinner. In the oak-panelled dining room two candelabras stood on the table set with fine china, cut glass and silverware. Tomáš was seated between Alice Masaryková and her brother. Opposite him, between Olga Revilliod and František Moravec, sat Miloš, who was examining his cutlery. The president and his wife took their places at either end of the table. The president's Alsatian dog, Toga, sat at his feet.

"The only thing our president has in common with Hitler," joked Jan Masaryk. "A love of Alsatians."

"Better that than the passion for Wagner you share with him, Jan," said his sister, Olga.

"Are you referring to Hitler or to our President, my dear?" Jan Masaryk asked her.

Tomáš was relieved when laughter broke some of the formality. He looked across at Miloš who smiled back at him with a quizzical look on his face.

"So, Sergeant Kovařík," said Beneš, as the soup was served. "Please give us your impression of the morale of our men."

"Morale is very high considering our circumstances, Mr President."

"Elaborate if you will."

"Most of the men feel as I do, sir. They have families they haven't seen for some time, and they worry far more about that than anything else."

"But what of their fighting spirit?"

"We're well trained, sir. We do nothing else. Every single one of us just wants to get home. We'd fight against any odds for that. We just want to be given the chance."

"What action have you seen up to now, Sergeant?"

"Sergeant Kovařík was interned in France, Eduard," said Alice Masaryková. "I told you earlier. He has had to leave his wife and daughter there in one of the camps. We are doing our best to help the sergeant locate them."

"Of course. I remember now. I do apologise."

"It's Sergeant Sobotka who has seen all the action, Mr President," said Tomáš

"And what do you think, Sergeant Sobotka?"

"Me? I've fought with our lads for four years, sir. Simple fact. They're the best fighters of the lot. Two reasons. Good officers and good training. But Kovařík's right. It's no good being the best if you don't fight. Oh, and another thing, sir, since you ask. The British tanks we've been given are rubbish. We had better tanks of our own in '38."

"You men must learn to be patient, Sergeant Sobotka," said General Moravec. "Barring a disaster it's just a matter of time before the Germans are beaten. They've lost North Africa and Stalingrad, and getting them out of Sicily won't take long. The second front in the west will come one day soon, but we must all be patient."

"And our men must be ready to play as big a part as possible when it does come," said Beneš. He put down his soup spoon and looked around the table. "Politically we have already come a long way. In 1940, when we first came to England, we found ourselves in the same position as we were in 1916. We needed recognition as the legitimate leaders in exile of our people. In the last war it was our Legions who earned it for us. This time it has been our brave pilots in the RAF and our brave soldiers like our sergeants here." His eyes moved from Tomáš to Sobotka and back again. "Soon the second front will give you another chance to restore your country to its former position, men. But I'm afraid it will not be we Czechoslovaks who decide when that time will be."

"Well, I don't wish to make light of all these earnest discussions, but there is one decision our fighting men *can* make for themselves," said Jan Masaryk. "Would either of you care for more wine?"

"Yes, sir. Don't mind if I do," said Miloš.

"And you, Tomáš? You don't mind if I call you Tomáš, I hope."

"No, Minister, I'm honoured."

"You must excuse my brother, Sergeant Kovařík," said Alice Masaryková. "He has always had an over-developed tendency towards informality."

"No, madam. I really am honoured."

"Then you must call me Jan, Tomáš."

"I could never do that, sir."

"Of course you could."

"No, sir. Really I couldn't."

"Why ever not?"

"Because of my father, sir."

"Explain."

"My father was one of the men you spoke of, President Beneš. He did not return from the war until 1920, after fighting his way from Galicia to Vladivostok with the Legion. I was the same age as my daughter is now when he came home. Three years and seven months. He had never seen me. My father taught me all my life that the greatest prize I could have in this world was to be a citizen of Czechoslovakia. And he taught me that the greatest Czechoslovaks of all were your father, Foreign Minister, and..." Tomáš looked towards the head of the table. "...you, President Beneš. My father would scarcely be able to believe that his child was sitting here today in the company of President Beneš and three of Tomáš Masaryk's children. He would want me to show the respect due to you all."

There was a brief silence and then Jan Masaryk patted the table gently. "Well spoken, Sergeant Kovařík. All formal titles will be reinstated forthwith." He raised his glass to Tomáš and drank.

"I think my father would forgive me though, President Beneš, if I ventured to ask you one question, sir."

"Your family's service to our country allows you much more than that, Sergeant. What is your question?"

"You have spoken this evening about the need for our men to fight to preserve our country, sir. I was an army reservist on the Austrian border in southern Bohemia on the 30th September 1938. My life would have been very different if you had let me fight then. Why didn't you?"

All sound in the room stopped. Beneš breathed out heavily and paused as if he needed to consider his reply.

"As you can imagine," he said, "that is a question I have asked myself countless times since the day I made that decision. Before I made it, I spent long hours agonising over the possible outcomes for our country and its people. I know I shall go to my grave wondering whether my final decision was the right or the wrong one. Can I answer your question by posing one of my own, Sergeant Kovařík?"

"Of course, sir."

"It concerns the assassination of Reinhard Heydrich last year. General Moravec and I planned that operation together here, and I gave the order for it to be carried out. Josef Gabčik and Jan Kubiš sat at this very table only days before they left on their mission. They and most of the brave men who went with them are now dead, of course. And so are the people of Lidiče and at least 13,000, perhaps even 30,000, other Czechoslovaks whom the Germans murdered in reprisals. You no doubt realise what my question to you is, Sergeant."

"Yes, sir. And I have my answer. You were right to order the assassination, Mr President, not knowing the outcome. You could only consider it wrong, had you known the outcome in advance."

"Based on the human cost I agree with you, Sergeant. But what if I tell you why the assassination was carried out, and what other outcomes flowed from it."

"I would be very interested, sir."

"Last year the war was not going well. Our allies, particularly the Soviet Union, felt that many countries under occupation had settled a little too easily into an accommodation with the Germans. We needed to show them that the Czechs had not. The audacity of killing Hitler's likely successor made our allies view us very differently. So too did the terrible sacrifice our people made in the reprisals that followed. Only days after the massacre at Lidice Churchill repudiated the Munich Agreement. Now Britain, Russia and America not only recognise us as the legitimate government in exile, they also acknowledge that the First Republic of Tomáš Masaryk continues to this day. And because the Munich Agreement now has no legality, all areas ceded under it will be returned to us after the war, and our 1938 borders reinstated."

"That's wonderful news, sir."

"In which case, Sergeant, do you not think now that ordering the assassination of Heydrich was the right decision, even if we had known about the reprisals in advance?"

"Please, Eduard," said pani Benešová, "remember that Sergeant Kovařík is our guest. You must not hector him." She stood up. "I shall ring for the fish course."

"Sergeant Kovařík has asked a question to which all Czechoslovaks deserve an answer, my dear."

"May I be allowed to address the question you just put to me, Mr President?" asked Tomáš

"I would like you to."

"The good outcome from Heydrich's assassination doesn't make the original decision a good one, any more than the bad outcomes make it a bad one. The question is, was it the right thing to do at the time?"

"Course it was, Tomáš," said Sobotka. "I don't know what all the argument's about. He was the Butcher of Prague. An evil 'b'... excuse me, ladies. I come from Prague. I tell you, there wasn't a man out there in the desert who didn't celebrate when we heard our boys had got Heydrich. We all wished we could've done it."

"Sobotka has given us all the answer, Mr President," said Tomáš. "Heydrich was evil. It was right to kill him. And our people will be stronger because it was done, regardless of what followed. Or perhaps because of what followed."

"I wonder if Sergeant Sobotka would have celebrated if his family was from Lidice and not from Prague," said Beneš.

"With respect, sir," said Tomáš, "that's not a fair question. I believe all of us would put the safety of our family before anything else if there was a straight choice. That is why it is good that we do not always know the outcome of our decisions. More than anything else I want to see my wife and child again. Nothing is more important to me. Not even my country. But I will fight for my country and risk death, because it is the right thing to do."

"Do you have no doubts at all then, Sergeant Kovařík, about what we should have done after Munich?"

"I'm afraid not, sir. Our country faced evil and injustice. Our people needed to confront it. We needed to fight."

Beneš shook his head.

"You judge my husband too harshly, Sergeant," said Hana Benešová. "He has worked his entire life in the cause of international peace and security. His decision after Munich saved the lives of thousands, perhaps even millions of our people. Think of the destruction of our cities."

"Of course, madam."

"And since then he has thrown his heart and soul into freeing our country. It's only due to him that we shall have a country to go back to after this dreadful war."

"Don't be too hard on our Sergeant Kovařík, Hana," said Jan Masaryk. "He is expressing a view which all Czechoslovaks need to consider. We may have preserved the bricks and mortar of our cities, but have we preserved the spirit of our people? I believe the British and French faced the same question following their disgrace at Munich. It has caused the French to lose their soul. The British have salvaged their spirit and self-respect only by the sacrifices they have made since. I believe we face the same challenge."

"That is why I say so much depends now on our soldiers in the Brigade," said Beneš. "They have a chance of restoring our nation's pride. As our pilots have done."

"Except there's only 4,000 of us, and the equipment they give us is useless," said Sobotka.

"That will be put right soon, Sergeant Sobotka," said Beneš. "I give you my word. Now you men from the Middle East have arrived, our mixed brigade will soon become a full armoured brigade with the best British tanks. I am coming to Dovercourt next month to see it for myself."

"Thankyou, sir. I'm sure the lads will look forward to that."

"And, of course we have our Czechoslovak forces fighting with the Russians. They have been invaluable in improving our standing with Marshall Stalin."

"That's surely one more reason why we need a second front as soon as possible, Mr President," said Tomáš. "So that we can liberate our country from the west before the Russians get there."

"I think we have to be realistic about that, Sergeant Kovařík. It seems most likely the Russians will enter our country from the east first. The important factor is that the liberating army will be spearheaded by Czechoslovak troops."

"But, sir, surely most of the Czechoslovaks who chose to go to Russia are Communists. We don't want Communists liberating our country."

"Perhaps I should tell you something about Russia, Sergeant, that most people do not know. Not all our allies deserted us after Munich. Stalin offered us help. He offered us thirty-five Russian divisions."

"Why didn't you accept them, sir?"

"You really cannot face both ways at once, Sergeant. You're against Communist forces entering our country at the end of this war, but you think I should have welcomed them in 1938. It makes no sense."

"Please, Eduard. Don't upset yourself," said Hana Benešová. "And even more important, do not upset one of our guests."

"Really, pani Benešová, I am not at all upset. Quite the opposite. As a citizen of the country we all love I feel privileged to be allowed to speak so freely with our President."

"Well, in that case... But I do insist that you do not neglect your food, Sergeant Kovařík."

"I shalln't, madam. Thankyou."

"May I continue then, my dear?" asked Beneš. His wife nodded her approval. "The reason I turned down Stalin's offer, Sergeant Kovařík, was because of one scenario I feared above all others. If we had accepted Soviet help after Munich, I knew Hitler would use it to characterise our country as a bulwark of Communism. He would have ranted on about us inviting Bolshevism into the heart of Europe. And knowing how powerful the appeasers were in France and Britain, I feared they might even take Germany's side against the Soviets. We would then have been stranded in an alliance which went against all that Tomáš Masaryk and I had set out to achieve. And the battle between east and west would have been fought out once more in Bohemia, as so many have been in the past. I did not want to put our people through it."

"And you were right not to, Mr President," said General Moravec. "I said so at the time, and I say the same now to our young guest."

"Thankyou, General," said Beneš. "But you and I know we cannot turn down help from the Russians now. The whole of Europe is depending on them."

"Quite right, sir."

"It is fortunate for our country that I enjoy such a good relationship with Marshall Stalin. He understands well enough that I oppose Communism as a way of life for our people, and he has made an open commitment to the restoration of the pre-Munich government after the war."

"But can you trust him, Mr President?" asked Tomáš.

"A lot more than I have learned to trust the French or British, Sergeant Kovařík. Stalin has guaranteed there will be no Russian interference in the internal affairs of our country after the war, and he has assured me that any Russian troops on our soil at the end of hostilities will be withdrawn within six months. I have received no such guarantee from the British or Americans."

"As you well know, Mr President, I tend towards Sergeant Kovařík's view on this," said Jan Masaryk. "I'm not so sure Mr Stalin can be trusted."

"Please, Foreign Minister, let us be a little more guarded on certain matters. I would not want our guests to go away with any wrong ideas about our official policy."

"No, of course. I do apologise."

"Perhaps I can be a little less guarded since I only express a personal view," said Tomáš. "The Communists I have met will say or do anything to further their cause. When it comes to brutality and contempt for democracy, there is little to choose between them and the Fascists."

"You have very firm opinions for someone so young, Sergeant," said Hana Benešová.

"The privilege of youth, my dear," suggested her husband.

"I lived under Pétain's Fascists for four years," replied Tomáš, "and my father fought the Bolsheviks for almost as long. He told me never to trust the Russians."

"So who is there left to trust?" demanded Beneš.

"Only ourselves, sir, and anyone like us who opposes Fascism and Communism."

"But the Russians are our allies."

"I remember something my grandfather used to say, sir. 'We need the snakes to kill the rats, Tomáš, but don't encourage them into the house.'"

"I think you should promote this young man, General," laughed Jan Masaryk, slapping Tomáš on the back. "He has an answer for everything. And furthermore I have to admit I agree with every word he says."

After dinner the party retired to the drawing room where coffee was served while Jan Masaryk played Smetana polkas on the grand piano.

"Your brother is very accomplished," Tomáš said to Alice Masaryková.

"Yes, our mother encouraged him from an early age. He is giving classical recitals in London next week to raise money for the Red Cross. Have you heard the recording he made with Jarmila Novotná?"

"The opera singer? No I haven't."

"They recorded Czechoslovak folk songs to commemorate the victims of Lidiče."

"I look forward to hearing it."

"Jan has become a great source of solace to our people. He makes weekly broadcasts to them from London, you know. It's illegal to listen to them, of course, but I believe thousands do."

"I've heard some of his broadcasts. Your brother is an inspiration to our people, madam. As was his father."

"Thankyou, Sergeant Kovařík. You always express such generous opinions about our family. Now, I must find General Moravec for you. I know how much you want to speak to him. I shall bring him over to you."

Tomáš watched as Alice Masaryková spoke to the general, who seemed reluctant to leave his chair. He came over to Tomáš alone.

"I have to tell you, Kovařík, I thought your comments over dinner were harsh," he said. "I suppose you understand such criticism of our president will not be tolerated once you return to your unit."

"Of course, General. But my opinions this evening were generously invited and respectfully given, sir."

"That may be, Sergeant, but our president is a man sailing a small craft between two treacherous shores. Someone of your obvious intelligence should see that."

"I do, sir."

"He deserves our full support at all times."

"Of course, sir."

"Now, what help are you after from me?"

Tomáš told Moravec about his visit to the Red Cross the previous day.

"I know all about Drancy, Kovařík. It's very unlikely your family will still be there."

"But it's information about where they are now I need, sir."

"To what end?"

"I wondered if anyone has tried to infiltrate the camps in the east."

"Why? Are you volunteering to go?"

"Yes, I am, sir. We need to know what's happening."

"Out of the question, Kovařík."

"Why, sir? No one has any answers to my questions. Isn't anyone interested in where the Jews are being taken, and what's happening to them?"

"You must understand, Kovařík, that such intelligence has no military value. We are all preparing for the second front. We need information about German strength on the Atlantic coastline, not about where civilian

Jews are being held thousands of kilometres away."

"So you won't let me go? Even though I accept the risk?"

"No, and for the same reason the British turned you down when you first arrived in England."

"You know about that?"

"Of course. It's my job to know. Personally I think you could make a good agent for the SOE, but for one obvious flaw. Your motives are too personal, Kovařík. To succeed in that job you have to be detached and dispassionate. Let me give you some advice."

"Yes, sir."

"Fight with the rest of the men to help free our country. Keep your opinions to yourself. And pray that when the war is over, you and your family will have survived."

Chapter Twenty-Three

April 21st, 1945

Tomáš waited outside the Czechoslovak Brigade Headquarters in Wormhoudt. An early-morning mist lay over the flat marshy land which surrounded the small Flemish town. He looked again along the road the lorry would take from Dunkirk. It was late. Seven thirty sharp he was told, and it was already a quarter to eight. Not that it mattered. Even his first twenty-four-hour pass since the Brigade arrived in France seven months before could do little to raise his spirits.

The whole sorry business had been one let-down after another. The men of the Brigade believed they were preparing to play their part in great events, on which the course of world history, the future of their country, and their families' lives depended. They were to be the new Legion. But they were deceived.

Tomáš stamped down hard with his right boot in frustration at the memory of it. It started in Scotland during their training for the second front. 'We want you combat-ready for the invasion by the end of the month,' the men had been told on the first of June '44. Five days later, when news of the landings in Normandy came over the radio, they were still stuck in Galashiels. Five more weeks they waited in the Scottish Borders, listening every day to reports of the fighting in France, but denied any opportunity to play a part.

In August they moved closer to the Channel ports. But still they waited. It was as if the Czech Brigade had been forgotten. That was the worst time for Tomáš, when news came through on August 25th that Paris had been liberated, and he was marking time in a makeshift camp in a park in East London.

A few days later came some relief when at last he disembarked at Arromanches and stepped back on French soil, the soil Anna and Eva might still be on, and only a few hours' drive away. His pleas to his commanding officer to be allowed to go to Paris to search for them were dismissed. But Major Sitek did at least do something for him. He discovered that the Swedish Consul-General had compiled a list of the 1,500 people still imprisoned in Drancy when it was liberated. Sitek informed Tomáš that he had sent for a copy of the list. When it arrived, the names of Anna and Eva were not on it.

Tomáš looked again along the tree-lined road from Dunkirk, where the Czechoslovak Independent Armoured Brigade had been in static siege positions for the past seven months. If the lorry arrived now, he would still be in Lille by ten o'clock. It would be good to have a change of scene. But he was not looking forward to meeting his fellow passengers. He knew what the other men called soldiers like him with a cushy number at Brigade Headquarters. 'Base rats.' But he had not asked to be sent there. It was the last thing he wanted.

He had trained for months with his seven-man crew on the anti-tank gun, only to be told the German garrison at Dunkirk would not be sending out any tanks against the Brigade. They would not be sending anything out. The Germans refused to surrender their fortress and were intent on sitting out the war behind their defences. The Czechoslovaks and the Free French did not have the strength in numbers to launch an assault on the port, so there was stalemate. The Brigade relieved the Canadians, who went off to fight the war, while Tomáš was sent twelve kilometres inland to headquarters, where his fluency in the four languages of the belligerents was considered 'vital for the war effort'.

Some children passed him on their way to school and the boys amongst them saluted him earnestly. He smiled back at them. This was not the vital role President Beneš had assured him he would be playing, when they met at Aston Abbotts two years before. But at least events were working out as Beneš had planned for himself, if not for the Brigade.

Tomáš had been dismayed, but not surprised, when he heard in early March that the President and the rest of the government-in-exile, including Jan Masaryk, had flown to Moscow at the invitation of Stalin. There they waited until the Red Army had secured the eastern part of their country, before Beneš temporarily set up the new government of Czechoslovakia in the town of Košice in southern Slovakia. Tomáš suspected it was no coincidence the Russians had already established their presence in his homeland, while the Czechoslovaks fighting with the western allies were abandoned on the Channel coast, more than a thousand kilometres from their country's border.

In the distance he heard the whine from the gearbox of a British army Bedford lorry. He raised his hand as it approached, as if he were stopping a bus, and then felt foolish, since he was the only person out on the street. The tailgate was thrown down and Tomáš put one foot on the step and pulled himself up with the help of a knotted rope hanging from the roof. There were about twenty men sitting along the wooden benches attached to either side of the truck. He returned the greetings offered by most of them in Czech and by a few in French. The ribbing he expected after being picked up from the headquarters of General Liška was more restrained than he expected, probably because of his sergeant's stripes.

"Seems like a nice place this, Sarge," someone ventured as soon as they moved off. "Not too quiet for you out here, is it?"

"Quiet? You must be joking, Private. I'm telling you, the sound those damned typewriters make can shred your nerves. You lads have got it easy."

It was enough. The new man could take a joke and would be left in peace. Tomáš preferred it that way.

They arrived in Lille soon after ten and were dropped off in the Grand' Place, where the Hotel de Londres had been requisitioned for the use of the troops containing Dunkirk. Four young women sitting in the lobby held unlit cigarettes to their bright red lips and smiled extravagantly at the soldiers as if in search of a light. While the men crowded around them, Tomáš went to the small reception desk and got his key. The room on the second floor had a wardrobe and four metal-framed single beds in it. He threw his haversack on the bed nearest the window and went downstairs and into the street.

Lille's Flemish buildings bore the scars of the present war and the last, but the people appeared determined to ignore the destruction and return to a normal life as quickly as possible. All the shops were open and market traders had set up stalls around the square. The tricolore and the flag of General de Gaulle with the Cross of Lorraine hung from every building. It was as if the Occupation had never happened and the France of Pétain and Vichy had never existed.

Tomáš bought a newspaper and took a seat in the morning sunshine at one of the pavement cafés. He sipped his coffee, still made from roasted barley and chicory, and watched the men who had been with him in the lorry cross the square and disappear into a bar. He wished he could join them, but knew he had no patience for it. It meant trivial conversation and weak jokes, which would get bawdier as the beer flowed. He looked at the plan of Lille he had been given, finished his coffee, and left five francs on the table. He hoped time would pass more quickly in the Palais des Beaux Arts.

At lunchtime he headed back to the estimanet in the Grand' Place where soldiers with leave passes received their meals. It was crowded and noisy. He queued for his food and felt lucky to find an empty table in a corner.

"Kovařík," someone called out. "Tomáš. Tomáš Kovařík."

He looked up and saw Miloš Sobotka walking towards him. Tomáš stood up to greet him. Sobotka put his beer on the table and shook his hand.

"It's good to see you, Miloš."

"And you, mate," said Sobotka pulling up a chair. "Haven't seen you since we landed. Heard you got a cushy number as a base rat. How did you work that then?"

"Some cushy number. All day turning French rubbish into Czech. Czech into English. It drives me mad."

"Warm bed. Three square meals. Sounds good to me."

"Believe me, Miloš, I'd much rather be where you are. At least you're seeing some action."

"That's not action. They lob a couple at us. We lob something back. Every so often we send out a raiding party to get ourselves a prisoner or two. Just to remind 'em we're still there."

Tomáš pushed his food away.

"But this isn't what we trained for, Miloš. Fast-moving armoured thrusts, they said. My crew could get that seventeen-pounder unhitched and ready in less than two minutes. This is just September '38 all over again. They're not giving us a chance to fight."

"All the lads are sick of it, Tomáš. Like a pal of mine says, we're just guarding a bloody big prison camp. The bastards in there know they can't go anywhere."

"All I do is sit around writing propaganda leaflets all day, trying to persuade them to be nice and come out. I've had enough of it."

Tomáš banged his fist on the table.

"You sound more wound up than any of us, mate," said Miloš.

"Maybe I am."

"Have you heard any news about your family? You've got a little girl, haven't you?"

"Eva. She'll be five and a half now."

"Did you ever find out where they are?"

"No. But I know they're not in Paris any more. They weren't there last August when the camp was liberated."

"Where would they have gone then?"

"Somewhere in the east, Miloš. Somewhere in the damned east."

"You don't mean one of those... something... camps?"

"Concentration camps."

"Yeah. Not that big one the Russians found where people..? Sorry, mate. I'm not thinking what I'm saying."

"It's alright, Miloš. I don't hide from the truth. I was on duty in January when the communiqué came though to our unit. The Russians called it an 'extermination' camp, but they've refused to offer one bit of proof. No photographs or documents. Nothing. Not even the names of the survivors they found."

"What was it called again?"

"Auschwitz-Birkenau."

"That's it."

"General Liška thinks the Russians are exaggerating it all to excuse some of the things their own troops are doing."

"That's probably right then."

"I know people have been killed in the camps, Miloš, but I have to believe my Anna and Eva will survive. What else can I do?"

"Nothing, mate."

"I need to get home as soon as I can to see if there's any news of them."

"It shouldn't be long now, mate. But it's bloody tough on you. I know a few Jewish blokes who are worried about family. Parents and uncles and things, but no one with a wife and kid."

"That's why I need to be doing something. It's been nearly three years since I last saw them. Sitting around is driving me mad."

"That's the army for you, mate. You just got to do what they tell you. Don't complain, and keep yourself dry is what I say. Mind you, that wasn't too hard in the desert."

"Even when I was with them in the internment camp I always thought I could keep them safe. If I tried hard enough I thought I could stop anything bad happening to them. Now I keep thinking if I could fight, I would be protecting them. I know it makes no sense."

"Fighting's alright, Tomáš, but so is staying alive. You're no good to them dead."

"But I need to fight for them, Miloš, before it's too late."

Sobotka took a long drink.

"You could always try to get yourself on this TF thing with the rest of us."

"What TF thing?"

"Shit, don't you know? I shouldn't have said anything then."

"What TF thing, Miloš?"

"I thought being at headquarters you'd know all about it."

"Tell me, Miloš. What is it?"

"You know the Americans have reached the border round Cheb?"

"I knew they were close."

"Well, someone high up reckons they should have some of us from the Brigade leading the way in. To make it look good, I reckon. The TF's the Token Force. They'll be the spearhead into Cheb, Pilsen and Prague."

"Who's in it?"

"There's 150 of us from the Motor Battalion going."

"One hundred and fifty. Is that all?"

"That's why we were told to keep it quiet, in case everyone wants to go."

"Of course everyone will want to go. Why have they chosen only from the Motor Battalion?"

"Because we travel fast and we're armed to the teeth. But your bloke from Anti-Tank is in charge of it all."

"Major Sitek?"

"Yeah. You could always ask him."

"I'll do better than that. I'll ask General Liška. This is my chance, Miloš."

"There you are, see. Being a base rat could have its uses after all. But you'll have to be quick. We're leaving in three days. Now, I'm going to get another beer. Do you want one?"

"Later, Miloš."

"Listen, Tomáš, you look like you've got the troubles of the world on you, mate. Why don't you come with me and a few of the lads this afternoon? Have some fun."

"Where are you going?"

"Have a few drinks and then to the Beauty Bomb Bombs."

"You mean *'La Boîte à Bonbons'?*"

"Yeah, that's it. When you've only got a few hours to enjoy yourself, you either pray for it or pay for it, I say."

"Thanks, Miloš. I appreciate the offer, but I can't."

Tomáš spent the rest of the afternoon at Lille's Citadel, walking beside the canals and rehearsing the case he would make to General Liška for his inclusion in the Token Force. In the early evening he headed back into the town centre.

The bars and cafés were beginning to fill up on a Saturday night. He looked across the Grand' Place at the estimanet where they would soon be serving the evening meal. He was not in the mood for company or for food. The lights of the cinema caught his eye and he went over to see what was playing. Bing Crosby in the 'Best Loved Picture of All Time'.

APRIL 21ST, 1945

'The Winner of Eight Academy Awards.' *'Going My Way.'* Why not? The film had already started but he was sure it would take little effort to pick up the story, and besides, Miloš was right, it was time he allowed himself some fun.

He was surprised how much he enjoyed the picture. It was an uplifting story with a happy ending, which he found improved his mood. He smiled at the French dubbing, which saddled Crosby with a thin, high-pitched voice, and was hopelessly out of synchronisation with what was happening on the screen. Thank God they at least allowed Crosby to use his own voice to sing.

He looked at his watch. Eight o'clock. There was just enough time to stay for the short second feature and still get some food before they stopped serving at nine. The lights went down, the curtains parted, and he settled lower in his seat. Before the film came on, he had to sit through the British Pathé News. The Pathé cockerel crowed and the title of the main story appeared on the screen with a fanfare of music. *'British Forces Liberate Nazi Camp'.*

He saw a scene which looked familiar. Rows of wooden huts on flat, sandy ground with a wide, open space behind. He heard the clipped English commentary. *"This is the concentration camp of Bergen-Belsen, recently liberated by the brave men of the British 11th Armoured Division. Nothing these hardened soldiers have experienced in nearly six years of war could have prepared them for the horror they have witnessed inside this camp."* The long-distance view of the camp in the opening scene changed to pictures of the inmates. Tomáš heard no more commentary.

He saw a procession of shuffling ghosts without flesh, dressed in rags. Each looked the same as the others. Hollow, blank faces and staring eyes which took in nothing. One on his haunches picking at something in his rags.

More of the same forms, lying abandoned, naked and motionless. Dozens of them. Hundreds of them. A mound of them piled together in outrageous, obscene poses, one on top of the other on the back of a lorry.

At last human figures, soldiers dressed in German uniforms. Dragging and throwing more of the mannequins with stretched, polished skin into a deep pit. A British soldier with a white mask over his nose and mouth driving a bulldozer. In front of the bulldozer another mound of the same white, floppy skeletons tumbling over one another, being pushed towards the pit.

Then children in striped clothes. Not the same as the others. They looked like children, rolling up their sleeves to show the camera numbers on their arms. Doing what they were told to do.

More recognisable people. A man, a live skeleton, clasping his hands in prayer as he was placed on a stretcher. A woman too weak to stand, sobbing and kissing the hand of a British soldier. German soldiers and women guards lined up to be filmed and shamed, but showing only blank indifference.

Tomáš heard shouting and cursing. *'Les cons! Les cons!'*

The lights in the cinema came on. Women were crying. Men were shouting, throwing coins at the blank screen. He sat motionless, his brain rejecting the question he was trying to ask it. Could that have been Anna and Eva?

He stood up, staggered forward, and found himself in a side street by the cinema. He was leaning against a wall, trying to catch his breath and clear his mind to reason. The British are in northern Germany. That's right. Then the camp in the newsreel couldn't be somewhere in the east. It would be different there. Not like Germany. The woman on the stretcher couldn't be Anna. The girl rolling up her sleeve couldn't be Eva. Not in Germany. The bodies... Not Anna. Not Eva. Oh, Anna. He fell to his knees on the pavement, then onto his hands, and vomited into the gutter.

Chapter Twenty-Four

April 24th – May 1st, 1945

"I intend to reach the Czechoslovakian border within five days," said Lieutenant-Colonel Sitek, the newly promoted commander of the Token Force.

"It will be our task to spearhead the liberation of Prague by the American 3rd Army before the arrival of the Russians from the east."

Anything more the colonel might have planned to say was drowned by the cheers of the 150 men assembled in the briefing room outside Dunkirk.

"Okay, men. Enough fine words. It's time to go."

Tomáš sat beside his co-driver in one of the ten Bedford trucks loaded with armour-piercing shells. Each truck pulled a six-pounder anti-tank gun. Sixteen more trucks carried the men, their equipment and armaments. Eight motor-cycle outriders provided reconnaissance. Five more days, thought Tomáš, as the convey pulled away, and he would be fighting his way back into Czechoslovakia.

It had not been easy for him to get a place on the Force. He knew General Liška would not allow his inclusion for any reason other than military necessity.

"I'm trained in languages, communication and liaison, sir," he told his commanding officer. "The Force will need all those skills passing through Belgium and Luxembourg and into Germany. And I know the terrain between the Bavarian border and Prague like the back of my hand. I'll be able to find alternative routes if any of the main roads are blocked." When Liška asked Tomáš if he spoke fluent Russian, he lied.

The Force made quick progress on the first day, reaching Bastogne on the Luxembourg border. The next morning they entered Igel, their first town in Germany. Sitek ordered a stop.

"We'll have a brew, men," he said, "and gauge the reception we can expect from the German population."

Tomáš did not care what reception they got. He wanted only to keep going. He stood alone and watched as some of the town's people, squatting in the ruins of their homes, ventured out to talk to the British soldiers.

He heard their surprise when told the convoy of armed troops massing in their square in such strength were Czechoslovaks. The Bürgermeister, smoking a proffered cigarette, recalled there had been some trouble over their country many years before, but was sure such distant events should now be forgotten. The children standing around listening to the conversations with this strange group of soldiers admitted they had not even heard of a country called Czechoslovakia.

Tomáš walked away and climbed back into his Bedford, slamming the door to encourage the others to get going too. He wiped the windscreen to get a better view of a woman and her two young children across the road, feeding a fire with wood from their smashed house. They had flesh on their bones and were together, alive. He felt no pity for them.

By the third day it became clear the convoy had to move faster. News arrived that General Patton had begun the American advance into western Bohemia, and the battle for Cheb had begun. But now the Token Force found all the bridges over the Moselle, Rhine and Main rivers destroyed, which meant long detours to find pontoon bridges, too new to be shown on any map. And, as night fell, the men had to locate American units which could provide them with petrol, spares and provisions for the next leg of their journey.

At the end of the fourth day Tomáš led a delegation of NCOs to Colonel Sitek and his British liaison, Captain Stephenson, to express the men's eagerness to drive through the night to reach Cheb. Permission was refused.

"Men entering battle in a state of exhaustion are a danger to themselves and to their fellow soldiers, Kovařík," replied Sitek. "You should know that."

None of Tomáš's objections would change Sitek's mind. The men were ordered to stop, service the vehicles and find billets. Tomáš could not sleep or rest. He stayed outside for hours in the night, looking to the east, imagining the fighting in Cheb. He climbed into his truck and sat there alone, waiting for the sun to edge slowly above the horizon.

The following day the convoy stopped fifteen kilometres from the border of Czechoslovakia.

"We could damn well walk to Cheb from here," Tomáš said to Miloš. "Doesn't anyone want to fight?"

But still they waited. And then it was too late. News came from Wormhoudt that the German commander in Cheb had surrendered to the Americans, and the men were informed they would spend two more days where they were, cleaning and maintaining their trucks, ready for a triumphal procession into Cheb and the raising of the Czechoslovak flag above the New Town Hall.

Tomáš was ordered to report to Sitek. "I'm told you're from Cheb, Kovařík," the colonel said to him. "I want to bestow on you the honour of raising our flag in the first Czech town to be liberated."

"Better to choose a soldier like Sobotka, sir, who has at least fought for the liberation of his country," said Tomáš. "Perhaps when I have had a chance to fight for Pilsen or Prague, you might ask me again."

On May 1st the 150 men from the Armoured Brigade were the first Czechoslovakian soldiers to enter their country from the west. But not as liberators. Cameramen and Public Liaison Officers from the U.S. 3rd Army, press photographers, and reporters were the vanguard, in position to record the crossing at the border village of Pomezi, three kilometres from Cheb.

"I can see now why they call us the Token Force," Tomáš muttered to Sobotka, as he did all he could to hide himself from the cameras. "We're not soldiers. We're damn film extras."

They entered Cheb shortly before noon. The wretched state of his town reinforced Tomáš's anger. The old railway station, the starting point of so many family journeys to Pilsen and Prague, was gone, lost completely in the recent fighting and the two American air raids which preceded it. Gone too was the Victoria Hotel, the former Gestapo Headquarters, where his father died a hero; and the Synagogue, whose destruction had not needed war, only the prejudice and hatred of the town's majority German population.

The theatre was badly damaged too, but not beyond repair. His eyes remained fixed on it as he drove past. He imagined walking into the foyer, as he had done so often with Anna, to visit her father at work. He looked back at the scarred façade in the truck's mirror and wondered whether people so closely linked to a place could, by some miracle, find their way back and be waiting there again.

He drove into the main square. The Town Hall was mostly intact. The fountain was badly damaged and so was most of the colonnade. But Müller's grocery and Hartmann's ironmonger's shop were still intact. How normal it would be to see his mother and grandmother standing together outside Müller's, or his father or grandfather coming out of Hartmann's. An empty, neutral feeling of helplessness gripped him. The past, so fixed, so permanent, was gone. There were no familiar faces. Only a few curious children, and a cordon of American G.I's guarding the square's every entrance.

The soldiers disembarked. Tomáš had dreamed of this so often with Anna during their years in France; the day of Cheb's restoration to Czechoslovakia. But now he was unmoved by it. When he saw Miloš raise the flag over the Town Hall he waited for the emotion he expected to feel. He knew without Anna there could be no joy, but he had expected to feel pride, and some satisfaction for the part he had played. But he could feel none of it. He stood watching his country's flag flying above the square, he heard Sitek's speech, and he sang his country's anthem, 'Where is My Home?', and all he felt was shame. He was an impostor again in his soldier's uniform, just as he had been the last time he came home to Cheb, on the night of Munich.

In the afternoon Sitek addressed the Token Force.

"You must understand, men," he said, "that the population of Cheb consists only of fanatical Germans. The Czechs and the few decent Germans amongst them were all driven out of the town over the past seven years. President Beneš has issued a decree from Košice, stating that all Germans and Hungarians who have shown disloyalty to the state will soon be expelled from Czechoslovakia. The population of Cheb is now aware of this new decree and is therefore likely to be very hostile to Czechoslovak troops.

"The Americans will soon be moving on. So for the next few days the Token Force will be taking over security in the town. A defensive perimeter will be set up around the main square, and patrols must only go out in sections of six. Force headquarters will be in the Town Hall and you will be billeted in the least damaged buildings. But these arrangements are only temporary, men. In a few days, I promise you, the Token Force will spearhead the final push into Prague."

Tomáš was put in charge of two sections and sent off in a Bedford truck to patrol the woods around the airfield on the outskirts of Cheb. It had been the last part of the town to surrender three days earlier, and German prisoners were still burying their dead under American guard. Tomáš's men went into the woods and were disappointed to find only liberated Russian POWs languishing in makeshift camps. Their hope of finding German soldiers there, ready to oblige them with a last stand, came to nothing.

Tomáš was relieved when his sections were ordered to the airfield, and not to the northern part of Cheb, to Štasný Lake where his grandparents' cottage had stood, and to the village of Skalka, where Anna lived before they moved Prague. They were places he wanted to visit alone. At six o'clock, when his patrol returned to the main square and the field kitchen opened, he waited until everyone was occupied. Then, with his rifle slung over his shoulder, he strolled down Krámařská Street towards the river.

He reached the pontoon bridge recently built across the Ohře by U.S Army engineers. The old bridge, which had carried the road to Františkovy Lázně for centuries, was gone. Only a few blocks of Bohemian sandstone lying on the far bank suggested it had ever existed. Tomáš looked to his left. His parent's house lay in ruins, along with those on either side of it, all victims of the bombing which had claimed the bridge.

Tomáš paused in the middle of the pontoon bridge at the spot where his mother loved to stand on summer nights, enjoying the coolness the river provided. He would sit at his window high up in the house, unseen, and watch her. He looked up at the window, forgetting for a moment that the upper floors of the house were no longer there, and saw only blue sky. He turned, walked off the bridge and took the path which led to the old Neumann house in Skalka.

He passed the turn-off leading down to the lake and his grandparents' chata. Nothing had changed here, and he felt the touch of the love and security which had been his life in this place. For a passing moment all that richness and permanence were his again, and he winced at the yearning it created in him. Movement in the woods to his right brought him back. He kept walking, neither looking around nor breaking his step, and waited for whoever it was to grow bolder. When the movement was as close as he dared allow, he turned and brought his rifle to his shoulder.

"Show yourself or I'll shoot," he shouted in German.

There was an abrupt silence and then frantic whispering in Russian, followed by the noise of people crashing through the undergrowth in the woods, as they turned and ran.

When he reached Skalka he was surprised to find the streets deserted. All the doors were closed, and the windows either had curtains drawn over them or were shuttered. But he knew he was being watched from every house he passed. He kept walking through the village to the river, his rifle once more slung over his shoulder. He reached the house which Ernst, Zuzana, Otto and Anna had left eleven years before, and walked up the garden path. He knocked on the front door, but no one answered. He knocked again more forcefully.

"Open up," he ordered in German. "You have nothing to fear, but if you do not open the door, I will break it down."

The door inched open. "Are you German?" asked a middle-aged man in workman's overalls.

"No, I'm a Czech serving with the Czechoslovak Armoured Brigade. We are now in control of Cheb and the surrounding area. I need to ask you something."

"I don't know anything."

"You're not in any trouble. I'm looking for a friend. Ernst Neumann. He used to live in this house many years ago. Has someone of that name called on you at any time?"

"I don't know anything," said the man and he started to close the door. Tomáš put his hand against it and pushed it back.

"Listen, I said you are in no trouble. But please answer my question. Herr Neumann is my father-in-law. I am trying to find him."

"Leave us alone. We don't know anything."

"His daughter is called Anna Kovaříková. Has she been here?"

"We don't know any Ivan women."

Tomáš reached in, grabbed the man by the strap of his overalls and pulled him through the doorway. "Show some respect, you German bastard. I asked you a polite question and you insult my wife."

"Please, sir. I don't know these people. Please leave us alone. We haven't done anything."

"You haven't done anything?" Tomáš tightened his grip and pulled the man down the garden path into the street. "Have you seen the state of the town? Do you know how many people you've killed?"

"The Americans destroyed Eger. I haven't harmed anyone."

"You Germans have harmed millions, you ignorant pig. Don't you care about anything you've done?"

A woman appeared at the front door. "Erich," she cried. "Please, sir, don't hurt my husband."

Tomáš turned to look at her and pushed the man away so violently he fell to the ground. "We have lost our son, sir," he whimpered. "My wife's sister was killed in the air raid on Eger."

"Cheb, you bastard. My town is called Cheb."

"Who says it is your town?" came a man's voice from behind Tomáš. He turned and saw seven or eight men walking towards him. He took his Lee Enfield from his shoulder and held it across his body.

"Don't come any closer. I haven't come here for trouble, but I warn you, I'll take no nonsense from you Nazi bastards."

"Haven't you Czechs done enough today?" said an elderly man standing in front of the rest. "You've already told us we must leave our homes. We have all lost sons or brothers. Our Führer is dead. Can we not be left to mourn?"

Tomáš clenched his fists around his rifle. "You think anyone should have sympathy for you people? After all you've done. Have you seen the camps? Have you seen what you Germans have done to people in the camps?"

"I have two sons in camps in Russia," said a man with a black armband around his right sleeve. He stepped forward. "We are all suffering."

"You deserve to suffer. You all deserve to be punished for supporting your bastard Führer. Nothing you people suffer will ever be enough. You've killed thousands of innocent women and children in your camps. Simply for being Jews."

"Well, if you're only talking about Jews...," said the man with the armband.

"What did you say?" shouted Tomáš.

"It was the Jews who started all this. And it's the only good thing to come out of it. There will be no more Jews."

"Come here, you Nazi bastard," screamed Tomáš. The man refused to move. Tomáš strode forward and, with his rifle clutched by the barrel in one hand, he grabbed the man's collar with the other. No one moved to stop him.

As he dragged the man away from his fellow villagers, Tomáš saw a larger group of men and women had come out of their houses. He threw the man to the floor and ordered the new arrivals to stand with the rest in front of him. They all obeyed, skirting around him.

"Repeat what you said," he ordered the old man on the ground.

"I don't want to. I didn't know you were a Jew."

"I'm not."

For a moment the man's face showed relief, but then he realised his words had only increased the Czech soldier's anger. He saw the rage in the soldier's face and knew he intended to kill him. He started to pray.

"Gracious Mary, Mother of God..."

Tomáš raised his rifle to his shoulder and aimed it at the man's forehead. "Stop that, you bastard hypocrite. Repeat what you said."

"No, I can't..."

"Repeat what you said about no more Jews or I'll shoot you dead." Tomáš screamed so hard that pain cut across his throat.

"I can't, I can't, I can't..." sobbed the old man.

Tomáš glanced quickly around to see where the other villagers were before he fired. They had not moved. They were cowering together, their arms around one another. He looked back at the man on the floor. One Nazi bastard. He took aim again. "Kill him..." he screamed at himself, "kill him, you damned coward." His arms started to shake, unable to support the weight of the gun. "I can't do it... Why can't I do it?" he mumbled. He turned towards the others, trembling, and his rifle slanted towards the ground in front of them.

"Someone has to pay," he said. The skin on his throat was raw. He felt the tears filling his eyes. "It should be you bastards. He stepped towards them. "You and your lunatic Führer have caused all this. But it won't be you who pays, will it? It will be your sons and grandsons over the next week. Their deaths will be your punishment." He stabbed his finger at them. "For every single one of you."

He put his rifle over his shoulder and, without looking back, stumbled down the road out of the village.

The light was fading when he came to the path down to the lake, and he could sense people's presence in the woods around him. His grandfather had taught him how to listen for wild boar at night, and hearing people trying to make no noise in the forest was easy. He kept his rifle over his shoulder, protected by anger and indifference, and did not stop.

He came to the lake. It was unchanged. Pink light moved gently on the surface of the water as the sun set behind the fir trees. It was all instantly familiar. He wiped the white blossom from his grandfather's seat beneath the cherry tree, slumped down onto it, and wept.

He had imagined being in this place with Anna so often over the past seven years. Whenever either of them made a wish, it was usually to sit here together. But he could not stay here now. Even this beautiful, sacred place had become too ugly and chaotic.

He walked over to the ruins of their grandparents' chata. Countless fires had been lit there since he last sifted through the broken tiles and stones, on the day he and Anna left for Prague to get married. He looked for a spot to hide something from everyone else but her. He removed a loose tile from the bottom of Babička's old oven and placed behind it a tin. In it was a message, *'Anna and Eva. I am alive and will keep looking for you. Your Tomáš and Táta, 1st May, 1945'.* He determined to return to Skalka in the morning, to place another tin with the same message somewhere in the garden of the Neumann house. On his way back to the main square in Cheb, he hid a third in the ruins of his parents' house by the bridge. Then he went to the Church of Saint Wenceslas to share with his parents and grandparents all that had happened since he was last in Cheb.

Chapter Twenty-Five

May 6th – May 31st, 1945

"Stand at ease, Kovařík. What do you want to see me about?"

"The other NCOs asked me to speak to you, Colonel. On behalf of the men, sir."

"You're becoming a bit of a spokesman, aren't you, Kovařík? The army's not a democracy, you know."

"No, sir."

"Say what you have to, Sergeant, although I think I can guess most of it."

"This is our sixth day in Cheb, Colonel. The men cannot understand, sir, why we are not moving forward. They know there's fighting in Pilsen. We could be there in two hours. They thought it was what we came here for."

"It's what we all thought we came for, Kovařík. But our first task as soldiers is to deploy as we are ordered to deploy." Sitek put down his pen and leaned back in his chair to look at Tomáš. "I'll tell you now what I shall be telling the men later. I was in touch with the headquarters of the 1st US Division this morning. I put in another strong request for the Token Force to be allowed to spearhead the attack on Prague. That is their reply." He pointed to a sheet of paper on the desk. "We are ordered to proceed to Pilsen tomorrow."

"Tomorrow? Why not today? Why not now? There are enough Czechoslovak militia in the town to keep order here."

"I know. Believe me, Sergeant, I'm as frustrated as you and the rest of the men."

"What lies behind it, sir?"

"I'm not prepared to theorise with you about that, Kovařík. All I can say is that the order to form the Token Force came from the very top. Supreme Allied Headquarters. Now it seems those very same people are reining us back."

There was a knock on the door.

"Come in."

A corporal handed Sitek a piece of paper. "This has just arrived from US divisional headquarters, sir," he said, and left the room.

"You won't like this, Sergeant Kovařík," sighed Sitek. "Message timed 16.32 hours today. The Americans have liberated Pilsen." He looked up at Tomáš. "Now Prague is the only prize left."

The next morning the Token Force left Cheb for Pilsen. Sitek and Captain Stephenson went ahead of the main column to US Divisional Headquarters to request permission in person for the Token Force to proceed directly to Prague. Permission was refused. The Germans still held the road between Pilsen and Prague in too much strength, they were told. There were reports of German units regrouping on the road between Cheb and Pilsen and, in case there was any truth in those reports, the Token Force was ordered to turn around, go back through Cheb and into Germany to find a safer route.

Miloš, who was used to following orders which made no sense, was becoming as angry and frustrated as Tomáš.

"What the bloody hell do the base rats think these are for?" he said, kicking one of the six-pounders. "Our men are so damn fired up I reckon they could walk through German stragglers with a damn bow and arrow."

But the men did as they were ordered and turned around. The column went back across the German border in order to approach Pilsen from the south, and a journey of only ninety minutes turned into eight wasted hours.

The men reached the outskirts of Pilsen at five o'clock in the afternoon. As soon as the inhabitants of the city caught sight of their first Czechoslovak soldiers in over six years, the column's progress was slowed to a walking pace. It seemed every last citizen of Pilsen had come out to welcome them. More than one hundred thousand people lined the streets, many waving handkerchiefs and all cheering at the top of their voices. Girls had changed into national costume and wanted to hug and kiss as many of their country's brave soldiers as they could. Children threw flowers and the older men and women wept and blessed their 'wonderful brave boys'.

For once Tomáš found himself able to share in the happiness and enjoy the acclaim. Although he had contributed nothing yet, word had at last come through that the Force would be proceeding to Prague the next day to fight for the liberation of the city. When the convoy stopped in Pilsen's main square in front of Saint Bartholomew's Cathedral, the wild cheering grew louder than ever and echoed around the tall merchants' houses which lined the square on all sides.

Slowly the sound of the crowd changed. The cheering and the waving died away, as news from Prague reached those standing at the back of the square and made its way forward. People were sharing hurried words with those around them, turning, talking, and then pleading. At last the words found their way to the men in the convoy.

"Help them. Help them," people shouted.

"They're alone. They need you."

"Go. Please go."

"What is it? What's happened?" the men shouted back.

"The SS."

"....attacking the people in Prague."

"Help our people. Help them."

"Please go. Go."

Sitek ordered the men into their vehicles. The crowds cheered and shouted their thanks. "Bless you. Bless you," they cried. Tomáš waved back. At last his chance had come.

A few kilometres outside Pilsen the Token Force stopped at the village of Kyšice. They were told to find billets.

"This is crazy, Miloš. Why don't we just keep going?"

"For once the pips are right, Tomáš. We'd be sitting ducks on that road in the dark. We wouldn't see what hit us."

"But I know other ways into Prague. We could be there in two hours."

"The city will be blacked out, Tomáš. They'd see us coming from miles away. Best get some sleep, mate. You'll get all the action you want tomorrow."

The next morning the men rose early. Reports of renewed fighting were already filtering through from Prague. The villagers of Kyšice stood watching the men's preparations and urged them on their way. The men waited by their vehicles for their commanding officer and his staff to appear from their headquarters by the church. After fifteen minutes the men started to drift away from their lorries and congregate in small groups on the green. Tomáš stood with the other NCOs discussing the possible reasons for the delay. After an hour passed, it was agreed that Tomáš should go to Sitek to find out why they were not moving.

Within minutes he was back. "The Colonel couldn't see me. I was told he's been in touch with General Liška. He's asking Supreme Allied Headquarters to release us."

"Release us? We don't need bloody releasing," said Miloš. "I saw the sense in stopping last night, but this is bloody cowardice. Our people are being slaughtered just down that road, and we're sitting here on our arses.

I'm going to tell that bastard what I think of him."

Miloš stamped his cigarette out on the grass and put on his beret. Tomáš grabbed his arm.

"No, Miloš. Give me one more chance to sort it out. Then you go and see him."

"Alright. But if he makes any more excuses I won't bother. I'm going down that road anyway."

"Please, Miloš. Don't do anything until I get back."

"Sergeant Kovařík. I thought it wouldn't be long before I saw you."

"The men need some explanation, Colonel Sitek. Is there anyone helping our people in Prague?"

"No, Kovařík. Even General Patton has been ordered to stay out. It's a mess."

"It's murder, sir. That's what it is."

"Choose your words carefully, Sergeant."

"What would you call it, sir? Civilians are taking on the German Army in our capital because they think we're coming. And we're standing here talking about it."

"We're soldiers, Kovařík. We obey orders."

"Not if they're criminal, we don't."

"You're going too far, Sergeant. You're very close to being on a charge."

"You can do what you want with me, Colonel. Nothing the army can do to me will be worse than having to live with this."

"For God's sake, man. We're a small country with an even smaller army. We cannot act alone."

"We should be grateful our legionnaires didn't think like that when they took on the Germans and the Russians in Siberia. Can you imagine them waiting here like this, knowing their people were dying at the end of that road? Your men outside are desperate to go."

"The Legion followed orders, Kovařík. They were desperate, too. Desperate to come home, but they stayed because President Masaryk ordered them to."

"But they used their own initiative when they knew enough was enough."

"You have an answer for everything, don't you, Kovařík? It borders on insubordination."

"My father was one of the men who instigated the capture of the railway to Vladivostok, Colonel. I was brought up to believe that a Czechoslovak soldier was never beaten."

"We're not beaten. We're awaiting our orders to engage."

"The people in Prague are ordering us to engage. Isn't that enough for you?"

"Who do you think you're..?"

"When we know something is right, Colonel Sitek, we have to do it."

"Listen to me, Kovařík. I'm waiting for word from General Eisenhower himself in Frankfurt. I can tell you that Montgomery and Patton are putting all the pressure they can on him to let us go in with the Americans this morning. I have no idea what's holding them up."

"You're waiting for Eisenhower?"

"Yes. Supreme Allied Headquarters."

"My God. Then I think we both know what's happening here, don't we?"

"I told you once before, Kovařík. I'm not prepared to theorise with you."

"You don't need to, Colonel Sitek. We left Dunkirk two weeks ago intending to reach Prague in five days. But we've been obstructed all the way. Now even the Americans have been told to halt in front of Prague, even though Patton has enough armour to go anywhere he wants."

"And you think you know the reasons for all that, do you, Kovařík?"

"I do know the reasons. I've been a fool not to see it before."

"Don't be so arrogant, man. How could you know?"

"What's happening today was decided years ago, Colonel."

"And how would you know that?"

"I was once invited to a very interesting dinner party."

"Now you're being a smart arse, Kovařík. I like that even less than insubordination."

"It doesn't matter any more, sir. We're not going to Prague, and we're not going to fight. Somehow we're all going to have to live with the shame of it. Again."

"If you say such things to the men before I receive our orders, I *will* have you on a charge."

"I won't say anything, Colonel Sitek. If I did, I think you'd have a mutiny on your hands."

"You will tell the men we have not yet received our orders to proceed. As soon as we do, we shall be on our way."

"Yes. I'll tell them."

"If it is any consolation to you, Sergeant, Prague's agony will soon be over whatever we do today. There will be an official announcement to all forces in Europe in one hour. The war will end at one minute past midnight tonight."

"I'm going, Tomáš. This is bloody stupid. I've never disobeyed an order in my life, but this makes no damn sense to me."

"But I've told you, Miloš, the war will be over tonight."

"I don't care. That's my city down that road. That's where my Saskie is. I'm not warming my arse round here while they do all the fighting. You've got to come with me, mate."

"You won't get through."

"Who says? I've had a word with a couple of the reccy boys. They say we can take their motor cycles."

"You still won't get through, Miloš."

"A few Germans aren't going to stop me. I've seen plenty of them off in my time."

"Listen, Miloš. It's not the Germans you need to worry about. It's the Russians."

"What are you talking about? We're wasting time."

"That's why we've been moving so slowly, Miloš. They've been keeping the Token Force this side of the Americans. They don't want us Czechoslovaks anywhere near the Russians. That's why the Brigade has been kept in Dunkirk."

"You're still making no sense. My people in Prague are fighting the Germans right now. I'm going to help. Are you coming or not?"

"No, Miloš, I'm not. I'm prepared to die fighting the Germans, but I'm not going to waste my life because of some deal Truman and Churchill have made with Stalin."

"What the hell are you talking about?"

"Don't you remember when you and I went to Aston Abbotts two years ago? Beneš told us then he trusted the Russians more than he trusted the British or Americans. They've done a deal, Miloš. You'll find the American 3rd Army are stopped just down that road. You won't get past them. And if you do, you'll find the Russians won't welcome you."

"Is this all you're going to do? Talk? If the bloody Americans were in front of us, they'd be on their bloody way to Prague already, wouldn't they?"

"Not if they were waiting for the Russians to go in first. You'll find Stalin will liberate Prague in his own good time."

"You think too much, Tomáš. Life's a lot simpler for me, mate. Prague's my home. Saskie's there, so that's where I'm going. And you should come with me. What if your Anna's there?"

"It's been three years, Miloš. I'll wait one more day and stay alive to find her. Saskie will want you to do the same."

"I'll buy you a beer when you do make it to Prague, Tomáš. I'm not sitting around here waiting for Sitek or for you."

Miloš went over to one of the motor cycles. "Good luck, base rats," he shouted as he got on. He opened the throttle, waved and disappeared down the road to Prague, leaving the loud cheers of the men of the Token Force behind him.

Prague was liberated by the Russians the following day. The Token Force had to wait in Kyšice a further three days before the Russians granted permission for them to enter the city. The welcome the convoy received was every bit as rapturous as the one in Pilsen. There was the same joyous waving and cheering from the crowds, the girls in national costume were as beautiful as before, and the older people wept once again with relief and gratitude.

Everything appeared to be the same as it had been in Pilsen, but for Tomáš everything was different. The people's joy seemed to make them unaware of the grim-faced Russian soldiers who lined every street; their battledress forming a brown frieze around Wenceslas Square. They were unaware, too, of how undeserving the Token Force was of so much adulation and affection. And in Pilsen Tomáš had not been searching for Anna, endlessly scanning the crowd for her face. He knew it would not be the way to find her, but she and Prague were linked so closely in his mind that he could not stop looking for her there. He looked for the Anna he knew, and for a gaunt, hollow-faced Anna. But he found neither. And as the dozens of faces he scanned became hundreds, and the hundreds turned into thousands, the hopelessness of the task drained him.

The next day he awoke with fresh determination to continue the search, but after morning parade the Token Force was ordered out of Prague, back behind the Chemnitz-Pilsen-Budweis Line, which Roosevelt and Stalin had agreed years before was to be the limit of Patton's advance into Czechoslovakia. All of Tomáš's requests to return to Prague alone were turned down. The Russians, he was told, would allow no Czechoslovak soldiers attached to American units to re-enter the city. For most of May he remained with the men outside Pilsen guarding German prisoners of war. No news reached him about the fate of Miloš Sobotka. All the men waited for Miloš to rejoin the unit, probably under guard, but he never appeared. While most accepted that either the Russians or the Germans had killed him, Tomáš liked to think of his friend lying in a cosy garret somewhere in Prague, with his Saskie in his arms.

Tomáš's chance to return to Prague did not come until May 30th, when a grand military parade was held to celebrate the nation's victory in the war. The main body of the Brigade at last arrived from Dunkirk, and was reunited with the Token Force in Pilsen. The 6,000 men were informed they would parade with their 20,000 fellow Czechoslovaks, who had fought with the Soviets to secure their country's liberation. All the men would wear the uniform of the new Czechoslovak Army, and it was hoped they would remain together to form the core of their country's new armed forces. But for those who wished to leave and re-enter civilian life, participation in the parade would be their final duty as a soldier.

Tomáš could not wait to leave the army. He did not even want to take part in the parade. He felt humiliated by his time in uniform and laid most of the blame at the door of the newly re-elected president. Beneš had arrived back in Prague on May 16. He was greeted by adoring crowds in a city bedecked with the nation's flag flying alongside the flag of the Soviet Union, and his portrait hanging next to Stalin's.

Beneš made a speech in the Old Town Square on the day of his return. Tomáš read it in full in one of the daily papers. The President announced that he had selected a cabinet uniting Czechs and Slovaks in a National Front government representing all the people. He confirmed there would be no room in Czechoslovakia for Germans and Magyars who had been disloyal to the nation. They would be stripped of citizenship and 'liquidated' out of the country. Never again, he pledged, would Czechoslovakia be undermined by ethnic minorities within its borders.

On the day of the parade Beneš took the salute in Wenceslas Square. Behind him sat the nation's military leaders and the twenty-five members of his new cabinet, eight of them from the Communist Party. Tomáš thought of his father as he marched through the square, and imagined how angered he would be by the sight of Russian soldiers and Russian tanks in his beloved city. Tomáš passed the spot from which he had watched his father marching on Independence Day in 1928. A legionnaire. He had been so proud of him.

Everything was so clear and certain then. Good and bad. Right and wrong. But Tomáš remembered something his mother told him when they returned home to Cheb. That his father did not like parading either, especially wearing his medals. Tomáš still did not understand why such a hero should have felt that way, but now it comforted him as he marched, knowing he shared a sentiment with his father from so long ago.

Tomáš remembered so much from that weekend in Prague. His father taking him to the Legion Bank in Na Porici Street, confiding in him like an adult and entrusting him with his medals. His Babička and Děda behaving more and more like naughty children. And Anna behaving so differently towards him for the first time. Wanting him to kiss her and hold her in a way he never had before. They were so young, but those days in Prague had changed the way they loved one another forever.

Tomáš was demobbed in Pilsen the next day, and immediately took the train back to Prague. The last of the old street names in the city were being reinstated. He left the station and crossed Wilson Avenue, walked to the Old Town past the buildings of Charles University and arrived at the Legion Bridge. There he turned left along the bank of the Vltava River, past the National Theatre and found a familiar apartment building. He went to the third floor, and rang the bell of the apartment where Anna lived with her father before the war. He heard someone approach the door and prayed it would be Uncle Ernst. The door was opened by an attractive young woman who smiled at him.

"Yes?"

"Good morning. I wonder if you can help me. I'm looking for someone who used to live in this apartment."

The smile disappeared. "Do you mean Neumann?"

"Yes, pan Neumann. He's my father-in-law."

"Are you German then?"

"No, my name is Kovařík. I'm a Czechoslovak, the same as pan Neumann."

"Neumann wasn't Czech. He was German. A Fascist. Everyone knows that. They took him last week. This place is ours now, so don't come here trying to say any different."

"That's not why I'm here, madam. I have no interest in anything other than finding pan Neumann. Did you say he was here until last week?"

"Yes, he was the first to go." She raised her voice and leaned towards the stairwell. "And the rest of you will be following him soon."

"One week." muttered Tomáš. He slumped against the wall.

"I want nothing to do with Neumann. I have to go."

"No, please." Tomáš stood back up and clasped his hands to his chest. "Please, madam. Tell me, do you know where they took him?"

"To one of the camps they took our people to, I hope." She went to close the door.

"Please, madam. One more question, I beg you. Has anyone but me come here looking for him? A young woman with a child. My wife and daughter."

"No. No one."

"Have any letters come for him?"

"No. This is our place now. All his things have gone. It all went out last week. It's time you people left us in peace. Neumann's daughter's not getting this apartment, whatever tricks you try on us. I want nothing to do with Germans or their families." She closed the door.

Tomáš waited, wondering whether to ring again. Before he had time to decide, the door of the apartment opposite opened.

"Perhaps I can help you?" said an elderly man in German. He wore an old cardigan, ill-fitting trousers, and slippers. "I knew Herr Neumann."

"Do you know where they've taken him, sir?"

"Theresienstadt, I expect. Most are sent there first. After that we're being sent across the border."

"But Ernst Neumann was a loyal citizen. He believed in Czechoslovakia."

"I know he did, but he had a Sudeten passport and a Fascist wife. That's why they took him first."

Tomáš put his hand to his forehead and turned away.

"But he only got that passport to help my family. My God, the world's gone mad."

He looked back at the old man.

"What did you say about his wife?"

"Ex-wife. She's Zuzana Gajda, you know. Married to Radola Gajda, the Fascist leader. They'll both hang. It was quite a shock, when I heard. Ernst never told me about her."

"Why should he? She left him years ago."

"Any Fascist in your family is enough to land you in trouble now. Especially if you're German."

"Did you know Ernst well, sir?"

"Very well. We played chess together every evening."

"Do you know if he heard anything from his daughter recently? She's my wife."

"You're Anna's husband. Ernst talked about her all the time. Would you like to come in?"

"Yes, thankyou."

"Excuse all the boxes. I'm trying to sell as much as I can. They've only given me until next week. I've lived in Prague for fifty-three years, you know."

"I'm sorry, sir. It's not what decent Czechs want."

"Sit down there, young man. I'm afraid you're wrong, you know. Most Czechs are like that woman across the way. They want us Germans out. All of us, no matter who we are. There's been a lot of violence, you know."

"I'm sorry, sir. I don't mean to be insensitive to what you're telling me, but may I talk to you about Ernst's daughter. Had he heard from her recently?"

"He got a card from her from Paris some years back. From a camp. He was very worried about both his children. All the time. His son is in Palestine, you know."

"When did he get the card from the camp?"

"It was at Christmas. Not last Christmas, or the one before that. It must be three Christmases ago. He hasn't heard from his son either. He was very worried. And he had a granddaughter. He'd never seen her."

"And he had no other news from Anna or Otto?"

"No. I felt terribly sorry for poor Ernst. It makes me pleased for once I have no family of my own."

"If Anna or Otto do come here, do you think I could leave a note for them, sir? My name is Tomáš Kovařík."

"You forget, Herr Kovařík, I won't be here. None of the German families will."

"Of course. I'm not thinking. I'm sorry."

"You can try to leave something with the Czech woman opposite, but I'm not sure she will help you. People have become very suspicious of one another over the past six years. "

"Is there anyone else here I could ask?"

"I'm afraid not. All the old families have gone. There were a lot of Jewish families here once, you know. Most were connected with the theatre like Ernst. They were all taken. Ernst got himself in a lot of trouble speaking out about it. Now all the Germans who moved in after them are being taken. It's all very sad and confusing."

Tomáš stood up. "I'm very sorry you're being treated so badly, sir," he said. "People are bitter because of all our country has gone through. Often the innocent are punished with the guilty. It is the story of our times."

"I'm afraid it is, Herr Kovařík. I wish you luck in your search for your family. If I meet Herr Neumann wherever it is they send me, I shall tell him I spoke with you."

Tomáš got no answer from the young Czech woman when he rang again. He posted a letter to Anna through her door. He sealed the envelope and wrote on it. *'From one loyal Czech to another. My wife, Anna Kovaříková has been in a German concentration camp. Please give this letter to her if she finds her way to your door. I thank you. Tomáš Kovařík.'*

Tomáš walked back to the Legion Bridge, crossed the Vltava and made his way to the streets which wound up the hill to Prague Castle. He soon reached Karmelitská Street. He had walked along this street so often with Anna on their way to meet friends when he was a student, but in all that time he never knew number 17 was the Headquarters of the Czechoslovakian Red Cross. He approached the heavy oak door, found it unlocked, and walked in. The entrance hall was cold and deserted. He heard voices coming from a room to his left and tentatively pushed the half-open door. There were two tables at the far end of the otherwise empty room, and half a dozen people were lined up in front of each. Behind the tables sat two women. Tomáš immediately recognised one as Alice Masaryková.

Tomáš took his place in the queue at Doctor Masaryková's table. All the people in front of him were there for the same reason as he, and none was having any luck. Each gave the name of the people they wanted to contact and left their own details in case anyone came searching for them. It took only a few minutes for Tomáš to reach the front of the queue.

"Good morning, young man," said Alice Masaryková. "Could you give me your name, please?"

"Kovařík, Doctor. Tomáš Kovařík."

Alice Masaryková looked at him more closely. "Sergeant Kovařík," she said standing up. "I didn't recognise you out of uniform." She came around the table and took his hand in both of hers. "How are you? It is so very good to see you again." She turned to the woman at the other table. "I have just met an old friend, pani Hadrová. Please ask Irena to take over from me. Excuse me, ladies and gentlemen, you will only be delayed a few moments."

She took Tomáš's arm and led him to a room on the other side of the entrance hall.

"Sit down there, Sergeant... Shall I continue to call you 'sergeant'?"

"I prefer Tomáš."

"Good. Now tell me, Tomáš, are you here about your wife and little girl?"

"Yes, Doktor."

"You still have no news of them?"

"No."

"Then give me a moment whilst I fetch the right folder for you."

The room was sparse. Full of bookshelves like the Doctor's study in London, but with none of the fine furniture and warmth. Tomáš became aware of the heavy silence and felt his stomach turn. Alice Masaryková came back into the room with a folder under her arm.

"Now let me tell you straight away, Tomáš, that I have no specific news of Anna and Eva, either good or bad. I can only give you the general information we have so far."

"You remember their names."

"Yes, dear Tomáš, I remember their names and I remember you. So does my brother, Jan. He enjoyed your company very much that evening together in Buckinghamshire."

"Thankyou, Doctor. You say there's no specific information about Anna and Eva?"

"No. I am afraid not."

Alice Masaryková opened the folder which lay on the coffee table between them. "I know the kind of man you are, Tomáš, so I shall tell you the unadorned truth as far as we know it."

She sat on the edge of her chair and held her hands in her lap.

"It is now becoming clear that those responsible for the camps have done all they can to destroy any evidence of them. We are just beginning to realise how long it will take to find out exactly what happened to so many people. Some of it we may never know. The French, for example, destroyed most of the records from Drancy. Anna and Eva do not appear on any of the lists we have so far."

"But that could be a good sign, couldn't it? Perhaps they weren't taken there after all."

"We know the Jews taken from Agde on the night of the 6th August 1942, arrived in Drancy on the 9th."

"How do you know if there are no records?"

"A Czech Jew taken to Drancy on that transport was found in another camp in January and gave us the information. His name is Josef Laskis. He confirms that the men, women and children taken from Agde in early August all went to Drancy."

"Found in January? What camp was he in?"

"Auschwitz, Tomáš. Laskis has told us that all the Jews in Drancy were sent to Auschwitz. We believe as many as sixty or 70,000."

"And what happened to them?"

"We know that very few survived."

"Josef Laskis did."

"And he was able to tell us what happened to the others, Tomáš."

"What did happen? Don't try to keep it from me."

"Laskis has told us that the old, the infirm and the women with children were not even entered."

"Entered? What does 'entered' mean?"

"They were not even registered on arrival, Tomáš."

"But what are you saying? I told you before in London, Doctor, I can accept the truth. Just tell me."

"Those not registered for work were killed soon after they arrived."

Tomáš stood up.

"You can't kill that many people as soon as they step off a train."

He walked to the window. A couple passed in the street, walking hand in hand, laughing. He turned to Alice Masaryková. She was looking down at her hands, now clenched tightly in her lap.

"It's just not possible to kill that many people," he repeated. "Besides I saw a film of a camp only a few weeks ago. Belsen. There were women and children there. The children looked well enough. Your Laskis has got it wrong."

"Belsen wasn't an extermination camp, Tomáš."

"You know, Doktor Masaryková, you shouldn't say these things unless you have evidence. What do you mean, Belsen wasn't an extermination camp? It looked like one to me. I can't imagine anything worse."

"People were simply left to die in Belsen, Tomáš. In Auschwitz they were murdered with gas. Those rumours we talked about in London two years ago were true. The Germans had gas chambers. We think they may have killed millions."

"No, no, no. You cannot say things like that without evidence. You can't kill millions of people."

Tomáš sat down again and stared at Alice Masaryková.

"I still believe they are alive, Doctor Masaryková. Don't ask me to explain it. I believe they are. I'll always believe it until I have evidence. Do you understand that?"

"Yes, Tomáš. I'm terribly sorry. I thought I was right to tell you all we knew. I thought it was what you wanted."

"It is what I want, but I won't accept my wife and child died like that, not without proof." He pointed towards the window. "There are thousands of people still out there. Displaced people. Refugees. People finding their way home. Anna and Eva could still be amongst them."

"Yes, it is possible. You saw for yourself. We see hundreds every day."

"There you are then. I shall keep looking."

"Dear Tomáš, you cannot look in every Displaced Person's Camp."

"There must be other organisations."

"There are, but copies of all their records are sent to Geneva. We get them eventually. I look every day for Anna and Eva. There has been nothing."

"I didn't know you had being doing that. Thankyou."

"I would like nothing more than to give you good news."

"What about the records from Auschwitz? Do we have those?"

"No, most were destroyed by the Germans before they fled. We know the Russians have some records, but they have not shared them with anyone yet. My brother has made a formal request to Molotov for copies of all those relating to Czechoslovak citizens. He thinks we shall receive something soon."

"And you will tell me as soon as you do?"

"Of course."

"Thankyou."

"What will you do now, Tomáš?"

"I shall stay in Prague. I believe at times like this we all try to make our way home. I shall wait here for Anna."

"Then I have a marvellous idea, Tomáš. Why don't you help us here? No one could understand better than you the needs of the people who come to us. We could not pay you much. But I could find you lodgings and enough to live on."

"I don't need pay, Doctor Masaryková. I have three years of army pay I never spent. Thankyou, I would like to work with you here. It's what I need to do."

What need have we for poetry?

When endless space is ours, Anna
What use poetic syllables, enchained,
Pointless in a space?

When faith is ours to live as to love,
What use my harrowed anger, squeezed
Into exquisite lines?

When faith connects us in reality
What need have we for abstract words
Lifeless on a page?

Alive we stay and keep our child alive,
Safe with you, Anna, blessed with
Knowing, logical faith.

My poetry, though scorned, I pray thee
Give me words, a word to hold,
A thought, an image.

I have it! It is this: a simple
Light, a particle too small to see
See it, Anna!

It makes its way through dark entanglement,
Pushing through evil's knotted mess,
Relentless. Slow,

Our particle of light is unassailable.
With faith await the sure dénouement.
Know it, Anna!

Tomáš Kovařík
Prague, June 12th 1945

Chapter Twenty-Six

June – September 14th, 1945

Tomáš found rooms in the Malá Strana, the Lesser Quarter below the castle. His lodgings were only a short walk from Karmelitská Street, but every morning he left home at daybreak and made a detour over Charles Bridge, before cutting back along the embankment to the Legion Bridge, where he stood and watched the Vltava. Looking upstream towards Slavic Island, Prague appeared unchanged.

Around five thirty the first trams of the day clattered across the bridge and other early risers walked past the National Theatre into the Old Town. Tomáš could see Ernst Neumann's apartment block from the eastern end of the bridge, and he could pick out the window where in his student days he and Anna used to sit looking down at the river. The Legion Bridge was now his favourite place to be.

The flow of desperate people through the door of the Red Cross never stopped in the months following the end of the war. People came from all over the country, looking for relatives who had been arrested or deported over the past six years and had not returned. And many deportees and conscripted workers who did return came looking for the families they could no longer find at the home they had left years before. And then there were the foreign refugees, often Jews from the east, passing through on their way to a destination as yet unknown, who came looking not for people, but for food and medicine to sustain them as they searched for a place of safety.

The most wretched of the people who came to Karmelitská Street were those from the camps. They had a sameness about them. They shuffled along in the queue and were the ones most likely to be lice-ridden, malnourished or diseased. Tomáš found they always looked down as they answered his questions, apprehensive and distrustful of the authority on the other side of the table. And they spoke in a monotone common to them all. Tomáš thought at first it must be a result of depression or trauma. Only gradually did he understand it was the practised way of speaking in the worst of the camps, employed by the inmates to spark no adverse reaction in the likely sadist who was questioning them. Tomáš took their details, added their names to the growing lists, and gave them all the practical help he could.

Alice Masaryková worried about him. She wondered if she had done the kindest thing, bringing him into such close contact with people who were repeated reminders of what Anna and Eva had probably suffered. But Tomáš insisted on staying. "It keeps me close to them," he said, "and it proves every day that people do come back."

On two afternoons every week Tomáš left Karmelitská Street to visit a new type of camp which sprang up throughout Czechoslovakia in the weeks following the end of the war. They were the camps containing Czechoslovaks of German ethnicity, who were driven from their homes, towns and cities by their fellow citizens. There were thirty-seven such places in and around Prague alone by the end of May, and Alice asked Tomáš to go to them all and list as many of the internees as he could. The camps reminded Tomáš of Agde. He loved Prague, but in the summer of 1945, during the 'Wild Transfer', he was ashamed of what went on there, as the German population was driven out.

Some of the worst excesses were carried out by the National Security Corps, a special force formed from pre-war policemen, Communist partisans and armed trade unionists to hunt down 'traitors' and 'collaborators'. People were dragged off the street, brought before People's Courts, and often executed within hours of a verdict without right of appeal. Tomáš witnessed for himself German speakers in Prague being harassed and bullied without any protection from the law.

More than once that summer, wearing the armband of the Red Cross, he intervened and narrowly escaped beatings himself. In some towns, it was said, Germans had swastikas painted on their clothes and foreheads, and were being made to scrub the streets in front of jeering crowds. It was rumoured that in Asch, a town close to Cheb where one of Anna's old school friends lived, hundreds of German civilians had been murdered by local Czechs.

Tomáš spent long days touring the camps, compiling reports for Alice, and searching without success for Ernst. At the beginning of autumn the expulsion of Germans from Prague became more orderly, and at last the city returned to some normality. The Russian soldiers, who were often part of the menace, began to behave less like an occupying force and more as tourists, strolling without weapons and mixing with local people. In September it was announced that the Russian and the American forces would both be withdrawing from Czechoslovakian soil in mid-November. Czechoslovakia would finally belong to its own people again.

***

The announcement of the withdrawal was made shortly before Alice Masaryková's brother, Jan, celebrated his fifty-ninth birthday. It was reason enough for a double celebration, Jan told her. He would hold a small party for family and friends at his apartment in Czernin Palace, and he asked Alice to extend an invitation to Tomáš. Tomáš accepted gratefully. He had formed an instant liking for Jan Masaryk when they met in England, and he looked forward to meeting him again. And there was always the possibility, he thought, that the minister might have some news for him.

Jan Masaryk enjoyed great popularity amongst his fellow countrymen, and received a hero's welcome when he returned home to Prague in May. *'Naš Honza'*, 'our Johnny', was the nickname people gave him, as they listened to his broadcasts from London during the war. Already popular for being a Masaryk and for his outspokenness over Munich, Jan was loved by ordinary Czechoslovaks for his irreverence, and for his understanding of what they had endured. He was no philosopher or leader of men like his father, but his cheerful manner and his music were valued as much by people as any fine words and high principles. And his presence as Foreign Minister in the new National Government gave people a sense of reassurance, which even President Beneš could not provide.

Prague was in the middle of a brief Indian summer on September 14th, the day of the birthday party, when Tomáš walked up the hill to the Castle Quarter. He had been this way many times, but had rarely walked in the direction of Czernin Palace, which contained the offices of the Czechoslovak Foreign Ministry and the official residence of the Minister. It lay only a few hundred metres west of Prague Castle but shared none of its intimacy and mystical grandeur. It was a large building of Baroque symmetry, more imposing than beautiful. According to Alice, her brother hated its austere marble corridors, and often told her he would willingly exchange his official apartment in the Palace for his cosy London flat.

Jan greeted Tomáš warmly, but as he was already surrounded by well-wishers, he allowed Alice to introduce Tomáš to the other guests. Their sister, Olga Revilliod, was there and she too remembered the young soldier from Aston Abbots who had challenged the President so forthrightly. Beneš himself was unable to attend, but his wife, Hana, spoke at length with Tomáš, seemingly unaware they had met before, until she surprised him just as they parted by asking if he had managed to find his wife and child. She seemed quite different from the person he met in England, more relaxed and informal now she was back in her own country. Tomáš recognised several government ministers from photographs he had seen in the newspapers, but he was disappointed none of the Communist ministers were there. He would have welcomed an opportunity to confront them.

The evening was a great success. Jan and his American fiancée, the author Marcia Davenport, were constantly doted on by small groups of people, laughing and swapping stories. Drinks and canapés were served throughout, and a large cake was produced, iced with the lettering, 'Happy Birthday to Our Honza and the UN', in celebration of the minister's recent attendance in San Francisco at the birth of the United Nations.

People started to leave around ten. Tomáš joined the informal line of guests thanking Jan and Marcia Davenport at the door as they filed past. Alice took his arm and drew him aside.

"Jan would like you to remain behind for a moment, Tomáš," she said.

"Does he have news?"

"No, I'm sorry, it's not that. He's just disappointed that he hasn't had a chance to speak to you this evening."

She led him back to the centre of the spacious living room, which was furnished in the French style of the thirties.

"I think Jan tires of talking only to politicians," she said. "He often says how refreshing it was hearing your views the first time you met. He can explain to you himself, but I think he is afraid the real voice of Czechoslovaks is not being heard. He would like the chance to talk to you."

The door closed and Jan Masaryk and his fiancée came back into the room.

"Ah, good. Alice has persuaded you to stay."

Jan walked towards them and reached out his hand. "My dear Tomáš, I have neglected you this evening. And I was so looking forward to speaking with you again."

"Likewise, Minister, but I could see how in demand you were."

"Now, if we are going to be friends, I insist you call me 'Jan'. I remember what you said about such informality in England and I respect it, but please..."

"If you would prefer..."

"I would. Alice tells me you still have no news of your wife and child, Tomáš. I am very sorry to hear that, but rest assured we will do everything to find out what we can for you."

"Thankyou."

"Now take a seat and we shall organise some coffee and brandy."

They all sat down in armchairs around the large coffee table.

"So, my dear Tomáš," said Jan, "Alice tells me you were visiting these holding camps over the summer."

"I still am. They're a disgrace."

Jan's smile disappeared.

"You feel that strongly about them?"

"I do."

"But don't you think our people's anger is understandable, when one considers the brutality they endured at German hands?"

"I understand their anger only too well, as you can imagine. Few people have more reason to feel bitterness towards Germans than I do, but our country stands for principles which do not allow us to mistreat people in that way."

"So you don't think we should expel them?"

"Yes, expel the Nazis, by all means. And the Fascist Hungarians from Slovakia too. But we must do it like decent, humane people, and use some discretion."

"Is it realistic to expect such forbearance after nearly seven years of oppression?"

"We must expect it, Minister. I've seen the brutality the Germans and French are capable of, and I had hoped never to see it in our own people. And I had hoped not to hear our own President encouraging it. Doctor Masaryková and I see the results of such barbarism every day. I never thought we Czechoslovaks would become a part of it."

"Eduard's use of language in his May speech was very regrettable, Jan," said Alice.

"It was, my dear. But people do not understand our President. Everyone thinks the main questions facing him now are, East or West? Capitalism or Communism? And of course they are vital questions. But I know the overriding priority for President Beneš is neither of these. His priority is to protect our country against renewed German aggression, and it is that which dictates all his decisions. He is removing our ethnic minorities so that Germany can never again use them as an excuse to move against us."

"I accept that and I see the logic of it," said Tomáš. "But fear of ethnic minorities does not give our people an excuse to act like Nazis. We Czechoslovaks either have humanity in our blood or we do not."

Jan's smile returned and he slapped the leather arm of his chair. "You have done it again, Tomáš," he laughed. "I have to admit I wholeheartedly agree with you."

Jan's butler brought in a tray with their drinks, and placed it on the coffee table. "Thankyou, pan Příhoda," said Marcia Davenport. "We shall serve ourselves."

"One of the problems I see," continued Tomáš, "is that our young people have grown up under nearly seven years of totalitarian rule. They have not seen how democracy works."

"But at least those seven years have given them a healthy dislike of Fascism, pan Kovařík," said Marcia.

"It has, madam. But our people now think there is no greater evil than Hitler and Fascism. And I hope they are proved right. But everyone must know that Stalin and the Communists are not democrats either. They may prove to be no better than the Fascists were."

"Now, Tomáš, I think you are being unfair," said Alice. "No one can doubt our President's commitment to democracy, and the Communists all recognise his leadership and our father's constitution. And not many of the cabinet are Communists, are they, Jan?"

"No, my dear. There are twenty-five of us. Only eight represent the Communist party."

"Yes, but look at those eight," said Tomáš. "They control nearly all the important ministries. Education, industry, agriculture, defence. And above all the Interior Ministry, which gives them control of information and the police. And I've seen for myself how the police are allowed to behave."

"I think you are overreacting, Tomáš," said Alice. "We have our dear President and our Jan to safeguard us. Our people believe in everything they stand for."

"Of course, Doctor, but Czechoslovaks are embracing Communism in ever greater numbers."

"That is because the Russians liberated them. It is hardly surprising they should be popular with the people. But the democracy our father founded is strong enough to contain the Communists."

"I hope you're right, Doctor, but what I have seen this summer has made me doubt it for the first time in my life."

"Your work is affecting your trust in people, dear Tomáš. Our people are committed to my father's democracy. It will always guide them. Say something, Jan."

"I say that I support all those who carry on the wonderful Bohemian tradition of opposing cynical and well-organised material dialectics."

"No, be serious, Jan. I want you to tell Tomáš he is wrong to doubt our President and our government."

"Of course, my dear. I can assure you all that neither the President nor I harbour any commitment to being ruled by Berlin or by Moscow."

"Jan. Please."

"Alright, my dear. I'm happy to give you the government's official view on all this, if you wish." He finished his brandy and turned the empty glass in his hand as he spoke.

"We all know our President is not a Communist, that he is a democrat to his soul. But he is also a Slav, and I believe for him Munich has sealed a bond between Czechoslovakia and the Soviet Union which will not be broken. President Beneš will never get over the betrayal of the western democracies. Personally, I share with my President his love of the Russian people, but I also share his dislike of their mode of government... Oh dear, I see I have upset Tomáš already."

Tomáš shifted in his chair. "It's simply the idea of the Russians being our friends. These are the people who turned on our legionnaires in 1918. The same people who allied themselves with Hitler in '39, then withdrew recognition of Czechoslovakia to appease him, and recognised his Protectorate of Bohemia and Moravia instead."

"What do you want me to say, Tomáš? Do you think I am not aware of such contradictions?"

"I'm sorry, sir. But I cannot understand why our President is returning to the old belief that the Russians will protect us. Why for once can we not stay neutral? Stand alone, confident in our own strength and democratic principles. I fear, when the democracies betrayed us at Munich, they destroyed something in our people. We must regain it and build faith in *ourselves*, not turn again to the Russians."

"The point is, Tomáš, President Beneš believes Czechoslovakia's Communists come from a different tradition to the Russians, that they are committed to our parliamentary democracy. And he asks us to share his faith. To be fair, their leader has pledged many times that his party will be truly democratic, that he will put our national interest first and only..."

"But Klement Gottwald was in Moscow with Stalin when he sold us out to Hitler," exclaimed Tomáš.

"I am explaining our government's official view, Tomáš. I am quite aware you do not support it."

"I'm sorry. I shouldn't interrupt you."

"Politics sometimes demands a strong stomach, Tomáš. Some of it is not for the faint-hearted. The point is we shall work with our allies and with the Communists in our government towards a national, democratic path to socialism. The programme of nationalisation will continue, and the land vacated by Sudeten Germans will be redistributed amongst our people. And I am pleased to say I have no trouble in giving these policies my full support. I hate Communism, Tomáš. I have never made a secret of that. But we have first-class democrats in the cabinet. You will have seen some of them here tonight. We must remain optimistic about the future, and above all retain our faith in our people."

"Hear, hear, Jan," echoed Alice and Marcia.

"I know our father's spirit is still alive amongst our people," said Alice. "They will not let you down, Jan. Or President Beneš."

Tomáš remained silent and everyone looked towards him.

"For once our young friend has nothing to say," said Jan. "Perhaps I have achieved the impossible. I have persuaded him of another point of view."

"I would like to be persuaded, sir..."

"Jan."

"I would like to be persuaded, Jan. I regard myself as a social democrat, or even a democratic socialist, much as you describe yourself. But the important word for me in all this is 'democrat', as I believe it is for all of us here. We are democrats before all else. Not like Communists or Fascists who subscribe to democracy only when it suits them. Our whole view of the world and our way of life flow from that word. It is what all four of us were brought up with. As a boy and as a student I felt the spirit of democracy in the buildings and in the air in Prague, and in the mood of our people. I felt the same thing in London while I was away. But in the three months since I returned, I'm afraid I have not felt it here."

Tomáš looked across at Jan Masaryk. Jan sat in silence, looking at his empty glass, turning it slowly in his hand.

Chapter Twenty-Seven

May 29th, 1946

All through the winter Tomáš continued his early morning walks to the Legion Bridge, but on the coldest days he lingered only briefly, watching the ice floes collect at the tip of Slavic Island. It became an article of faith for him to stand and pick out the window of Ernst's apartment. When the light went on there every morning just before seven, it was his cue to head away to Karmelitská Street.

One morning in late May he stood on the bridge in the warming sunshine, for once not looking upstream, but absorbed in the newspaper he had hurried to buy from the vendor at Charles Bridge. He was too agitated to rest against the parapet wall. He stood in the middle of the pavement, his arms spread wide holding the broadsheet, studying the results of the parliamentary elections. He lowered the paper and cursed out loud. "Damned idiots." Only twelve months after the defeat of Fascism, Czechoslovaks had made the Communists the most powerful party in the country.

Tomáš read the details in disgust. It was in the Czech part of the country, in his own Bohemia and Moravia, that the Communists were most popular. Forty percent of the vote. Far more than Beneš's National Socialists in second place. How could people be so stupid, so naive?

He turned and spread the newspaper on the bridge's wide parapet. At least the Slovaks had shown some sense and given two-thirds of their votes to their own Democratic Party. But the Communists still had enough support across the country to install the Stalinist Klement Gottwald as the new Prime Minister. Tomáš winced at the thought of this drunken bully leading the National Government of the country his father had loved so much.

"You damn fool, Beneš," he muttered, "trusting Gottwald or any damn Communist to respect democracy." But maybe Beneš wasn't such a fool after all. He knew how popular Uncle Joe Stalin and the Russian liberators were. Keeping them and Gottwald as allies had allowed him to remain as President.

Tomáš rested his arms on the paper and read on. It appeared Jan Masaryk had agreed to remain, too, as Foreign Minister, and sit as one of the thirteen non-Communists in Gottwald's new cabinet. Tomáš looked upriver, shaking his head. Beneš, perhaps. But how could Jan possibly join a Communist-led government controlled by Moscow? Surely his only loyalty was to his father's democracy? He had said so often enough during their many conversations since the birthday party in Czernin Palace. They had become good friends since then. Jan even visited him occasionally in his rooms in the Malá Strana and he had never once hinted at this. His actions only added confusion to Tomáš's anger.

He could see how clever the Communists had been. They had worked with Stalin for years taking the country in a pincer movement from above and below. As soon as the Red Army entered the country in September 1944 they set up their own National Committees. To administer the liberated territory on a local level, they said. But they made sure most of the committees were dominated by Communists. Even in his own small district of Malá Strana he had seen them slowly gaining control. All the local policemen were Communists. It was an open secret. And so were most of the civil servants he dealt with through his work. They all wore their party tie-pins and lapel badges quite openly. All the managers in schools, factories, and farms were mostly Communists too. But that was hardly surprising, since the education, industry and agriculture ministries were all led by Communists. And now they had Gottwald as Prime Minister, they had control from the very top, just as Stalin had always intended.

It infuriated Tomáš to see how his countrymen had fallen for it. He looked around at all the people walking over the bridge to work. A man in a suit and tie passed by on a bicycle, clips attached to his trouser legs and a small hammer and sickle flag attached to his handlebars. Did these people not realise what they had done? Did they really think Communism meant no more than a continuation of Tomáš Masaryk's democracy with just a few socialist policies added to it?

Tomáš closed his newspaper, folded it roughly, and set off for Karmelitská Street. He knew some of his younger colleagues at the Red Cross were caught up in the enthusiasm for the Communists. The mood for change, the paper called it. As he approached number 17, he expected many of those inside to be celebrating, and he was only too ready to tell them exactly what he thought.

But in the room where everyone met for coffee before work there was no rejoicing. People seemed embarrassed when he walked in. When he looked towards them, they lowered their eyes or turned away.

"I see you've all read the papers then," he said.

No one spoke.

"What's the matter? I expected most of you to be celebrating this morning."

"Doctor Masaryková wants to see you, Tomáš," said Hana Hadrova, Alice's deputy. "She's waiting for you in her office."

Tomáš smiled, searched their faces for a moment, then turned and hurried across the corridor.

"Come in," Alice called out. "There you are, Tomáš. You are a little later today. Please take a seat."

"Is there a problem?"

Alice sat down opposite him. "We have news, Tomáš."

"Oh yes."

"The Russians have released some documents at last."

"I see."

"Jan got them to me this morning, as soon as he could."

"Yes. And what do they say?"

"There is one which confirms what I think we already knew, Tomáš. Anna and Eva were sent to Auschwitz."

He looked at the thin sheet of light brown paper she was holding. He saw the black typewriting on it.

"I never knew any such thing," he said. He folded his arms, crossed his legs and rocked forward. He looked at Alice. "What sort of document is it? It doesn't seem like much to me."

"It is one page from a list of people transported to Auschwitz from Drancy on February 13th 1943."

"I see."

"Anna's and Eva's names are on it. Do you want to see it?"

Tomáš did not move. He gulped in short breaths of air and exhaled slowly. "Who made the list?"

"The French in Drancy. This is the stencilled copy which accompanied the transport. It was found in Auschwitz."

"Where's the German list?"

"I think I told you before, Tomáš. The Germans only made lists of people who were kept in the camp to work. The old, and mothers with young children were..."

"I know. You don't have to say it. And you think that's what happened to Anna and Eva."

"Yes, Tomáš."

"Let me see it then."

Tomáš reached across and took the paper from Alice as if he were indifferent to it. The paper was thin and of the poorest quality. "It's just the stencil of the main copy," he said.

"Yes. The main copy would have remained in France."

'*Départ du 13 février, 1943. WAGON 3,*' it said at the top. There were three columns. Name. Date and place of birth. Address. There were about thirty names. Tomáš looked down the list. Halfway down he saw them.

KOVAŘÍKOVA Anna 5.12.16 Tchécoslovaquie Route de Rochelongue, Agde
KOVAŘÍKOVA Eva 9.11.39 Tchécoslovaquie Route de Rochelongue, Agde

A German clerk had scribbled some notes at the bottom in black ink. '*Abschubliste Nr 48   13.2.43 von Drancy n. Auschwitz*'

"Is this all there is?"

"Yes."

"Can I keep it?"

"I'm afraid not. I brought you the original found in the camp files. I knew you wouldn't accept a typed copy as proof. Jan has to hand it back."

"But it's all I have. What use do the damn Russians have for it?"

"I don't know, Tomáš."

"I'll write out my own copy then. I want a list of all the people. All the ones who were with them in that wagon."

"I'll get Irena to do it for you, Tomáš. You stay here with me."

"I don't believe it. I won't believe it. Not what you're trying to say."

"It's hard for anyone to believe."

"I know Anna would have protected Eva. I know she would not have allowed anything to happen to her."

"She would have protected her, Tomáš. They would have been together all the time. All our reports say that young children like Eva stayed with their mothers."

"I always thought they would come back. I still think they will come back."

Alice leaned forward, closer to him.

"You know the first part of recovery is to accept the truth, Tomáš. You have seen enough of it yourself over the last year. The sooner it starts the better."

"It's different for me. I do not see how Anna can be gone. I can't imagine her not being alive somewhere."

"Dear Tomáš, just think how few people we have seen here who have come back from Auschwitz. Seven. Only one of them a woman. And no mothers."

"Why are you being so cruel?"

"Because I think you must accept what has happened. You are still a young man who must live his life."

"I have only ever lived my life for Anna. And for Eva. Without them there's nothing."

"You must not say that, Tomáš. We see thousands of people who have suffered loss. They all carry on."

"I know you are trying to help, Doctor, but what you say doesn't work. That's the tragedy of all the people we see. No one's loss is lessened by seeing others suffering the same. However normal you try to make it, it can never be normal. I won't think of a life without Anna."

Tomáš stood up. "I'm going for a walk. I'll come back later for the list. I need to work out what I can do."

"You will come back, Tomáš? You will promise me you will come back, won't you?"

"Yes, Doctor. I will come back and Anna will come back."

Tomáš walked along Karmelitská Street towards Charles Bridge. He was angry, and people stepped out of his way as he strode past. How dare Alice Masaryková try to persuade him Anna and Eva were not coming back? She had no idea of the kind of woman Anna was. He continued along the Smetana Embankment and realised he was talking out loud. He didn't care. All these people going about their business as usual. They didn't know Anna. And neither did Alice Masaryková. Not as he did. He knew how beautifully stubborn she was. She would never give up. And neither would he.

He turned across the Legion Bridge and thought about stopping in his usual place, but he had no patience for it. He kept going. He wasn't going to be like all those people who came to the Red Cross and gave up when faced with the horror of it all. They listened to Alice Masaryková telling them death was merely a gateway to eternity. It was no such damn thing. Death was about people not being there and never being there again. He wasn't going to accept that. And he didn't want any of the hope they ladled out either. Hope meant doubt, and there was no doubt about Anna. She was somewhere. He knew it. He knew it.

He took out her picture and slowed down to look at it. "But where are you, Anna?" he said. "I know you're searching for me, darling. I'm here. Here in the obvious place. Why don't you come and find me?" All the times he had looked up, whenever the door opened, to see if it was her. Every day. Hundreds of times. But perhaps... perhaps not so much recently.

No, he was not going to allow thoughts like that into his head. "Keep them out, Tomáš," he said. "Keep those damned thoughts out." What had the Doctor said about no women coming back? It was strange. They came back from the other camps but never from that one. "Just don't think it, Tomáš. Don't think it." He took out the picture of Eva taken on her second birthday. It was the most recent one he had. He wondered what she would look like now. She would be six and a half. He might not even recognise her. He smiled. He would have to explain to her who he was when he saw her again.

It was a long time for a child, four years. How old would she have been on February 13th, 1943? Three and a half. Still recognisable when they say she went to that place. What did they do to her there? "Don't think it! Don't think it..."

He stopped, leaned on the parapet of the bridge and closed his eyes. He knew what they did... He knew... They killed her. And they killed Anna. It was true. It was true. He knew it was true... She would have found him by now... He would have found them... Why didn't he protect them? He should have protected them...

He looked down into the water. He was surprised he wasn't sobbing, but he didn't need to. Not now. He could stop worrying now... now he knew. Anna and Eva. There had been so many. His grandparents. His father and his mother. She must have looked down into the water like this. He understood her at last. He understood everything. He leaned forward towards the Vltava and felt the weight leave his feet.

Strong hands gripped his shoulders.

"Grab his legs," he heard someone shout, and then he was looking up at the sky. He stared at the circle of strange faces looking down at him.

"What's the matter with him?" a woman said.

"I don't know, but I've been following him for the past ten minutes. He's been stopping and starting and shouting out. I think he must be a bit simple. Stupid fool was about to jump."

Chapter Twenty-Eight

February 21st – February 25th, 1948

Jan Masaryk finished his tenth cigarette of the two-hour journey from Prague to Sezimovo Ústí. He stabbed the end into the ashtray, as his chauffeur turned into the long driveway leading to the modern, white summer home of President and Hana Beneš. Snow covered the slopes of the spacious grounds, where in happier times Eduard Beneš liked to ski. Jan looked out to see Hana Benešová standing at the door, ready to greet him.

They entered the hall together without speaking, and a maid took his hat, scarf and overcoat.

"How is he?" asked Jan in a hushed voice.

"Shocked, like the rest of us. But he thinks he can turn it to his advantage."

"He's not going to accept the resignations, is he, Hana? That would be a disaster."

"I'm sure not."

"I cannot believe all twelve democratic ministers would resign from the cabinet without my opinion even being sought. I feel dreadfully ignored."

"Poor Jan. I'm sure it was not intended that way."

"Did the President know of their plans?"

"I don't know, Jan, but please remain calm when you see Eduard. The doctor was here again this morning. He says Eduard might not survive another stroke. You know the last one was quite severe."

"Is he well enough to receive me?"

"I think so. Yesterday's events have taken a lot out of him, but his thoughts are as focussed as ever. I'll tell him you are here."

"Thankyou, Hanci."

Beneš was sitting in an armchair next to a picture window overlooking the snow-covered rockery. Jan shook the President's limp hand and sat down opposite him.

"I'm sorry if this has come as a shock to you, Jan," said Beneš. Jan detected a slur in his voice.

"The only shock is that no one warned me. Surely you knew of their intentions in advance, Mr President."

"Prokop Drtina did tell me they were considering it. The final straw, of course, was Gottwald sacking all the non-Communist police chiefs. The twelve clearly decided they had to make a stand."

"But this puts me in an appalling position, Mr President, being the only non-Communist minister left. My presence in the cabinet means Gottwald has a majority to carry on. You must allow me to resign too."

"There is no need, Jan. I have no intention of accepting the resignations, and the twelve do not want me to."

"Then why do it, and leave me appearing to side with the Communists? Can you not see how intolerable it is for me?"

"Drtina has explained that it was merely a gesture to show our people the true nature of the Communists."

"Good God. If our people don't know their true nature after the best part of two years... The armed Workers' Militia are everywhere in Prague this morning. There are truckloads of them. They're guarding all the public buildings and bridges. And the main roads. I had to pass one of their checkpoints to get here. I've heard they've even closed our borders. It already amounts to a coup, Mr President."

"No, Jan. You exaggerate the threat. I believe Gottwald has played right into our hands by acting in this way. Our people were already disaffected enough with the Communists. When they learn the reasons behind the resignations, and see Gottwald's overreaction, they will desert them in droves in the May elections. I am confident the Communist vote will collapse."

"That's if they allow the May elections."

"Now you are going too far, Jan. I know Klement Gottwald is not an easy man ..."

"He is a vulgar, boorish drunk."

"That may be, but I still believe he is at heart a reasonable man, who believes in parliamentary democracy."

Jan took out another cigarette. "Do you mind if I smoke?" Beneš nodded. Jan took a long draw and breathed out heavily.

"It concerns me when you say that, Mr President. The belief that Gottwald supports my father's constitution is a hoax the Communists have perpetrated on our people. I almost believed it myself in the beginning. But look how they've used the Interior Ministry to defame our democratic parties. Accusing your own National Socialists of spying for the West. Destroying the Slovak Democratic Party with the absurd claim they were planning an armed insurrection. My God, six months ago they even sent parcel bombs to Drtina, Zenkl and me."

"It was never proved it was the Communists."

"Drtina proved it. He stated it openly in parliament. That's why they hate him so much."

"Prokop Drtina is a brave man, but not necessarily right about that."

"I know he's right. I have the proof, but the police won't act on it, of course. You know, Mr President, of all the ministries we agreed to give the Communists in '45, our biggest mistake was giving them the Interior Ministry. With the police in their pockets they control everything."

"You know as well as I do, Jan, it was never my intention to let them have the Interior Ministry."

"Then why did we allow Stalin to persuade us?"

"It wasn't a question of persuasion, Jan. You know very well that if I'd said no to Stalin in Moscow, there would have been no train to bring us home at the end of the war."

"Stalin is behind all of this, of course, Mr President. You do realise that at last, don't you? He has agents guiding the Communists in everything they do."

"It won't matter, Jan. I still believe Gottwald has calculated very poorly. I think their losses in the elections will surpass even their own worst forecasts.

"Do you really believe the answer to this mess lies in the May elections, Mr President?"

"Yes, Jan. I do."

"Then I believe we are faced with two choices."

Beneš looked up. His eyes showed interest at last.

"And what are they?"

"The first is to do nothing. Do not accept the resignations. Let the government limp on with a divided cabinet until we get through to May. The Communists will carry on their programme of bullying and intimidation against anyone who opposes them, but we shall put up with it as best we can, and they will lose the election even more heavily because of it."

"That is precisely what I intend to do."

"Good, then we do not need to consider anything else. But over this weekend, Mr President, you must instruct the twelve to return to cabinet. I shall stay away until I know they are going back, otherwise I shall be giving Gottwald the quorum he needs to carry on without them."

"I shall do exactly that, Jan."

Jan leaned over to return his ashtray to a side table. When he turned back, President Beneš was looking out of the window. For the first time Jan noticed the trembling in his left arm and the sallowness of his cheeks. He seemed to have aged twenty years in as many weeks.

"Just out of interest, Jan, what was your second option?" Beneš asked, still staring out at the snow.

"Does it matter now?"

"I would like to know."

"Accept the resignations and let me resign too. Then Gottwald has no cabinet to lead. He must resign and new elections must be called. But I believe that would be a dangerous strategy."

"Why, if it would bring the elections forward?"

"Unlike you, Mr President, I have no confidence any more in Gottwald's commitment to democracy. If you accepted our resignations, Gottwald would portray the situation as a crisis and declare an emergency. He will fill the cabinet with Communists and there will be no elections. No, we must limp on until May. You must not accept any resignations, sir. Are we still agreed?"

"Yes, Jan. Don't worry. We are as one over this."

"I am very relieved. I believe we Czechoslovaks have a heavy responsibility to the world at this moment. Of all the countries liberated by Stalin we are the only one left not to have fallen under his yoke. If we go, I believe his influence could spread to the West. To Italy, and perhaps even to France."

"It is a great comfort to have you sharing such burdens with me, Jan. In 1938 I bore it alone. I do not think I have the strength to do so again."

"We will see it through together, Mr President."

"Good. Good. Will you stay to dinner, Jan? I know Hana would be pleased. She enjoys your company so much."

"I'm afraid I have to return to Prague, sir, if our plan is to work. I must go back to my residence and concoct a bout of something which keeps me away from cabinet. If I am known to be here, it might look as if we're conspiring in some way."

"Yes. You are quite right, of course."

"Before I go, may I put to you again a question you did not answer earlier?"

"You may ask me anything, dear Jan."

"Why did you or Drtina not seek my advice about the resignations, or at least warn me they were going to happen?"

"I think the others felt no obligation to ask you because you have no party affiliation with them, Jan. As for myself, I knew you would not be compromised by the resignations, since I had no intention of accepting them."

"But what if I had resigned too, not knowing that?"

"My dear Jan, I hope you will forgive my presumption, but perhaps given my present state of health I should acknowledge it now. I know your loyalty to me as your president is total. I knew you would never resign without asking me first."

Tomáš heard the commotion in the street beneath his rooms in Malonstranské Square. He did not bother to look out. There had been so many marches and demonstrations in the city in the five days since the resignations. All Communist demonstrations, of course. Each one timed to show a spontaneous outpouring of support for the 'people's democracy'. Each one calling on Beneš to accept the resignations and allow Gottwald to form the government the people demanded.

"Stupid fools. They deserve what they get."

He leant against the sink and surveyed the mess in the room. It was only four o'clock but the light was already fading. He knew he ought to eat something. He had walked all over the city today. Five appointments, all in different districts, and he couldn't afford the tram. But he was grateful to Alice for getting him the work. There hadn't been enough to occupy him at the Red Cross for a long time, and anyway she was right. He couldn't have coped with any more of what he saw there.

He hated February. It was the fifth anniversary of Anna and Eva's transport and he was relieved to be back in his room. It was typical of Alice to come and see if he was alright. She had wanted to take him out somewhere, but he did not want to be out in the world. He just wanted to be alone with them. But Alice gave him addresses of more people she and Jan knew who were 'desperate' for his English lessons, and she made it clear he must not let her down. Every day for the past two weeks she had kept him constantly busy.

The noise in the street was getting louder. It wasn't normal for the Communists to hold demonstrations in the Malá Strana. Wenceslas Square and the Old Town were their usual territory. He had walked through Wenceslas Square today and heard the same old nonsense from the Trade Unionists and the Workers' Militia. The twelve were plotting an armed conspiracy against the Communist Party and the State, which in the Communists' minds were the same thing, and the people were demanding Gottwald's protection. There was even a rumour that Red Army troops were at the Austrian border, ready to come to the rescue of the people's democracy. He could believe that.

He took his coat from the back of the chair and walked slowly down the stairs to the street. His body ached. He would buy some bread at the corner and perhaps some ham and pickles. He opened the main door and was met by a tide of people making their way through the Square towards Nerudova Street. He held the door and watched them for a moment, wondering whether to go back inside. From their dress it was clear most of them were students. They were walking purposefully, a few shouting, but the majority saying very little. He stepped out into the stream and was carried along by it. When they reached Nerudova Street, they joined hundreds more coming up the hill from Charles Bridge, all making their way to the Castle.

"What's going on?" he asked a young couple.

"We're going to breathe some spirit into the President," the young man said. "We've heard Gottwald has gone to the castle to see him."

"We're here to save our country's democracy," insisted the girl.

"You think you can?"

"We're the Third Resistance," said someone from behind them. "First it was the Hapsburgs. Then the Nazis. We're not going to let the Communists dictate to us."

"Perhaps one day you'll learn to fight before it's too late to change anything," Tomáš called after them, as he stepped into a doorway.

He watched the couple climbing the hill away from him, hand in hand. He followed the girl's white hat and the boy's dark hair as they disappeared into the dusk, talking and taking strength from one another, confident that what was right must win through. He noticed the address plate on the wall next to him and remembered this was Nerudova Street. The same street he and Anna had climbed during the crisis of September 1938.

He stood there for several minutes and realised the flow of people passing in front of him was slowing down. Then it stopped completely. Explanations filtered down through the crowd from the top of the hill. The police had set up a cordon at Jansky Vršek. The way to the castle was blocked. Then news came up the hill from the town. There had been an announcement in Wenceslas Square. President Beneš had accepted the resignations. Gottwald was to form a new government. But Jan Masaryk had not resigned. There were looks of disbelief amongst the crowd. Jan Masaryk had agreed to stay on in the cabinet with Gottwald. But how could 'naš Honza' support the Communists?

There were shouts of protest and denial. The students in front of

Tomáš tried to push forward towards the castle and began to chant, "*Third Resistance. Third Resistance. Third Resistance...*" Further up the hill people started to scream. The screaming and shouting grew louder and louder until the tap, tap, tap of machine gun fire in the middle distance brought instant silence. For a few seconds there was no sound or movement at all. Then, as one, hundreds of people turned and started to run down the hill. The screaming started again, as Tomáš witnessed the mad scramble to get away. The running, terrified crowd in front of him gradually thinned until only the injured and shocked limped and stumbled past.

He stepped out into the street to help a girl who was bleeding heavily from a gash across her forehead. He put his arm around her and looked up the street to see a line of National Security Corps with machine guns and clubs descending towards him. The girl could no longer stand. He picked her up and carried her to the doorway.

"Thankyou," she whispered to him.

"You have nothing to thank me for," he said. He knelt over her and waited for the blows to start.

Chapter Twenty-Nine

March 9th – March 10th, 1948

Jan knew he was being followed. The two leather-jacketed thugs were not even trying to make a secret of it any more. Their black Tatra car had tracked him all the way to Sezimovo Ústí that morning, and had waited at the gate before trailing him back to Prague. He looked behind him as he crossed Malonstranské Square. There they were. They stopped when he stopped, folded their arms and stared at him. He felt bad leading them to Tomáš's lodgings, but it was a risk he thought his friend would approve of him taking.

He paused halfway up the stairs to catch his breath. He clutched the handrail, listened and heard no one behind him. It seemed they had decided to wait at the front door. Perhaps they did not care which rooms he was visiting. At Tomáš's door at the top of the house he paused again. All he could hear was his own wheezing. His bronchitis was bad and he was carrying too much weight. He resolved to take more care of himself once all this was over, if only for Alice's sake and Marcia's.

He knocked and heard movement inside. When Tomáš answered, Jan held up a bottle of single malt whisky. "I thought we might both benefit from some fortification, my dear Tomáš," he said.

"Jan. I wasn't expecting you. Come in. Please come in."

The room was dark, cold and stale.

"Do you mind if I let in some light, Tomáš?"

"No. Please do. I'll move some things off the chair. Do you mind if I just lie on the bed?"

"Of course not. You look after yourself. I'll get some glasses."

Jan poured the drinks and handed one to Tomáš.

"What are we drinking to, Jan?"

"The future?"

"I admire your optimism. To the future." Tomáš attempted to laugh but winced in pain.

"How are you now, Tomáš?" Jan sat down on a chair at the foot of the bed.

"Do you mean physically?"

"Yes."

"The head's nothing. It's the ribs that stop me from sleeping. But I'm just pleased to be out of that damn prison. Did you have something to do with that?"

"My reward for being a good lap dog."

"That means all 200 were let out because of you, Jan. People ought to know that."

"It doesn't matter."

"It does. I, for one, am very grateful."

"People like you and those students put me to shame, Tomáš."

"It's not like that, Jan."

"It is for me. That's why I had to come to see you. I cannot explain or apologise to every Czechoslovak for what I've done, but perhaps I can to you."

"Why me?"

"Because you have always believed in the things I believe in, and have always had the courage to say it. Sometimes I've been too circumspect, Tomáš. I regret that now."

"That's not how people see you, Jan. You've always been their voice. You're still a hero to them."

"No, Tomáš. That pedestal was built for my father. I was allowed to stand beside it for a time, but the real Czechoslovaks, people like you who believed in my father and his republic, must feel I have betrayed them."

"No. We may not understand why you've acted in the way you have, but we still have faith in you."

"Thankyou, my friend."

Jan got up to pour Tomáš another drink. "I have to confess to you now, Tomáš, that I always knew you were right about the Communists. From the very beginning when I first went to Moscow, Gottwald and Stalin made it clear they would only follow parliamentary democracy for as long as it gave them what they wanted."

"Then why did you always defend them, when I said those things?"

"I wasn't defending Gottwald and Stalin, Tomáš. I was supporting my President who still believed in them. They have made fools of us all. And of our republic."

"What was it Engels said? 'The parties of order die by the legal state which they created.' Gottwald and Stalin understand that as well as Hitler did."

"It sickens me, Tomáš. The Czechoslovak Communists have not one ounce of patriotic pride. They are slaves of Moscow and take pride in their servitude. I only realised last September how damaging that servitude was."

"When they tried to kill you?"

"No. Not then. The parcel bomb was Gottwald's doing, not Stalin's. No, I'm talking about Stalin vetoing the millions of dollars the Americans were offering us for reconstruction. Even Gottwald saw the sense of us having that money. But Stalin forbad it. He ordered me to Moscow, you know, and told me in very plain language that, if we accepted money from the Marshall Plan, we could expect to see Red Army troops back in Prague within days."

"But, of course, that's not what the public were told."

"No, of course not. It was humiliating, Tomáš. I went to Moscow as the Foreign Minister of a sovereign state, and came back a stooge of Stalin like everyone else. I have suffered the greatest anguish of my life since that day."

"I'm sorry, Jan."

"They even used my father's name at the rally on Sunday to justify their treachery. They said he would have approved of their 'new course'. That he would have been proud of his son's place in a Communist government. I feel so ashamed."

Jan emptied his glass and poured himself another. His hands shook as he lit a cigarette.

"I have to ask you, Jan. Why in God's name have you stayed on? And why did the President accept the resignations in the first place?"

"The answers to both questions are much simpler than you can imagine, Tomáš. The President accepted the resignations because Gottwald threatened him with civil war if he refused. The Communists were ready to fight and call in the Red Army, if necessary."

"He should have told him to go to hell."

"The President is a very sick man, Tomáš. The thought of civil war terrifies him. I saw him this morning. 'The state must go on, Jan,' he said. 'The nation must survive and be governed.'"

"Even if it's a Communist state, and the nation is enslaved to Russia?"

"Yes. And who is to say he's not right?"

"Me, for one."

"And what would you do, Tomáš?"

"You know what I would do. I would fight. Or rather, I would if I cared enough any more."

"I cannot believe you don't care, Tomáš."

"I see no point in caring. This is just another Munich. Decent Czechoslovaks would fight if Beneš called on them. But, of course, he won't. He thinks he's avoiding bloodshed. But there was plenty of blood shed under the Nazis after Munich, and it will be no different under the Communists. This really is the end of us, Jan."

"Czechoslovakia will live on."

"But not its spirit. We shall never recover what we had under your father."

Jan put his glass down on the floor and held his head in his hands. "You're right, Tomáš. God, you're right. What can we do?"

"It's already done, Jan. We have to find a way of living with what is unbearable."

Jan picked up the glass and poured himself more whisky. "Churchill would have agreed with you about fighting. I remember what he said to me in 1940 when the British were beaten and he wouldn't surrender. 'Nations which go down fighting, Jan, rise again'."

"And that's the lesson Beneš never learned from your father. Tomáš Masaryk would have fought in '38, and he would fight now. We both know it."

"I shall carry on the fight, Tomáš. I promise you. Those people will learn that the name Masaryk still means something in this country."

"What are you planning?"

"It would be unfair to tell you. All I can say is that Marcia is now safely out of the country, and I do not believe they would harm Alice. I am free at last to act."

"Weren't you before?"

"No, Tomáš. I haven't been free for years. I was never free until four hours ago."

"I don't understand."

"You asked me just now why I stayed on in the cabinet after the President accepted the resignations. I stayed because President Beneš asked me to. He wanted me there as a democratic presence in the government for as long as possible."

"You should have refused."

"I couldn't refuse." Jan took a drink and sat back in his chair. "You see, many years ago I swore an oath that I would serve the President in any way he asked. Why else do you think I allowed myself to sit in cabinet surrounded and abused by Communists? Why do you think I stood in the Old Town Square and allowed them to abuse my father's name? Because of that oath."

"But Jan, that's ridiculous. Even swearing an oath to Beneš doesn't mean you have to act against your own conscience. No one could expect it of you."

"I did not swear the oath to Beneš, Tomáš. I swore it to my father. He asked me on his deathbed to do anything and everything the President demanded of me. I vowed to do it, and I have always done it. Today, at last, the President discharged me from that oath."

"The people need to be told this, Jan. They need to understand."

"They will understand one day. What I do now will tell them."

"You're not planning to do anything stupid, are you, Jan?"

"Kill myself, you mean? God no. I will admit that in my darkest hours I have considered it. But I'm a coward, Tomáš. I cannot stand physical pain. I think of poor Drtina jumping from that window and spending the rest of his life with a broken body. No. That sort of gesture is not for me. I intend to live and to restore honour to my family's name."

"I'm very pleased to hear it, Jan."

"And what will you do, my dear Tomáš?"

"I shall do nothing. Stay in Prague and see it through."

"You are a good patriot."

"If you think that, I'm afraid my reasons will disappoint you. I shall stay simply because for me this is where I remain closest to my wife and child. Even though Eva never set foot in her own country, I feel this is where they both are."

"Has it not got any easier for you, Tomáš?"

"No. Sometimes I wonder how it is possible to stay alive whilst feeling such pain. If it were anything but grief, I would think it was a sign of mortal illness."

"I am sorry, Tomáš. I wish I could offer you some solace, but I know there are times in life when we have to find our own way."

Jan got up and walked over to the bed. He poured whisky into Tomáš's glass.

"In case we do not meet again, I propose a toast to us both, Tomáš." He offered Tomáš his hand.

"Over the hills, my dear friend."

They touched glasses.

"Over the hills, Jan."

Jan sat up in bed in his official residence preparing his speech for the Polish-Czechoslovak Friendship Society the following afternoon. He had to keep up appearances. No one must suspect it was the last duty he would carry out as a government minister. In the evening he would leave to take the cure which had long been planned and which would provide cover for his escape to England. Then the people would learn the truth about the Communists, when he started his broadcasts again from London.

He read the speech aloud. He was pleased with it. Through his open window he heard the carillon of the Loreta Church ringing the hour. He loved the beautiful sound of those bells. Midnight. When they stopped, there was perfect silence in the courtyard outside. He placed the speech on his bedside cabinet, turned out the light and was asleep within minutes.

"Minister. Minister Masaryk. Wake up. Come on. Wake up."

Someone was shaking him. "What is it? Who is it?" The light went on. Jan saw two men, strangers, standing by his bed. They were wearing dark blue workmen's overalls. One was holding a tool bag.

"What's the matter? Is there something wrong?"

One of the men sat down on the bed. He was short and stocky with blond hair and strong Slavic features. The other was tall and thin with even lighter hair. Jan sat up and leaned back against the headboard. "Who the hell are you?" he asked.

"My name is Kral," said the man on the bed. "This is Schramm. We need to talk to you, Minister."

"At this hour? What time is it?"

"Three in the morning. Yes, at this hour. We need to talk to you about a problem."

Jan fumbled for his cigarettes on the bedside table. Schramm passed them to him. "Would either of you like one of these?" Jan asked.

"No, thanks, we prefer our own," said Kral. "The problem is a very basic one, Minister. We do not believe you are loyal to our country's Communist government."

"Why would you say such a thing? I have always shown great loyalty."

"Yes, but do you intend to in the future?"

"Yes, yes. Of course. I see no reason..."

"We believe you intend to leave and arouse false bourgeois sentiments amongst our people from abroad."

"No, I don't have any plans..."

"So you intend to stay?"

"Yes, I'm delivering an official speech tomorrow. Here it is on the bedside..."

"Then that leaves us with another problem, you see. We believe your continued presence in the country could be divisive. You could become a focus for anti-Communist agitation."

"I don't see why."

"You're not a member of the Party, are you? That's a problem, you see."

"Lots of people are not..."

"But you are the Foreign Minister. If those people follow you rather than the Party, you would be responsible for setting one Czechoslovak against another. Don't you think that would be a bad thing?"

"Yes, I suppose..."

"You suppose? Arousing false bourgeois hopes, preventing the government from getting on with its business, standing in the way of internal peace. Do you think these are good things?"

"Well, no. Clearly not."

"Then we must ask you, Minister, to perform one more valuable service for your country."

"Of course."

"You must accept that your presence is a threat to internal security and leave."

"Where do you want me to go?"

"Get on with it, Kral."

"Shut your mouth, Schramm. I'm trying to provide the man with some dignity. Give me the tablets."

"What..? What do you want..?" Jan mumbled.

"We want you to take these, Minister Masaryk." Kral emptied six pills onto the palm of his hand. "To help your country, and yourself."

"You want me to kill myself?"

"We want you to accept that Czechoslovakia would be better off if you were dead."

"I won't do it."

Schramm cursed. "Come on, Kral. It's getting fucking late. Quarter past three."

"I told you to shut up. Look, Masaryk, these pills are painless. You will go to sleep and that's it. Everyone will be told you took your own life because of all the criticism you've had from the West. You'll be a martyr. You'll have a state funeral."

"I won't do it. I won't. I can't. Please."

"Listen. Smoke a cigarette and then decide. You have other choices. You could shoot yourself. Or you can go out that window."

"Oh, my God, no. Please..."

"You will do one or the other."

"No, I won't. I warn you. I will not give up without a fight." Jan wondered where his words came from.

Kral stood up. "Get out of bed, Masaryk."

"No. I will not."

The two men looked at one another and then grabbed hold of his arms. They dragged him head first from the bed.

"Don't leave any marks on the old fool," ordered Kral.

Jan managed to scramble to his feet and push Schramm against the bedside cabinet. The cabinet toppled over and Jan's books, water jug and glass fell to the floor. Kral forced Jan's arm up his back and marched him to the open window. As he approached the opening, Jan turned and struck Kral on the side of the face. Free now, he ran into the bathroom and tried to force the door closed. He shouted at the top of his voice for help. Over and over. He felt the door slowly being pushed open. An arm appeared through the gap and then a leg, and Jan felt his strength draining away. He fell back onto the floor as they burst through.

Kral stood over him, red in the face and breathing heavily. "Shut the fucking door and open the fucking window," he shouted at Schramm. "You stupid bastard, Masaryk. Now we're going to have to get you through there." He nodded towards the smaller opening of the bathroom window.

"You can fucking try, you Communist bastards," Jan panted.

He kicked out as they dragged him to his feet. He refused to stand. He saw Kral take a short, thick metal rod from his pocket. Then he felt a sharp, blunt blow behind his right ear. All power went from his arms and legs, and he was dragged backwards towards the window.

He was raised up until he was sitting on the window sill. He felt them pushing him backwards. At the last moment some strength returned and he grabbed at the wall on either side of the window to prevent himself falling back. He felt his fingernails digging into the plaster.

"This is no good. Someone will see his fat arse sticking out of the fucking window," said Kral. "We'll have to soften him up first."

"You said no marks."

They dragged Jan back into the bathroom. He sat down on the edge of the bath exhausted.

"Get two pillows from the bed, Schramm," ordered Kral.

Jan looked up. Kral was standing in front of him looking around. Jan stood up and, with no strength left, used his heavy frame to propel Kral into the wall cabinet. It crashed to the ground and covered the floor with glass.

"Get him in the bath. Don't let him cut his feet. People don't cut their fucking feet and then kill themselves. What a fucking mess. Give me a pillow."

Jan felt the smothering softness on his face. It was the worst of all. He chewed at the pillow as his chest tightened. If only they would stop this, he would go quietly. He stopped struggling and felt every muscle in his body give way.

"Oh, for fuck's sake. What now?" shouted Kral. "The old bastard has shit himself. Get him up. Sit him on the fucking toilet."

Jan was spent. He was too exhausted for any more physical or mental effort. He felt nothing. Too tired for any emotion. Even fear. They were dragging him. He was being raised up again. He sensed sudden movement and a split second of cool air...

"That's it. He's done. The old bastard landed on his feet. How could that happen?"

"Is he dead?" asked Kral. "That's the only thing that matters now. This is one holy fucking mess. Get some razor blades out, Schramm. Tie a pyjama cord to the door handle. Make it look as if he was weighing up how he was going to do it."

"We'll have to clear up all this shit, Kral."

"There's no time. They'll make up some story to make it all fit. I'll tell you what though. Masaryk was a tough old bastard in the end. He had plenty of fight in him."

Tomáš read the typewritten note pushed under his door during the night.

They know he spoke with you. You are a marked man. Get out while you can.

Chapter Thirty

December 14th – December 19th, 1956

Fran hoped the French teacher would be on the bus. If he were, he would be on the top deck having a cigarette. She would go upstairs, feign surprise to see him and take the seat next to him. What should she call him? She couldn't say 'Good morning, Mr Colman'. He was a colleague, after all. 'Hello, Tom. Mind if I sit next to you?' No, that was no good either. Too casual. He always looked so severe. A lot of the boys were afraid of him. But there was something about him somehow. He had a kind face. More sad than severe. She'd not even spoken to him really. Just a 'Good morning' or 'Good night' in the corridor. But he always smiled at her. Well, half a smile.

She looked up Islington High Street. There was a bus coming, but not the 21. He might not even be on it, when it did come. More often than not she passed him somewhere on route, walking in his gabardine mac, head down and shoulders hunched. Usually smoking a cigarette. Wasn't he too old for her anyway? He must be at least forty-five, even more. He had grey flecks in his hair. But he was still very good looking.

If only he were more approachable. She thought many times of talking to him in the staff room, but he always sat on his own, engrossed in a book. He left one on his chair once. *'The Poems of Rainer Maria Rilke'*. Fran had not even heard of her. No one she spoke to seemed to know much about Tom Colman either, in spite of his being at the school for the past seven years. Wendy said he came from Czechoslovakia, but you could never tell from his English. It was perfect. Well almost. Sometimes he stressed the wrong part of the word, but that only added to his attraction. Poor Tom. It couldn't be easy teaching French to boys in a secondary modern.

Oh Lordy, the 21 was coming. The blond in front in the queue patted the back of her perm and climbed aboard, careful not to get her heels caught in the grooved wooden floor. Fran checked her hairgrips and straightened her best tortoiseshell glasses. The floor would present no problem for her shoes. The conductor stepped aside for her and she wound her way up the stairs. She entered a fug of smoke. Condensation ran down the windows. There he was. Sitting on his own, reading. Last minute nerves made her hesitate, but people behind pressed her forward.

"Is this seat taken?" she asked.

"No. Please." He did not even look up from his book.

Don't leave it too long, she thought, or it will become too embarrassing.

"You're Mr Colman, aren't you?"

He looked up at last. "Yes. I'm sorry. I do recognise you, but ..."

"Fran Whitaker."

"Yes, of course."

"I only started in September. Geography."

"Right."

"You're French, aren't you? I mean, you teach French."

"Yes, that's right."

"Do you enjoy it?"

He closed his book and gave her a resigned smile.

"I never really thought about it. It's just what I do."

"Surely you have to enjoy it to be able to do it. It's not exactly easy, is it?"

"No, it's not easy. But it's a simple equation. Work, money, live."

"Lordy. That sounds depressing. There must be things you enjoy?"

He held up his book. *George Sand*. She'd not heard of him either.

"I'm sorry. I'm talking too much and asking questions I shouldn't. I'm always being told I do that."

"This is our stop," he said. He extinguished his cigarette on the stubber and dropped the butt to the floor.

"I suppose we ought to walk separately into school," said Fran. "You know how they gossip. People think all sorts of things."

"I don't give a damn what anyone thinks, as long as you don't."

She liked the idea of them being involved in something daring together.

"No, I don't mind. Whatever you say."

Fran hoped Tom Colman might choose to seek her out at some time over the following week, but he never did. He sat alone as always during breaks and lunchtimes, his nose in a book, courteous in his dealings with everyone, but hardly ever initiating contact with anyone. She found it upset her more than she wanted it to. On the last day of the Christmas term, when the boys had gone and the teachers were enjoying a drink together in the staff room, she decided to approach him again.

"Hello, Tom. All by yourself?"

"Yes. I'm happy enough."

She sat down opposite him and sipped her rum and blackcurrant.
"Do you have any plans for Christmas?" she asked.
"Not really."
"Some of them are going for a drink later. I thought I might join in. Would you like to come along? There'll be quite a group. I shall only stay for a short while."
"It's very nice of you, Fran, but it's not really something I enjoy very much."
"You enjoy a drink. That's your third already. Not that I was watching or counting or anything." She put her hand over her eyes. "Lordy, how embarrassing."
"It's alright."
"Not really. I always manage to say something silly like that."
"No, you don't. It's just that I prefer my own company."
"Oh, I see." She stood up. "I was only trying to be friendly. I didn't mean to cause offence."

She was crossing the playground when she heard him calling after her.
"Fran. Miss Whitaker, would you wait a minute?"
She stopped and he caught up with her.
"Fran. I was very rude to you earlier. I didn't want you to go off for two weeks upset by something I'd said or done. I'm very sorry."
"It's not too late to catch the others up."
"No, I didn't mean that. It's really not for me. I find other people's company quite a strain sometimes."
"Oh, I see."
"No. I don't mean you. I mean large groups. I can't join in."
"I understand. I'm always feeling awkward."
"I'm afraid with me it's something worse. I just don't have the patience. But anyway, have a nice Christmas. Thanks for asking me."
He held out his hand. She shook it and he walked away. Fran knew how much regret she would feel over Christmas at her parents if she let him go.
"Do you like the cinema?" she called out to him.
He stopped and stood for a moment before turning slowly.
"Not really," he said, stretching the words out. "I'm not very good company for that sort of thing."
"I think you are. I feel awkward on my own and there's something I really want to see."
He trudged back towards her. "What is it?"

"Anastasia. Ingrid Bergman's in it. Everyone's talking about it."
"Perhaps after Christmas."
"Yes, alright. I understand. Perhaps after Christmas."
He gave her one of his half smiles. "Is it local?" he asked.
"The Empire in the High Street. But it finishes this weekend."
"How about tomorrow then?"
"Really? What time?"
"I don't know. What time are films?"
"I'll meet you tomorrow evening at seven in front of the Empire."
"Alright, Fran. I'll see you tomorrow at seven."

She couldn't help talking too much. The film had been wonderful.
"I love mysteries like that. I wonder if she really was the Tsar's daughter. It didn't really say one way or the other in the end, did it? Only hints. I suppose no one will ever know."

He seemed to be heading straight for the bus stop. She wished he would slow down. She wasn't used to heels, and they were starting to hurt her feet.

"I know if she was the Tsar's daughter. Do you want me to tell you?"
"Are you joking?"
"No. I was told years ago by someone who was there."
"Slow down a minute, will you, Tom?" She tugged lightly at his sleeve. "Don't be in such a hurry. How can you know, when all the people in Hollywood don't know?"
"It's a fact. The Communists murdered the Tsar, his wife, the Tsarevich, and all four princesses."
"Even Anastasia?"
"Yes. No one escaped. And I can tell you why they did it, if you want."
"Goodness. You are a mystery man. Please tell me."
"In the summer of 1918 the Communists were sure an attempt would be made to rescue the Romanovs. A rumour spread that Czech legionnaires were on their way to free them. In fact the legionnaires were simply heading for Yekaterinburg on their way east along the railway out of Russia. They didn't even know the Tsar's family was being held there. But their captors panicked, took them down to the basement in the middle of the night, and murdered them to prevent a rescue."
"How do you know all that?"
"My father was one of the Czech legionnaires. He told me the story when I was a boy." Tom stopped to light a cigarette. "My father said they took the town only a few hours after the murders. He spoke to one of the

guards, Nikulin, who told him the whole family and their four servants were dead. Nikulin said he only helped carry the bodies out, but my father always suspected he was one of the murderers."

"Lordy, that's incredible. Your father should tell the Hollywood people his story."

Tom had stopped outside a pub. "Do you fancy a drink, Fran?"

"Ooh, yes please."

"There you are, Fran. A rum and black." He put his whisky down on the table. She had noticed him drink one at the bar first.

"Thankyou. The story about your father is fascinating. Does that mean the rumours about you are true? You come from Czechoslovakia?"

"Rumours?"

"Only innocent chit-chat. People are interested, that's all."

"Well, the chit-chat's right. I left Czechoslovakia when the Communists took over in 1948."

"So your name's not really Colman?"

"It is now. I needed British citizenship to get residence and a teaching job. I thought it would be easier with an English name."

"So what are you really called?"

"I don't really want everyone at school knowing, Fran. You know what kids are like."

"I'm sorry. I always ask the wrong questions." She blushed.

"It's alright, but I prefer no one else to know. My name was Kovařík. Tomáš Kovařík."

"Tow-mash. I like it."

"But don't use it."

"I won't, if you say so. My full name is Francesca, but only my parents still call me that."

"It's a lovely name."

"It's too grand for me. People expect a Francesca to be glamorous and mysterious. I prefer plain Fran. It feels more me."

"Fran is a nice name for a nice person."

"Thankyou, Tom," she said and blushed again. "Is your father still in Czechoslovakia?"

"No, he's been dead for eighteen years now."

"Do you still have family there?"

As soon as she said it, she knew she had asked too much. He finished his drink and stood up. "Would you like another?" he asked.

She shook her head. She was relieved when he went to the bar and not to the door. When he came back with his whisky she apologised again.

"I'm just not used to talking about it, Fran, that's all."

"I shouldn't pry."

"The fact is, I have no family left in Czechoslovakia. My parents and grandparents were all killed by the Nazis in 1938. In one way or another."

"Oh, dear Lord, I'm so sorry. You poor man."

She wanted to take his hand, or put her arm around him, but she knew neither would be welcome. "But surely the war didn't start until 1939," she said instead, and immediately regretted it.

"It did for us. It always amazes me how uninformed people here are about my country."

"I'm sorry. But I think all the Iron Curtain countries are a bit of a mystery to us."

"Czechoslovakia wasn't always an Iron Curtain country. We were a democracy like you for twenty years, before the British and French fed us to the Nazis."

"I'm sorry, Tom."

"It doesn't matter."

"I was only twelve in 1938."

"Well, I'm a lot older than that. I still have a very clear memory of it all."

"How old were you in 1938?"

"You don't mind asking personal questions, do you?"

"I'm sorry."

"You don't need to keep apologising." He drank some whisky. "I was twenty-one when the Nazis took over."

"So you're only nine years older than me?"

"Ten. I was forty last month. Try not to look so surprised."

"I'm sorry."

"I'm sure there's a rumour I'm much older but, to be honest, I don't really care."

"Please don't get so tetchy. I'll only blame myself for it later. And we were having such a nice time."

Tom emptied his glass.

"Maybe I should apologise. I know what I get like in company. I find simple things annoy me when they shouldn't."

"Perhaps the whisky doesn't help."

Tom laughed. "You really are priceless. You're completely honest without intending to be."

"My parents say I'm gauche."

"Gauche? Do they mean it kindly?"

"I can't imagine they do. I think I'm quite a disappointment to them."

"Why should you be?"

"They're both very successful. I don't think teaching geography in a London secondary modern is what they had in mind for their only child."

"It's not up to them what you do."

"Don't you think so?"

"Of course it isn't. Do you want another drink, Fran?"

"No, thanks."

"Will you excuse me while I get myself one?"

She watched him at the bar. At least he had asked her a question about herself at last, and had seemed interested in her reply.

"We all need to make up our own minds about things, Fran," he said as soon as he sat down again. "I cannot stand people dictating to others what they can and cannot say or do."

"Aren't we doing that all the time with the boys at school?"

"Not me. They can do and say whatever they like as far as I'm concerned."

"But you have a reputation for being so strict. Sorry, I shouldn't have said that."

"I'm strict about good manners and hard work, but I have nothing against independent thinking and the freedom to express it. If you want to teach geography at Islington Boys' Secondary Modern, whose business is it but yours?"

Fran smiled and sipped her rum. "Thanks, Tom. It's nice to hear you say that."

"What is it your parents do anyway that's so wonderful?"

"They're both senior lecturers at Oxford University. That's where they met."

"What do they teach?"

"Mummy teaches English literature and my father teaches philosophy. They write papers and books and have all these clever friends. I think they expected to have bright, beautiful children and... oh, I don't know. It's not really important."

"Yes, it is. You mustn't let people dictate to you about your life. It's important to stand up for yourself."

"It's just that when I go home tomorrow, I know the house will be full of my father's friends. I know I'll just feel foolish in front of them. Someone like you could join in with them, but I can't."

"Someone like me?"

"You're clever. You're always reading. You understand history and politics and things like that. You know a lot about Communism."

"Your father's not a Communist, is he?"

"Yes. He's very important in the British Communist Party."

"And you think he's very intelligent and wise?"

"Well, he is."

"Let me ask you something, Fran. You must have read over the last few months about the uprising in Hungary."

"Yes, of course."

"What did you think when the Russian Army went in and stopped it?"

"I don't know. I think I wondered why people in Hungary weren't allowed to do what they wanted in their own country, I suppose."

She was pleased to see Tom give her a full, unreserved smile.

"And what did your father think about the Russians going in?"

"He never talked about it with me, but I know he wrote an article about it for the Communist newspaper."

"The Daily Worker?"

"Yes, he writes a lot for them."

"Well, the Daily Worker said the Hungarians were counter-revolutionaries who had to be stopped from destroying socialism. If your father thinks that, he doesn't have half the common sense you have."

"How can you say that?"

"I had a very good friend back in Prague who understood very well what makes a good political system. He said to me once that he had only one wish for Czechoslovakia. It was that every citizen could stand without fear on any street corner in the country and shout, 'I hate my Prime Minister'. You understand what my friend meant, Fran, and why it is so important. Your father doesn't understand. And that makes you much cleverer than him."

Fran opened her handbag, took out a handkerchief and dabbed her eyes. "Do you really think so, Tom?"

"Yes, Fran. I really think so."

Chapter Thirty-One

January 3rd – February 16th, 1957

"Morning, Fran. Have a good Christmas?"
"Yes, lovely, thanks, Julia."
"Good morning, Miss Whitaker."
"Good morning, Headmaster."

The door opened again. It was the young PE teacher. Fran counted for nothing in his world. He didn't even bother to acknowledge her, let alone speak to her. She looked around as the staffroom filled up. It was funny how cliques formed. People came in and sat down in the same place with the same group every day. It would be making a bold statement to come in one morning and sit somewhere different.

Cliques never formed around her. She wasn't pretty enough like Penelope in her last school, or opinionated enough like Brian Curtis here. How wonderful it would be if Tom came in now and sat with her. That would make them all look. Where was he? She looked at her wrist watch. The Deputy Head's notices started in ten minutes and Tom was always here long before that. All the mornings she had come in and seen him sitting there reading and had not spoken to him. Now, on the very morning she had so much to tell him, he was late.

She saw Mr Sturridge enter the staffroom and tried not to catch his eye. Oh Lordy, he was coming over. He was wearing the same clothes he had worn every day of the previous term. Not just the same stained jacket and trousers, but the same shirt and tie and pullover. The boys inevitably called him 'Stinker Sturridge' and he had a reputation for varying his history lessons as much as he varied his clothes. It was cruel, but Fran could not help thinking it was bad luck he was in the same Humanities Department as her.

"Good morning, Fran," he said, as he sat down next to her. "Have a good Christmas?"

"Yes, thankyou, Walter, and you?" And just as she asked the question, Tom walked in and she could do nothing but attend to Walter's reply. Tom smiled and nodded and walked to the far end of the staffroom where he took his usual seat by himself. She looked over at him as the Deputy Head stood up and read the first announcements of the new term.

Tom did not reappear in the staffroom all day. She thought of going up to his classroom at the end of school, but knew it was too out of the ordinary. She sat marking books in the staffroom instead, and at last he appeared. She wasn't going to let him go. She got up and joined him as he cleared his pigeonhole.

"Hello, Tom. Did you have a good Christmas?" It was a question she had been asked a dozen times today, but put now to him it seemed stupid. The look he gave her confirmed it was.

"Christmas is like any other day as far as I'm concerned, Fran. But thanks for asking."

"I've been finding out all about Czechoslovakia while I was home."

"Really?"

"All about Jan Hus, the Hapsburgs, and the Battle of White Mountain. And the president you have now. Oh... What's his name? Zopo... Oh, drat."

"Zápotocký. He took over after Gottwald. But he's not my president."

"No, of course not. He's a Communist. I did what you told me. I stood up to my father over his Communist nonsense."

"I didn't tell you to do that."

"No, but you said we should all stand up for what we believe is right."

"Yes. We should."

"But I didn't understand all the things my father said. I thought you might help me."

"How?"

"By explaining it. I thought we could meet up again and we could talk about it."

"I don't think so, Fran. I'd be happy to lend you some books."

"Or we could go to the cinema again and then a drink afterwards. I really enjoyed it."

"I'm not interested in the cinema, Fran."

"Something else then."

He sighed.

"You don't make it very easy to be your friend, Tom, do you?"

"I don't know what to say to you, Fran. I just want to be left alone."

"Yes, I think I realise that." She rummaged for something in her bag, but wasn't sure what. "I'm sorry. I thought we could talk about some of the things I learned about your country. And some of the things my father said. Over a drink or something. I feel very foolish now."

He sighed again.

"Wait, Fran. I'm sorry. Over a drink. Let's talk over a drink."

"Really? When? Tonight?"

"At the weekend. Saturday evening. In the same pub."

"What time?"

"I'll meet you at eight o'clock in front of the cinema, in case I'm delayed. It's not nice for a lady to wait on her own outside a pub. We'll walk together from there. And I apologise again if I upset you."

"You got all that from the Encyclopaedia Britannica?" Tom laughed. "That's a strange way to spend your Christmas holiday."

"I really enjoyed it. It was like studying again. Like a project. And thanks for explaining all the Marxist-Leninist things this evening. I can't wait for half-term now. My father was shocked enough over Christmas. He won't believe how much I know when I see him next."

"Remember when you discuss all this with him, Fran, that you should argue from conviction. Someone as academic as your father will try to catch you out by bringing in something they think you don't know about. They want you to believe their intellectual training has given them access to a higher truth."

"By knowing that Communism follows in the tradition of Plato's Republic and... don't tell me... Thomas More's Utopia."

"Well done. You remembered. Yes, things like that."

"I can't believe I'm able to talk about such things. And that it's so enjoyable. You make everything so interesting. But there is something that still confuses me. How can it be that sometimes you make Communism sound like a good idea?"

"But that's what I'm trying to explain, Fran. I have nothing against Karl Marx as a philosopher. He wasn't the first to think of a Communist Utopia. It's what people like Lenin and Stalin and Gottwald have done with the philosophy that's the problem."

"And Zápotocký."

"Yes, him too. To achieve Marx's first step of socialism they're prepared to abolish individual choice and crush a person's right to freedom of expression. They create a system in which everyone must feel and believe the same things, and we never will. The human spirit won't fit into a straight-jacket."

"I love the way you say things."

"I've lived under Fascism and under Communism. Both systems turn the decent world on its head. Honesty and kindness aren't rewarded. Goodness and innocence don't stop maltreatment or even murder." He took a drink. "Sometimes people who have lived their whole lives in a democracy stop appreciating what they have."

"Like my father?"

"Especially institutionalised academics like your father. He needs to see what's been done to my country."

"My father says the way the Communists came to power in Czechoslovakia was a perfect example of how it should be done."

"I'm sorry, Fran. I've never met him, but I don't like the man."

"He was quite excited when I told him I had a new friend who came from Czechoslovakia. He was disappointed when I told him you weren't a Communist."

Tom pushed back his chair and stood up.

"What's the matter? Did I say something wrong?" Fran said.

"No, I'm getting another drink. Do you want one?"

"Not at the moment, thanks." She watched him go to the bar. She knew she had said something to upset him, but couldn't be sure what. And just when everything was going so well again.

He sat down and didn't speak.

"Do you ever drink beer?" she asked. "That's another thing I've learned. Czechoslovaks drink more beer than anyone else in the world."

"I might drink it if I could ever find it here. But I prefer this."

"Why whisky?"

"I had a friend who drank it. For me it has more affinity with my country than beer ever could."

She wanted to ask him about his friend but knew she mustn't. "You're full of mystery," she said.

"I don't try to be. I don't try to be anything."

"I know I've said something to upset you, but I don't know what."

"You haven't said anything."

"I wasn't discussing you with my father. I only mentioned you, and not by name."

He didn't speak.

"This happens so often. We're enjoying ourselves and then suddenly you seem to go all depressed."

He shuffled in his seat and she knew it was really best not to say any more.

"My mother says depression is anger without enthusiasm."

"Oh, for God's sake," he said, and he brought his whisky glass down hard on the table. "This is what I can't stand. Questions. Small talk. Having to think about how I am to people. I told you before, Fran, I just want to be left alone, but you never take no for an answer."

"I'm sorry."

"And stop saying sorry all the time. It's ridiculous. What are you always apologising for?"

"I don't know."

"This is exactly what I want to avoid, Fran. I don't want you to have expectations of me. Why can't you understand? What I have already is enough."

"I'm sorry," said Fran. "I want to go." She took her camel coat from the back of the chair and put it over her arm. "Stay where you are, Tom. Don't get up. I'll get a cab outside."

A month went by. She didn't try to approach him, even though he was the only person who had any chance of making her feel better about herself. He didn't speak, but at least the nods and half smiles he gave her seemed more apologetic than begrudging.

Another week passed and then Tom wasn't there at all. Fran went to the school office to ask after him. The Headmaster's secretary eyed her suspiciously and was prepared only to inform her that Mr Colman was signed off as a result of ill health. The news added worry to Fran's misery.

She sat in the staffroom at lunchtimes in her usual chair opposite the door, eating her sandwiches and drinking chicory coffee from the flask which rested on the chair next to her. Her colleagues did not seem to mind covering Tom's classes for his first few days away, and she enjoyed taking her turn, sitting at his desk viewing the world as he must view it. But when Tom's absence stretched into a second week, Fran had to listen to disgruntled voices in the staffroom speculating about what could be wrong with him.

"Have you ever seen him eat anything?" asked someone from the large circle which started and ended with Brian Curtis. "That can't be good for him."

"Haven't you heard?" said Curtis. "He survives on a special diet from the Highlands of Scotland. Liquids only." Everyone laughed.

"It's not really fair though, is it?" said Walter, drawing on his pipe. "I had to take his fifth-year French lot again this morning."

"I had them yesterday," said Bert Wilson, the longest serving member of staff. "Mind you, give the man his due. He's got the boys well drilled."

Walter took his pipe from his mouth. "I don't know how he does it. Never uses a cane or a slipper."

"Perhaps he's a conscientious objector," said Curtis to more laughter.

"Is Mr Colman French?" asked the new PE teacher. "The boys think he is."

"Ah, there's the question," said Curtis. "He's British now, but we've always reckoned he started off either Polish or Czech. Polish probably. They like their firewater." He turned towards Fran. "You must know, Miss Whitaker," he said across the room. "Is our Mr Colman Polish or Czech?"

Fran blushed. "I have no idea. You must ask *him*."

Curtis turned back to his circle. "We would if he'd come back and do some work."

"I don't think it's very fair to make fun of him when he's not here," said Fran. The circle went quiet.

"You're not sweet on him, are you, my dear?" said Curtis.

"Steady on, Brian."

"No, Walter. We had people in the army like him. Loners who relied on the rest of us to do all the work."

"Tom Colman works hard enough. He gets them through."

"But I know his type, Walter. They come here and show no gratitude for all we did for them."

"What in heaven's name did we do for Czechoslovakia?" asked Fran from her corner, more loudly than she intended.

"Ah, well that answers one question then," said Curtis looking around his circle for approval. He turned to Fran. "We fought to protect them, my dear. That's what we did."

"We didn't fight for Czechoslovakia. We handed them over to Hitler."

"Then that shows how little you understand, Miss Whitaker. Chamberlain was being very clever there. He was buying us time to rearm."

"That's nonsense. We gave them up because we hoped we wouldn't have to fight at all."

Curtis waved his arm as if he was dismissing her.

"You don't know what you're talking about, young lady. This country freed the whole of Europe from Fascism. Without us your friend Tom Colman's country wouldn't be free now."

"But it's not free."

"Of course it is. It's not up to you to judge people for wanting to live in a Communist system. And who's to say it's not better than ours anyway." He turned to his circle. "Aren't I always saying how we're at the bottom of the class system here? First the public schools, then the grammars, and then dumps like this for the working classes. And mugs like us have to pick up the pieces."

There were murmurs of approval. Fran collected her things and went over to the circle.

"You should be ashamed of yourself for some of the things you're saying, Mr Curtis. It seems to me you take against Tom Colman because he gets good behaviour from our boys without seeing the need to beat them, and because he doesn't choose to hang on your every word."

"You're a very silly woman, Miss Whitaker, who clearly doesn't know what she's talking about. You can go now."

Fran took a few steps towards the door before she stopped and turned back towards Brian Curtis.

"You know, you really are a disgrace, Mr Curtis. You sit there enjoying the freedom to give your opinions about all sorts of things you know nothing about. And if you dared to do the same thing in the country Tom Colman comes from, we wouldn't see you here tomorrow or ever again. You should leave the man in peace."

The next day was the start of the half-term holiday. Fran got Tom's address from Walter Sturridge and delayed her journey home to visit him. She rang the bell of the basement flat in Chadwell Street and heard Tom coughing as he made his way to the door.

"Fran. What do you want?"

He turned and shuffled back inside without waiting for an answer. Fran closed the door behind her and followed him into the sitting room. He was already slumped in an armchair.

"I've brought you some fruit and some medicine. It's for coughs and flu. I guessed that might be what's wrong with you."

"It's bronchitis. I've had it before."

She saw the cigarette burning in the ashtray on the arm of his chair and decided not to comment. "I've come to help you, that's all. Maybe cook you something or do some shopping. There's no ulterior motive like the cinema or anything."

"You'll be lucky."

She took her coat off without being asked and looked for somewhere to put it down. Every available space was covered in books and papers. Empty glasses and cups littered the floor and mantelpiece.

"I haven't been able to tidy. There's a hook in the hallway."

"I'm going to clean all this up and cook you something," she said when she came back in. She knew from the tone she used there would be no objection.

As she prepared a meal, she felt the frustration building up inside her. How could a person so capable and talented allow himself to sink this low? She put the cottage pie in the oven and went into the sitting room to clear things away. He sat in the chair, his head in a book, coughing and smoking and taking no notice of her. She returned to the kitchen and wiped away tears of exasperation. She heard him unscrewing the top from a bottle and from the kitchen doorway watched him pour whisky into a cup.

"It's eleven o'clock in the morning. What the hell do you think you're doing?" she said.

"I thought you said you came here with no ulterior motive."

"I did."

"Then stop sticking your nose into my life. I don't need you here."

"You do. You need me to stop you from killing yourself."

"Don't be so melodramatic. It sounds ridiculous."

"Don't you understand how you sound? How your life looks to other people?"

"Do you think I care how my life looks to other people?"

"You can't live like this." She spread her arms wide and looked around the room. "You're not brilliant or mysterious. You're just bitter and feeling sorry for yourself."

He didn't reply.

"I thought your books made you wise and clever, but you're just like my father. They're just a way of cutting yourself off from real life."

"That's a very interesting observation, Fran. So you're telling me I shouldn't look for wisdom or insights amongst the world's great writers and thinkers. I should look to the likes of Walter Sturridge and Bert Wilson and you instead."

"That's cruel."

"My God." He took a large drink of whisky. "If you knew what effort it takes to live and work every day. To bother with the triviality of other people's lives."

"People like me, you mean?"

"If you could feel the weight of it all."

She sat down on a chair at the small dining table.

"I'm not sure I can help you, Tom. I thought we might help one another. All I know is, you mustn't waste your life with all this bitterness. It's making you so unhappy. You have to see a future."

He closed his book and raised his head to look at her.

"Why won't you understand? I'm not interested in the future."

"Only the past?"

"Yes."

"But why?"

"Because that's where all the people are I loved and who loved me."

"So is no one ever allowed to love you again?"

"No. They would be intruding. Like you are now."

Fran stood up. "I'll leave the food for you in the oven," she said. "And I'll tidy up before I go. I said I would. Can I do anything else for you?"

"You could go to the shops."

"Alright. What shall I get?"

"Cigarettes and a half bottle of White Horse."

"You're a horrible man, Tom Colman. I thought you were so nice... do you really think I'd go and buy the things you're using to kill yourself?"

She went into the kitchen and closed the door behind her. She leant against the sink listening to him moving about. Then she heard the front door slam.

She planned to tidy up and clean before he came back. She cleared the room of dirty crockery and carried it all to the draining board. She picked up his papers from the floor and placed them on the table without rearranging them. The writing looked like heavily annotated poetry in a language she supposed was Czech. Such things were not going to interest her any more.

She replaced the books strewn on the floor in the few empty spaces left on the bookshelves. The shelves covered an entire wall and continued into an alcove next to the chimney breast. Most of his books had English or French titles, but directly on her eye level in the alcove she noticed two small, thin books with no title. She looked towards the door, took the first and opened it. It was full of more poems written in Tom's handwriting. They were all dated from 1934 to 1938 and written in Czech; all except the last one which was in English. It was dated October, 1938. She read the title, *'Treachery'*.

I love thee, Mother
I love thee, Father
I love thee, Czechoslovakia
My Trinity

She read the rest quickly, listening for his key in the door. *Land of Shakespeare... I learned your language fair... Thy words spew false across the page.* She knew she should not look at any more but she wanted to understand. She put the book back and took the second. It too was full of poems written in Czech. No, there was one in French. It had no date, only a title, *Anna*.

Mes lèvres touchent ton nom
An-na, ils dansent
An-na, ces deux syllabes
Ma vie, ma joie

She couldn't read on. She understood just enough to know it was something too personal. She flicked through the remaining pages intending then to return the book to its place. At the end were two loose sheets of paper. One in French, the other in English. She read the title, '*For Eva*'.

Sit on your horse, I'll rock you
Turn the page, I'll read to you

She came to the last line.

Together we'll know where

She heard his key in the door. She put the book back on the shelf and quickly wiped her eyes. She knew Tom was looking at her from the door but she could not turn round.

"I knew I'd upset you, Fran. I'm really sorry. I have no right to get so spiteful. I've brought you a peace offering. It's only a box of chocolates. I'll put them on the table."

She could not face him.

"You've made a real difference here, Fran. I really am sorry. Won't you turn round?"

"I can't."

"I understand. Sometimes I can't help myself. I'm alright most of the time. It's this time of year..."

"I think I may have done something terrible."

"What? You're alright, aren't you?"

"Yes. I haven't done anything to myself. I've done it to you." She turned around. "I was tidying your books. I looked at your poems."

"Really?"

"I'm sorry. I needed to understand."

"But you can't read them."

"Who are Anna and Eva?"

He took off his scarf, folded it and placed it on the table.

"They are my wife and child."

"Where are they?"

"They're with me. Safe."

"Tom, I know I did a bad thing looking at your personal things. But I think it could turn out to be a good thing if you let it. Tell me about them."

Tom sat down at the table. He lit a cigarette. "Get me a drink, Fran."

"No. Tell me what happened to Anna and Eva." She watched as he exhaled the smoke. He stared down at the ashtray.

"I loved them both every day of their lives. I still do. I keep them safe with me."

"But you're not keeping them safe, Tom. Because you're killing yourself. Tell me about them."

"If I tell you, it becomes real again."

"No, it doesn't. The only thing that stays real is your love for them and their love for you. If you let me help you, you can keep that alive for a long time. I won't ask anything from you, and I'll never tell another soul."

He looked up at her.

"Anna and Eva died fourteen years ago this week."

"Yes."

"Anna was Jewish."

"Yes."

"They died in the camps, Fran. I couldn't save them."

Chapter Thirty-Two

April 9th, 1968

Tom reached out his hand. Fran took it, and he pulled her up the last few steps. She flopped down next to him on the rocky outcrop which capped Fern Tor.

"We've been very lucky with the weather again," she said, catching her breath. "Just look at this. It's got to be one of my favourite views."

"Mine too."

They looked down to Lynmouth and the Bristol Channel. Fran turned and shielded her eyes to gaze back over the moor towards the Brendon Valley.

"I don't think I can ever remember rain on our first day."

"I can. One year we couldn't leave the hotel 'til the Wednesday."

"I think you're getting a Devon accent, Tom Colman."

"It's not surprising. The number of times you drag me down here."

"You're not complaining, are you?"

"No. I'm not complaining. How could I complain after all you've done for me?"

He helped her off with her rucksack and put it down on the ground between them.

"What have I done for you, Tom?"

"You're not fishing for compliments, are you?"

"No. I really would like to know. You never tell me."

"I don't need to tell you. It's obvious."

"Not to me it isn't."

She watched a boat coming into view around the headland. She wondered if Tom was going to answer her question and then felt him squeeze her hand. "You've been a wonderful friend, Fran. Always there. Constant."

"Unthreatening, you mean. Always letting you stay exactly as you are."

He looked at her and she smiled back at him to lighten the weight of her words.

"My, Fran Whitaker, you have become wise. What's all this about?"

"Nothing really. I just wish you would come on the trip with us next week, that's all."

"Oh no, not that again, Fran." He let go of her hand. "I've explained to you why I can't go back there."

"I've checked. Montpellier is only an hour on the train from Clermont L'Hérault and the village. It would help you move on."

"I've told you. I don't need to move on. I'm happy the way things are."

"You're content. I don't think you're happy."

"I could say the same about you."

"What do you mean by that?"

"You've stayed content with our friendship over the years, instead of finding real happiness with someone. I've told you often enough you should."

"Now you're trying to upset me."

"I would never want to upset you."

"Then come with me to Montpellier. It makes no sense anyway, the most experienced French teacher in the school not taking part in the exchange."

He bent forward and looked up at her, smiling.

"Is this Miss Whitaker, the Deputy Headmistress, speaking now?"

"No, it's your friend, Francesca, as well you know."

He put his hand on her shoulder. "Please can we change the subject, Fran?"

"You're so stubborn. You're always the same."

Fran reached down to open her rucksack and took out a flask and two enamel mugs. Tom moved away as she placed them on the rock between them and poured the coffee.

"You know, Tom Colman, I don't want you to think I've never had romance in my life. I was engaged once."

"I didn't know that."

"You wouldn't. It was before I came to Islington. His name was Stephen. You helped me get over all that."

"Did I?"

"Not at first. But when you finally let me into your life."

"Really?"

"Yes. When you let me help you. And when you told me I was clever. No one had ever said that to me before."

"You are clever, Fran. And wise."

"You gave me so much confidence. I would never have got promotion without you."

"Rubbish. You're where you are because you deserve it."

"But I would never have applied without you."

"Of course you would."

Fran smiled to herself. He always had such belief in her. And he had such self-belief. Perhaps that's what made him appear so obstinate sometimes. The certainty he felt about everything. About her. About the world. And especially about Anna. He hardly ever spoke her name, but she and Eva were always there. Fran could feel them around him even now as they sat in this beautiful place. She welcomed them.

"Do you want to know what else you've given me?" she said. "Because I know you're never going to ask."

"Yes, of course," Tom replied, but she wasn't sure if he had really heard the question.

"Honesty."

"What about it?"

"It's what you've given me. You've always been honest with me. You've always given me the chance to make my own choices."

"I hope so."

"Without that I couldn't have settled just for our friendship. But I'm glad I have."

"Are you, Fran?"

She shook the last drops from her mug onto the floor. "Yes, because I know what love is. And I don't regret not having children. Not when I see the state the world's in."

"What's making you say all this?"

"I don't know. Sitting here away from it all. Everything's so peaceful. The rest of the world seems so crazy somehow. The war in Vietnam, and all the protests everywhere. And what they've done to poor Martin Luther King."

"I know. He was a brave man."

"Why is the rest of the world so ugly, Tom? Why can't people just be happy?"

"What happened to Luther King will be the work of a madman, Fran. But the protests and sit-ins aren't necessarily a bad thing. As long as they're done peacefully."

"I feel there's real change coming over our world. Young people today are so different. They're never happy. They question everything."

"I think that's good."

"How can you say that when they're always so anti everything?"

"I just think it's not an easy world for young people to understand, Fran."

"The world's not so different from when we were young."

"It is. If you think about it, all our boys and even some of the staff now were born after the war. They're not naïve like we were."

"Speak for yourself."

"I do. My childhood was full of innocence. I didn't grow up with images of the Holocaust and mushroom clouds. But kids today see war on the television and all the hatred between East and West, and they're scared. They don't trust one side or the other, and they're searching for something to believe in. The trouble is they're looking in the wrong place."

"What do you mean?"

"Well, in the past people looking for a better society always looked to Russia and the great socialist experiment. People like your father."

"Please, Tom. I was enjoying myself."

"But even diehards like him can't defend thugs like Stalin and Brezhnev anymore."

"I'm sure my father can."

"Well, the young can't. So they look for new revolutionary heroes and turn to the likes of Che Guevara and Ho Chi Minh. They parade their pictures next to the red flag and sing the Internationale, while at the same time demanding freedom from oppression. They just don't see the joke."

"There was a time when I wouldn't have seen it either."

"They'll learn eventually that any politician who puts socialism or nationalism before all else is going to lead them to disaster."

"Why do you defend the protests then?"

"Because it's part of democracy. But what we need to teach our young people is that democracy itself should be their only goal. It's not a means to an end. It is the end itself."

"But we do teach them that."

"We try. But they still think something is missing from our world, when all we really need is the freedom to live life with the people we love." She saw a familiar look appear on his face. "Free to write and think. Free to talk, read, worship. Totally unmolested by the state. What I would have given just to be allowed to do that in my life. But men with power always want to make it impossible, and people don't appreciate it until it's taken from them."

Fran shuffled closer to him and linked his arm. "Don't upset yourself. Have you noticed the paddle steamer making its way up the Bristol Channel?"

"I've been watching it for the last ten minutes. It'll have come from Ilfracombe, going across to South Wales."

"Barry."

"That's a strange name for a paddle steamer."

Fran pushed him and stood up. "Come on, funny man. Let's head back for some lunch."

Fran followed him down the worn path which led to the gorge carrying the River Lyn to the sea. He was walking purposefully, as if getting back to the hotel had become a task to be completed as efficiently as possible. Fran was going to find it difficult to have the conversation she wanted unless he slowed down.

"Ease up, will you, Tom?" she called out to him. "We're not in any hurry."

He stopped and waited for her.

"You're turning this into a forced march," she said, as she approached him.

"Sorry, Fran. I was in a world of my own. I hadn't realised."

They carried on walking together at a slower pace. After a few minutes Fran broke the silence.

"I was thinking, Tom. You must be very pleased about what's happening in Czechoslovakia now."

"I'm not sure yet, Fran. I'm withholding judgement."

"But you must be pleased about Dubček's Action Programme. What does he call it? 'Socialism with a Human Face.'"

"My, you have been doing your homework."

"No, there was an article in The Times about it on Saturday. He's abolished censorship and given complete freedom to the press."

"I know. I read it."

"You haven't mentioned it to me."

"I'm not that interested."

"But he even says he wants to allow other political parties."

"I know. I said I read it."

"I thought you'd be pleased."

"Alexander Dubček is still a Communist, Fran. He's the Party First Secretary. You know what I think about Communists."

"But isn't he different? Isn't that what the Prague Spring is all about?"

Tom stopped to face her. "It's simple for me, Fran. I've learned not to trust any Communist. The only reason Dubček is loosening the reins now is because the country's economy is in such a mess, and the Party's afraid of people's anger. I'm pretty sure he hasn't suddenly converted to democracy."

"That's not what it said in The Times."

"Fran, the Communists took one of the richest industrial nations in the world and strangled the life out of it, with their pathetic Five-Year Plans and their obsession with controlling every part of people's lives. I can't see how Dubček or any other Communist is going to change that."

He turned and carried on walking.

"Lordy be, Tom, you can be such a cynic sometimes. You could at least give the man a chance."

"I said I was withholding judgement."

"It doesn't sound like it."

"Even if Dubček is Czechoslovakia's messiah, Fran, there's one simple word that guarantees he won't be allowed to succeed."

"What do you mean, one word? What word?"

"Russia."

"No. The whole world is on your country's side. Russia can't do anything with the whole world watching."

She heard Tom laughing. "I guarantee you, Fran, there will never be a democracy in the Soviet bloc."

"Then Czechoslovakia might have to leave it."

He stopped again and Fran walked up to him.

"You have to understand something, Fran. For Russia this isn't really about Communism and democracy at all."

"Surely it is."

"No, it's about controlling the Slavs and keeping the Germans in check. That's all the Russians have ever wanted, and since the war they've had both for the first time ever. And they'll never allow anyone to challenge it. Certainly not a few million Czechs and Slovaks."

"So all your countrymen are holding out these hopes for nothing?"

"I'm afraid so. I would love to be wrong, but I'm pretty damn sure I'm not."

"Why don't you go there and find out for yourself?"

"Don't be ridiculous."

"It's not ridiculous. Anyone can go to Czechoslovakia now. The article said Dubček has allowed complete freedom of movement. It said Prague's full of hippies, and people are free to do and say whatever they like. Go back. Be part of it."

"What are you doing? Are you trying to get rid of me?"

"You know better than that. I just want you to be happy."

"I've told you. I am happy."

"No, you're not. This is your chance. Go back, and find those happy memories you had with Anna. Move forward. You could even start writing again."

"Stop this, Fran."

"No, Tom, I won't stop it. You say how you want to preserve Anna's memory, but you won't go to France or even to your own country where she existed for real. I don't want to watch you drifting into old age only half alive. You must confront all this, or your life will just peter out."

"I thought we got past all this years ago."

"We did, but what's happening in your country now seems such a wonderful opportunity for you."

"Why the hell can't you just leave things alone?"

"Because unlike you the world moves on, Tom Colman. But I'll leave it alone if you want. I'll see you back at the hotel."

Tomáš watched her walk down the path as it steepened towards the gorge. He was anxious not to lose sight of her and followed at a distance. He couldn't be angry with her, or even impatient. Not when she had always been so patient with him.

But go back? Was she mad? Go back to the people who let in the Communists? Czechoslovaks who turned on the Jews in their own party, and killed Jan Masaryk and anyone else who opposed them. There was so much she didn't understand.

But how could she? How could anyone understand? Even he couldn't understand how his country could submit in the way it had. The only country in the whole Soviet bloc that had once been a democracy. And what a democracy it had been, so strong and healthy. The people had understood instinctively what it meant, and it had suited them. And it suited Prague

Fran was still too far ahead of him. He walked faster to keep sight of her. What had she said? 'Prague is full of hippies, and people are free to do and say whatever they like.' If that was true, it must be something like the Prague he knew before the war. Except the shops then had been full of beautiful things his country produced and sent all over the world. His father had been so proud to show him. What did he used to say?

"To be born a Czechoslovak, Tomášek, is the greatest gift you will ever have."

He smiled at the thought of his father's optimism. He paused and looked at the river hurrying over the rocks down to the sea.

Was it possible? Was it just possible that his country's people still had something of Masaryk in them? Could something of his spirit have survived the Nazis and the Communists? His father would think so. He had such faith.

But no, it wasn't possible. And even if it were, Fran was wrong about Anna and Prague. She wasn't in Prague. She was with him. Wherever he was, she was. Wherever he was...

He walked on again, quickening his step.

"Fran, wait," he called out. She stopped and he ran towards her.

"What is it?" she said, as he caught up with her.

"Fran, I will come to France with you next week. Then I'm going back."

Chapter Thirty-Three

April 17th, 1968

Tomáš stepped down onto the single platform and looked around. The rendered walls were painted in the same light yellow-brown, and the doors and windows were the same municipal light-turquoise. The lack of change at the station at Clermont L'Hérault came as a shock. Only the large marshalling yard was different; it was quieter than it had been back then; there was little activity now and no steam.

He had thirty minutes to kill before the connecting train to Castiran arrived from Lodève. He walked through the ticket hall and looked up the *Allée Roger Salengro*. He had forgotten it was a Wednesday. The avenue was lined with stalls under the horse-chestnut trees. It was the morning of the weekly market from which Milan never returned.

He went back to the station and waited. He resisted the craving for a cigarette and the even greater temptation to return to Fran in Montpellier. He boarded the train to Castiran at the last moment. Within minutes he was passing through the vineyards on the plain of Languedoc below the Montagnes Noires. The train stopped briefly at Castiran's station, and he got out.

The small station building stood outside the village amid the same ocean of vines, which grew up to its walls and threatened its single track. He showed the stationmaster his ticket, and walked up the lane leading to the village a kilometre away. Soon he could see the clock tower of Father Benoît's church at the top of the slight incline. He walked past the cemetery where Milan lay, and reached the first property at the bottom of the Rue Jean Jaurès. He stopped at the open gates, and through the overgrown trees and bushes caught a glimpse of the Château de Monteux.

He trod lightly up the driveway until he reached the courtyard. It was deserted. The winery, the château and the row of five houses had been left to fall into disrepair. The old horse-drawn carts lay piled up in one corner. Tall weeds grew everywhere through the gravel, and some of the shutters hung from single hinges. He looked at the house where he and Anna had lived. The hopeless state of its roof and windows told him the time was past. So much time. So much decay. He should not have brought her back to this.

"What's your business, monsieur?" someone called out to him.

Tomáš turned to see a young man in baggy trousers and a stained collarless shirt standing at the door of the winery, wiping his hands with an oily cloth.

"Excuse me, monsieur. I didn't think anyone was still working here."

"Well I am. What do you want?"

"I used to work here myself years ago. When it was owned by the family Musil."

"Never heard of them."

"Then it was taken over by Arnaud Bousquet."

"Never heard of him either. This is all owned by the municipality. I look after it for them."

"I thought I would come back and take a look at the old place. I'm sorry if I disturbed you."

"Best thing you can do is ask at the mairie. There's not much happens in Castiran that Henri doesn't know about."

"Do you mean Henri Fauchery?"

"Yes, that's him. He's been there for years. He'll be able to put you right."

"Thankyou, monsieur. I'll do as you suggest."

Tomáš strode back down the driveway, the emptiness and sadness replaced. He marched up the narrow backstreets, which were the quickest way to the Place du Peyrou, past the water troughs that Eva used to love playing in. Nothing here had changed. The same sunless grey houses and passageways which only Anna could light up. He paused at the back of the Bar de la Poste. The window was open. The window where Gaston Daguenet had appeared on the morning of their arrest. He heard laughter and the sound of someone playing bagatelle. It was still the village bar.

He stepped out into the sunlight, crossed the square towards the mairie and glimpsed the blue sign with white lettering on the wall. A new name. *Place de la Libération*. A small man with thinning black hair stood up at the counter as Tomáš entered the mairie. The man looked out of the window over Tomáš's shoulder, as he waited for him to speak.

"Monsieur Fauchery?"

"Yes."

"I've come from the Château de Monteux. A young man there said you might be able to help me."

"How, monsieur?"

"I'm looking for someone who used to live there. Arnaud Bousquet."

Fauchery looked at Tomáš for the first time. "You're going back a bit, monsieur. That place hasn't been called a château for years. The village owns it now. It's part of the coopérative."

"And Bousquet?"

"Are you a tourist?"

"I'm an academic. I'm doing research into the German occupation of the Hérault Département during the war."

"Arnaud Bousquet was killed before the Germans occupied this part of France."

"Killed?"

"Yes. He was murdered at the château, as it was then. Had his throat cut in his own bed."

"Who was responsible?"

"No one ever found out. But Bousquet upset a lot of people here in those days. We assumed it was our local maquis."

"I see. Were any other civilians killed during the war, or taken away?"

"Only the priest."

"Father Benoît?"

"You've seen the plaque in the church, have you?"

"No, not yet. But I do a lot of research before I visit a new town or village. I knew his name."

"Our priest was a very brave man. He kept speaking out from the pulpit, even though the Germans warned him to stop. You should see the plaque, monsieur. He died in Buchenwald concentration camp. We're all very proud of him here."

"When did he die?"

"February, 1944."

"And when was he arrested?"

"I'm not sure of the exact date."

"What did he speak out about? Was it the treatment of the Jews? Or perhaps the internment camp at Agde?"

"I'm not sure, monsieur. I don't remember every detail."

"Were Jews taken from the village by the Vichy authorities?"

"Jews? No. Not from here."

"You worked for Vichy, so you can confirm that, can you?"

"All functionaries worked for Vichy. It was the legal government back then." Fauchery looked at his watch and stepped away from the counter. "Now, I have a lot of work to do, monsieur. I don't want to be rude but I must get on."

"I understand, Monsieur Fauchery. But there is one more person I'm interested in tracing. His name is Émile Durand."

Fauchery looked down at the floor and rubbed his right hand over the back of his neck.

"He was a local gendarme during the war," prompted Tomáš

"Durand? Oh yes. I remember him now. But he wasn't here long. I think he moved to Paris."

"You don't remember me, do you, Henri?"

Fauchery looked up, his hand still on the back of his neck.

"September 16th 1941. I came in here with my wife and child, and you rang a little bell on that counter. Do you remember? It was the signal for Bousquet to appear with Durand and another Fascist gendarme from that room."

Fauchery took a step back.

"I know who you are now. You're that Czech Kovařík."

"Oh, so you do remember Jews being arrested here, do you?"

"You weren't Jewish. You were a saboteur. That's what Bousquet said. You could have been shot. Bousquet only interned you instead."

"Oh yes. He only interned us."

"I remember Bousquet saying the little girl didn't have to go. But you insisted."

"What are you saying? That it was my fault my daughter was sent to die by you Vichy bastards."

"But you can't blame me for that. I didn't decide anything about her, or you, or your wife. I just happened to be working here at the time. Like I do now. I didn't make any of the regulations then, and I still don't."

"You're a pathetic little weasel, Fauchery. I used to drink with you in Daguenet's bar over there. Either of you could have warned me that morning."

Tomáš stepped towards the gap at the side of the counter. Fauchery backed further away.

"But you chose not to warn me, didn't you, Fauchery? And for that you and Daguenet both have my family's blood on your hands. I'm going over to his bar now to tell the cowardly bastard the same thing."

Tomáš stopped at the door. "I'll tell you something, Fauchery. If I thought for a second you were as guilty as Bousquet or Durand, I would come round that counter right now and choke the life out of you."

Tomáš walked up the steps to the Bar de la Poste. There was a billiard table by the door now and a juke box, but the chairs and tables looked the same, and so did the customers. Old men played cards and a few younger ones stood at the zinc bar. Tomáš joined them and ordered a small beer.

"Is Gaston Daguenet still around?" he asked the young man drawing his drink.

"Father," the young man said without looking up from the glass he was filling. "Someone here for you."

Tomáš turned to see who responded. An old man in the far corner by the window raised his head slowly and looked towards his son. His head nodded constantly as he waited for more information. Surely this could not be the same Gaston Daguenet.

"This gentleman is asking after you, Father."

Tomáš thanked the barman and took his drink over to Daguenet's table. The frail old man looked up at him. The round, ruddy face had become thin and sallow, and his hair had thinned too and turned grey.

"Do you remember me, Gaston?" Tomáš put his beer on the table and sat down opposite him. "I'm a ghost from your past."

Gaston studied him and smiled as if he were being set a friendly riddle. "I'm sorry, monsieur..."

"Your wife had coffee ready for us. And you promised my daughter a pain au chocolat."

The head stopped nodding and Gaston's eyes turned liquid. "Thomas with the beautiful wife," he muttered. "Is it really you?"

"Yes, Gaston. It is."

"Thank God you're well. I'm so happy to see you. Are your wife and child here with you?"

"No, Gaston. They only survived for seventeen months after you spoke to them from that window."

The old man took a handkerchief from his sleeve and wiped his eyes.

"Are you alright, Father?" his son called out.

Gaston raised his hand to wave away any concern. "I'm so sorry, Thomas," he said. "I've thought about your little family so often. And poor Monsieur Musil."

"Have you, Gaston?"

"Of course. They were terrible times. We all made so many mistakes. I ask no forgiveness."

"I have none to give you."

"I saw the gendarmes go in with Bousquet. I knew they were after someone. I had no idea it might be you."

"You knew, Gaston. That's why you went back inside."

"I couldn't be sure."

"You should have warned us. I might have been able to save them."

"Why say such things? What good does it do any of us now?"

"What good? Haven't you people learned anything? Is there no one in this place trying to put things right?"

"How can we put it right? Life must move on, Thomas."

"Life hasn't moved on for the thousands Vichy murdered."

"But what can any of us do about that now?"

"You astound me, Gaston. Has no one in the village thought of restoring the château, and returning it to the Monteux family? Or to the Musils? Does anyone ask why Fauchery is still working in your mayor's office after all he did? Of course you don't expect forgiveness. None of you think you did anything wrong."

"They were difficult times, Thomas."

"You make me sick, Gaston. You act as if you're sorry. You behave like a broken man, but you take no responsibility."

"I am sorry. I watched you and your family being taken away across that square. Every morning I have to wake up and look out at it."

"That's not remorse, Gaston. That's self-pity. I know the difference."

"Why have you come back here, Thomas? Just to accuse us?"

"Our daughter was born here. We had happy times here with the Musils. I hoped to recall some of them. And I needed to confront the bad memories."

"And have you?"

"Far more than you French have." Tomáš pushed back his chair. "I see no hope for you people, Gaston. But I'll tell you when you will be ready for forgiveness. When you add another plaque to the one commemorating Father Benoît. You should put it on the wall of the mairie next to the new name you've given the square. It should commemorate the people who came to this part of France in hope, and were murdered by you and your government."

Tomáš stood up. "I'll be on my way now. I shall leave you as I found you." He drank the last of his beer. "But at least I've discovered one good thing this morning. Arnaud Bousquet got the punishment he deserved. I only wish the same could be said of that swine Durand."

Gaston puffed his cheeks. "I agree with you there. He's still a nasty piece of work."

Tomáš sat down again. "What do you mean 'still'?"

"Durand's still around."

"Where?"

"Here in the village. In that white house next to the old château. Just off the rue Jean Jaurès."

* * *

Tomáš walked back past the Château de Monteux. He paused at the corner of the Résidence Mazérand, a cul-de-sac of modern, single-storey villas, and studied the first property on the corner. He took several deep breaths and approached the front gate. It was locked. He rang the bell. The speaker on the gatepost crackled.

"Is that you, Kovařík?"

"It is."

There was a buzz and the gate clicked open. Tomáš walked up the gravel path between neat beds of Mediterranean plants. He smelled rosemary and lavender. As he reached the tiled steps leading up to a veranda, the front door opened. A tall, upright man wearing smart cotton trousers and a short-sleeved white shirt appeared. He stood with one hand behind his back.

"I suppose Fauchery tipped you off," said Tomáš.

"Of course."

"You were the last person I expected to find back here, Durand." Tomáš put his foot on the first step. "I hoped to be told you were dead."

"You're a surprise too, Kovařík. I was sure you died in the camp." Durand retreated into the hallway as Tomáš approached. "You can come in and sit down in there on the sofa, but I warn you, I've got my service pistol here."

"Always the hero, weren't you, Durand?"

Tomáš went into the living room. He crossed the room and sat down on the sofa in the far corner. Durand stood by the open double doors and put his MAB gendarme's pistol on top of a low bookcase.

"Why have you come here?"

"I didn't come to Castiran to see you, Durand. But once I heard you were here, I had no choice. I need to know what you did to my family. Then I'm going to do my best to kill you."

Durand picked up the pistol. "You're crazy. I didn't do anything to your family. I tried to save them."

"Stop your bloody lies, you bastard. You took them to Drancy. I know what people went through there. And you took them knowing I had my own plan to save them."

"Any plan you had would never have worked, Kovařík."

"They died in Auschwitz, you mad bastard. How well do you think your plan worked?"

"I did all I could for them. I got them food. I kept them together. I got them medicine."

"Why? Were they ill?"

"Anna was very anaemic. Eva had an ulcer on her right eye, but the medicine I got for them helped."

Tomáš stood up and walked to a window.

"Sit down, Kovařík."

"Fuck you, Durand. You took them. You tricked us. Even now when they've been gone so long..." Tomáš sat down again and put his head in his hands. "...I can't bear to think of them suffering. You're going to have to shoot me, Durand. I can't go over all this again and let you live."

"Listen, Kovařík. I did all I could for them. Believe me, they were alright in Drancy. I made sure of that. We gendarmes didn't know where people were being sent. How could anyone imagine that?"

"My God, you people never stop, do you?" Tomáš looked up at him. "I've seen the transport lists with their names on it, you bastard fool. The list was drawn up by the French. It had Auschwitz as the destination."

"We knew the name, but we didn't know what was happening there. Who could imagine anything like that? The people at the very top may have known, but we didn't. I risked my life to help people in Drancy."

"The same old excuses. You persuade yourself you're innocent... you even think you're a damned hero... when Auschwitz could never have happened without you, and thousands like you, all doing your little bit."

"Didn't you do your little bit? You worked with Bousquet to supply the German army."

"Very clever, but pathetic. I didn't round up women and children and stand guard over them until their murder could be arranged. I made wine, Durand, for God's sake. Can't you see the difference?"

"All I know is, I did all I could to help those people. If we'd refused to guard them, how do you think the Germans would have treated them?"

"Just more excuses." Tomáš bent forward, his forearms resting on his thighs, his fists clenched. "Nothing any of you says changes the truth. Vichy France was unoccupied, but still you French sent Jews to the gas chambers. You were the only people to do that."

"Damn you, Kovařík. I was decorated for what I did in the war. I was badly wounded during the liberation of Paris. They made me chief of police in Clermont for what I did. I served this district for fourteen years."

"That only confirms what I suspected. France is still full of Fascists bastards like you in positions of power."

"You should shut your mouth. I will shoot you, you know. I have the right. You threatened Fauchery and you've threatened me."

"I've already said you'll have to shoot me. Otherwise people are going to find out what you did to my wife and child, and how you planned to have me murdered. You don't deny that last bit, do you?"

"I wanted you out of the way. I don't deny that. But I never told anyone to kill you."

"Damned liar. I'll make sure people learn the truth about you."

"I'm getting tired of you, Kovařík." Durand slammed the gun down on the bookcase. He was breathing heavily and looked down at the floor as he spoke.

"I think there's something you need to know, Kovařík. I would never have hurt Anna or Eva. I loved Anna. All I wanted was to help her. To save her. I just wanted you out of the way. But I'll tell you something you will like." His eyes filled with tears. "Whatever I did for her made no difference. She only ever wanted you. Even when we were loving, I could feel she only ever wanted you."

Tomáš leapt to his feet. "What did you say?" he roared. Durand looked up to see him charging across the room. Durand reached for the pistol on the bookcase and grabbed it just as Tomáš crashed into him. They fell together through the doorway onto the floor of the hallway. Tomáš grabbed Durand's wrist as the Frenchman tried to level the pistol towards him. With the palm of his right hand Tomáš hit Durand under the chin. His head cracked against the tiled floor, his body went limp and he began to moan.

"You raped her. You raped her," Tomáš screamed at him. He prised open Durand's fingers and took the gun. Durand opened his eyes and Tomáš spat into them. He put the gun to Durand's temple and tried to pull the trigger. It wouldn't move. He searched for the safety catch.

"No, no, please... I didn't rape her... I didn't... please... we lived together... as man and wife. I looked after them."

Tomáš found the catch.

"I looked after Anna... and Eva..."

He put the gun to Durand's temple.

"...and your son. I looked after your son."

Tomáš's hand froze around the gun. "What did you say?" he screamed.

"You had a son... please... it's true. Anna was pregnant when she left Agde."

"You bastard, Durand. What pathetic game are you playing now?"

Tomáš's hand shook as he pressed the end of the gun as hard as he could into Durand's forehead.

"I'm not playing. It's true... please... you have a son." Durand struggled to turn his head away. He closed his eyes. "That last night in Agde... you must remember. I arranged for you and Anna to be together. You gave her a child."

Tomáš released the pressure for a second, then stabbed the muzzle into Durand's face.

"You pathetic bastard. You can't even work that out right. She went to Auschwitz six months later. There was no time for a child. Why don't you just accept you're going to die?"

"But she wasn't on the transport." Durand started to sob. "Please stop... please. I wrote down their names... but it wasn't them on the train. You have a son. You have a son."

"Don't lie to me, Durand. I warn you. Don't lie to me any more."

"I won't. I won't. I'll tell you the truth, but you mustn't kill me."

Tomáš got up and stood over him.

"I'll spare you..." He gulped in air. "...only if I *know* you're telling me the truth."

Durand curled up on his side, with his back to Tomáš, sobbing.

"I got them out of Drancy. I told Anna you were dead. I thought you were. We lived in Paris. I wanted them to stay. But she left me."

"What the hell are you saying? What happened to them, man? For God's sake tell me."

"I made sure they were alright. They're alive, Kovařík. They send me Christmas cards."

Tomáš felt all strength leave his body. He slumped to the floor.

"Don't let this be a lie, Durand," he mumbled. "For God's sake don't let this be a lie. Alive? Where are they?"

"It's not a lie. I'll show you the cards... and the photographs. All three of them are alive. They're in Prague."

Chapter Thirty-Four

April 23rd – April 30th, 1968

"Doctor Fialová, there's a telephone call for you in the administrator's office. She's not very happy about it."

Eva thanked the nurse, put down her knife and fork, and picked up her spectacles from the table. She was exhausted, and now she would not have time to eat her lunch. She left the canteen and checked her watch as she walked down the corridor. She had been on duty since five o'clock that morning and still had three more hours of her shift in front of her.

The administrator passed her the telephone, but did not release it into her hand until she was sure Eva had registered her disapproving look.

"I think it's your mother, Doktor Fialová. I must insist you remind her of our rules regarding personal calls. And don't block the line for too long." Eva gave her a weary smile. It was the first time her mother had ever contacted her at work. Her first thought was of Lenka.

"Hello, Máma. Is everything alright?"

"Yes, darling. I need to talk to you."

"Where are you phoning from?"

"From the block supervisor's office. I told him it was an emergency."

"It's not Lenka, is it?"

"No, she's at the nursery. I'll collect her later. But listen, Eva. I've had the most incredible news. You're not going to believe it..."

The line went quiet.

"Are you still there, Máma?"

"Yes, darling..."

Eva could hear her mother crying. It hardly ever happened. Her mother was able to cope with anything. But she always reached for Eva when she faced great changes in her life. When they left Uncle Émile's. When Opa died. And the first night in Prague, when she was eleven and Lukáš eight, and the three of them knew no one. Those were the times when Máma took her into her bed and held on to her all night. But she hardly ever cried.

"Máma, calm down. You're worrying me. Tell me what's happened."

"I came home for lunch, Eva, and found a letter. It's from your father..."

The line went quiet again.

"You're not making sense, Máma. Breathe steadily. What do you mean 'my father'?"

"Your father. Tomáš. He's alive... he's been living in England all these years. Can you please come home, darling? I need to show you."

Eva turned to look at the administrator and knew there was no chance of that.

"I'll be home as soon as I can. Will you be able to collect Lenka?"

"Yes, yes, of course. He found Uncle Émile in France and got our address. I recognise his handwriting. It is him. It's a miracle."

"Just stay calm, Máma, and don't get your hopes up too much. How can it be him? You have his death certificate."

"It is Tomáš, Eva. He's applied for a visa. He's coming to Prague."

The administrator reached out across the desk, her fingers beckoning for the receiver.

"I have to go now, Máma. I'll be home as soon as I can. Don't forget Lenka."

She handed the telephone to the administrator, who returned it to its proper place.

"I'm surprised your family has time for such matters," she said, "when there are so many important things to be done."

Anna climbed the stairs of her apartment block in Smíchov, south of the Malá Strana. Her hands shook as she unlocked the door of her one-bedroom apartment on the third floor. She sat on the couch, which had so often doubled as her bed over the past seventeen years, and read the letter for the fourth time, still unable to believe it could be true. The sight of his handwriting made her look again at his name at the end. *'From your adoring husband Tomáš'*. She kissed the paper and stood up to release her joy. It was a miracle. Tomáš was alive and would be with her within days.

She caught sight of herself in the mirror on the wall above the electric heater and stepped forward to confront the image. She leaned closer and tried to smooth the skin under her eyes and on her neck. She took the clips from her hair and let it fall. It hung unevenly, the ends split and dry. Cheap dye had thinned it over the years and taken its lustre. She held her hands up in front of her face. The skin was thick and cracked from all the detergents she had to use in her cleaning work. None of it mattered. Nothing else mattered. Her Tomáš was alive.

She turned to the side, pulled her hair tight above her head and smoothed her other hand down her body. Her breasts were firm and she had put on very little weight. "Thank God for the food shortages," she said, and laughed at herself in the mirror.

She breathed deeply and fought to relax. She sat down again to concentrate on every detail of the letter. He had searched for her everywhere. And he had searched for Ernst too. Poor Tomáš. If only he could have written to Otto in Palestine, as she had done to find her father. The poor, poor man. Living half his life thinking she and Eva had died in that terrible way.

How could Émile have deceived her so cruelly? Showing her the newspaper report of the uprising in the camp, and offering comfort to her as he unfolded Tomáš's death certificate. She had felt so grateful to him over all these years. How could he have maintained the deception for so long? She had even made Eva and Lukáš send drawings to him on his birthday. But he had saved their lives. He had taken such risks for them. She wondered if he had told Tomáš all the details of their relationship. It could not matter now. It must not matter. She returned to the letter

'I have not remarried, darling Anna, or looked for anyone else, because there is no one who could ever replace you. I have always kept you with me.' She put the paper to her cheek, closed her eyes, and rocked gently back and forth. He had become a teacher like his father and was now a British citizen. She imagined him in a smart suit, mature and handsome with slightly greying hair, and she felt her cheeks flush. But he would be accustomed to such luxury in England, and used to seeing such refined women. It did not matter. She would borrow some of the nice clothes from her friend, Hana, and get Eva to do something with her hair.

Every word was written by the Tomáš she knew. Nothing about him had changed. He wrote of his love for Eva and Lukáš and his pride in them, without even knowing how well placed such confidence was. At least there was no risk of disappointment for him there. And he wrote of his passion for her. He had breathed it into the paper in the way he was always able to do. His love and desire for her had never changed. He had lived his life for her and only now, as he waited to see and to touch her again, had his love become too much to bear.

Anna put the letter down on the couch next to her and leaned forward with her head in her hands. Would he be shocked to see what had become of his young, beautiful wife? Surely he would understand that the innocent girl, so reckless and sure of the world, had gone forever. How could all the fear and hardship not have changed her? Paris had been the worst. Depending so much on Émile. The constant need to keep him happy to ensure he protected the children. Pretending to love him. It had been worse even than Dresden. At least with the Russian soldiers there had been no pretence; it was only ever a transaction. And then the years here, where the Party constantly demanded individual sacrifice, and the slightest feeling of self-pity was seen as a crime against socialism.

She picked up the letter again. *'From your adoring husband Tomáš.'* She smiled. He was still so sure of himself and of her. It did not even occur to him to ask if she had remarried. She stood up and looked out onto Bozděchova Street. He was collecting his visa next Monday and leaving the same day. In one week they would be walking along that street together. It was no fantasy. All her prayers were being answered. Tomáš was alive and coming back to her.

And it was the best time for him to come, just as Prague too was full of renewed hope. She was sure she could go back, and everything could be as it once was. She watched a young man in blue jeans and a polo-neck jumper handing out leaflets on the street corner. It was spring in Prague, and he was being allowed to carry on unmolested. She felt sudden elation and intense happiness. She kissed the letter again and wept.

Tomáš threw his suitcase into the corridor of the boat train and climbed in after it. He found an empty compartment and, before he even had time to put his suitcase on the luggage rack, a whistle blew and the train pulled out of Victoria Station. He breathed a loud sigh of relief. What a crazy morning it had been, but thank the Lord he had not missed the train. He shuddered at the thought of Anna waiting for him at Prague Main Station tomorrow evening, and him not being there at the time he had given her. He fell back onto the seat by the window.

The damned Embassy, making him wait so long just to collect his visa. He took his passport out of his pocket to check the stamp. Three months the Czechoslovak Socialist Republic had allowed him. He smiled. They didn't realise how unimportant their petty restrictions were, since he never intended to leave again. Once he had re-established himself as a citizen and renewed his passport, Fran would send all his belongings over and he would stay with Anna forever.

Dear Fran. She had been so upset yesterday. "They're tears of happiness for you, Tom," she insisted. "I have lived with Anna and Eva for all these years and I feel they have come back for me too." And they had. She alone had brought them back. And, on top of all that, she had arranged compassionate leave for him, so he could serve out his notice. "Doing it properly will protect your pension," she told him. "You'll need it one day." Dear, dear Fran. A time would come, he promised her, when they would all meet.

The train passed through the Kent countryside. Everything was too slow. He could not settle. He picked up the newspaper and immediately threw it down unopened. He checked the visa stamp again. Finally, he reached into his jacket pocket and took out the black and white photographs Anna had sent with her letter. At last he relaxed as he looked once more at his wonderful family. His three-year-old granddaughter, Lenka, in the arms of her father, Vilém. And Eva holding Vilém's arm and looking so happy and so proud. He was struck again by Eva's resemblance to his mother. He balanced the picture on his knee and looked at the others.

There was Lukáš. *'Intense and serious, just like his father,'* Anna had written, *'and just as passionate about the world.'* She wrote with such pride about both their children. She had performed miracles to keep them safe and raise them so well, and nowhere did she mention her struggles, only their successes. He read her words out loud in the empty compartment.

'They both have degrees from Charles University, just like you and Uncle Pavel. Lukáš studied Slavic Languages and Literature and Eva studied medicine. Lukáš is doing his Master's now and Eva is an anaesthetist at the old Francis Hospital. She met her husband there. Vilém's a surgeon, and very handsome as you can see. They have an apartment in the same block as me and are very happy. They always remind me of how we were at their age, darling.' He looked out of the window and smiled at his reflection. Could there be anyone on Earth happier than he was now? Tomorrow he would be with his wonderful, beautiful Anna again.

He looked at the only photograph she had included of herself. It was a shame he could not see her more clearly in it. She was standing in the middle distance, wearing a winter coat down to her knees and with her hair up. She looked very serious, and he wondered why she had chosen to send that picture. Perhaps it was the most recent one she had. Or perhaps there was a message contained in it. She did say in her letter not to expect too much of her apartment or of the life she now lived in Prague. *'We work, we eat, we sleep. The only thing to live for here is your family. There is nothing else.'* The words made his impatience even greater. He needed to tell her how he understood what life must be like for her, and how proud he was of her for what she had achieved. If only the time would pass.

He could not eat on the Ostend ferry or rest on the overnight sleeper from Cologne, but in the morning they seemed to be making quicker progress. They were in Würzburg by nine, Bayreuth at ten thirty, and a few minutes after eleven the train pulled into Schirnding on the German side of the Czechoslovak border. He was elated. He knew Schirnding.

Prague lay only 150 kilometres to the east, and they were not due there for another eight hours. He thanked God there was no chance now of being late. He sat, patient at last, and waited. For half an hour, then a full hour, and still there was no sign of movement anywhere. He went to a window and called out to a West German customs official on the platform.

"What's the hold up?"

"It's always like this," the official said, approaching Tomáš. He seemed pleased to be able to educate a naïve tourist about life behind the Iron Curtain. "We have to wait until the Czechoslovak authorities are ready for you on the other side. They like to keep us all here for at least two or three hours."

"But why?"

"To show their power. Because they can."

"But it's pointless."

"You don't have to tell me. Just imagine the poor devils on the other side who have to live with this nonsense all the time."

Permission to proceed was not given until a few minutes after two, exactly three hours after they arrived. The West German officials left the carriages, and the train began to creep towards the border. Tomáš looked out of the window for the red, white and blue flag which would tell him he was back in his homeland for the first time in twenty years. Sparse woods of pine, chestnut and birch bordered the single track. Beyond them he was able to glimpse meadows in the distance. Then the train slowed to a crawl and the woods ended abruptly. But there was no meadow here, just a wide cleared area where only low undergrowth and the stumps of trees remained. Looking from the carriage to his left and his right he saw the cleared strip extend to both horizons.

Then came the first fences. Three lines of them, each over two metres high and three or four metres apart. He still could see no Czechoslovak flag, but at last there was a sign at the start of a wide, ploughed strip of land. *'Nebezpeči min,'* it said. And below in German. *'Achtung Minen.'*

"My God," muttered Tomáš, "the bastards have laid minefields." Other passengers ignored him.

At the end of the ploughed strip was another fence, higher than the others and topped with grotesque white electrical insulators. The train was crawling now more slowly than a man could walk, and he was able to look along the length of the fence in both directions. It too extended as far as the eye could see, and every fifty metres or so stood watchtowers with guards and searchlights, able to scan the whole area. Beyond them the woods had been cleared for another 100 metres, and then at last came the sign he had been looking for. *'Československá Socialisticka Republika'*. But surely that couldn't be right, he thought. And then he realised he had been back in his country for the past twenty minutes, but the Communists, who had scarred the borderland to keep their people imprisoned, were too ashamed or too cowardly to claim it as part of Czechoslovakia.

A short distance from the sign the train made an unscheduled stop. There were no station buildings, only two bare platforms lined with Czechoslovak soldiers. Two entered each door of the train and remained in the corridors smoking and talking loudly. The train started to move and picked up speed until it stopped again about fifteen minutes later. This time Tomáš could see it was a large station, built of functional grey concrete with no adornment save the name of the town it served. Cheb. The soldiers got out and were replaced by dozens of men in dark blue uniforms and black knee-length boots. Each wore a blue cap encircled by a red ribbon confirming who they were. *Sbor Národni Bezpečnosti.* State Police. Tomáš took out his passport and waited for one of them to approach him. He decided there and then to speak only English and to give his address as the Interhotel in Wenceslas Square, where he had booked a room as a condition of his visa application.

He waited for thirty minutes before two of the men came into his carriage. They worked their way along the passengers until they came to him. He handed one of them his passport and was surprised when he was addressed in reasonable English.

"The purpose of your visit, Mr Colman?" the policeman asked politely.

"I'm going to Prague on holiday."

The policeman wrote down his reply and copied details of his passport.

"Where will you stay?"

"The Interhotel in Wenceslas Square."

"How long will you stay there?"

"Two weeks, perhaps longer, if I'm enjoying myself."

The policeman looked at him and made more notes. Then he handed back his passport and saluted. "Enjoy your holiday in the Czechoslovak Socialist Republic, Mr Colman."

Tomáš mumbled his thanks and for the first time realised how nervous he was. He imagined the man returning and addressing him by his 'real' name and asking him to explain his reasons for leaving Czechoslovakia twenty years before. He decided to stay in his seat and feign sleep. An hour passed, and then another. After three hours the train moved.

Tomáš looked at his watch. Five o'clock. The train was due in Prague at seven. He should still be on time. Every few minutes he checked his watch. The train stopped in Pilzen. As they pulled away the guard came through the carriage and announced the next stop. Prague. He imagined Anna leaving her apartment, being as nervous and anxious as he was. He looked out of the window at the countryside he knew so well. The sun was low in the sky as the evening began to set in. He checked his watch again. Six forty-five. They had reached the outskirts of Prague.

The train entered the bridge over the Vltava, and people began to stand up and take their luggage from the racks. He collected his suitcase and put it on the floor next to his seat. They reached the railway sidings leading into the station and then the end of the platform. He looked out the window and saw the sign he had waited so long to see. *Praha*. The passengers were making their way to the doors now. People were waiting on the platform, but he could not see her. The train came to a stop, the doors opened and the passengers filed out. He stepped down onto the platform and still could not see her amongst so many people. He waited for the crowds to thin, until only one figure remained. The figure from the photograph, dressed in a winter coat with her hair up. Anna.

There was no sound or movement. They stood there, each taking in the physical reality of the other. This was not a thought or a wish; they were alive, together, at the same time in the same place. Tomáš walked towards her. He stopped a few paces from her and they looked at one another.

"Ahoy, Anna."

"Ahoy, Tomáš."

They smiled. He was just as she imagined. A little broader now but still very handsome, his hair at his temples turning to grey. She was just Anna, her beautiful, young face as clear to him as ever. They threw their arms around one another; their bodies felt instantly familiar and they laughed and cried.

"We did it, Anna. We did it."

"I know. I know. Tomáš... my Tomáš..."

"I thought I'd lost you, Anna. I'm so sorry I didn't keep faith with you." He felt her soft cheek next to his. "I knew you'd keep our Eva safe."

"I thought I saw you at the fence. I thought I saw them take you away. He said you were dead."

"I know, darling. I know what you've been through. I'm so sorry."

They stood back to look at one another again and laughed as they wiped away their tears.

"I was afraid you wouldn't recognise me," said Anna.

"Not recognise you? I've seen your face every second of every day for twenty-six years."

"But I've changed so much."

"You haven't changed at all. You're my beautiful Anna. Exactly the same."

Tomáš picked up his case and without speaking they locked arms, and walked to a bench at the rear of the platform. They sat down, each looking into the other's face, and they kissed.

"I've kept you and Eva with me every moment since that day, Anna."

She lowered her eyes.

"I tried to hold on to you, darling. But there are places I've been where I didn't want you there. Sometimes I thought I could die from needing you so much."

"You'll never feel like that again. I promise you."

She stroked his face, kissed him, and put her head on his shoulder.

"How will we ever be able to make sense of everything, Tomáš?"

"Are you happy at this moment, Anna?"

"Oh yes, my darling. Yes."

He took her gently by the shoulders and looked into her eyes.

"As long as we are happy now, Anna, we must accept everything that has brought us to this moment. We're together and we'll stay together forever. Nothing else matters."

"Yes, darling Tomáš." She wrapped her arms around him. "Just hold me," she said. "Never let go."

Chapter Thirty-Five

May 1st, 1968

"I do love you, Tomáš. I hope you're not too disappointed this morning."

"Come here, Anna."

She stood next to his chair at the breakfast table. He put his arms around her hips and rested his head against her stomach.

"You still say the silliest things," he said, looking up and smiling at her. "Those were the happiest hours of my life. It was enough just to be next to you."

She stroked his head and held him against her.

"I love you so much, Tomáš, and I know I still have all those feelings. But it's been so long and... I can't explain."

He drew her down onto his lap and she laid her head on his shoulder. "Don't think about anything, Anna. I want nothing except to hold you. I can't stop holding you."

She stayed, inhaling the scent of his neck, as he smoothed the thin material of her skirt over her thigh. She kissed his cheek and stood up to pour more coffee.

"Sit down with me, darling. Relax and have some breakfast," he said. "Tell me what the plan is for today."

"Eva will be here in half an hour. She's so anxious to see you. She's very upset they made her work last night."

"I still can't believe I'm going to see her. I'm so impatient."

"She's wonderful, Tomáš." Anna sat down and reached for his hand across the small table. "She looks so much like Auntie Karolína. You'll be so proud of her."

"I am already. Are you sure she doesn't remember me?"

"She was too young, darling. But I've told her so much about you over the years. About your poetry and how you looked after us."

"But I didn't."

"Yes, you did. You did everything you could for us. You told me not to be silly. Now I'm telling you. I don't want you to say that again."

"Tell me more about her eyes."

"You won't notice much. Her glasses are really only for her right eye with the damaged cornea. You can see a slight milkiness if you look closely. I thank God you and that Red Cross nurse insisted on her going to hospital." She squeezed his hand. "Do you see the things you did for her that you don't even realise?"

He nodded without looking up.

"And wait until you see little Lenka. Your heart will melt."

"I know. Eva's child. I can't believe it."

"You'll adore her."

"And I'll meet Lukáš this afternoon?"

"Yes, at the parade. But you mustn't mind if he's a little distant. Lukáš is so involved in all the student politics these days, he hardly bothers with any of us. He'll be marching this afternoon."

"I can't imagine what a Communist May Day in Prague will be like. On the television back in London all we ever see is a parade of tanks and missiles in Red Square."

"Moscow will still be like that, but Lukáš says we're all in for a surprise here. He's one of the students on the organising committee."

"Really?"

"He says Dubček and the Presidium are allowing it to be very different this year."

"Are things really changing here, Anna?"

"Not for ordinary people like us. Dubček and the reformists have promised a lot, but it hasn't made any difference to our daily lives."

"Has it been very hard for you?"

Anna pulled her hand away from his and took a handkerchief from the sleeve of her cardigan. She held it ready in both hands on the table.

"The children make it nice, of course. But apart from them, life here is terrible, Tomáš. Everyone has a job, but most do little work. There's no point. We get our pittance whatever we do, and there's nothing in the shops to spend it on anyway. Look how we live." She looked around the cramped, sparsely-furnished room. "I can understand how disappointed you must be."

"In my country perhaps, Anna, but never in you. Never."

She dropped her handkerchief on the table and reached out for his hands. "You always had a way of saying the right things, Tomáš."

"Life's going to be good for us from now on, Anna, whatever happens out there in the world. I promise you. "

"Lukáš is very optimistic about it all. He says now Dubček has abolished censorship everything will have to change, even the Party."

"He may be right. A free press is the first step towards democracy."

Anna poured more coffee and put in some sugar. He watched her stir it for him.

"You wouldn't believe what gets written in the papers now," she said. "I'm surprised half of it is allowed."

"What sort of thing?"

"Criticism of Moscow for what they've done to our industry, and of the Party for creating so much apathy amongst people. Criticism like that was unheard of before."

"It's a good start. And is the press calling for democracy?"

"All the time. But it's not so much politicians saying it. It's mostly writers and intellectuals. They're behind what you read in the newspapers."

"I thought Dubček wanted it too."

"I think he does, but it's all too slow. Nothing's really changing for people."

"Well, it will now for you and me."

"Yes, darling Tomáš, it will for you and me." She stood up and kissed the top of his head. "You can talk to Lukáš about all this tonight. Eva and Vilém have invited us all to eat with them in their apartment. Lukáš knows far more than the rest of us about what's going on." She started to put away the cheese and rye bread. "All I know is my work never changes, and neither does the money I get."

"But you won't need to work now, Anna. I have lots of money saved. And when I renew my citizenship, I'll find a teaching job here."

"But I have to work, Tomáš."

"Of course you don't."

"You don't understand, Tomáš. It's illegal to be unemployed in Czechoslovakia."

The door bell rang.

"Oh no, that's them. We've been talking and I haven't even cleared the breakfast things."

"I'll do it, Anna. You go and let them in."

Tomáš heard talking at the front door as he put the dishes as quietly as he could into the sink. He had imagined this moment so often over the past two weeks, and now he was unsure whether to venture out and greet everyone or to wait.

"Is he here?" he heard someone say. Eva's voice. His body locked in position and he felt it might break if he moved. He took several deep breaths, made himself turn slowly and walk to the kitchen door. Across the living room he saw a young woman with fine features and auburn hair, just like his mother's. She looked at him. The words he had prepared were lost to a guttural sound, and he clasped his hand over his mouth to stifle it. Eva hurried towards him.

"It's alright, Táta." She put her arms around him. "It's alright. Everything's alright now." He held Eva and wept over her shoulder into the empty room.

"I'm so sorry, darling. I'm so sorry."

"Don't be sorry, Táta. Everyone is alright now." Anna came over and put her arms around him too. He held on to them both and, for no reason he could understand, said a silent thanks to his father. He saw the anxious face of a child peering around the door frame from the hallway, and he broke away and went back into the kitchen.

"Are the grown-ups being silly, Lenka?" he heard Anna saying. "Come here to Babička."

Eva followed him into the kitchen. She put her hand on his back as he leaned over the sink. "Máma has told me everything that happened, Táta. This must be very hard for you."

"It's wonderful for me, Eva. I'm usually able to control my emotions… I hope I haven't upset you or Lenka."

"Of course not."

"I'm afraid if I turn round and look at you, I'll start again."

"I don't mind, Táta. Turn around and let us see one another."

Tomáš turned and slowly raised his head to look into her face. He put his hand on her cheek. "I can still see the child you were, my precious Eva. You're still so beautiful."

"And I have a táta who's as wonderful as I always dreamed he was."

"Thankyou for calling me 'táta'. I was worried you might not."

"You've always been my táta. I used to make up stories about you, and I must have read the poem you wrote for me a thousand times."

"Your birthday poem?"

"It's helped me all my life. You've always given me such strength."

"My darling Eva. My lovely child." They held one another again and cried.

"Come on," said Eva. She patted his back. "I want you to meet your granddaughter and the other wonderful man in my life."

Vilém stood up as they came back into the room. He was tall and had a kind, open face. He reached across the table and offered his hand. "It's an honour to meet you, sir," he said. "Your wife has told us so much about you."

"Thankyou, Vilém, it's a pleasure to meet you too. I must apologise for the way I'm being…"

"Please, sir. I only have to think of my Lenka to understand what this must be like for you. No explanations are necessary."

"Thankyou." Tomáš turned to Lenka, who had burrowed herself into Anna's lap and was eyeing him suspiciously. "Your silly Děda has a present for you, Lenka," he said. He went into the bedroom and reappeared carrying two bags from Harrods of Knightsbridge.

"This is for you, Lenka. All the way from London."

"What is it?" she asked, sitting up and reaching out her hands.

"It's called a teddy bear, darling," said Tomáš, "and you must choose a name for him."

"Děda bear," she repeated, and everyone laughed.

"That's a wonderful name," said Tomáš. "Děda Bear from your Děda."

"And I have something here for your táta." He took a box from the bag and passed it to Vilém.

"My, what's this? A transistor radio. A Grundig from West Germany. The very best. That's very generous of you, sir."

"You're very welcome, Vilém. And please call me Tomáš."

"Thankyou, Tomáš."

"And just as they've unblocked the BBC and Radio Free Europe," said Eva. "It's perfect timing, Táta."

"I've got one for Lukáš too. You'll have to change the plug, I'm afraid, and I've got some spare batteries in case it's difficult to get them here."

"Thankyou, Tomáš," said Vilém. "You're very thoughtful."

"Good. And now my beautiful wife and daughter. I didn't know what to get you. I thought of books and music, but a very good friend of mine from work told me I had to get cosmetics or clothes. She came with me to choose. I bought this for you, Eva."

Eva unwrapped the outer paper and then gently unfolded the tissue paper inside. She took the pale-pink jumper by the shoulders, stood up and held it in front of her.

"It's fabulous," she gasped. "Look, Máma."

"It's so soft," said Anna. "Is it wool?"

"Yes, one hundred percent cashmere, but in the shop they said it's very light for wearing in the spring or summer."

"I love the narrow fit," said Eva. "I'm going to wear it today for the parade."

"I was told you must team it up with this. Is that the right expression?" said Tomáš. He took a dark-pink suede belt from the bag.

"Oh my, that's beautiful too," exclaimed Eva. "I don't know what to say."

"I was told it's for slim figures, so it will suit you perfectly."

Eva came around the table, put her arms around his neck and kissed him. "It's the most perfect present, Táta. Thankyou so much."

"I'm just relieved you like it."

"You could wear it with your black trousers, darling," said Anna. "You'll look lovely in it."

"And now my beautiful wife. I hope you like this, Anna. I was told it's the height of fashion and I could just picture you in it." He put the present on the table.

Anna unwrapped it and lifted the tissue paper. "My goodness." She put her hand to her mouth. "You hold it up for me, Eva."

Eva stood up and unfolded the white linen dress. "It hangs beautifully, Máma. Look, it has a satin lining. Stand up. Let me see what it looks like against you."

"It is lovely, Tomáš," said Anna, "but it's too much for me."

"Come on, Máma, see what it looks like."

Anna stood up, and Lenka walked over to Vilém. Eva held the dress in front of her mother.

"They call it 'A'-line," said Tomáš. "It's perfect for you, darling."

Anna looked down at the dress. It had a scoop neckline and stopped just above the knee. The sleeves came down to the elbow and each was decorated with a single purple button. Three larger purple buttons decorated the neck.

"Wear it today, Máma. You'll look fabulous."

"Perhaps not today, Eva. It's a lovely dress, Tomáš, but I think I'll save it for another occasion." She stepped away from the table.

"Whatever you say, darling," said Tomáš. "Wear it when you're ready." He felt Anna's hand on his shoulder and she sat down next to him. He saw her turn her handkerchief over in her hands.

"I hope you don't all think I've overdone it," he said, "but I have something else for you here, Eva and Anna. My friend picked out a selection of cosmetics and things for you. There's no hurry. They're in this bag when you want to see them."

"Pass them over, Táta," said Eva with a large grin on her face. She reached into the bag and took out one package after another. "My goodness. Look at this, Máma. Chanel perfume. I've heard of that. Isn't it very expensive? L'Oréal moisturiser and lipsticks. And what's this..?"

"Will you all excuse for a moment," said Anna, and she pushed back her chair and disappeared into the bedroom, closing the door behind her.

"Oh dear, was I getting too carried away?" said Eva. "I'll go and see what it is."

"No, Eva, I'll go," said Tomáš, standing up. "I think I might know."

"Come on, Eva, let's get going," said Vilém. "We'll see you downstairs in an hour, Tomáš. I think Anna wants us all to walk to the parade together."

"Thankyou, Vilém." Tomáš kissed Eva and stroked Lenka's head. "I'm sure your máma will be fine. We'll be in the entrance hall in an hour."

Tomáš knocked on the bedroom door. When there was no answer, he opened it slowly. "Can I come in, Anna?"

"Yes."

She was lying on her side on the bed with her eyes open. She reached out a hand to him. Her eyes did not move.

"You haven't done anything wrong, darling," she said.

He sat down next to her, took her hand and held it to his lips.

"Your presents were wonderful. It was a lovely thought."

"Do you want to tell me what upset you?"

"Not really."

"Can I do anything for you?"

"Stay patient with me. Keep loving me."

He leaned over and kissed her.

"That's the easiest thing I've ever been asked to do," he said.

Chapter Thirty-Six

May 1st, 1968

They watched Lenka skipping along in front of them, holding her parents' hands and swinging into the air after every few steps. "Again, again," she demanded, as soon as her feet touched the ground. Eva and Vilém kept the game going until Lenka tired, planted herself in front of her father, and reached up to him.

"Now she wants to be carried," said Tomáš, laughing. "She's a little monkey." He felt Anna grip his arm and lay her head against his shoulder.

"She's exactly the same age as Eva was when I last saw her in France," he said.

"Yes, just coming up to three."

"I can hardly believe it, Anna. Only two weeks ago I was in Castiran, trying to relive memories of us there, and here I am now with you and Eva and Lenka walking by the Vltava."

"It's wonderful, darling. A miracle." Anna kissed the sleeve of his jacket, and they strolled on together in silence, matching one another's steps. Tomáš noticed Lenka watching them over her father's shoulder and he waved to her. Lenka waved back and then buried her face in Vilém's neck.

"You know, Anna, the real miracle in all this is the way you kept our children safe. I want you to know how much admiration and gratitude I have for what you did."

Anna looked away across the river.

"You don't have to talk about it if you don't want to, darling," said Tomáš, "...but I have wondered... how you got Eva and Lukáš out of the camp in Paris."

"Didn't Émile tell you?"

"Not about that."

Anna kept her face turned towards the river and began to walk more slowly. He heard her sigh.

"When I realised I was pregnant, I begged him to help us, and he used the excuse of taking Eva to hospital."

"Was it that easy?"

"I think it was for him. It was chaotic in that camp. The guards all did favours for one another. He took me in the car with Eva and drove us to his apartment. I don't think he found it difficult removing the name of a mother and child from the camp records."

"It was that simple. He removed your names, and you no longer existed?"

"No, Tomáš. That's not what he did at all."

Anna stepped from the shade of the chestnut trees lining the embankment and leaned on the wall by the river. Tomáš followed and stood next to her. She did not look at him as she spoke.

"You said you saw our names on the transport list to Poland. Émile must have removed two other names from the camp records and sent those poor people in our place. Whoever that mother and child were, he made us disappear with them."

"I see... But that's not your fault, Anna. And it didn't change anything for those unfortunate people. I learned from the Red Cross that no Jewish women or children from Drancy survived. I'm afraid they would have been transported anyway."

"But I had no idea Émile was such a wicked man. He was so good to Eva and Lukáš. He treated them like his own. Eva even went to a French school after the war."

"You stayed in Paris?"

"I had no choice. He showed me your death certificate. We had nowhere else to go. I left as soon as I heard from Otto that Vati was alive in the Russian zone in Germany. It was March '46. Émile tried to stop us, but it was too late by then. As soon as I knew Vati was alive, I had somewhere to go. Émile lost his hold over me."

"I understand."

"The madness of it is, I even felt I was being ungrateful by leaving him at the time. Now I feel... I don't know what I feel... as if there's an ugly stain on me I can never remove."

"We were all deceived by Durand, Anna."

"But I'm not who I was before all that, Tomáš. There were other things... I'm not who you think I am."

"Listen, Anna. You're everything I think you are and more. The world hasn't allowed you or me to stay as we wanted to be. But as long as we've always acted for the right reasons, the essence of us hasn't changed. My love for you hasn't changed."

He turned towards her and hoped she would look back at him, but her eyes remained fixed on the far bank of the river.

"The only thing that's changed for me, Anna, is the realisation of just how brave you've had to be, and how wonderful you are. I place you higher now than I've ever done before."

She took his hand and he put his arm around her waist.

"Now we've talked about it, Anna, shall we agree not to mention it or even think about it ever again?"

She nodded, still without looking at him. He pointed to Eva, Lenka and Vilém, who were waiting for them in the spring sunshine.

"Look, Anna. There's our life now, not Durand or Agde or Drancy. I don't want my coming here to bring all that terrible time back to you. I was wrong to mention it. It's over. Our lives can be about you and me and our family now. Nothing else."

She put her arms around his neck and hugged him. "You are a very special man, darling Tomáš. I love you very much."

"And I love you, my Anna. More than ever."

The others turned towards them as they caught up.

"Come on, you two lovebirds," said Eva. "I know May 1st is Love Day, but we'll be late for Lukáš. We said twelve o'clock by the Jan Hus statue."

"I thought the procession was in Wenceslas Square," said Tomáš.

"It ends there, but everyone who wants to parade has been told to assemble in the Old Town. Look at all those people in front of us. The whole of Prague is turning out."

"It is very impressive."

"It's special this year, Tomáš," said Vilém. "It's the first time people haven't been forced to attend. The hospital authorities usually insist Eva and I go."

"And why haven't they this year?"

"Because the parade hasn't been organised by the Party. It's been left to the people to do as they please. It's getting late. We need to get going."

"We'll have to keep an eye on Lenka in all these crowds."

"Don't worry, Anna. I'll keep a tight hold of her," said Vilém.

They continued along the Lenin Embankment past the National Theatre. Tomáš looked across the Legion Bridge and noticed the change of name. Karl Marx Bridge. People were streaming across it from the Malá Strana.

"Are you nervous, darling?" asked Anna.

"Why do you ask that?"

"Because you've been so quiet for the last few minutes. It's not like you. I thought you might be nervous about meeting Lukáš."

"I suppose I am. Tell me what I should expect, Anna."

She pulled him closer to her.

"I don't want you to be disappointed by his reaction, darling. You mustn't expect him to greet you with open arms and call you táta like Eva did. He's not like that. He's quite serious about everything, and he'll be very distracted by all that's going on. And you have to remember he's been the man of the family since he was eight, when Vati died."

"I understand. I can't wait to meet him, but I am being realistic about it. I know I can't just walk into his life and expect to be what my father was to me."

They reached Charles Bridge.

"Will you excuse me a moment all of you," said Tomáš. He ran to the newspaper vendor and came back clutching two papers. "Look at this, Anna," he called out as he approached her. "I can't believe my eyes. He's selling English newspapers. It's the Daily Mail. Do you remember back in '38..?"

"Yes, darling, of course I remember."

He looked at the front page. "It's the last thing I expected, a Communist country allowing English newspapers."

"You wouldn't have found it a few weeks ago," said Vilém.

"Come on," insisted Eva. "It's five past. You know what Lukáš is like. He'll lose patience and go."

Tomáš had never seen the Old Town so packed, even in the days of Prague's deepest crises and greatest celebrations. And everyone seemed pleased with themselves and with each other, talking and laughing and smiling at complete strangers, as if they knew they were bonded by a special happening, unique to this time and to this place.

"If we get separated, we'll see you by the statue," shouted Vilém, as he merged into the crowd in front of them with Eva and Lenka. Tomáš reached his right hand above his head, raised his thumb and mouthed his agreement. With his other hand he held on tight to Anna.

"Look at all these hippies," she said. "They can't all be from Prague."

"I'm sure they're not. And where are all the workers on May Day, I want to know? Most of these people must be either students or tourists."

"Just keep moving and don't let go of my hand," Anna shouted back.

"I won't, my darling. I won't."

They reached Old Town Square and made their way to the meeting place in front of the Jan Hus statue. Tomáš spotted Vilém standing next to Eva with Lenka in his arms. He was about to wave and call out when he noticed a slim, young man in blue jeans and a blue and white Paisley shirt talking to them. He had brown hair hanging loosely over his ears and collar, and as he talked he kept sweeping his hair back from his forehead with his right hand, and then gesturing towards different areas of the square. In his left hand he held a placard turned inwards with the shorter edge resting on the ground.

"Is that..?"

"Yes, that's Lukáš." Tomáš felt Anna squeeze his hand. "Lukáš," she called out before Tomáš had time to stop her, and the young man looked over and waved.

"God, why am I so nervous, Anna?" said Tomáš, as they walked the short distance towards him. "It will be alright," she whispered.

"Ahoj, Máma," said Lukáš, and he bent forward to kiss her. "And you must be Tomáš." He reached out his hand. "So what do you think of Prague?" His handshake was firm.

"I thought I knew the city well, Lukáš, but it feels very different today."

"It is different. Everything's different, and we're going to make sure it stays that way."

"How will you organise today with so many people?"

Tomáš studied his son as he answered.

"We've got everyone here separated into their groups. What's great is that lots of them have never been allowed to parade before." He had the gentle features of Anna's father. "The Sokol and the Junak over there were banned until recently." His face was full of energy and enthusiasm as he spoke. "And you've got your veteran groups over there." Tomáš could see the child in him. "The legionnaires are allowed back for the first time in twenty years, and so is the Masaryk Association. But look over there. That's the best of all."

Tomáš watched as Lukáš turned and waved at two groups waiting outside the Tyn Church. He felt intense pride and a stinging sense of loss.

"The one this side is KAN. It's for non-Communists who want to form an opposition party." Lukáš smiled broadly and looked at his mother and sister for approval. "See how far democratisation has come. The party is so confident, we're allowing opposition parties in the May Day parade. Next to KAN, that's the K-231. They're a pressure group supporting the victims of Stalin and Gottwald. They're allowed here too now. Isn't it fantastic?"

"Yes, my love," said Anna. "It's all very exciting."

"It's more than that, Máma. What you're witnessing here is our whole country waking up politically. We're showing the whole world what real socialism can achieve."

"It's wonderful, my love."

Lukáš looked at his watch. "It's nearly twelve thirty. We'll be off soon. Now listen all of you. The parade is being led by President Svoboda and First Secretary Dubček. They will be followed by the groups here, and then comes the most important part - you, the people. You must wait for the groups here to leave, and then you can join in the march with everyone else. First Secretary Dubček and the rest will review the march-past in Na Prikope Street. I'll try to catch you all in Wenceslas Square on the steps of the National Museum at three o'clock."

Lukáš reached out his hand to Tomáš again. "It's nice to meet you at last, Tomáš. You'll probably bump into a lot of other English visitors here today. People have come from all over the world. Prague is the place everyone wants to be."

"But I'll be seeing you tonight at Eva and Vilém's place, won't I, Lukáš?"

"Oh yes, I forgot. Sorry, Eva. I'll be there. I must go."

They all watched him join a group of students a short distance away. They formed loose ranks and raised their placards high in the air. Tomáš looked for the one held by Lukáš. *'Democracy at all costs,'* it read.

"I like that placard," said Eva. "*'I would like to increase our population, but I have no apartment.'* Lukáš should be carrying that one."

The parade moved off. Everyone cheered and the students chanted Dubček's name. The same messages were held aloft on a thousand placards. *'Socialism with a human face.' 'Fewer monuments, more thoughts.' 'Make love, not war.' 'Support Polish students.' 'Free elections.'*

The crowds applauded as all the groups passed. The last were the legionnaires and the Tomáš Masaryk Association.

"It's the first time I've ever seen pictures of Masaryk displayed in public," said Eva.

"Or anywhere else for that matter," added Vilém.

As the legionnaires marched past, Tomáš stood to attention and saluted them.

"We can follow them now," said Eva. "That's the last group." She took hold of Tomáš's hand. "That was nice of you, Táta. Saluting them like that."

"They created our country, Eva. They deserve our respect. You know your grandfather Kovařík was a legionnaire in Russia, don't you? That he received an award from Masaryk himself for his bravery?"

"No, I didn't." Eva looked at her mother.

"You must understand, Tomáš." said Anna, "Legionnaires have been persecuted for the past twenty years for fighting the Communists in

Russia. I'm still not sure you should be telling Eva about her grandfather. If the hospital knew..."

"Don't worry so much, Máma. I think Lukáš is right. Things really are changing here. I haven't seen any secret police around today, have you?"

"No, but I still don't trust people not to report what they overhear. They always have before."

"I'm sorry, Anna, it's my fault," said Tomáš, taking her hand. "I didn't realise."

"You weren't to know."

"Are we all ready then?" said Eva. "How about you, Vilém?"

"Yes, we're fine, aren't we, Lenka?"

Lenka laughed as she sat astride her father's shoulders with both hands clasping his forehead.

"Well, Lenka's happy, and I certainly am," said Tomáš, "walking through Prague with the two most beautiful women in the world."

He put his arms around Anna and Eva, kissed them both, and they walked along hand in hand in the midst of the crowd. The route was lined with cheering people, and more and more joined the procession as it passed.

"Na Prikope Street is just around the corner," shouted Vilém. "The podium with all the officials should be in view soon. There they are. Up there on the left."

The parade slowed and wild cheering filled the air at the sight of Dubček on the low platform. Some marchers broke away to reach up to touch him. Uniformed policemen rushed forward to protect him, but he waved them away and leaned down to touch hands with as many people as he could. As the crowd moved slowly along, Tomáš came close to him. He saw a tall, thin man with a sad face behind a faint smile, which he maintained for everyone who wanted to greet him.

"We are with you," people shouted at him, until it became a chant which spread through the crowd.

Tomáš shuffled past the platform amidst the throng of people. He noticed stern-faced men sitting behind Dubček, making no effort to hide their disapproval at what was taking place in front of them. Soon Tomáš's section of the crowd had passed the platform and was turning right towards Wenceslas Square, still chanting their support for Dubček. There was more space now, and Tomáš felt Anna and Eva slacken their grip on his hands.

"So what do you think of Dubček then, Táta?" Eva shouted into his ear above the noise.

"It's not my place..."

"Yes, it is. Even if Lukáš has forgotten you're a Czechoslovak, I haven't. Tell me what you think of it all."

"I'd rather not..." Tomáš shouted back.

"Tell me, Táta. I want to know."

"I think Dubček has an impossible job, Eva."

"Why?"

"Because he can't keep everyone happy."

"What do you mean?"

"I mean, he has to show the world he's a reformer... but persuade the old guard in the Party he's not. And all the time he has to show Moscow he can be trusted. Our people expect too much of him, Eva. My fear is... the Russians won't allow him to deliver it."

"I'm sorry I'm late, Eva," said Lukáš. "We reckon there was a quarter of a million people there today. It took five hours for them all to pass the podium."

"Come and sit down, my love," said Anna. "You must be exhausted."

"I'm too fired up to be exhausted. We've just come back from the Polish Embassy. We're demonstrating against their anti-Zionism, and the attacks on students in Warsaw. We're going back in the morning."

"Would you like a beer, Lukáš?"

"Thanks, Vilém, that would be great."

"How about you, Tomáš?"

"No, thanks, Vilém. I'll just have another apple juice, please."

"You've been in England too long, Tomáš," said Lukáš, sitting down opposite him. "All us Czechs drink beer."

"I fell out with alcohol many years ago, Lukáš. We haven't bothered with one another since."

"I didn't know that," said Anna. She stood up, went over to him and kissed him on the forehead. "My darling."

"It's alright now, Anna. I'll tell you about it one day."

"You and Lukáš talk. I'll go and help Eva bring out the food."

"I suppose you and my mother have a lot of catching up to do?"

"Not really, Lukáš. We've known one another all our lives. It's you and Eva I really need to catch up with. For your mother and me it's as if no time has passed at all."

"She always told us you were a poet. I'd like to read some of your work."

"I'm afraid I'm a lapsed poet, Lukáš. But I'd be pleased to show you later what I have with me."

"Perhaps all the great things happening in Prague will inspire you again. What did you think about today?"

Vilém came in with the drinks.

"Thanks, Vilém. Of course, today was special for me anyway, Lukáš, meeting you and spending time with you all. But I must say, I haven't seen Prague so full of hope and happiness since I was a boy. Since the tenth anniversary celebrations back in 1928."

"But surely today beats that. We're witnessing the real birth of Czechoslovakia now. A new type of politics. The third way."

"What do you mean exactly?"

"I mean we're building something totally different here." Lukáš leaned forward holding his beer in both hands. "Czechoslovakia is a very special case, you see, Tomáš. The one thing that makes us such a good model within the Communist bloc is that we chose socialism democratically after the war. But we didn't choose the crazy Stalinist model Gottwald imposed on us. Now we're rid of that, we need to ditch the useless command-economy. It's nearly destroyed us."

"I agree with you there."

Lukáš took a few gulps of beer.

"But neither do we want a crass consumer society of witless shoppers, such as you have in the West, buying your moral values at the supermarket." He placed his glass on the table to free his hands as he spoke. "We want to harness our people's genius and allow them to use their initiative within socialism to produce what people need. We want to develop new technologies in medicine, agriculture and engineering for the general good. Socialism with individual freedom. A third way."

"And who decides what people need?"

"It's common sense, isn't it? People need food. They shouldn't have to queue for hours like Máma does to buy everyday items for the table. Clothes, furniture... it's obvious what people need. But we don't need countless factories competing to pamper to people's vanity and whims. A chair is a chair. A shirt's a shirt. We need different sizes obviously, and some choice of colours, but any more is a waste of resources and human endeavour. It's common sense."

"And what about people's opinions? Must choice be limited there too?"

"No, because we've reached a stage in our socialist development where people have choices within a shared vision. You saw it in action today."

"I saw mostly students and tourists today. I didn't see many workers."

"A lot of workers have lost faith in the Party, it's true. But that's because the old Stalinist system didn't cater for their basic needs. The Party recognises that. That's what all the reforms are about. Better housing, more good-quality products in the shops, and a greater say in our lives at a local level." He paused and removed his glass from the table, as his mother came in to put plates down. "We have freedom of speech and of the press now, and we can travel freely. Lots of westerners I've met in Prague love our new system. They recognise us as the vanguard Communist country, ushering in a new type of socialism."

"Sit up around the table," ordered Anna. "It's lovely to see you both talking, but the food's ready." Eva followed her in with more dishes. Tomáš watched Lukáš drain his beer and put his empty glass back on the table. He looked tired, but still full of energy.

"I'll check on Lenka before we start, Eva."

"Thanks, Vilém. Careful not to wake her."

"This looks fabulous, Eva," said Lukáš, pulling his chair up to the table. "How did you manage to get all this?"

"Máma started queuing a week ago, as soon as we heard our táta was coming to visit us."

"The two of you ought to know that your táta hasn't just come to visit us," said Anna. "This is permanent. Your táta is staying with us for good." She put her hands on Tomáš's shoulders and he reached up to hold them. "We won't ever spend another day apart, will we, darling?"

"No, my Anna. Not one day."

"Well, I'm delighted," said Eva.

"And so am I," said Vilém, emerging from the bedroom. "I think this calls for a toast. He picked up his beer. "Help yourself to another, Lukáš. I give you all 'Anna and Tomáš'."

"Anna and Tomáš."

"Thankyou, everyone," said Tomáš. "Being here with you all... I did not think it possible to ever feel such happiness again... thankyou. This is like the wonderful evenings we used to spend in Cheb at our grandparents' chata, isn't it, Anna?"

"Yes, darling. Precious family times. Just the same."

Tomáš kissed Anna's hand and everyone ate in silence.

"So, Lukáš, how long have things in Prague been so different?" asked Tomáš.

"Yes, just the same," said Anna, laughing. "Always politics. Your grandfathers were always talking politics, Eva and Lukáš."

"Politics shape our lives, Máma," said Lukáš. "There is nothing more important." He turned to Tomáš.

"To answer your question, Tomáš, the tourists have been coming for a couple of years now, but nothing like the numbers this spring. Politically the backlash against Stalinism started here late, when they had to abandon the third Five-Year Plan in '61. But two things happened last year that finished President Novotny, and brought in the reformers."

"And what were they?"

"The first was the Fourth Writers' Congress last June. Have you heard of the writer Milan Kundera?"

"Yes, I've just finished reading *The Joke*."

"Well then, you probably know Kundera was a Stalinist, but at the Congress he joined up with non-party writers like Ludvik Vaculík and Václav Havel, and they spoke out together against censorship and the Party. They asked the question we were all asking. In order to have socialism, do we really need to have a centralised power system controlling every aspect of people's lives?"

"And what was the answer?"

"Of course we don't need it," said Eva. "It drives us all mad."

"And that's why we're changing it," snapped Lukáš. "But I keep telling you, Eva, it will take time."

"But look what the Presidium did to those writers. They expelled Kundera from the Party and got the Ministry of Information to censor the lot of them."

"But that was Novotny, not the reformers."

"Dubček was in the Presidium. He agreed to it."

"But he wasn't First Secretary then. He didn't have the authority. But he's abolished censorship completely now. Why must you always be so damned negative, Eva?"

"Please don't shout, Lukáš," said Vilém. "You'll wake Lenka."

"I'm sorry, Vilém. But honestly..."

"What was the second thing that changed things, Lukáš?" asked Tomáš.

"Oh, I've got the scar to prove this bit's true." He raised the hair from his forehead and leaned towards Eva. A raised pink scar ran five centimetres along his hairline. "I got this from the State Police last October during the first student protest..."

"But you were only protesting about the lack of heating in the student dormitory," said Eva.

"Please, Eva," said Vilém, "you're being mischievous. She gets like this, Tomáš."

"I know," said Tomáš returning her smile. "I remember."

"But that's the whole point, Eva," said Lukáš. "We were only asking for light and heating so we could study, and the police beat us senseless just for that. It was the biggest mistake they made. Most of our parents are Party members, and their complaints went right to the top."

Tomáš noticed Anna's face redden, as she looked down and busied herself with her food.

"It also caused one hell of a backlash amongst ordinary people about the heavy-handed way the Party always dealt with everything," continued Lukáš. "In the end Novotny had to invite Brezhnev to Prague to support him."

"I read about that back in London. Brezhnev refused to support him though, didn't he? And that's when Dubček took over."

"That's right."

"But doesn't it worry you, Lukáš, that Brezhnev didn't block Dubček's appointment?"

"Why should it worry me? We're not slaves of Moscow. The Russians don't decide who leads our Party. We are an independent country, you know, in spite of what you people in the West might think."

"Don't get too heated, Lukáš," said Vilém.

"Yes, I think that's enough," said Anna. "I am going to be like my Babička now, and insist you all concentrate on the lovely food Eva has prepared for us. This is our first meal together as a family."

"I'm sorry, darling. I do apologise to you all," said Tomáš. "It's just that I'm interested in knowing about your lives, and how you all feel about everything."

"For most of us, Tomáš, life is about family and work," said Vilém. "The same as anywhere else, I expect."

"Except here we all earn the same whatever work we do and regardless of what we put into it," said Eva.

"But you're happy at the hospital, aren't you, Eva?"

"Yes, Táta, I'm happy enough, but it's very hard for us. Vilém and I both work long hours, but we still can't afford anything more than this one-bedroom apartment. We can't bring another child into this."

"Wage equality is one of the things the Party will change, Eva," said Lukáš more calmly. "I know it's hard for you, but you will be rewarded. You just need to be patient."

"It's hard in the West for a lot of people too, you know," said Tomáš. "Some families don't have places as nice as this."

"There, what have I been telling you?" said Lukáš, smiling at last.

"But surely surgeons and anaesthetists in London live better than this, Táta?" said Eva.

"Well, yes, darling, they do. It's a meritocracy in Britain. Some people are very rich and some are very poor. Most are somewhere in the middle."

"Well, here we're all poor."

"But they've got protests in the West against their system too, Eva," said Lukáš. "We see all the riots in Paris and London and Berlin on the television. And America's even worse."

"Yes, Lukáš is right," said Tomáš. "The protests in the West have turned violent." He put down his knife and fork. "I think a lot of young people there just take their freedoms too much for granted and don't know how lucky they are. I must say, I was impressed today how orderly you young people are keeping things here, Lukáš."

"I think Czechoslovakia has had enough of radicalism in the past," said Vilém. "From the left and the right. That's the difference."

"I agree, Vilém." Tomáš turned to Lukáš. "Young Czechoslovaks like you, Lukáš, seem to be a lot more measured and patient than protesters in the West. For all our sakes I hope you succeed."

"Thankyou, Tomáš."

"Well said, Tomáš," said Vilém.

Anna took his hand and Eva smiled and gently nodded at him from across the table.

"Before you all thank me too much, I'm afraid I do have one reservation about the situation here."

"And what's that?" asked Lukáš.

"The attitude of the Soviet Union to all this."

"Oh, we know how to handle them." Lukáš swept his hand through his hair and grinned. "Didn't you hear Dubček's speech after the parade."

"No, we had to leave early for Lenka."

"Dubček told them how committed we are to socialism and to our alliance with our 'great friend and ally', and so on and so on. The Soviet ambassador was smiling and applauding all the way through. And he shook Dubček's hand afterwards. Dubček knows how to deal with the Russians. He grew up there."

"Then he ought to know Russia only sees the world in one way, Lukáš. Divided between East and West. It always has. And it's always wanted supremacy for itself in the East. When I was your age, Russia saw Germany as its great rival, now it sees America. Yesterday I passed through our country's frontline border with the West." Tomáš felt the blood rising in his scalp. "The Russians will never allow anything to happen here which threatens the strength of that border."

Lukáš leaned forward with his forearms on the table. The grin had gone. His voice was calm and strong.

"I think you need to have more confidence in us, Tomáš, and not look at the world in such a narrow way. The system of socialism we propose can be a model not just for our Communist neighbours, but for the West too. Czechoslovakia is a great country, capable of much more than we have achieved in the past. We are a strong, resourceful people who just need to seize our chance."

Lukáš looked around the table in search of enthusiasm from the others, but no one spoke. "Don't you all see..?" His eyes moved quickly from one person to another, as he became more animated. "...we are going to create something here which can build a bridge between East and West. It can be a model for this whole alienated world. We just have to believe in ourselves."

Tomáš saw the look on his son's face and wanted only to reach out to him. Vilém and Eva sat gently nodding polite approval. Anna looked towards Tomáš, her eyes pleading with him to offer some words of encouragement.

"Lukáš," Tomáš said, and then hesitated. "... I'm going to pay you a great compliment. When you speak about Czechoslovakia and its people, I hear the same passion and faith I used to hear from your grandfather Kovařík. Don't you think so, Anna?"

Anna turned to their son with a look of relief.

"Yes, I do think so, Lukáš. You sound just the same."

Chapter Thirty-Seven

May 2nd – July 1st, 1968

Anna returned to work after May Day. Every morning she and Tomáš walked together to the offices of the Department of Education on the Lenin Embankment where she started her day's cleaning. They kissed, Anna would try to make light of the work imposed on her, and Tomáš would continue to the Charles Bridge to buy the Czech, English and Russian newspapers, which on fine days he read sitting outside a café in the Old Town. He had never seen Prague or Anna looking more beautiful, nor felt the city or himself so full of hope. Only his continuing apprehension about the Russians prevented a feeling of total contentment.

After May Day he asked Lukáš for help in deciphering the Cyrillic script in the Moscow editions of *Pravda*, in order to judge the mood of the leaders in the Kremlin. And it became clear to him that Brezhnev and Kosygin disapproved of the events of May Day as much as their puppets, who witnessed it from the platform in Na Prikope Street. Even the students' long hair and bell-bottomed jeans were regarded by *Pravda* as 'reactionary subversion' and were a sign, one editorial insisted, of Czechoslovakia's ingratitude for all the Soviet Union had done during and since the liberation.

Lukáš's naivety about the threat from Russia worried Tomáš. Two days after the parade Lukáš and his fellow students organised a pro-reform rally in the Old Town, which drew 4,000 peaceful protesters. Ignoring Tomáš's advice, Lukáš carried a placard all the way from Anna's flat proclaiming, *'Poland awaits its Dubček'*. The morning after the rally Dubček and Oldrich Černik, the Prime Minister, were summoned to Moscow.

Rumours spread throughout the country of Warsaw Pact troops gathering on Czechoslovakia's borders. Special units were equipped with radio-jamming equipment, it was reported, and Soviet secret police carried lists of Czechoslovak dissidents who were marked down for arrest. After forty-eight hours Dubček was returned to Prague in an attempt to calm his people's nerves.

Anna and Tomáš went up to Eva and Vilém's flat that evening to watch Dubček's broadcast on their television.

"Our friendship with the Soviet Union does not depend on diplomatic niceties," Dubček told the nation. "It is reasonable that we listen to our friends' concerns."

But any reassurance provided by his reappearance soon evaporated when he announced he had agreed with Moscow to allow Warsaw Pact training manoeuvres to take place on Czechoslovakian soil in June, and that it was perhaps best over the coming months if the pace of change in the country were to proceed more slowly.

"What does the silly man mean by the pace of change?" exclaimed Eva. "I can't see how any protests or Action Programmes have changed our lives one jot."

"We must give the man a chance, Eva," said Vilém.

"But our work and our wages haven't changed. And there's still nothing worth buying in the shops, not even decent food half the time. And what about this place, Vilém? It'll be years before we get an apartment with another bedroom. I'll be a grandmother before we can have another baby."

Tomáš noticed Vilém take Eva's hand and then felt Anna's hand on his. He knew everything Eva said was true. As far as he could see, there was only one thing gathering pace in Czechoslovakia as spring approached summer: the criticism of Moscow and of the Communist Party in the country's media. And he understood, with faint satisfaction and much misgiving, something Dubček clearly did not; that abolishing censorship had let a cat out of the bag which was not going to crawl back in of its own accord.

There was no part of the past twenty years of Communism which was not being scrutinised in the press, on the radio, or by the country's writers in their own publication, the *Literární listy*. The main preoccupation of writers and other intellectuals was the need for free elections and the removal of hardliners opposed to Dubček's reforms. And their agitation delivered a remarkable result. The Party Congress to pass Dubček's Action Programme into law was brought forward from a date originally set for 1970, and was now to be held in early September. Lukáš treated the news as a great victory for the reformists, and a clear sign the Party was really independent of Russia and moving towards democratisation. When Tomáš pointed out the difference between democratisation within the Party and democracy in a multi-party state, he was shocked by Lukáš's vehemence towards him.

"You have the cheek to criticise us, but look at your western democracy at work in France. They have ten million workers on strike. The whole country's at a standstill, and what does that fascist de Gaulle do? He bans demonstrations and calls a so-called free election, knowing he'll win because he controls the media and has the army on his side. Compare that with the peaceful way we socialists are changing things here."

Anna was relieved when Tomáš chose not to take up the argument, and she wondered if he felt the same way she did; that any issues surrounding events in the country were far less important than the risk of Lukáš becoming disillusioned, or much worse, disaffected.

"We need to encourage his optimism, my love," she said later, when they were alone together in their apartment. "He has such faith in Dubček and the people. Life has been so bad here, Tomáš, and he really believes his generation can change things. And maybe he's right. Maybe they will be allowed to decide their own future this time."

"I hope so, Anna. I feel the same as you, darling. The last thing I want is for our son to suffer the same humiliation our generation did. We rid ourselves of the Germans, and now it's the damned Russians. I wonder if our country will ever be left in peace."

The 'manoeuvres' the Russians planned for June remained Tomáš's chief concern, and he sought to understand as quickly as he could the tensions behind the politics reported in the newspapers. Because this time, if a crisis did come, and the Russians did move against Dubček and the reformers, he was determined to be forewarned, and to keep his family safe.

He found it strange that the nation's press made so little of the Russian threat. The main focus of all the newspapers during the spring and early summer surprised him. The editorials contained the usual musings about the nature of democracy, freedom and socialism, but for week after week the headlines concentrated on only one theme: justice for the crimes committed in the late forties and fifties during Gottwald's Stalinist terror. And the person for whom the press demanded justice before all others was Jan Masaryk.

Every day during May Tomáš read and reread the front-page reports of the special commission set up to investigate the suspicious death of his friend. For the first time in twenty years the Masaryk family became the centre of the nation's attention again, as the inquiry into Jan's death remained headline news well into the summer.

Tomáš wanted to approach the commission to tell them of Jan's visit to his rooms on the night he died, to provide them with clear testimony that Jan Masaryk had been in no mood to commit suicide. God knows, thought Tomáš, Jan deserved justice. It was time people knew what a brave and principled man he was. But he remembered the note pushed under his door that night. *They know he spoke with you. You are a marked man.*' To give evidence to the commission he would have to reveal his true identity and, according to reports in the newspapers, that was an increasingly dangerous thing to do.

In early spring Dr Josef Brestansky, Vice President of the Supreme Court, and one of those responsible for reopening the investigation, was found hanging from a tree in Babice forest south of Prague. Three weeks later the Chief of Prague CID was found hanging near the same spot, only twenty-four hours after one of the physicians who had examined Jan's body in the courtyard died from a bullet wound to the head.

Tomáš shared his fears with no one. He decided to postpone declaring his Czechoslovak identity to any officials until the hysteria and danger surrounding the Masaryk case died down. But then the director of the secret police in the Interior Ministry at the time of Jan's death was also found hanged in the same forest, and Tomáš realised he could only tell what he knew, if Dubček's reformists won the day. If the hardliners prevailed, he could never reveal his true identity and reinstate his Czechoslovak citizenship. And without citizenship he would be unable to remain permanently with Anna in Prague. If Dubček failed, he would be left with no choice. He would have to persuade Anna and the rest of his family to return with him to England.

"A holiday in Cheb, Tomáš, that's a wonderful idea, darling. When did you think of it?"

"It's been on my mind since I arrived. And you said you had two weeks off at the end of June. I've reserved a week in the Hotel Hvězda from next Saturday, the 22nd."

"The Hvězda in the Main Square? You took me for dinner there on my 16th birthday."

"I know."

Anna came over to the chair where Tomáš was sitting, stroked his hair and kissed him. "It was just before Christmas in 1932," she said. She turned and walked to the window. "It's funny, isn't it? I remember that evening so well. What I wore, what I thought, even what we ate. I remember feeling so grown up, as if I understood everything about life. But I knew nothing at all. Neither of us did."

Tomáš stood behind her and put his arms around her waist. They looked out together onto the street as a tram clattered past. "We knew one thing that has never changed, Anna. We knew we loved one another."

She held his arms and pulled them tighter around her. "Yes, darling, we knew that. I can't remember a time when we didn't know that."

"Come on, Anna. Sit down on the couch. I'll bring you a cup of your herbal tea and a slice of Bábovka. You need a rest."

Tomáš stood in the kitchen waiting for the water in the saucepan to boil on the weak gas flame. He would be glad for once in his life to get out of Prague. It had become a confusing place. A city of contradictions. It was bustling with tourists and buzzing with more cultural activity than ever before. The theatres and cinemas were full every night, and every basement in the town centre had become a mini-theatre or a beat club, or even just a place for drop-in discussion and drinks. Talking. That was the passion in Prague now. People gathered everywhere in the Old Town, along the embankments and bridges, and talked, played music and smoked, and talked some more.

They were still mostly young people, students and tourists, boosted by a few middle-aged intellectuals who joined in with them from time to time. But there was no involvement from working people, from people who could not escape the practicalities of family life and the need to earn a living in the world as it was. The people the reformers would really need if they were to carry the country with them. Workers such as those he had met today at the repair shop, where Eva's bicycle was being mended. People, who had been robbed of all ambition and aspiration and had settled for a life of torpor.

"Maybe next week, comrade, if you're lucky," he was told, while half the workforce stood around smoking cigarettes and chatting.

But why should they be any different? thought Tomáš. It was no wonder such people did not welcome Dubček's reforms. They had no one to envy and no ladder to climb, and they had made a virtue out of a common saying: a poor day's work for a poor day's pay. They saw no reason to change anything. The government was obliged to give them a job and, in a strange way, Tomáš realised, they could even feel pampered by Communism. Workers in the different factories and shops had created a market to satisfy their consumerism through pilfering and barter, and managers turned a blind eye for a quiet life. As he walked away from the repair shop, Tomáš knew that if a need arose within the market, there was no chance Eva would ever see her bicycle again.

The water was bubbling and Tomáš took a towel to lift the pan by its metal handle, which seemed to be the part retaining most of the heat. He took Anna's tea through to the living room.

"I heard the water boiling for ages," she said. "I thought you'd gone to sleep out there."

"Yes, I'm sorry. I was lost in my thoughts."

"Good ones?"

"Not really. I was thinking how pleased I'll be to get away from Prague."

"That's not like you. I thought it was the place everyone wanted to be."

"It's all a veneer, Anna. What you and Eva say is true. All the activity and openness is on the surface. There's nothing changing at the grass roots. And look how nervous everyone gets as soon as anything appears in the papers which might offend the Russians. Did you get a chance to read that Václav Klaus article in the *Literární Listy*?"

"When do I have time, darling?"

"Of course. I'm sorry."

"Was it important?"

"Only because it made the Russians so mad they called Dubček to Moscow again and he refused to go."

"I heard people talking about that. Good for him, I say."

"Yes, but I don't know how much more they'll take from us."

"You always were a worrier, Tomáš." She sipped her tea. "You don't really think there could be a problem, do you?"

"No, I don't think so for a minute." He went over to her and kissed her forehead. "You know me. Always thinking too much. You enjoy your cake."

He sat down at the table and watched her. She looked tired and she ate slowly. He knew he must not tell her what he really thought. That Dubček was probably only too anxious to go to Moscow to placate the Soviets, but dare not for fear of the reaction in the Czechoslovak media, now hopelessly out of his control. Moscow would look to Prague and see Dubček as a hostage in his own country, which was clearly the reason the thousands of Warsaw Pact troops on manoeuvres in Bohemia and Moravia had not left last week as originally agreed. 'Transportation problems' was the official reason given in the Party newspaper, but surely no one really believed that. Everyone must realise it took just one phone call from Moscow to turn those troops into an army of occupation...

"You're miles away again, Tomáš. Are you going to tell me what's on your mind?"

"Nothing really. I was thinking about Cheb. How much it might have changed."

"It won't have changed that much. The lake will still be there, and the beach by the river at Skalka. I'm so looking forward to it."

"I'm pleased, darling. So am I."

* * *

"It's desecration, Tomáš. To leave it in this state."

"The manager of the hotel said there's not a single Jew living in Cheb now."

"I don't blame them when I see this. Why haven't they cleared the rubble? Why just leave it piled up like that, with weeds growing through everywhere? They've had nearly twenty-five years to clean this up."

"I know, Anna. It's dreadful. There's a memorial over there,. Do you want to see what it says?"

They stepped over the uneven ground, and Tomáš clambered over the rubble to reach a granite block. He read out the inscription. *'Here stood the Cheb Synagogue and Cemetery, constructed in 1463 under the protection of George of Poděbrad, King of Bohemia, and destroyed by Nazi barbarians on September 23rd, 1938. On this site lie the mortal remains...'* There's not much more."

"Read it, Tomáš. I'm hardened to these things."

'On this site lie the mortal remains of 139 Jewish men, women and children taken from a transport on route from Auschwitz on January 22nd, 1945. Respect this place.'

"Respect this place. What hypocrites."

"I doubt whether the Town Council understands irony, Anna. Are you sure you're alright?"

"I'm upset that my mother's grave isn't marked. But you did warn me I might not find it. Was it the same as this when you were here at the end of the war?"

"No, it was much worse then. The synagogue was a burned-out ruin. At least someone's levelled it since."

"Come on, Tomáš. I don't want to leave the flowers here. I'll put them with yours on your parents' grave. My mother will understand."

Tomáš took Anna's hand to help her back over the rough ground. They reached the road and walked towards the main square and the Church of Saint Wenceslas.

"I'm afraid all this makes me even more disillusioned with Czechs than I was already," said Anna.

"I didn't know you were."

"Then I've hidden it well. I still can't forgive the people who treated my father so badly. Did you know they put him in the concentration camp at Terezín?"

"I suspected it. It was one of the places I went looking for him. But he had gone by the time I got there."

"Bless you for doing that, Tomáš. They didn't keep him there long.

As soon as he had his stroke, they took him to the German border and abandoned him. He never told me how he made it to Dresden."

"Thank God you found him in the end, Anna."

"If Vati hadn't written to Otto I would never have known what happened to him. I had made up my mind to go to Palestine with the children, you know, until I learned Vati was alive."

Tomáš put his arm around her and pulled her towards him.

"Thank God you didn't. I would never have found you."

"It's so strange, isn't it, Tomáš? The things that determine our lives. I think of my mother. Her religion was so important to me. My earliest memory of her caring for me created such a strong connection to her. I clung to my Jewishness in France because of that memory. But do you know what I discovered from Vati before he died?"

"What?"

"The woman I remembered wasn't my mother at all. It was your mother. Auntie Karolina."

"*My* mother?"

"Yes." Anna stopped and stood with her head bowed. "Vati talked a lot about your mother towards the end. He told me she helped him with Otto and me after our mother passed. So all the time I was growing up, and when we were in the camp, I had no real memory of my mother at all. But I attached such meaning to what I thought was her. I was so stubborn in France, and for the wrong reason. I promised myself I'd never tell you all this, but coming back here..."

Tomáš put his hands on her shoulders.

"It's alright, darling. It doesn't matter who the person caring for you was. Your commitment was always to your mother, no one else. And you were right to have those feelings."

"But when I think of what my stubbornness led to. Why do we attach so much importance to things when we're young? Why are the young so stubborn?"

"Are you talking about Lukáš now?"

"I see the same thing in him. He won't compromise his principles for anything. I worry about where it will lead him."

"Come on, let's keep walking," said Tomáš. They strolled arm in arm towards the main square. "You can let me worry about Lukáš if you like, Anna. I want to be a father to him. I'd welcome the responsibility."

"Oh, Tomáš, please do. Look after him. Make him listen to you."

"I will, darling. You don't need to worry. I won't let anything bad happen to any of you ever again."

They entered the square and passed the Town Hall.
"At least this hasn't changed," said Anna. "I've always loved the square. The lovely buildings and the colonnade. Do you remember how we used to splash around in that fountain after school?"
"Yes, darling. I remember everything."
"We were so innocent."
"I wasn't. I always saw it as a chance to look at your legs."
"Tomáš Kovařík." She looked at him and smiled. "And do you think I didn't know that?"

They put their flowers on the grave shared by Pavel and Karolína in the Church of Saint Wenceslas. Anna waited for Tomáš by the fountain while he spent time alone with his parents. When she saw him coming from the churchyard she made her way over to him. She took his hand and they strolled, without speaking, down Krámařská Street towards the river.

In front of them they saw the concrete, single-span bridge which had replaced the medieval stone bridge destroyed at the end of the war. They walked onto it and stood looking over the iron railings.

"My God, Tomáš, what's happened to the river?"

Below them the River Ohře was no more than a shallow stream barely two metres wide. On the dry river bed on either side lay paper and bottles and pieces of twisted metal. Tomáš called out to a man crossing the bridge on the other side of the road.

"Excuse me, sir. What's happened to the river?"

The man kept walking. "Been like that for the past three years," he said looking straight ahead. "Since they built that bloody useless dam at Skalka."

"This is awful, Tomáš," said Anna shaking her head. "Is there nothing these people haven't spoiled? Have you seen your parents' house?"

"It's the first thing I noticed. It was in ruins when I was last here. I knew it wouldn't be rebuilt the way it was before the war."

"But it was such a beautiful house. All that lovely wood and white plasterwork. Does it upset you?"

Tomáš looked at the terrace of tall, thin buildings. The steep gable of the Kovařík house had been replaced by a flat roof, and the medieval frontage by uneven, grey rendering.

"We can't let everything that changes upset us, Anna. After all we've been through, does any of this really matter?"

"I know you're right, but this is all so typical of the way we live. Everything's so functional and bleak. There's nothing to lift the spirit. I'm tired of it."

"Do you want to go back to the hotel? We could have an early lunch."

"No, I want to see the lake. I've waited years for that."

They crossed the bridge and took the path to Skalka. Soon they turned off to the right along the track through the forest of oak, birch and fir down to Štasný Lake.

"You mustn't be disappointed again, Anna. Remember our grandparents' chata isn't there any more. It could all be a real mess."

Anna gripped his hand but did not reply. After two hundred metres they reached the clearing. They walked through the overgrown grass to the spot where the cottage once stood. Only the foundations remained. They stood together and looked out over the carp lake to the fir trees on the far shore. To their left the sun was at its highest point in a clear sky.

"What in the Lord's name is all that?" said Anna.

They looked at a ring of blue-green algae reaching out into the lake for fifty metres from every part of the shore.

"It's like scum. And it stinks. Like rotten vegetables."

"It's because of the pollution, Anna."

"And look at the fir trees over there."

Tomáš looked to his right following Anna's outstretched arm. The tops of the tallest fir trees skirting the lake to the north were stripped of their pine needles and stood with their light-brown skeletons exposed, stark and naked.

"It's from all the industry in the north," he said. "The sulphur dioxide dissolves in the rain and strips them." He shielded his eyes from the sun and looked around the lake. "All the trees are affected to some extent. They're just worse on that side."

"I can't stay here, Tomáš. It's too depressing. Cheb, Prague, the whole country is depressing. There's nothing beautiful or unspoilt left anywhere anymore."

Tomáš faced her and placed his hands on her arms. She would not look up at him. "Anna, there's still beauty here for me." She turned away.

"I have an idea, Anna. Why don't we leave Cheb for a few days and get the train to Karlovy Vary? We could stay in the Hotel Pupp. You could wear your white dress to dinner..."

"I didn't bring my white dress."

"Oh, I see."

"Let's go, Tomáš. There's nothing left of us here, or of our family."

"No, wait, Anna. Perhaps there is." Tomáš took her hand and led her to the corner of the chata's foundations where the kitchen once stood. He bent over and scraped at the soil. "I wonder..."

"What are you doing, Tomáš?"

"Yes, it's still here." He stood up holding a green porcelain tile in one hand and a rusty tin in the other. "Look, Anna. There is still something of us here. Open it."

Anna forced the lid from the tin and took out a piece of browned paper. She unfolded it. *'Anna and Eva. I am alive and will keep looking for you. Your Tomáš and Táta, 1st May, 1945.'*

"I left it here because I knew this place would draw you back one day. I left one at your father's house in Skalka. And in a couple of other places."

She stepped towards him and pulled him to her. "Oh, my darling Tomáš. Here am I feeling so sorry for myself and you went through so much for us. I feel so ashamed. Please forgive me."

"I love you, Anna." He smoothed her hair as she rested her head on his chest. "This place will always be a part of our lives, Anna. I'm not saying we belong here any more. Just that the memories we have of it will always belong to us. It will always hold meaning for us, and one day, in better times, we'll come back. It's the same with Prague and with our country. They will always belong to us... but we could leave and come back when life has improved."

"What do you mean, Tomáš? What are you saying?"

"I'm saying there's no reason for you to put up with life under the Communists any more, Anna. You're married to a British citizen. You and I could live together in London."

"London? But Eva and Lukáš. I could never leave them."

"I know you couldn't. Neither could I. We must persuade them to come with us. England won't turn down a surgeon and an anaesthetist and a bright young man like Lukáš."

"Are you serious?"

"I am. Eva isn't happy here, and I sense Vilém would do anything for her. And you would have a wonderful life in London, Anna. I want to see you happy again."

"But Lukáš would never leave. He thinks Czechoslovakia is about to become the most perfect country in the world."

"If it does, then none of us need leave. I'm a Czechoslovak before I'm ever an Englishman, Anna. I'd love to stay here. But if the Russians lose patience and take over, our family must come before our country. I'll have to make Lukáš understand."

"How will we know if something is about to happen?"

"I think the signs will be clear enough. But first we need to discuss it with the three of them, so we're all agreed to go if it does become necessary."

Anna stepped back and fixed her eyes on his. He was afraid he had upset her, but then a broad smile spread across her face. "Alright, darling," she said, "I'll do it."

"You will?"

"Yes, but you must promise you won't say anything to Lukáš or Eva without speaking to me first."

"Yes, Anna. Of course."

Anna smiled again and leaned forward to kiss him.

"All of us together in London. It's such a wonderful thought, Tomáš. You've always found ways of making things better."

"I have another idea right now. Shall we get away from this horrible smell and go back to lunch?"

"Yes, my darling. Please."

They skirted the long grass and walked by the lakeside with their hands over their nose and mouth. They passed a sign, *'No Fishing. No Swimming'*.

"More irony from the Town Council," said Anna, and they both laughed through their hands.

The smell from the algae became more bearable as they left the lake and approached the track. They passed a tree with bright green leaves and ripening red fruit, standing alone at the edge of the forest. On the ground around its trunk lay lengths of decaying wood, which had once been fashioned into a seat. The summer air above the tree was calm, and the waters of the lake silent, as they made their way laughing up the track.

Chapter Thirty-Eight

July 21st, 1968

"Are you mad?" Lukáš turned to his mother. "Is this what he came here for? To persuade you to leave, thinking we'd all follow you like little children?"

"Lukáš, that's offensive to your mother and to me," said Tomáš. "Your mother knows I came here to stay with you all for the rest of my life." Anna smiled at him from the other end of the table. "But things have changed, Lukáš. You must see the reforms will never happen now. The Russian troops should have left weeks ago. Brezhnev will keep them here until Dubček backs down, and then life is going to get a lot worse for everyone."

"So you'd prefer us to run off to a fascist country like England, would you? Rather than stand up for our principles and show the Soviets what they can gain from a new Czechoslovakia."

"But you'll never convince the Russians to allow a multi-party state, Lukáš."

"Well, I certainly won't if I'm stuck amongst fascists in England."

"Stop saying Britain is fascist. That's just ridiculous propaganda the Party's fed you."

"That's strange. Most people I meet from the West agree their countries are fascist."

"Well, they would. Idiots like that think Fidel Castro is a democrat."

"Your country supports West Germany, doesn't it? Are you trying to say the West German government isn't still full of Nazis?"

"There are probably some."

"Some? Then I think *you've* swallowed too much propaganda, Tomáš. I'd rather believe *Pravda* before the lies your English newspapers feed you."

"So you believe what Brezhnev tells you, do you, Lukáš? That there are American spies in Czechoslovakia preparing an invasion from West Germany?"

"Stop it, both of you!" said Anna. "You're both treating this like a game, seeing who can score the most points." She looked directly at Tomáš. "You told me the situation here had reached crisis-point, Tomáš, and we needed to discuss it urgently with everyone. But this isn't discussion. Eva,

JULY 21ST, 1968

Vilém and I may as well not be here."

"I apologise, Anna." He paused for Lukáš to apologise too, but Lukáš took a gulp of beer instead. "I've explained what I think," Tomáš continued. "I do believe we have reached crisis-point. The '2,000 Words' article has changed everything here. It's a clear call for action against the Communist Party, and the Soviet response is an open threat to our country. Refusing to meet Brezhnev again may be brave of Dubček, but it's foolhardy too. When Russian soldiers are sent to Prague, as I expect them to be, the city will become a battleground. We should leave while we still can. That's all I have to say."

"A battleground? That's a ridiculous thing to say," said Lukáš. "Russia attacking us would be like America attacking Canada."

"What do you think, Vilém?" asked Anna.

"You know me, Anna. My work takes up too much of my time for me to bother much with politics. Personally I feel quite angry with Ludvik Vaculík for writing that article, and with the others who put their names to it. It just causes trouble when things should be allowed to progress naturally. You learn that as a doctor. Go gently, allow the body to heal itself. You don't go digging around with a scalpel like some of those writers do with their pens."

"Well put, Vilém," said Lukáš, and he looked at the others around the table. "Vilém's right. We should all relax, trust Dubček, and not make such a fuss about everything."

"Well, I like the idea of living in London," said Eva. "I know it would be difficult at first with the language, but you could teach us, couldn't you, Táta?"

"Of course, darling."

"We could get a bigger apartment, Vilém, and have another baby. I might even get help with my eyes. I could take up my surgeon's training." She took Vilém's hand. "What do you think, my love?"

"Anything's possible, Eva. I'd go if it was that important to you, and it was right for Lenka."

Lukáš slumped back in his chair and wiped the condensation on his beer glass with his thumb. "How incredibly shallow and ungrateful my family is," he said. "I suppose I should thank you really, Tomáš, for coming here and opening my eyes about you all."

"Lukáš..."

"No, Máma." Lukáš sat forward at the table, his shoulders hunched. "How can any of you think of leaving now, when every Czechoslovak is needed here? I know people are on edge about the Russian troops, but there's such a fantastic spirit here. Can't you feel it? For the first time in my life there are no Czechs or Slovaks any more, or Bohemians or Moravians. For the first time we're a country only of Czechoslovaks."

He sat back again sweeping the air with his hand. "And all any of you want to do is leave."

"It's because some of us have been through it before, Lukáš," said Anna. "Thirty years ago your father and I felt the same way, and all the people around us did too. We thought, if we all stick together and our leaders stay strong, we can win against anything, but..."

"Oh, don't go on about Munich again, Máma. All we hear from your generation is damned Munich. You're so negative all the time. Can't you see this is different?"

"But there is no difference, Lukáš," said Tomáš. "The rest of the Warsaw Pact talk about the 'Czechoslovakia problem'. They met last week to discuss it without us. Dubček himself said we're like defendants in the dock. It's exactly like Munich."

"But the Soviets aren't the Nazis. We share the same philosophy and values with them. The troops here aren't invaders..."

"They refuse to leave."

"What hypocrites you westerners are. England is full of American troops, and so is most of Western Europe, but you don't call them invaders."

"Because they'd leave if we told them to."

"Ha, you really believe that, do you?" Lukáš shook his head. "Don't you see the Russians are only staying here because they don't trust the West? I know Brezhnev comes across as a hardliner, but Russia changed for good under Khrushchev. It's more liberal now than any of you seem to realise. They even admit they were wrong to go into Hungary in '56. They're not going to make the same mistake again."

"Lukáš could be right, Tomáš," said Anna.

"At last. Thankyou, Máma. I don't think any of you should do anything until the reforms become law in September. Just give Dubček a chance to explain to our allies what we're doing."

"I still don't know what you *are* doing," said Eva.

"Well, that's typical." Lukáš looked at his sister and spoke in a slow monotone. "We are trying to return the Party to the way it was after the war. The leading party in a National Front of parties. Understand, Eva? Leading, but not all-powerful. A people's democracy with all the freedoms we're enjoying now."

"The problem is, Lukáš, when Communists say 'leading' they mean dominant," said Tomáš.

"What makes you so damn cynical all the time?"

"Because in a democracy no party can be sure of a permanent leading role. To have a real democracy you have to have uncertainty."

"What the hell does that mean?"

"There has to be a chance the Communists can be voted out."

"Well, they could in theory, I suppose. But it's very unlikely. Just about everyone here supports a socialist system. No one wants capitalism."

"But what if they do want it one day? Vaculík is right, Lukáš. There are too many contradictions in what Dubček says. He says he wants democracy, but the Party must always play a leading role. He wants to free the economy by adapting to market forces, but there can be no private ownership or private capital. And he wants local solutions to local problems, but everything must be checked by the Party in Prague first. None of it makes any sense."

"There's your western cynicism again. If Dubček is so wrong, why do so many people in the West support what he's trying to do?"

"Simple. Leftists love him because they think he's showing the inherent goodness of socialism. And the right because they think he's showing the universal appeal of liberalism. But most of all, we like him because he's standing up to the Russian dictators in the Kremlin."

Lukáš pushed back his chair and got to his feet. "There you go again. Everything you say comes down to your hatred of Russia, and you're determined to turn my family against everything good here because of it. I'm getting sick of your negativity, Tomáš. You forget Russia liberated us from fascism, and our Communist Party rebuilt this country after the war. And they did it democratically."

"Please sit down, Lukáš," said Anna, "and don't upset yourself. Tomáš, please don't argue over everything. I thought we wanted to persuade everyone, not fight amongst ourselves."

"I'm sorry, Anna, but until Lukáš accepts the truth, there's no chance of any of us escaping from what's going to happen here."

"Escaping? Are you mad? Escaping from what?"

"From the bloodbath there'll be when Russian tanks enter Prague."

Lukáš turned away and threw his arms in the air. "He's mad. He's completely mad. Máma, you never told us you married a madman."

"Lukáš, darling..."

"I understand your idealism, Lukáš..."

"Don't you patronise me."

"I'm not patronising you. I'm your father. I'm trying to help you. [1]

all of you."

"Oh, great. Help from an Englishman who's completely lost touch with our country."

"Alright, Lukáš. You're so damned stubborn... I'll spell out the real truth to you, shall I, about your Russian liberators and your precious Communist Party?"

"Spell out what you like."

"In May 1945..."

"Oh, here we go again."

"... in May 1945, when the uprising against the Nazis began in Prague, the Russians said they couldn't get here to help in time. But did you know the British and Americans were just outside the city, but your wonderful Communist Party wouldn't allow them in, and thousands died because of it?"

Tomáš stabbed the table with his finger. His voice trembled.

"And don't say the Communists came to power democratically in '48. They staged a coup d'état before elections could be held which they knew they were going to lose. They terrorised people, bullied President Beneš into accepting them, and persecuted one of the few men who stood up for democracy. Jan Masaryk."

"Puh. Propaganda and nonsense. For a start, everyone knows Masaryk was nothing but a playboy, who chose to kill himself when he realised the family dynasty was over. And how would you know any of the rest?"

"Because I waited outside Prague with the British in 1945, while the Communists let our people die," shouted Tomáš, "and I was beaten senseless by Gottwald's thugs during the takeover. And Jan Masaryk was my friend..."

There was silence around the table. Tomáš glanced at Lukáš who was leaning against the doorframe, looking up at the corner of the room with his arms folded.

"I see only two ways Dubček can prevent the Russians coming to Prague," Tomáš said in a quiet, tremulous voice. "He must either give them what they want... censorship and the guarantee of a one-party state... or... he must act decisively and show them we'll fight to keep our independence... But I don't hold out much hope of the second one."

"Well, I'd fight, I can tell you," said Lukáš, stepping towards the table. "My generation won't give up like yours did, that's for sure. But you're mad suggesting all this." He leaned towards Tomáš. "I can see what you're doing, you know. You're scaring Máma and Eva so they'll go back to England with you. You've got a damned cheek coming here..."

"Don't you dare speak for me, Lukáš," shouted Eva. "I don't want to stay in this awful country, and I'm sure Máma doesn't either. Do you know how hard we all have to work to get nothing back... nothing at all? Perhaps you've haven't noticed, because you're so wrapped up in yourself all the time, but I've never seen our mother happier than the past three months since Táta came home."

"But he's not home, is he? He's an Englishman, not a Czechoslovak. He doesn't care about our country. He's just saying all this to get us to go to London with him, where he really wants to be."

Tomáš stood up, his face flushed with anger. "That's enough, Lukáš. I'm your father. And I am a Czechoslovak. How dare you question my love for my country."

The violence of his voice and the anxious look on the faces of Anna and Eva shocked him into silence. He felt his legs weaken and he slumped down onto his chair. He put his head in his hands. "I love my country," he said, and his shoulders shook. "But I always loved your mother more, Lukáš. Your grandfather understood. I always loved Anna more. I must keep her safe."

Chapter Thirty-Nine

August 3rd – August 21st, 1968

The Russian troops left Czechoslovakia on August 3rd.

The whole country was jubilant. Within half an hour of Dubček making the announcement on television, Lukáš appeared at Anna's front door. He put his arms around her and lifted her off her feet.

"I told you, Máma. I told you. What did I say? We only needed to trust Dubček and everything would be alright."

"I know, darling. We've been so worried, but you were right. I'm so pleased for you after all you've done."

"I hope you're going to apologise for being so cynical about everything," he said to Tomáš, who had got up from the couch and walked to the hallway to offer Lukáš his hand.

"I'm as delighted as anyone, Lukáš. It's a great relief to us all."

"But you're not going to apologise?"

Tomáš dropped his hand to his side. "I'm not sure it's my place to apologise, Lukáš. They've only withdrawn over the East German border. They could be back at any time within hours."

"I really give up with you, Tomáš." Lukáš shook his head and turned to his mother. "The whole country is celebrating out there. Prague is one huge party tonight, and he stays here cynical and miserable."

"Your father's not miserable. We were just about to put our coats on and walk up to the Old Town."

"No, Lukáš. I'm not miserable at all, I promise you. I know sometimes survival alone is victory enough, and we're surviving."

"We're not just surviving. We're winning. Didn't you hear on the television? Brezhnev has agreed to the Party Congress next month. All the reforms are going to be passed into law."

"That's very good. But I also heard what Dubček said. We have to stop the media attacks on the Soviets and the Party. And he warned us again. Our sovereignty depends on Russia."

"Yes, because they protect us from the West. Not because they're the threat."

"I'm not sure that's what he meant, Lukáš."

"Oh. I give up with you. I'm going back to the celebrations."

Lukáš kissed his mother. "Don't let him get you down, Máma. And

no more talk about leaving. Everything's going to be alright now. It's fantastic out there. I've never seen people so happy. I'm off back to where the fun is." He kissed her again. "Try to cheer up. Bye."
"Bye, darling. Be careful."
"Bye, Lukáš," Tomáš called after him.

Tomáš returned to his chair. The television flickered in front of him. Dubček's broadcast had been followed by a display of gymnastics by Young Pioneers.

Tomáš understood well enough why people were celebrating tonight. The row with the Kremlin caused by Ludvik Vaculík's *2,000 Words* had turned into a crisis over the past two weeks. A crisis which had left the country on the brink of war. Brezhnev accused counter-revolutionaries of driving Czechoslovakia into the arms of the western bourgeoisie and risking the security of the entire socialist bloc. Dubček, he said, was 'unprincipled and irresolute' for allowing it. Such a situation, he warned, could not be tolerated and would need to be 'normalised'. The Kremlin then went silent.

Tomáš witnessed the changing mood in Prague, as people were gripped by fear. And it seemed Dubček and other Party leaders shared the people's fear, as every day the newspapers reported their efforts to secure talks with Brezhnev, in an attempt to stop Warsaw Pact troops moving against them.

There was general relief when, at the end of July, the Kremlin announced Brezhnev was prepared to meet with Dubček, in order, they said, to find a lasting solution to the 'problem' of Czechoslovakia. The meeting would take place over four days in Čierna nad Tisou on the Slovak-Ukrainian border.

Before Dubček left for the meeting, an article appeared in the Literární Listy praising him for his ideals and urging him to remain strong in the face of Soviet threats. 'We are with you,' the article ended. 'Be with us!' Within hours the same rallying cry appeared on walls all over the country and was chanted by crowds in the centre of Prague. 'We are with you, be with us!' The article was redrafted into a petition, signed by more than a million people, and a single symbolic sheet was handed over to Dubček as he left for the talks from Prague Main Station. Tomáš remembered that night less than a week ago. It was the only time during the crisis that Lukáš had called at Anna's apartment. He had been to the station to wave Dubček off. Tomáš had seen tears in his eyes.

Nothing was heard from Dubček during the four days of the meeting, and rumours spread through Prague of his arrest and imprisonment.

When the meeting ended, the only words came from Brezhnev. A second conference would take place immediately in Bratislava, he said, and the outcome of those talks would be broadcast that evening. Like all Czechoslovaks Tomáš and Anna had waited all day and, when they turned on their television, it was Dubček's face they saw.

He looked exhausted and spoke slowly and quietly. He assured his people the entire socialist bloc was now firmly united. A new opportunity to proceed with liberalisation has been created, he said, due to the continued goodwill of Czechoslovakia's Soviet comrades. He left it until the end of the broadcast to announce that all Warsaw Pact troops would leave Czechoslovakia immediately.

The gymnastics display was still on. Tomáš got up, clicked the dial to the left and watched the picture contract into a dot in the centre of the screen. Anna came in and handed him his coat. He took it, too distracted to thank her, and they went out to join the celebrations.

"I'm so pleased to see Lukáš so happy, Tomáš. This is all he's wanted for months. Years. You do think everything will be alright now, don't you?"

Tomáš put his arm around Anna's shoulders as they walked along the embankment.

"I hope so, Anna. God knows, our country and our people deserve to be left in peace."

"You don't think the Russian troops will come back?"

"Not if we behave ourselves."

"It's such a lovely evening. The sound of the river. The castle all lit up, and everyone celebrating. I don't understand why anyone would want to disturb any of this."

"My father used to say it's the curse of our geography. I think he was right."

"But you do think we're all safe here now, don't you?"

"Yes, darling. Don't worry. We're safe."

"Thank goodness. I know how worried you've been." Anna stopped and placed her hands on his cheeks and kissed him. "But I think everything will be alright now. Everyone's got what they want. And Lukáš is happy. I want us to enjoy the rest of the summer, darling. Don't you?"

"Of course."

"Shall we do something nice tomorrow? Hire a boat. Celebrate. Have a picnic on the island. I could wear the dress you bought me."

"Really? Oh yes, Anna." Tomáš put his arms around her and felt her press her body against him. "My darling," he said, "it would make me very happy if you wore your dress."

"That's settled then. Come on. Let's do what Lukáš is doing. Go to the Old Town and have some fun."

"Rowing isn't one of your strengths, is it, darling?"

"The oars won't stay in the damned... whatever they are."

"Don't worry, we're nearly there. Careful. Mind out!"

The boat hit the jetty and Tomáš tipped backwards off his seat. The boat rocked as he tried to stand up. He gave up and lay on his back watching Anna laughing. The sun shone over her shoulder and all he could see was her silhouette. She moved her head slightly to the side, blocking the sunlight, and her whole body came into focus.

She had taken to wearing her hair up most of the time now, and he thought how much it suited her. It showed her thin neck and the still fine outline of her jaw. Her eyes had remained as bright and as beautiful as ever, and when she laughed her face lit up as it had done as a child and as a young woman.

The white dress suited her more than she probably realised. The low, round neckline complemented the way she wore her hair and led his eyes to her breasts. And the sleeves stopping just above her elbows made her look as if she had just walked from Carnaby Street. He noticed how she kept pulling at her hem in a vain attempt to cover her knees, but as she laughed she rocked back and forth and the dress rode up her legs. His brain took a photographic image of her, which he knew would stay permanently in his head. He felt his mouth go dry and his cheeks flush, and recognised his all too familiar desire for her.

"You blasted fool, are you going to go to sleep down there? Look what you've done to my boat."

The boatman secured the craft to the jetty and helped Tomáš to his feet. Anna was laughing so much she couldn't move from her seat.

"Come on, young lady. You won't think it's so funny when I give your boyfriend the bill for this damage."

Tomáš took Anna's hand and helped her onto the jetty. He reached into his pocket and pulled out several hundred kroner. "Will this cover it?"

"Well, yes. I suppose it'll do," said the boatman, hardly able to believe his luck at being so well compensated for retouching some scraped paintwork.

Tomáš retrieved the picnic hamper and started to walk away. Anna caught up with him and took his arm, still giggling.

"I don't see what's so funny, Anna. That was bloody embarrassing."

"Your face," she said. "Being rescued by an old man." And then she laughed some more.

"At least it's nice to see a bit of capitalism alive and well in this small corner of our country. The thieving so-and-so."

"I liked him. He called me 'young lady'."

"You are a young lady, Anna. Young, and very beautiful."

"Come here, Tomáš." He turned and Anna took him by the collar and kissed him on the lips. "You're still my hero, even if you do make a rotten sailor. It's just as well Czechoslovakia has no navy."

"Well, it's funny you should say that, because it did have one once."

"What are you talking about, silly socks? I think you must have bumped your head."

"No, my father told me when I was a boy. I told the story in school once... about the Battle of Lake Baikal... You... Oh, it doesn't matter. Shall we have our picnic over there?"

"Yes, under the tree." Anna took his hand and squeezed it hard. "Oh, Tomáš, this is so perfect. I haven't felt this happy for years. Everyone so relaxed at last, enjoying the sunshine and the river. And we're together in Prague with our family. I can't believe it."

"Believe it, Anna."

They sat on a blanket under the chestnut tree and ate Bramborak and drank Moravian wine. They talked about their lives together as children, and dug for happy memories which had long been buried under trauma and the common cares of adulthood. They fell asleep in the shade to the sound of hippies strumming guitars by the river's edge, and woke up in the late afternoon with their arms still around one another. The crowds had thinned and the hippies moved on, probably to the Old Town to spend the evening strumming, talking and smoking. In their place a well staffed team of men and women were collecting the few items of rubbish people had left behind.

Tomáš and Anna stayed until they were the only ones left, sitting talking about their plans for themselves and their children. Anna hoped the new reforms would allow her to give up her job, and she had heard talk of people being allowed to start their own enterprises, as long as they employed no one. She thought they might be allowed to open a small shop or a café, and she had plenty of ideas for things she could make and sell. Any doubts Tomáš may have had about the future of his country counted for nothing, as he watched Anna's spirit return, and she renewed his faith in a carefree future together.

Only the cold on Anna's bare legs, as the sun dipped below the horizon on the other side of the river, alerted them to the fact the boatman had left and they were now alone on the island.

"Don't worry, Anna, I'll find a boat and row us back to the old Legion Bridge."

"In the dark? I don't think so, Tomáš. Not if we really want any future."

"We've got to do something."

"We can do something. We can stay here. We have this blanket, and there's another in the basket if it gets colder."

"Are you serious?"

"Of course I am. Come here, Tomáš."

Tomáš sat down on the blanket and Anna knelt in front of him. I haven't been very fair to you, have I, darling?" she said.

"It doesn't..."

"No, don't say anything. I know I haven't. You've been so patient with me, and so loving. You always were. I want to make it up to you."

"Anna."

She twisted her body and put her right hand on the nape of her neck. "Unzip my dress."

She turned back and pushed the dress from her shoulders. She stood up and let it fall to the ground. Tomáš looked at her with the red sun setting behind her. His Anna.

"General Secretary Brezhnev is on the telephone for you again, First Secretary."

Alexander Dubček took the receiver. He had been expecting the call. He put his hand over the mouthpiece. "Please leave us, Andrei. I'd like to talk in private."

"Of course, First Secretary."

"Hello, Comrade Brezhnev," said Dubček. "How kind of you to call again."

"How are you, Sasha? Ambassador Chervonenko informs me you have been under some strain."

"Not at all."

"I must tell you bluntly, Sasha, the Ambassador's latest report gives us great cause for concern."

"Really. In what respect?"

"In the respect that you seem to be doing little to honour the agreement we made at Čierna nad Tisou."

"We are drawing up the necessary measures, Comrade Brezhnev."

"More vague talk, Sasha. It won't do. Why have you not disbanded the SDP, KAN and K-231, as agreed?"

"Measures to do so are being drafted, Comrade Brezhnev. But such matters can only be decided by the Central Committee."

"Well, get them to decide it then!" shouted Brezhnev so vehemently, that Dubček had to hold the phone away from his ear. "These are vacillations, Sasha."

"The Central Committee will meet shortly."

"Has a date been fixed?"

"Possibly August 19th."

"Possibly? No, this will not do. What have you done about removing that rightist television director Pelikan? And the Ambassador tells me you still have not sacked Kriegel and Cisař."

"Once again, Comrade Brezhnev, they can only be removed by a decision of the Central Committee."

"Well, what can I say to you, Sasha? These procedural excuses sound like a new deception. I can call it nothing else. I believe you are deceiving us. And I will be completely open with you. If you are unable to resolve these questions, it seems to me you and your Presidium has lost all power."

"That's not the case, Comrade Brezhnev."

"Deal with the rightists, Sasha. We have come to the conclusion here that the rightists are carrying out subversive work against the decisions taken by us at Čierna. Everything depends now on how you deal with the rightists."

"We are drawing up measures to deal with spontaneous demonstrations and…"

"They are not spontaneous! They are being organised by Cisař and Kriegel. Sack them, and join forces with Bilak! And tell your media they must observe the ceasefire we agreed at Čierna."

Dubček did not reply.

"Is that you crying, Sasha? Are you not well?"

"I will be fine, Comrade… It has not been easy. I have spoken to the editors."

"Listen to me, Sasha. It is not enough. Tell me, my friend, how we can help you?"

"I assure you, Comrade Brezhnev, we need no help. The Presidium will take any measures against the rightists they deem necessary."

"More vague talk, Sasha. I must be honest with you. There are many here who believe the main struggle is going on not with the counter-revolutionaries, but within you. You must show decisive action. Let the StB loose on the demonstrators."

"We prefer at the moment to choose the path of persuasion, Comrade Brezhnev."

"You prefer? I must tell you, Sasha, that without tough measures, without tough helpers, we fear you will allow the rightists to drive you into the arms of western capitalists."

"No, Comrade..."

"Listen to me, I must underscore that we are all now living through a crucial moment. A certain uneasiness is already arising here that decisions we made together as friends are not being executed. You must think on this, Sasha. Find the time and ways of executing what we agreed. In my opinion this is very important now."

"Perhaps you think I should quit my post as Party leader, and return to humbler work..."

"Pull yourself together, Sasha. Take control of yourself and of the situation in Prague. You must understand the impression you are leaving in people's minds here. Ambassador Chervonenko will report again in one week. We must then assess anew this whole state of affairs, and possibly adopt new, independent measures."

"I assure you, Comrade Brezhnev, like any other state we shall impose order within our own borders."

"Good, Sasha. We must both remember that the whole meaning of our meeting at Čierna nad Tisou lies in the great trust of a friend for a friend."

"Thankyou, Comrade Brezhnev."

"I wish you goodnight, Sasha. I put my faith in you. I wish you well."

"Thankyou. Goodnight, Comrade Brezhnev."

Brezhnev put the phone down and remained behind his desk, staring straight ahead.

"Well?" asked Premier Alexei Kosygin.

"The man is unstable, Alexei. He has completely lost control of events."

"Goodnight, Anna."

"Goodnight, Tomáš darling."

"Anna, thankyou for making the past two weeks so special."

"They've been very special for me too." She put her arm across his chest and he felt her bare skin pressing against him. "I never expected to have these wonderful feelings again," she whispered. "But you've made me feel beautiful again. I can never have enough of you."

Tomáš turned towards her and they kissed. He felt Anna's hand on the back of his neck, and she kicked the bedclothes from their bodies. They made love again.

The moonlight filtered through the thin curtains, and he lay looking at her as she slept. He felt himself drifting into a contented sleep. His dreams took him back to Castiran. He was walking past the Cave Coopérative on his way to the Musil vineyards, but he was not the young man he was then. This was him now. The Tramontane was blowing gently, but as he continued walking it grew in strength. He had to bend into the wind to stop himself from being blown over by it. The sound the wind made was unlike anything he had heard. It did not howl or whistle. The trees bending wildly all around him made no sound. The wind rumbled. He leaned further into it, but he was losing the fight. He could not move forward, the rumbling grew louder, and he was blown violently off his feet and into the air.

His body jerked as if electricity had passed through it and he woke up, sure he was falling out of bed. He lay on his back, his heart pumping fast. He looked at Anna. She was sleeping peacefully. He was sure he was awake, but he could still hear the rumbling, and it was growing louder. He covered and uncovered his ears to make sure it was real. No question. And he knew that sound from somewhere. From where? Dunkirk. He knew it from Dunkirk. The rumbling was coming from outside their window in Bozděchova Street. He got out of bed and stood in front of the closed curtains. He knew what he was going to see, and wanted a few more moments before he had to face it. He closed his eyes and moved the curtains just a fraction apart. When he opened his eyes again, he saw the tanks.

Chapter Forty

August 21st, 1968

"What's going on, Tomáš? What's that dreadful noise?"
Tomáš sat on the bed and took Anna's hand.
"I don't want to tell you, Anna. I don't want you to know." He put her hand to his lips. "My darling... I'm sorry."
Anna sat up in bed.
"What are you talking about? What is it out there?"
"They've done it, Anna. The Russians. They're taking Prague."
"No. That's not possible."
Anna got out of bed and went to the window. "Oh, God in heaven." She clasped her hands to her cheeks. "Lukáš. Where's Lukáš?"
The door bell rang. Tomáš put on his dressing gown and took his father's watch from the bedside table. It was one thirty-five.
"Who is it?" he called out through the door.
"It's me, Tomáš. Vilém."
Tomáš opened the door and Vilém stepped inside. "Have you seen them?"
"I'm afraid I have."
"Where's Eva?" asked Anna.
"Sitting with Lenka. She's sleeping right through it."
"Is Lukáš with you?"
"No, Anna. Why would he be with us?"
Anna turned and went into the living room.
"Lukáš, Lukáš..." She went back to Tomáš and grabbed his sleeve. "You have to find him, Tomáš. He'll do something stupid. I know he will." Tomáš put his arms around her and guided her to the couch.
"You must find him."
"Where will Lukáš be, Vilém?" he asked.
"At the student dormitory, I suppose." He leaned towards Tomáš and whispered. "But he'll go to Wenceslas Square. They all will."
"Look after Anna. I'll go and find him."
"Don't be crazy, Tomáš. You can't go out there on your own. You'll get shot."
"Take Anna upstairs, Vilém. I'm going."
Tomáš hurried back into the bedroom and got dressed in the darkest

clothes he could find. He put on his hiking boots and grabbed the rucksack he took on walks with Fran. Outside, the sound of the tanks had been replaced by the heavy drone of low-flying aircraft using the river to guide them on their approach to the city's airport. Tomáš went to the bathroom and put in two towels and some iodine. Then into the living room. Anna looked up at him as he walked past her on his way to the kitchen. He filled his flask with water and crammed bread and fruit from the larder into the rucksack. Back in the living room he took the transistor radio Lukáš had left on the sideboard.

"Right I've got everything."

He knelt down in front of Anna on the couch. "I'll find Lukáš, Anna." She put her hand to his cheek and he leaned forward to kiss her. "He'll be safe. I promise you."

Tomáš stood up and put his arms through the straps of the rucksack. "Take Anna upstairs when I've gone, Vilém. Keep everyone together."

"Are you sure this is a good idea, Tomáš?"

"Just ask yourself what you would do twenty years from now if it was Lenka."

"Well, stick to the side streets then. And for goodness sake stop if they tell you to."

"I will, Vilém. Keep your radio on. I have one with me. That way we'll know we're all getting the same information. Whatever happens, don't any of you leave here."

"Don't worry. We won't."

Tomáš opened the front door of the apartment block and looked to his left and right. The tanks were still there, guarding the major crossroads leading to the bridges over the Vltava. During the one-minute intervals between the transport planes passing overhead he could hear the tick-over from their diesel engines. They sat like predators under the neon street lights, daring anything to cross their path.

The night was fine and still, and there was too much moonlight. Tomáš walked slowly across the road towards the river. There was no challenge. He disappeared into a cobbled side street too narrow for any tank and walked down it, keeping close to the walls of the houses. He heard urgent whispering ahead and then it went quiet. He kept going.

"What's happening out there, comrade?" came a voice from a doorway.

Tomáš turned to see three anxious faces peering at him. "We're being invaded. There are Russian tanks on Bozděchova Street."

"I told you," said the man to the two women. "I said the bastards wouldn't leave us alone. I said that sounded like tanks. That's what the announcement will be about."

"What announcement?" asked Tomáš.

"Radio Prague says there'll be an announcement at two o'clock. From the Central Committee."

Tomáš looked at his watch. Ten minutes.

"Come in and listen with us, if you like, comrade."

"Thanks, but I'll keep going. I have to meet someone."

"Please yourself, but you won't catch me going out there tonight. I know those Russian peasants. They'll be drunk soon. Then they'll have their fun. Come on, Hana, Mařenka. Let's get inside."

Tomáš walked quickly and was soon at the river. He climbed down a grassy embankment and sat in the dark out of sight. He searched his rucksack for the radio, switched it on and held it to his ear. He heard only static, until at two o'clock a calm female voice came over the air.

'This is a statement from the Central Committee of the Czechoslovak Communist Party to all the people of the Czechoslovak Socialist Republic'

Tomáš turned up the volume as another plane passed overhead. Across the black water, streaked with silver moonlight, he could see the headlights from a constant column of vehicles moving along the embankment. He looked upstream to his right and searched for the outline of the iron railway bridge he hoped to cross during the night. The calm female voice spoke in his ear again.

'Yesterday, 20 August 1968, at 11pm, the armies of the Soviet Union, the Polish People's Republic, the German Democratic Republic, the Hungarian People's Republic and the Bulgarian People's Republic crossed the state borders of the Czechoslovak People's Republic. This action took place without the knowledge of the President of the Republic, the Presidium of the National Assembly, the Presidium of the government, and the First Secretary of the Communist Party Central Committee.

'The Presidium calls upon all citizens of the Republic to remain calm and not to resist the advancing armies, since the defence of our state borders is now impossible.

'For this reason our army, the security forces, and the People's Militia were not given the order to defend the country. The Presidium of the Central Committee of the Czechoslovak Communist party considers the present action to be contrary not only to the fundamental principles of relations between socialist states, but also a denial of the basic norms of international law.'

Tomáš switched off the radio and lay back on the grass. He had not expected for a moment that Dubček's government would fight. He accepted now his country never fought. But at least Dubček had told the world the Russians were invaders. No one would now believe the Czechoslovaks had invited them in to save their country from counter-revolution. There was a measure of defiance in that.

He got up and made his way to the Smíchov railway bridge. It was unguarded and he was able to cross unmolested. He walked along the right bank and turned into the New Town. The main streets were clogged with armoured cars, lorries and tanks, come to a standstill under street lights, their drivers standing by their vehicles like confused tourists studying maps. He allowed himself a smile. All the signposts and plaques showing the names of the streets had been removed, and the hapless Russians had no clue where they were. And no one was going to help them.

The number of people making their way to Wenceslas Square was growing by the minute, and they were doing nothing to hide their anger. More and more emerged arm in arm from darkened side streets carrying torches, all chanting the names of Dubček and President Svoboda.

Outside the Botanical Gardens he broke away and stopped next to a small group of protesters, gathered in a semi-circle in front of four Russian soldiers. The protesters stood by the kerb, stabbing their fingers at the confused invaders and demanding to know why they were there.

"You liberated us once. Why do you now invade us?"

"We don't need saving from ourselves."

"We are socialists the same as you."

"Just go home."

The young Russians, told by their leaders they would be welcomed as liberators, shifted their feet, searched one another's faces for support, and offered no reply. Tomáš enjoyed their discomfort. They may have been looking forward to pretty girls, grateful and eager, throwing flowers at them as dawn broke, but this is what they were getting instead. Jeers and curses and spittle from a dark, angry city.

He rejoined the protesters converging on Wenceslas Square and the Old Town. The crowd was different this time. These weren't just students and hippies. There were workers too and professional people of all ages, and they were coming in their thousands. He regretted his rash promise to Anna. How would he find Lukáš amongst a crowd as crushing as this?

When he reached the Square, thousands were already there, waving the national flag, chanting, remonstrating with the invaders, and surrounding the tanks which lined both carriageways. He stopped at the statue of Saint Wenceslas and looked up at the young men clinging to their patron saint, tying a blindfold to shield his eyes from the shame of it all. A banner hung from one side of the plinth, 'Truth Prevails, but it will take time.' Tomáš stood in awe. The invaders were powerless in the face of so many protesters. And still the people kept coming. Fifty metres away flames shot into the night sky. A burning rag had been thrown onto an auxiliary fuel tank, secured to the rear of a Russian tank, and set it ablaze. The crowd around the flames ran in all directions, as soldiers rushed to the burning tank, trying to beat out the flames with their tunics, but they soon retreated too. The tank crew scrambled from the turret and the crowd cheered.

The protesters became bolder and surrounded a second tank. Two young men waving the Czechoslovak flag clambered onto the hull. The tank swung around on one track trying to dislodge them and gore the people on the ground taunting it. The gears meshed and it turned the other way forcing those closest to scramble to safety.

More young men ran forward, waving flags trying to distract the beast. It drove straight at them, then stopped abruptly to avoid hitting them. The crowd shouted encouragement and the young men kept running forward. The tank charged again, swung around and this time did not stop. It tossed one of the men in the air and he disappeared under the grinding tracks. People ran screaming from the scene, more fearful of the sight of the crushed head and body than the threat of the tank, which was now still, its hydraulics swivelling the gun turret from side to side, challenging its tormentors.

The other tanks on both sides of the Square copied the manoeuvre, and the crowds fled to the central reservation, leaving the monsters in control of both carriageways. The tanks' engines revved in anger as the people continued to taunt them with chants and gestures. Tomáš forced himself to look at the body of the young man lying crushed a short distance away. 'Please don't let it be him.'

"We can't leave the poor boy lying there," he said to two of the older men around him, and he rushed forward. To his relief they followed. He turned the rag doll body over. Brown eyes. It wasn't him. He covered the boy with a flag and helped carry him to the sanctuary of the central reservation. Young men came forward to dip their flags in the martyr's blood and wave them high in the air, stoking the crowd's fury.

For more than an hour the standoff between metal and flesh continued, until the first light of dawn appeared above the National Museum at the far end of Wenceslas Square. With each passing minute the menace the darkness bestowed on the Russian tanks diminished. Small groups of young men left the sanctuary of the central reservation and began to encroach again on the tanks' territory. Soon swarms of people gathered around the tanks, refusing to move and neutralising their threat. The benign light of the summer dawn brought a new strategy. Talking.

Tomáš walked away. For two hours he patrolled the Square looking for Lukáš amongst the groups trying to engage the Russian soldiers in debate. He could not see him. The daylight was bringing more and more people to the Square and he knew the chance of finding him was becoming more and more improbable.

As improbable, he knew, as any chance these people had of persuading the blank-faced invaders to go home; of persuading them that they had been lied to. There was no one here for them to fight. No NATO. No CIA. No counter-revolutionaries. Only bewildered Czechoslovaks once again suffering a brutal foreign army in their city, come with the same criminal excuse of wanting to protect them.

"It's Dubček. Dubček's on the radio."

Tomáš took out Lukáš's transistor and tuned it again to Radio Prague. It was seven o'clock. Everyone around him fell silent at the sound of Dubček's clear Slovakian voice.

"*My fellow Czechoslovaks. Comrades. Your government remains intact. The people you chose to lead you are still in post, and will not step down to lend legitimacy to this act of betrayal by our allies. This deed was done without your government's knowledge or approval. Yet I still believe, Comrades, that we can persuade our misguided friends to see the grievous mistake they have made, and encourage them to withdraw their forces shortly from our country. While negotiations continue, I must ask you to adhere to the following directives for the sake of our country's integrity. Stay calm. Go about your business as usual. Above all, I urge you, fellow Czechoslovaks, stay proud and resolute, but do not resist...*"

The broadcast was cut short. The crowds stood silent, clustered around radios wondering how to react. "Dubček!" someone cried, and thousands began to chant their leader's name. Tomáš watched people all around him punching the air with their fists, fighting with their voices. He felt conspicuous and alone, unable to join in the self-deception. He pushed through the crowd, impatient to get away.

Was Dubček so stupid that he still believed he could negotiate with the Russians? And did these people here, the scales surely at last fallen from their eyes, really think they could persuade these young, clueless tank crews to just turn around and go home?

He stepped into a shop doorway. In front of him young mop-haired men in tight jeans and polo-neck jumpers clambered onto the tanks to talk to the soldiers. Girls in mini-skirts and white boots attempted shouted conversations with the blank-faced tank crews from the pavement, and some older men and women simply stood and wiped away tears. Tomáš looked on, detached from his fellow Praguers and exasperated by their stubborn, pathetic belief in a communist brotherhood.

But somewhere within him he felt a begrudging pride too. All these Czechoslovaks were alone again in their fight, and they knew it, but in spite of everything, they still tried to talk and to reason.

There was sudden movement at the far end of the Square by the National Museum. People were running towards the Museum's steps and veering left towards Vinohradská Street.

"It's the radio building."

"They're moving tanks down there."

"They want to shut down Radio Prague."

The younger protesters in front of Tomáš began to run too. He turned and walked slowly towards the National Museum, unwilling to add to a drama he knew none of these people rushing past him could affect. When he reached Vinohradská Street he saw the first barricade. Two buses and a tramcar had been strung across the road and overturned, as if uprooting them would make them a greater barrier to tanks. People were filtering through a narrow gap at the side to reach the radio building. Many more took fright and were turning and hurrying back the way they had come. Tomáš went through. If this was to be the centre of resistance, he knew this is where Lukáš would be.

Outside the modern headquarters of Radio Prague youths were prising paving bricks from between the tram tracks, and by the main glass doors a small group was preparing Molotov cocktails. He looked about him. All the roads leading to the building were blocked by barricades of overturned cars, buses and trams.

Within the stronghold the number of resisters could be counted in hundreds rather than the thousands of protesters congregated in Wenceslas Square. They were mostly young men. Students probably. There were a few girls and a few older men like him. He questioned whether he should leave for Anna's sake, but then it was too late. From the direction of the National Museum he heard the low rumble of tanks.

Behind him the young men formed lines across the road. In the front line twenty or so held petrol bombs. Behind them were several hundred more, armed with bricks.

And then Tomáš saw him.

"Lukáš!" He ran to where his son stood in the middle of the front line.

"Lukáš."

"What the hell are you doing here?"

"You've got to get out of here, Lukáš."

"Get out? I'm not getting out. Open your damned eyes. We're about to fight."

"You mustn't do this, Lukáš. It's not fair on your mother. Or on me."

"What? You pathetic man. We're invaded and you want to take me home because it's not fair on you? Get out of my way." He pushed Tomáš aside. "We're not going to surrender like you did. Just go home and gloat about how right you were. And leave us to fight."

"But you don't understand, son. You can't fight tanks with your bare hands. You'll be killed. And that will kill your mother too. Please, Lukáš. For Anna's sake, come with me."

The rumbling grew louder and they could hear the grating sound of metal tracks turning on concrete.

"They're coming. Now get out my way and get home to my mother. That's all you really care about anyway." He shouted to the others in his line. "Here it comes. Ready, everyone?"

Tomáš saw one of the buses sliding towards them, propelled by an unseen force. Then the muzzle of the tank's gun appeared high above the bus, followed by the front of the hull and tracks. The bus stopped moving as the centre of it was crushed by the weight of the tank dropping down onto it.

"Fucking hell," shouted one of the brick throwers. "How did it do that?"

Tomáš looked at Lukáš who seemed unsure what to do in the face of such power. One of the young men in the front row lit the rag hanging from his bottle, ran forward and hurled it at the tank. It exploded into flames on the front of the hull. The tank kept coming. Three more men ran forward with flaming bottles which whooshed through the air in an arc before hitting the tank, covering it from front to back in fire.

But still it kept coming. An explosion ripped through the auxiliary fuel tank and flames reached out instantly to cover the whole of the barricade and climb up the walls of the buildings on either side. The tank stopped and the crew baled out. One. Two. Three. They jumped through the flames at the rear and were gone. The hundreds of resisters cheered, shouted obscenities and threw bricks at the burning wreck.

"There should be four," shouted Tomáš. An arm appeared through the turret amid the flames, then another and then a torso. The crowd fell silent as the radio operator, screaming in pain and panic, struggled to get out. He levered his body up and fell through the burning petrol onto the ground twenty metres away. He lay there, his head and upper body burning. Tomáš ran forward, slipping his rucksack from his back. He tore off his coat and laid it over the Russian, smothering the flames.

Behind the barricade he could hear a second tank approaching. He put the rucksack over his shoulder, picked up the young Russian, and ran with him to a shop doorway opposite the radio building. The boy's clothes were still smouldering and he was unconsciousness, probably from the impact he made with the ground after baling out. Tomáš poured water onto a towel and laid it over the deep compression across the boy's forehead.

The second tank sliced through the barricade and stopped in front of the burning vehicles, sizing up the protesters. A barrage of bricks hit the hull and bounced off. Tomáš looked towards Lukáš who had not moved since the action began.

Four men in his line lit the rags hanging from their petrol bombs and approached the tank. The turret opened. One of the tank crew in khaki uniform grabbed the heavy machine gun with one hand, flicked back the safety catch with the other and within seconds fired a burst above the heads of the young Czechoslovaks. The four men tossed their petrol bombs in the vague direction of the tank and turned and ran for their lives. The bottles exploded on the ground metres short, and the gunner lowered the muzzle of the machine gun. Lukáš had still not moved and Tomáš yelled at him above the chaos.

"Drop, Lukáš! Drop!"

Lukáš was jolted from his trance as the gunner fired at the four fleeing bombers. They were all hit by the same burst. The bullets kicked their bodies up and forward and ripped off pieces of flesh and bone, which landed on the road several metres from where their corpses fell. Lukáš had thrown himself to the ground and was crawling away through the bloody mess. The gunner raised the muzzle and fired another burst at the hundreds of fleeing men. Tomáš saw many of them fall. The sound of the gunfire made Lukáš stop crawling. He lay face down in the road, immobile. Tomáš lifted the Russian's head and shoulders from his lap and laid him on the ground. He had stopped breathing.

Tomáš ran to Lukáš, knelt down next to him and put his hand on his back. He was trembling and moaning in shock. Tomáš turned him over, put his forearms under his armpits and started to drag him away. He looked up at the tank. The main gun had been elevated and was pointing at the centre of the radio building.

Flames shot from the muzzle and the tank reared back on its tracks as the shell left the barrel. The shock wave knocked Tomáš off his feet, and his ears registered no sound as a large part of the front of the radio building crashed to the ground. Next to him Lukáš was sitting up staring at the tank. Tomáš saw the tank commander speak into his intercom and point to where they were. The tank turned and drove straight towards them.

"Move, Lukáš!" screamed Tomáš. "Move! Move!"

There was no time to drag him. Tomáš stood up and walked towards the tank, fixing his eyes on the commander in the turret. He stopped a few metres in front of Lukáš and the tank kept coming. Tomáš raised his arms above his head, clenched his fists and stabbed at the air in the direction of the tank.

"Get out of my country, you Russian bastards!" he screamed. He stepped towards the tank shaking his fists at the Russian. "Get out! Get out of my country. Leave us in peace."

When he reached the tank, he beat his fists against the hull.

"What makes you people think you can do this to us?" he shouted, still pounding his fists on the dense metal. "It's our country, you bastards. This is our country."

The tank stopped. The commander climbed from the turret and stood on the hull, intrigued by the madman attacking his tank with his fists. He took his pistol from his holster and waved the muzzle to the side, indicating Tomáš should move.

"You move, you Russian bastard," said Tomáš, glaring at him. "Turn your tank around and get out of my country."

The Russian pointed the pistol at him. The look on his face had changed. He was not curious or amused by this madman anymore. He held up three fingers and then returned them to a clenched fist. He raised one finger and started to count. "*Raz*". Tomáš asked Anna to forgive him. The Russian raised a second finger. "*Dva*". At last, after all these years, he understood how and why his father died. He looked into the Russian's bulging eyes. "Get out of my country," he said. The Russian raised a third finger. Tomáš heard him say "*Tri,*" and then he felt the bullet enter him and he fell back. He hoped his head wouldn't hit the concrete too hard. He waited for the impact and was surprised to feel himself being held. And then carried. He opened his eyes and saw Lukáš's face. He felt his son's arms on him and heard his voice.

"Táta, Táta," he was crying. "You stupid, stupid man."

Chapter Forty-One

April 23rd, 1968 – April 17th, 1969

"Tomáš. Can you hear me, Tomáš? Take your time."
"Is that you, Vilém?"
"Don't move, Tomáš. You're in the Francis Hospital. Don't move. You must stay on your side."
"Lukáš…"
"Lukáš is fine. He brought you here. He was in shock at first but we gave him something. He's fine now."
"What happened to me?"
"You were shot, Tomáš. In your right shoulder. The bullet hit your scapula."
"Scapula?"
"Your shoulder blade. We've repaired it as best we can, and mended the nerve and tissue damage, but you were very lucky."
"Was I?"
"Very lucky. The subclavian artery tends not to respond well to a bullet, but Lukáš got you here in time for us to stop the internal bleeding."
"Where's Anna?"
"She's here. I'll tell her you're awake. She's refused to leave since you were admitted."
"How long?"
"You were brought in at eight thirty on Wednesday morning. It's now four o'clock on Friday afternoon."
"Anna's been here all that time? I must see her."
"You mustn't move. I'll get her."
"No, wait. Give me a moment, Vilém. How's Eva?"
"She's here too. Working. I can send for her when you're ready."
"Please, but not yet. I need a few moments to collect my thoughts. Why are my hands bandaged?"
"You tried to knock out a T-55 with your fists, Tomáš. You broke metacarpals in both hands. I had no idea you were so foolish."
"Oh, God. I remember now. It's strange. My hands hurt more than my shoulder."
"Your shoulder's full of painkillers. You'll forget about your hands when they wear off, I'm afraid. Shall I tell Anna you're awake?"

"One more minute, Vilém. Are there many casualties?"

"Twenty-seven dead in Prague since Wednesday. Scores more injured. Some from bullet wounds. Most through drunken Russians driving their vehicles at people."

"Are they still fighting out there?"

"Much less than the first day. The Russians have control of most of the city now, but they can't get the people out of Wenceslas Square. There are as many there as ever."

"Our poor country, Vilém."

"You really mustn't move, Tomáš. Shall I get Anna now? She'll want to know you've come round."

"Yes, would you, please?"

Vilém put a chair by the side of the bed. Tomáš heard him leave the room. Within seconds the door opened again. He saw Anna's legs and tried to look up at her but couldn't move his neck. She leaned over him and kissed his cheek and smoothed his hair from his forehead. He felt her tears on his face. She sat down, looked into his eyes and tried to smile.

"Sorry, Anna."

"You mustn't say sorry, darling. Lukáš told me what you did for him, and for the Russian boy. You nearly died."

"Don't cry."

"You saved Lukáš, and then he saved you."

"Don't upset yourself, Anna."

"But Lukáš is still out there. He won't listen to me."

"He's not a little boy, Anna. We have to let him do this, if he feels he must. He's a man who loves his country."

"You two. One minute you can't agree on anything, and now you're his hero and you're defending him."

"Hero?"

"He hasn't stopped talking about it. How you stood there... to protect him..."

"Anna. Darling."

"I think he feels he has to prove himself. He says he watched you, but he could never do what you did."

"Oh, the poor boy." Tomáš closed his eyes. Anna took a handkerchief from her sleeve and wiped her eyes and cheeks. "Why must you men be like this? Look what our fathers had to go through."

"It's forced on us, Anna. We have never asked for it. All any of us ever want is to be left alone to live in peace."

"I hate this country. All the wars. All the misery."

"That's not fair, darling. Czechoslovakia has never sought wars."
"I want to leave. I want us all to leave. So does Eva."
"Have you spoken to her?"
"Yes. She hates all this too. She's been on constant call here since early Wednesday morning. Lenka has had to stay with pani Nováková downstairs. And what's it been for? Dubček has gone anyway."
"Gone?"
"He's been arrested."
"Where have they taken him?"
"No one really knows. Radio Prague says he's in Moscow with Černik and the rest of them. President Svoboda left this morning to try to get them released."
"I don't think there's much chance of that. But didn't the Russians take the radio building, then?"
"Yes, but what you all did allowed a lot of their people to escape. They've set up new stations all over Prague."
"That's wonderful news."
"No, it's not, Tomáš. It just keeps all this trouble going. Eva can't be with Lenka. Lukáš is God knows where in all sorts of danger. When will it all stop?"
"You didn't always feel like that, Anna. You wanted me to fight after Munich, remember? You even wanted to come and fight with me."
"But I didn't have children then. I was young and naïve. I didn't understand the misery all this brings. I've been through too much, Tomáš. I want peace in my life. In all our lives."
"I know, darling."
The door opened. Eva and Vilém came in.
"Táta. How are you?" Anna sat back as Eva leaned over to kiss her father. "We've been so worried about you."
"I'm sorry, darling."
"Lukáš phoned the hospital just now. He was asking after you. He says he'll come and see you as soon as he can."
"So he's alright?" said Anna. "Thank God." She got up and stood at the window with her back to everyone. Tomáš watched her. Eva sat down on the chair and put her hands on her father's arm.
"How long must I stay here, Eva?"
"About two weeks, I imagine."
Vilém nodded his agreement. "Your arm will be in a sling for about three months," he said. "The wounds and bones will take anything from three to six months to heal. But I must warn you, Tomáš, that shoulder

may give you trouble for the rest of your days."

"I understand, Vilém. I'm just grateful for all you've done."

There was a knock at the door.

"Come in," Tomáš called out from his bed.

"Hello, Tomáš."

"Lukáš, is that you? Come in. I can't turn around, I'm afraid. Vilém insists I lie facing this way."

"Don't try to move then."

"I've been a whole week like this. It's driving me mad. Come this side where I can see you. Sit here next to the bed."

"Thanks. How are you, Tomáš?"

"Better for seeing you. You look well."

"I wish I could say the same for you. Are you in much pain?"

"Not too bad. I just wish I could lie on my back."

"I'm really sorry for what happened, Tomáš. And for taking so long to visit you. I've wanted to thank you for what you did for me."

Tomáš moved a hand towards him. "And I've wanted to thank you, son. They tell me if it weren't for you, I wouldn't have survived."

"I only did the obvious thing. What you did was incredible."

"Foolish, according to Vilém."

"I couldn't have done it. Everyone's talking about it."

"But it's nothing compared to what you've done over the months, Lukáš. You've worked so hard to make things better for all of us."

"There's still a lot more we can do. Did you hear Dubček on the radio yesterday?"

"Yes I did. And Svoboda."

"Svoboda was a disgrace. Telling us we must accept the troops until everything is normalised. As if it was all our fault. The man's a fool. His speech stirred up more anger than the Russians have."

"What about Dubček? What do people think about what he said?"

"He's more popular than ever now. It's obvious he understands how we feel. And we trust him. So everyone's done what he asked us to do. Cleared the streets. Stopped the protests."

"He sounded very emotional on the radio."

"Doesn't he have a right to be? Don't we all? But at least he understands what people want."

"The Russians out."

"Of course. And if he says he can do it, provided we all cooperate with him, then we will. But it doesn't mean people aren't showing the Russians how they feel."

"What are they doing?"

"No one will give them any food or water." Lukáš grinned. "People ignore them in the shops and on the street. And it's working. It's as if they're not there." Lukáš got up and went over to the window. He looked up over the river towards the Letná Heights. "I've never seen people so united. Everyone out there feels they have a role to play in all this. It's real politics, Tomáš. Everyone's involved."

"It's good to hear you being so positive, Lukáš. I'm proud of you."

Lukáš turned to face the bed.

"Thankyou for saying that, Táta. I think we can all be proud of ourselves."

"Do you think we did enough?"

"Yes. If everyone hadn't gone out on the streets that first night, I don't think Dubček or the others would still be alive. The Russians certainly wouldn't have allowed him back to lead us again. But with everyone protesting and the radio still broadcasting, they had no choice."

"You're probably right. Come and sit down where I can see you, son. You know, I can see why the Russians didn't want to make a martyr of Dubček, but I wonder if they would have let him back if they thought they couldn't control him."

"Still the cynic, aren't you?"

"Perhaps I am. But I'm pleased you can smile when you say it now."

Lukáš sat forward and bowed his head. "I think you've more than earned your right to your opinion," he said.

"I think we all have."

"I can't sit down, Táta. I'm too pent up. I need to move about."

"That's alright. I understand."

"But what you say about Dubček is too cynical," said Lukáš, looking once more out the window. "You must see he has more authority today than ever before. Everyone out there is behind him and the reforms now."

"I don't want to say anything to annoy you, Lukáš, but we do have half a million foreign troops occupying our country again. He's hardly free to do as he pleases."

Lukáš turned and sat against the window sill with his hands in the pockets of his jeans.

"Dubček will get the troops out with the same method he has for everything. Patience and persuasion."

"I hope you are right, son. But I do a lot of thinking lying here. And I wonder if it might have been better if he'd refused to take control again until the troops left."

"And where would that have got us?"

"The Russians would have been forced to impose martial law. The world would have seen them for the oppressors they really are."

"I don't want to argue with you either, Táta. I'd rather just say I understand your opinion, but I disagree. I think Dubček will be able to return things to normal."

"Normalisation with a human face, eh?"

"Very good," said Lukáš forcing a smile.

"I'm sorry."

"It's okay. We don't have to agree about everything. But I will admit there is something you have changed my mind about."

"Really?"

"I agree with you now about the Russians. They can't be trusted."

"It's very sad, Lukáš. Your grandfather learned that in the First War. I learned it in the Second. Now they've managed to alienate a whole new generation of Czechoslovaks. The truth is, the Russians have never really protected their fellow Slavs. They just bully us."

"I know that now. They thought they could just walk in here and we Czechoslovaks would jump to attention and accept any stooge government they gave us. They got a damned shock."

"They did, son. I think we all did rather well, don't you?"

"You did. The fighting's not over for me."

"For God's sake don't say that in front of your mother."

"I won't."

"You have nothing to prove, Lukáš. All I did was lose my temper. Getting yourself killed like that isn't fighting."

"Has Máma told you she's determined to leave? And Eva."

"Yes, she has."

"I realise you haven't tried to persuade her this time. I'm sorry for what I thought before."

"I understand. I know it must have been hard for you to accept me in all your lives. I hope that's changed."

"It has. I heard the conversation you had with that damned tank. I know how you feel about your country. I know if you want to leave and take Máma with you, it's for a good reason."

"Will you come with us, Lukáš?"

"No."

"Perhaps if you had a wife and children you would."

"Is this a father and son talk?"

"If you like."

"Perhaps it would be different if I had someone I loved and needed to protect. But I haven't."

"I understand. It's the only reason I took your mother to France in 1938. It's why I want you to leave with us now."

"I appreciate that, Táta. But all I want to do now is help my country. And to do that I have to stay."

No one took any notice of the young student standing on the steps of the National Museum. He stood by the wall overlooking the fountain, gazing down the length of Wenceslas Square. No one noticed the small package at his feet.

He decided to spend a few more moments in the mid-January sunshine. There was little traffic. Lovers sat around the plinth beneath the statue of Saint Wenceslas. A boy was taking a picture of his self-conscious girlfriend. The shops were open but doing very little business. Everything appeared normal. But that was the problem. Too much had returned to normal.

Where was the hope of the previous spring? Where was the defiance of August? All gone. Even the faith in Dubček when he returned from Moscow was gone, and the deal struck with a trusting people proven worthless. And they had accepted so much. The return of censorship, the closure of Literární Listy, and the banning of any group which challenged the leading role of the Party. Bans and censorship were 'temporary', Dubček promised. Restrictions on free assembly and travel 'exceptional'. But still the Russians were here. Withdrawn from the centre of Prague perhaps, but still here, and their presence made lawful by the man the people had trusted most. His endless appeals to reason had been no more than appeals to compromise and cowardice.

The student picked up the package at his feet. The people had accepted too much. This would shake them from their lethargy. All the people of talent and courage, who had emerged from nowhere during last spring and summer, would be jolted from their hibernation again by what he was about to do. He unscrewed the top from the small can of petrol. "Never betray your conscience, Jan," he said to himself,

He had seen the newsreels of Buddhist monks in Saigon protesting against the war. He would stand here on the steps and, like them, he would not move as the flames enshrouded him. Jan Palach poured the petrol over his head and felt it trickle over his face and down his collar. He waited a brief moment for it to soak into his jacket and then struck the match.

Oskar Jarmil, a tram driver on his way home from work, thought he must be witnessing a street performance. Only when the blazing figure ran towards him screaming did he realise this was something else. The figure fell on the pavement in front of him. Oskar took off his driver's jacket and tried to smother the flames. The young man's eyes were open, pleading with him. He lay still as if trying to make Oskar's task easier. Two more passers-by came forward to help beat out the flames, until there was only smoke, and the stench of petrol, burnt hair and flesh.

"Wake up," Jan muttered to them. "You must all wake up."

Jan held on to his life for three days, knowing he could not survive. The government, fearing a violent backlash on his death, agreed to allow Prague's students to organise his funeral, in return for their assurance there would be no protests. Lukáš, as one of the student leaders, visited Jan Palach in the burns unit in Legerova Street to hear his wishes.

"Tell people... this was not an act of desperation, Lukáš," Jan told him. His voice was hoarse and weak. He had inhaled the flames and could breathe only in gasps. "Tell them... it was an act of hope... that the defiance of August can be revived."

"I shall, Jan."

"The people must... find their spirit again. They must argue... protest, strike. They must wake up."

"Yes, Jan."

"But tell them... no one should copy what I have done. Tell them... the pain is too great."

"I shall tell them that too."

One hundred thousand people walked behind the coffin, and two hundred thousand more lined the route. There was no need for protest. The silence of the crowd was enough. Thousands wept openly for the young life sacrificed to shine a light on their own demoralisation and indifference. And many wept, too, out of anger and frustration with Alexander Dubček, whose main concern on that day seemed to be to avoid any actions or words which might annoy the Russians.

"Jan's act has revived our people's spirit today," Lukáš told his father later that evening, "but I'm afraid on this same day our pact with Dubček has finally been broken."

Tomáš did not confide in his son his own fear that Jan Palach was just one more martyr in a long line of Czech martyrs. He would be heralded by the people, and then they would use his sacrifice as an excuse not to take any decisive action themselves.

After Jan Palach's funeral it seemed only a matter of time before Brezhnev and Kosygin found a reason to replace the wounded Dubček.

The opportunity presented itself at the end of March, when people throughout Czechoslovakia took to the streets again, in greater numbers than ever before. This time they came not to protest or to mourn, but to celebrate. Dubček's great socialist experiment ended not because of invasion, repression or political manoeuvring, but because of an ice-hockey match.

The Kovaříks and Fialas watched the match together in Vilém and Eva's apartment. For the second time in eight days Czechoslovakia played the Soviet Union in the Ice Hockey World Championships, and for the second time they won. At the final whistle the door of every household in Prague opened, and people came out to dance, sing and cheer in the streets. If Czechoslovakia's army could not see off the Russian invaders, at least the country's ice-hockey team could provide a surrogate victory.

Tomáš, Vilém and Lukáš made their way cheering and laughing to Wenceslas Square, where the celebrations would really begin. Only later did Tomáš understand the significance of the pile of cobblestones he noticed neatly stacked up outside the Soviet Aeroflot office on one side of the Square. They were the cobblestones used later in the evening to smash the windows and doors of the office, shortly before the building was torched by men dressed in smart leather jackets and neatly ironed jeans.

In Moscow Brezhnev waited by the telephone for confirmation that the assault on Soviet property and prestige had taken place, and immediately denounced the 'mass hooligan attacks' as the work of 'rightist extremists' and 'counter-revolutionaries'. It was to be the final sign that Dubček had lost control of public order in the country, and the perfect excuse to offer him an ultimatum. Either he must step down or the Warsaw Pact troops would move back into Czechoslovakia's towns and cities. When Dubček resigned as First Secretary of the Czechoslovak Communist Party on April 17th, no one was surprised by it, and few were moved. Most Czechoslovaks had, by then, long since mourned the passing of the Prague Spring.

With Dubček gone, Tomáš and Anna hoped Lukáš would at last agree to join Eva, Vilém and Lenka, and leave with them for England.

"Why would you want to stay now?" asked his father. "The purges will start soon. The hardliners will crack down on anyone who had anything to do with organising the protests. We have a week or two to get out, Lukáš. Your mother and sister have waited for months for you to change your mind. For their sake, please see reason."

"I'm sorry, Táta. Take them with you. You have my complete understanding and total support. But I cannot run away."

355

Chapter Forty-Two

May 20th – May 21st, 1969

"As soon as you have the necessary documents from the Czechoslovak Ministry of the Interior, we shall be only too happy to issue your family with entry visas to the United Kingdom, Mr Colman."

"Thankyou, sir. And you don't think there will be a problem with their applications for full residence?"

"I cannot give guarantees on behalf of the Home Office, but residence for your wife, son and daughter, and granddaughter, should be a formality once you're all in London."

"And my son-in-law?"

The British consul got up from his battered, leather armchair and took his pipe from his mouth.

"Given Mr Fiala's profession and his position within your family, I see little likelihood of his residence application not being viewed favourably. That's strictly off the record, of course."

"Of course. Thankyou, Mr Bedford."

"I shall wish you good luck with the Czechoslovak authorities then, Mr Colman."

The consul offered his hand.

"Thankyou, sir. I hope to be back to see you very soon."

Tomáš walked out into the sunlight of the Malá Strana and headed down the hill towards the Charles Bridge. 'The necessary documents,' he muttered to himself and kicked a stone into the gutter. He thought of Anna and Eva, and the endless visits they had made to the Ministry of the Interior over the past five weeks in an attempt to secure passports for themselves and Vilém and Lenka, and for Lukáš too, in spite of his continued insistence on staying. Tomáš kicked out at another stone. He knew Lukáš would never leave. And he knew the Czechoslovak authorities had no intention of issuing passports to any of them. But Eva and Anna would not give up.

"There's only one way to do this, Táta," Eva kept saying, "and that's to show them we're as stubborn as they are. Besides, we have nothing to lose now anyway."

They all knew she was right. The simple act of applying to leave meant Vilém's career and her own were now permanently blighted under the new hardline regime.

There was only one possible solution left, blurted out a few days ago by a ministry official exasperated by the two women's persistence. Anna, Eva, Lukáš, Vilém and Lenka would all be stripped of their Czechoslovak citizenship if they insisted in this folly, he said, and issued with stateless person's documents. It would mean they might one day be able to leave, but they could never return, and they would become totally reliant on someone somewhere granting them citizenship. Anna and Eva realised it was a way out, and they were determined to pursue it.

Tomáš reached the Old Town Square and took his usual seat at his favourite café. He checked his watch. He had half an hour before he was due to meet Anna from work and take her to lunch by the river. He sipped his coffee and looked around the square. There were far fewer tourists in Prague this spring. So few it was hard to imagine the numbers drawn to the city only twelve months before. He felt nostalgia now for that brief time, and a large measure of regret for the cynicism he had shown towards Lukáš, however well founded it had proved to be.

It was hard to imagine any of it had happened. The recent May Day had passed without notice. The students had all returned to their libraries and lecture theatres, and the rest of the population to their lethargy. The purge of reformists was well under way, and Jan Palach's sacrifice reduced officially to well-intended but misguided idealism. The State Secret Police were back on the streets too, and making little effort to remain secret. Tomáš watched two across the square staring at people as they passed, making sure everyone was aware they were being monitored. They were supposed to be plain-clothed, but their leather jackets and pressed jeans were as much a uniform as the apron and bow tie of the waiter serving Tomáš his coffee. They knew people feared them again, and they were enjoying it.

Tomáš took another look at his watch and got up to leave. He made his way back to the Charles Bridge and turned left along the embankment, quickening his pace, anxious not to keep Anna waiting. The traffic had thinned to almost nothing by the time he passed the old Legion Bridge. A tram clattered across it, and he remembered the morning pilgrimages he used to make there just after the war. He glanced back at the bridge over his shoulder and caught sight of a black Tatra car crawling along on the other side of the road. He thought how ugly it was, swept back in one line of bonnet, roof and boot, where it ended in a point. He turned away and waited for it to pass. When it didn't, he decided not to look around again, but to take a detour up the steps of the National Theatre. Behind him he heard the squeal of tyres.

"Mr Thomas Colman," someone called out.

Tomáš turned and saw the two StB men in leather jackets standing at the foot of the steps. The rear door of the black Tatra hung open.

"Come here, please. We must talk with you."

"What do you want? I have to meet my wife."

"Well, you won't find her in there, will you? Now come with us."

One of the men got into the back of the car and slid across the seat, while the other held the door open for Tomáš. He got in and soon found himself squeezed between the two policemen. Neither spoke to him as the driver pulled away. A hundred metres down the road they passed Anna waiting outside the office block.

"Can I..?"

"No."

The car turned left and doubled back behind the National Theatre. It stopped in front of a building of reddish-brown brick resembling an apartment block. Tomáš knew, as every Praguer knew, that it was the Headquarters of the State Secret Police.

He was allowed to walk freely into the building. He followed one of the men up the marble stairs to the first floor. He could hear the second man behind him. Neither of them spoke as they approached a dark varnished door. The first man knocked gently.

"Enter."

The room was stark. The curtains were drawn and the only light came from an Anglepoise lamp on one of two desks positioned at right angles to one another. Behind each of the desks sat a man in a shiny grey suit. One of the men, jowly and overweight, was busy studying papers from a file. The other was sitting upright in front of a Remington typewriter. A straight-backed chair stood unoccupied in front of the fat man's desk and Tomáš, thinking it must be for him, sat down on it without being invited. He looked across at the man with the typewriter and nodded. The man stared straight ahead and did not respond.

The fat man studying the papers still did not look up. Tomáš noted the pictures on the wall behind him. They were photographs, at least double life size. One was of Leonid Brezhnev. On his left was Gustáv Husák, who had replaced Dubček as First Secretary, and to Brezhnev's right was President Svoboda. Both Czechoslovaks were looking towards the Russian leader in the centre. The photographs were cheap and massed-produced, their garishness providing the only colour in the room. Tomáš noticed dark stains on the wall in the far corner. The fat man spoke.

"Do you know why you have been brought here, Mr Colman?" He looked up at Tomáš at last and smiled.

"No, I don't."

Tomáš heard the metallic tapping of the Remington.

"Do you have your passport with you?"

"I'm afraid not."

"It doesn't matter." The man took some papers from the file in front of him. "We have copies." He glanced down at them. "It appears, Mr Colman, that you have overstayed your tourist visa. It expired on the 30th of July last year."

"Yes, I'm sorry about that."

More tapping.

"Why did you not apply for an extension? I'm sure, given the mood of the country last July, it would have been granted easily enough."

"I think I just forgot. I'm very sorry."

"One of the conditions of your visa was that you should reside at the Interhotel on Wenceslas Square during your visit. And yet, you have not spent one night there. Why is that?"

"I decided to stay elsewhere."

"Elsewhere? Do you realise that you have committed a criminal offence by remaining illegally in the Czechoslovak Socialist Republic?"

"I'm very sorry. It was an oversight. But I'm not a criminal. Is it too late to renew it?"

"Too late? Oh, yes. It's certainly too late. At the very least you will be deported."

"But my..?"

"Yes?"

"Nothing."

"The bigger question is whether we investigate further to see if there are more sinister reasons for your presence here. Why have you made five visits to the British Embassy in the past month?"

"I was seeking advice about the visa."

"On five separate occasions? Such an obvious lie makes me even more suspicious of your real intentions here. Have you anything to say?"

"No, honestly. The visa was an honest mistake."

"Because we are well aware there were many western agents at the root of the counter-revolutionary sedition in our country last year. And we are determined to get to the bottom of it."

"That's ridiculous..."

"Ridiculous!" boomed the fat man and he slammed his fist on the desk. "You find it ridiculous that an agent of the West, who poses as a tourist and stays illegally in our country, should be suspected of anti-state activity?"

"It's just not true."

"Why were you hospitalised last year?"

"I'm sure you know why."

"Yes, we do know why. And I think you can see the evidence building up against you, Mr Colman."

"You're making it build up."

"We are doing nothing of the sort," shouted the fat man. "Let's stop this charade, shall we, Mr Thomas Colman, and make it clear what's going on here. We know who you really are. How many Englishmen do you think speak such perfect Czech? Do you think we're stupid?" He held up a sheet of paper from the file. "You are Tomáš Pavel Kovařík, born on the 21st of November 1916 in Cheb. You are married to Anna Esther Kovaříková, a Czechoslovak citizen, and father of two more Czechoslovak citizens, one of whom is a known counter-revolutionary seditionist and traitor to the Czechoslovak people."

"No, no, no. That last bit's wrong. Please..." Tomáš stood up and was immediately grabbed from behind by the arms and shoulders and forced back down onto the chair.

"And now your traitorous family, knowing the net is closing in on them, are doing all they can to find a means of escape."

"No, no, no. Please, this is all wrong. I'm not an agent and my family aren't traitors. But if you'll just believe me about them... if you leave them in peace, I'll admit to anything you like about myself."

"Ah, it appears you may have seen some sense at last. You admit to your own role?"

"Only if you leave my family alone. My son took part in student demonstrations last year, that's all... but then most of the wretched population did."

"Only because traitors like you and your son tricked them with lies and western propaganda."

"You can say that of me, but not of him. Unless you assure me that my family is safe, I'll admit to nothing. And remember I'm a British subject."

"Well, you do have something there, Mr Colman." The man's voice softened again. "I must admit the trial and imprisonment of a British subject may not be in either of our country's best interests at this time. But your son? I do not see how we can ignore that. The best he can hope for is a commuted death sentence and a lifetime in a uranium mine. You probably know the Jáchymov uranium mines near Cheb. Nice places..."

"Please. What do you want from me?"

"The problem we have with you, Kovařík, is that your treachery goes back such a long way."

"I don't understand."

"All the way back to those tools of western imperialism, the Masaryks."

"Oh. I see..."

"I hope you really do see, Kovařík, because we have a separate file on you which goes all the way back to 1948. I would say it's even more disturbing than the one we have on Thomas Colman, or on your son."

"Alright, I'm listening. I'll ask you again. What do you want from me?"

"Your cooperation. Your silence over certain matters. In return we are prepared to show you some socialist clemency."

"And my family?"

"It could extend to them too, if the appropriate conditions were met."

"Go on."

"You will be deported the day after tomorrow for visa irregularities. Your son can go with you if you wish. We don't want his sort here."

"He won't go."

"He's applied for a passport."

"His mother applied on his behalf. He's a loyal Czechoslovak in spite of what you say. He won't leave."

"Be that as it may. Your wife can certainly go if she wants. Her loyalty to the Party has long been suspect in any case."

"What do you mean, 'her loyalty'?"

"Your wife was a loyal member of the Communist Party from September 1957 until May of last year. Did she not tell you?"

"Yes, she did. It was the only way she could secure university places for our children. Try again."

The fat man smiled. "You can believe that if you wish. Anyway, she can go. Your daughter and son-in-law can't."

"But my daughter wants to leave."

"Do you think we train our surgeons and doctors so they can tend the bourgeoisie in the West? Their place is here. Besides, we need to keep someone close by to secure your silence."

"But you'll have Lukáš."

"Too unreliable, Kovařík. Your daughter and her family stay. No discussion. Otherwise we put all of you on trial. Your wife can go if you still want her. You can grow old together in your bourgeois decadence."

"You still haven't told me what you want from me."

"It's very straightforward. For the rest of your life you will not say or write one word to anyone about the conversation you had with Jan Masaryk on the evening of March 9th 1948."

"You mean, when he told me how much he was looking forward to joining Marcia Davenport in London, and telling the world how Gottwald really came to power? That conversation?"

The fat man waved at the other man to stop typing. "Don't push your luck, Kovařík."

"I think I can push it a bit. Perhaps I have a letter from Jan Masaryk back in London telling me what his plans were. Perhaps I've made a deposition to the British consul in case anything happens to me or my family."

"Now you listen to me, Kovařík, you traitorous swine. You have this one chance. You can go back to London in two days or go on trial here. Your choice. Your wife and son can go with you or they can face a trial too, and the death penalty. Your choice again. Your daughter and her family will stay anyway, and they'll probably do very well in their careers with your cooperation. Or they can end up working for a Forestry Department somewhere in Siberia. You choose, Kovařík."

"Alright, alright. I accept your offer. Will I be allowed to see my wife and family before I go?"

"You can see your wife for one hour tomorrow. Then you either leave under my conditions or all your lives will become a hell you can't imagine. Cooperate and those in your family who remain will be well looked after." The fat man looked past Tomáš to the two StB men standing by the door. "You two, take Kovařík to a cell. And pick up his wife in the morning."

The cell door opened. Tomáš stood up and Anna appeared.

"Tomáš, we've all been so worried. Why have they got you here?"

Tomáš put his arms around her and they sat down on the blanket covering the bare springs of the bed.

"Vilém and Lukáš spent all night checking the hospitals..."

"I'm sorry, darling. I'm really sorry. I'll explain everything to you later. But we only have one hour, and there are things we have to decide."

"One hour? What are they going to do to you, Tomáš? What have you done?"

"It's alright, Anna. They're not going to harm me, or any of us, but we have to do what they say. Try not to speak. Just listen to me." Tomáš whispered in her ear. "Remember they're probably listening to every word we say."

"Okay. Okay. Just tell me."

"I'm being deported back to England tomorrow, Anna. No, don't speak... just listen. I didn't renew my visa. That means I've been staying here illegally. Now they're trying to say I came here as a western agent to stir up trouble." He looked up at the light fitting and shouted towards it. "But they know it's all damned nonsense."

"Tomáš, how could you forget to do something so important? I don't understand."

"I'm sorry, Anna. I can't explain it all to you now... but do you remember I told you once I was a friend of Jan Masaryk?"

"Yes."

"Well, I know things about Jan, Anna, which these people never want the world to know. I can't tell you what it is... it might put you in danger too. But they want to buy my silence, Anna. They'll let me leave if I give my word never to speak about what I know. And they'll let you come with me."

"Tomorrow?"

"Yes, darling. Tomorrow."

"But what about the children and Lenka?"

"Lukáš can come with us, but not Eva, Vilém or Lenka. They must stay here to ensure my silence."

"But that's impossible. We can't leave them."

"I have to leave them, Anna. I have no choice. If I stay they'll put me on trial. And you and Lukáš too. And Eva and Vilém's lives will be made intolerable."

"But will Lukáš come with us?"

"No, he won't. You're the only one now with a choice, Anna. I have to go. It's the only way to keep our family safe. But you can come with me, or you can stay here with Eva and Lukáš. When I'm gone, you'll all be allowed to live in peace. I believe them when they say that. They wouldn't dare hurt any of you."

"But how can I choose between you and the children? How could anyone expect me to do that? It's too cruel."

"It shows how far the Communists have come, Anna. My father told me the Tsars used to do this to people."

"Would I ever see you again? If I go with you, would I ever see the children again? Or little Lenka?"

"We have to be realistic, Anna. As long as the Communists are in power in our country, neither of us could ever come back."

Anna sat in silence. She took Tomáš's hands in hers and squeezed them hard.

"Are you alright, Anna?"

"Yes, I am, darling." She relaxed her grip. "I really am alright, because I realise these people can never harm us. Not you and me. They're trying to make everything as unbearable for us again as they can. And we won't let them. Will we, darling?"

Tomáš looked into her eyes.

"No, Anna. We won't."

"We won't let them break our love for one another, Tomáš. Or the faith we have in one another. They can't break our love for our family. They can never win. And we can never lose, whatever we decide."

"No, Anna, you and I can never lose."

"There is no decision to make, is there, Tomáš?"

"No."

"There's always the two of us together, whatever happens. Everything will be alright, my darling. It always has been."

"Yes, my wonderful Anna. Everything will be alright."

"I love you, Tomáš. I've always loved you. I always will love you. Kiss me."

Chapter Forty-Three

November 9th, 1989 – August 18th, 1990

Tomáš placed the flowers against the light-grey marble and stepped back from the graveside. Peruvian lilies were always Fran's favourite. She said they represented friendship and devotion. He knew little about flowers, but she knew everything about friendship and devotion. Whenever he visited her grave and Peruvian lilies were in season, he brought her a bouquet arranged with the best the florist could provide.

It was cold and blustery and it looked like rain. His shoulder ached. He read the words on the headstone again. *Francesca Annabelle Whitaker. Teacher. Born 17th May, 1926 - Died 15th June, 1982. Rest in Peace.* On every visit he regretted not having chosen a more worthy inscription for her. It had been down to him. She had no immediate next of kin and he had been closer to her than anyone. She deserved to have more said about her.

She was such a loyal and generous friend. He knew how she felt about him, and yet when he turned up on her doorstep after the deportation, he could see she was genuinely disappointed to see him there. She knew what it meant for him, and the pain he felt was more important to her than any feelings of her own. She had found him a teaching job at the girls' school where she was headmistress, and supported him again in his old life, caring nothing for the gossip her loyalty to him attracted.

Tomáš turned up the collar of his overcoat. 'See you soon, Fran.' He walked back to the car. It was only a five-minute drive to Fran's house in Kensington. He still thought of it as her house, although now legally it was his, as was everything she had once owned. He pulled into the gravel driveway and parked in front of the steps leading up to the front porch of the Victorian villa. As he opened the front door he looked down at the mat and saw two familiar envelopes. He picked them up and found a third lying underneath. All three were postmarked *'Praha'*. There was the usual one from Anna, a second from Eva, and... he smiled... a letter from Lukáš at last. He put them on the hall table and went into the kitchen. He would sit down and take his time reading them later with a cup of coffee in the lounge.

He looked out through the drizzle onto the back garden as he waited for the kettle to boil. He still couldn't get used to Fran not being there.

Even after seven years. And he had only moved in with her right at the end. At first she had hated the thought of him nursing her. But then, when she knew she had no choice, she allowed him in, and finally needed him with her constantly. "You take away the fear, Tom," she said. She had been peaceful at the end. Happy even. He felt he had helped with that.

The kettle clicked off. He sighed and took a mug from the cupboard. It was his greatest fear that the same might happen to Anna or Eva, and he wouldn't be able to get to them or do anything for them. He tried not to have such thoughts. He was determined not to be unhappy. He poured his coffee and went into the lounge.

He had made a pact with Anna in the police cell that they would live full and enjoyable lives, separate but never apart, and he had done all he could to stay true to that. He had been as good a teacher as he was capable of being, and since his retirement in 1981 he had published a collection of his poetry, and written the story of his and Anna's life, so that one day their grandchildren and great-grandchildren would know of the events which had shaped their world.

And he read a lot too, mostly news articles about Czechoslovakia and the Eastern bloc, and the banned plays and novels of the Czechoslovak dissidents, Pavel Kohout, Milan Kundera and Vaclav Havel, which he could buy easily enough in his local bookshop. His life was full, and he took care of himself and stayed healthy, so that his life would also be long. Long enough to take him through to a time when it might be possible to see his family again.

Recent events in the Soviet bloc had given him a faint reason for hope. He sat in his armchair and sipped his coffee. It probably began when Mikhail Gorbachev became leader of the Soviet Union in 1985. No, that wasn't right. It began earlier than that, with Lech Walesa and Solidarity in Poland back in 1980. But without Gorbachev's *glasnost* and *perestroika* Solidarity would never have won the landslide in the Polish elections last June. To think, the Poles elect a non-Communist government and the Soviets raise not one word of objection. Gorbachev and the Russians encouraging 'openness' and 'economic restructuring'. The very things Dubček wanted during the Prague Spring. The very things that caused the damned Russians to invade his country, and for him to be deported to London for the past twenty years. He put down his mug of coffee. He mustn't allow himself to get angry or frustrated. He had his pact with Anna.

Perhaps he should allow himself to hope a little. He had never known a Russian leader as popular in the West as Gorbachev. People seemed to believe him about wanting change. And he had stuck to his word so far about Russia not interfering in the affairs of other Eastern bloc countries. He had let the Hungarians take down their border with Austria in May, and thousands of people had poured across it ever since. And the Russians had done nothing so far to stop them. But he shouldn't get his hopes up too much. Knowing the Russians, it wouldn't be long before Gorbachev was ousted and some hardliner sent in the tanks.

He picked up the three letters from the coffee table. He would open Eva's first. After all, today was her special day. Her fiftieth birthday. God, Eva fifty. It was hard to believe. He peeled away the sellotape left by the censors. They weren't always so obvious, but it felt as if there were photos in this one, and they couldn't get those out with their damned tweezers. There was no glasnost in Czechoslovakia. Husák and his hardline Communist cronies in Prague were seeing to that.

He looked at the photos first. Eva had included one of her Uncle Otto and his family in Tel Aviv. It was a wonder they could all get into one photograph. And there was one of herself with husband Vilém and their Kamil on their recent holiday in the Tatra Mountains. Kamil was seventeen now. He was a fine young lad with his father's blond hair and broad smile, although it looked as if Vilém's hair had started to turn grey and thin a little. Eva looked well. She was smiling and looking very proud.

He looked at the next. It was of Eva holding Lenka's boy, little Tomášek. He was a big lad, too, for only two months. Eva looked so proud of her grandson, as she had a right to be. And there was a photo of Lenka with her husband, Jarek, both looking down at Tomášek in Jarek's arms. So much had happened in twenty years. He had missed so much. But they were all well and happy. That was the main thing.

He looked at the last photo. It was of Anna with their children, grandchildren and great-grandson. She was sitting on a chair in Eva's back garden. Behind her stood Lenka and Kamil with their arms around Eva, and then Lukáš with his wife, Irena, and their daughter, Izebela. My goodness. What a beautiful young woman she was becoming. You wouldn't think she was only the same age as Kamil. Anna was holding Tomášek, who looked fast asleep and oblivious to everything that was happening or had ever happened in the world. It was a precious photo. He would take it to be enlarged and framed. It could take pride of place on the sideboard with all the others.

He read Eva's letter. He was pleased the handbag and gloves had arrived safely. She was thrilled with them, she said. He had been worried they might get 'lost' on the way. But, to be fair, that hardly ever happened.

The deal he made with the StB man twenty years ago had been honoured in full. The post and parcels were all opened, but as long as everyone was careful with what they said and sent, they usually got through. A few from Lukáš never made it, but that was not surprising since his views had hardly moderated over the years. And yet he had been allowed to do well in spite of it. They all had.

He didn't think Eva ever understood why she and Vilém were offered a new apartment soon after he was deported, and then a few years later a house with its own garden. Something unheard of for non-Party members. She and Vilém had both got promotion, and Lenka was offered a place at Charles University in the department where her Uncle Lukáš lectured. Tomáš stood up and leaned against the sideboard, looking at his collection of framed photographs. The sacrifice had been worth it.

He sat back down and opened Anna's letter. She was as loving and positive as she always was, and wrote mostly about their family, as she always did. She knew it was what he wanted to hear about most. Her life had improved, too, after he left. She had been allowed to give up work at sixty, after being promoted to cleaning supervisor, and her years of retirement continued to be wonderful, she said. She got such pleasure from their growing family, as she was sure he did, and she was still enjoying the opportunity to follow the creativity her father had always encouraged in her. She had stopped painting for the time being, and was now designing and writing pop-up children's books with Tomášek in mind. She hoped he was happy and well, and she was leaving it to Lukáš to tell him of the exciting developments in Prague. "*I hope you enjoy Eva's photographs, my darling. You know I love you more with each day that passes. Your absence can only be counted in time and distance. I feel you are always beside me. Your Anna.*"

Tomáš raised himself from the armchair and walked into the kitchen. He stood by the sink and looked out again onto the garden. It never got easier. Never. Then he remembered the 'exciting developments in Prague' and went back to the lounge and sat down with Lukáš's letter. The tweezers had done their job on this one. He opened it and saw thick black lines drawn through much of what Lukáš had written, but he could still manage to get the gist of it.

The mood in Prague was very much like the spring of '68, Lukáš said, but only because the government had to allow reform now the people knew the Soviets would never intervene again. The Poles and Hungarians had tested the ground. They had turned their back on Communism, and the Soviet Union had not reacted. The tables were turned. The Russians were the reformists now and Husák was... the rest was blacked out, but he could guess that whatever lay beneath the censor's ink was not complimentary. But things were moving in the right direction, Lukáš insisted. Husák had recently put forward a new draft constitution which no longer mentioned the leading role of the Communist Party. Lukáš was clearly optimistic, and his idealism had not dimmed over the years. Tomáš was pleased about that.

He read on and came to a paragraph which was heavily censored. He tried to piece together what Lukáš was describing from what he had learned from the BBC news and the Times. East Germans were coming in their thousands to Prague. He already knew that. They were camping in the grounds of the West German embassy, waiting for a chance to get into Hungary, then through the open border to Austria and on to West Germany. He knew that too. But it appeared from Lukáš's letter that the Czechoslovak government had opened its own border, near Cheb, and was allowing East Germans to cross directly into Bavaria from there. The rest of the letter was blacked out, except for the last line. "*I wish you well, Táta. We all continue to miss you. Your loving son, Lukáš.*"

Near Cheb. My God. Czechoslovakia had opened its borders near Cheb. A crack had appeared. At last. He stood up. Could this be the chance to get them out? But there was nothing in the paper or on the television about it. What should he do? He looked at the carriage clock on the mantelpiece. It was twelve fifty-five. He switched on the television and waited for the lunchtime news.

It was the second item behind Margaret Thatcher's speech on climate change. But the news wasn't about Czechoslovakia opening *its* borders, only calls by the Husák government for East Germany to open its own borders to the West to stop the flow of 'escapees' into Prague. The Czechoslovak government spokesman saw no irony in complaining about his Communist neighbour keeping its borders closed, and 64,000 East Germans arriving in Prague over the past four days, while his own country's frontier remained steadfastly closed to the West. No mention about Czechoslovakia's borders being open at all. Had Lukáš got it wrong? The item closed with Václav Havel from the dissident group Charter 77 calling for all Eastern bloc citizens to be granted the basic freedom to travel wherever they wished. The reporter returned to the studio for the next item about Neil Kinnock's attack on Thatcher over the government's education policy and...

Tomáš got up and switched the television off. What could anyone expect? Nothing but talk, talk, talk... It was always best not to get your hopes up about anything. The main thing about today was Eva's fiftieth birthday. Forget everything else. He would go and get the photograph framed. Then he would buy a bottle of non-alcoholic wine to toast her over dinner. He put on his coat and outdoor shoes in the hallway and took his umbrella from the stand. He would have lunch at Rodrigo's.

The wine was remarkably good. English sparkling from Sussex. If he didn't know it was non-alcoholic, he would swear he was feeling a little light-headed. It was nine o'clock. Time for the evening news on the BBC. He hated the music that introduced it. He sipped his drink and turned up the volume, as the East German border story came on as the main item.

A picture of someone he had never seen or heard of before filled the screen. Günter Schabowski. Who the hell was he? A spokesman for the Central Committee of the East German Communist Party. He had announced earlier that evening that East Germany's borders with West Germany were to be opened, in order to relieve the pressure on his country's fraternal neighbours. An Italian reporter had then asked him when the open-border policy would come into effect. Unsure of the answer, Schabowski had hesitated and replied, "As far as I know, that goes into effect now. Immediately".

"We go over to our political correspondent, Brian Hanrahan, who is in East Berlin. What can you tell us, Brian?"

It was a confused scene. Thousands of East Berliners were congregating at the five main checkpoints along the Berlin Wall. They were demanding the border guards allow them through to West Berlin in line with the government announcement, but the guards seemed not to have received any orders to let them do so.

Behind the bespectacled reporter East Berliners of all ages were chanting, "*Gorbi, Gorbi, wir wollen raus!*" We want out.

"As you can see, there is a real sense of expectation here. This is Brian Hanrahan. East Berlin."

"Thankyou, Brian. We shall return to East Berlin later in the bulletin if there are any further developments in that story. And now in other news tonight..."

Tomáš kept the television on. What could be happening over there? He sat drinking his wine, with the sound down, through a situation comedy and then some film or other. If only he could call someone who could tell him more. But who? Calls to Prague had always been impossible. He looked at the carriage clock. Eleven o'clock. It was getting late. Time for bed. The film was interrupted by a newsflash. He turned up the volume.

"We interrupt this programme to go over to our political correspondent, Brian Hanrahan, in Berlin."

"Sensational news here. You may see from the scenes behind me that only a few minutes ago the checkpoints all along the Berlin Wall were opened by the East German border guards, and East Berliners are pouring through to be greeted by friends and family in the West, who some have not seen for the best part of fifty years..."

Tomáš sat forward, watching the euphoria on the faces of the people walking through the checkpoints, as bemused guards looked on at a scene which a few hours before would have taken place only in their worst nightmares.

People with joyous, beaming faces leaned out of the windows of their Trabants and waved at the cameras, as their vehicles inched through the openings in the wall. A lone figure climbed on top of the wall, a suicidal act earlier in the day, but now the spell was broken. The fear was gone. More and more people were lifted up, until dozens stood on the barrier between East and West and danced up and down and cheered. From somewhere a pickaxe was found and passed up to a young man on the wall, and he began hitting the reinforced concrete with little physical result, but with a huge psychological impact on the people watching. They cheered and laughed and cried and hugged one another.

Tomáš got to his feet, eyes glued to the television. His hands shook. He raised his wine glass and toasted the scenes in front of him. East Germany was open. My God. It was impossible now for the Communists to go back on this. "Anna," he mumbled. "My Anna." He put down his glass, slumped in his chair, and buried his face in his hands.

The snow was still falling outside Eva and Vilém's house in Bohnice in the northern part of the city. In their dining room the Christmas carp and potato salad had been cleared away, and Anna brought in gingerbread and fruit cake for the nine of them around the table. Tomášek lay fast asleep upstairs.

"I dare say this must be the best Christmas any Czechoslovak has ever had," said Lukáš.

"I don't know. We had some wonderful Christmases before the war," said Anna, placing more food on the table.

"Yes, but I'm thinking of what's happened since the Wall came down, Máma. I don't think our country has ever seen such change. And without any fighting or bloodshed. It's incredible. A miracle. A Velvet Revolution. I like that. It sums it up rather well, I think."

"I think you've had too much wine, darling," said Irena. Izabela and Kamil looked at one another and laughed.

"You two can laugh. But you don't know how incredible this is for us older ones. For the Communists to just give up power without a fight. It's... it's..."

"Incredible?" offered Izabela.

"Well it is. When we fought in '68, the Russians clung on for dear life."

"But I think it was 1968 that allowed all this to happen, Lukáš," said Eva. "It showed the whole world what the Soviets really were. The Russian people have a lot to thank Gorbachev for, ending the Cold War and showing a different side to them."

"We all have a lot to thank him for. He's a brave man," said Jarek. "When he said 'no more Iron Curtain', that was the moment. The Communists here knew then it was all over. It was a great moment."

"Do you know what the greatest moment was for me?" said Lukáš.

"I'm sure you're going to tell us, darling," said Irena.

"It was seeing Dubček and Havel together on the balcony in Wenceslas Square, the day the Presidium resigned. I'll never forget it."

"Do you think Havel will be elected president on Friday, Uncle Lukáš?"

"I do, Kamil. I can't imagine a single person in the country not voting for Civic Forum. Without them none of this would have happened. The demonstrations. The general strike."

"I thought the students organised that." said Kamil.

"They did, but the hardliners have never negotiated with students. It was Civic Forum who convinced Husák and the rest of them their time was up."

"Your Uncle Lukáš was quite an agitator himself in his student days, you know," said Eva.

"What do you mean 'was'. He's been agitating all his life," said Anna, and everyone around the table laughed.

"It's a wonder you kept your job sometimes, dear brother, considering some of the things you've written over the years."

"You know, Eva, I've often thought that myself. I've seen colleagues held back for doing much less than I've done, but they never seemed to bother with me. Perhaps I wasn't as outspoken as I thought I was."

"You've been lucky, Lukáš," said Vilém. "But I think we all have over the years, haven't we?"

"You all have your táta to thank for that," said Anna.

"What do you mean, Máma?" asked Eva.

"Nothing really..."

"Nothing?"

"I only mean your father set a good example to us all. He made us try hard in everything we did. He has watched over us."

Vilém filled everyone's glass during the silence.

"I'm surprised none of you has mentioned him this evening," said Anna.

"We didn't want to upset you, Máma. We've all been wondering why Táta hadn't come back to Prague already. I have asked him, but he won't say anything in his letters."

"He can't come until he's sure the Communists have gone forever, Eva."

"Are you going to join him in England now, Máma?" asked Lukáš.

"No, my darling. If Václav Havel wins the election next week, your father's going to get a flight to Prague right away. He's going to come back to us. For good."

"Is that really the house where you were born, Děda?"

"Yes, Izabela, it is."

All ten members of the family, eleven with Tomášek asleep in Jarek's arms, stood on the bridge over the Ohře in Cheb and looked at the tall, narrow house with its dull grey render and flat roof.

"I hope you don't mind me saying, Děda, but it's not very nice, is it?"

"It was once, darling. And do you know what I'm going to do?"

"No."

"I'm going to buy it, and then I'm going to make it look as it was when I was a boy and I lived there with my mother and father. It will have a beautiful tiled roof, and black beams showing again on the outside, and all the rest painted white. It will be a late Golden Wedding present for your Babička, and a holiday home for us all."

"Did you like living there, Děda?"

"Yes, darling. Very much."

"What were my great-grandparents called?"

"Pavel and Karolina."

"What were they like?"

Tomáš looked at his granddaughter and smiled.

"They were everything that's good in the world, Izabela. They would be very proud of you all."

"And of you, Děda."

"Thankyou, darling. That's a lovely thing to say. Now, let me show you where my grandparents and Babička's grandparents used to live."

They walked along the road to Františkovy Lázně and turned off onto the track leading to Skalka. Izabela ran to catch up with Kamil and they walked together, chatting and laughing. Lenka walked behind them with her husband, Jarek, who was still carrying Tomášek. Eva and Vilém followed with Lukáš and Irena. It was a fine summer day. Anna and Tomáš stayed back, watching their family walking together in front of them.

"Turn right down through the woods in about a hundred metres," Tomáš called after them. Without looking back Lukáš raised his hand to acknowledge his father's instructions. Tomáš looked at Anna and they smiled at one another.

"Come on," she said.

"Wait a moment, Anna. Let me just watch them for a few more moments. We haven't done badly together, have we?"

"No, darling Tomáš. I think we've done rather well. I can't wait for Otto and his family to meet them all next week. I'll be so proud." She took his hand. "Come on. I want to show Eva and Lukáš the lake."

When they reached the clearing at the end of the track through the woods, everyone was standing by the water's edge.

"I did warn you," said Tomáš, "about the pollution. But at least the dreadful smell has gone."

"Have you seen the sign over there, Tomáš?" asked Vilém.

Tomáš looked over to where the chata once stood.

"What does it say? I can't read it from here."

"It's in German, as well as Czech. A Munich company is going to build holiday flats here. They're going to clean up the lake and create a beach where we're standing."

Tomáš looked at Anna. "My goodness, Anna, what would our grandparents say? And my father?"

"I dread to think."

"Is it progress, Anna?"

"I don't know, darling. It's change. But I think you and I can deal with change, don't you?"

"I think we can." He leaned forward and kissed her.

"Babička and Děda, would you like me to take a photo of you both by the lake?"

"Yes, that would be nice, Kamil."

"Why don't you take it over there by that tree?" said Eva. "It will look beautiful with the red fruit."

"What do you think, Anna? Shall we?"

She put her arm around his waist and he put his arm around her shoulders, and they walked together to the cherry tree at the edge of the wood. Everyone followed and watched as Kamil took his photos.

"I've taken six. Is it alright if Izabela and I go for a walk round Štasný Lake now, Auntie Irena?"

"Yes, I don't see why not. But take some water with you. It's very hot."

Tomáš stood under the tree and watched the two young people walk off together. As they turned along the lakeside path, and they thought they were out of sight, he saw them take each other's hand. He looked over at Anna sitting in the shade under the tree with Tomášek. She was watching their children examining the last remnants of the chata. She looked serene and very beautiful. He looked down at Tomášek.

"No, no, Tomášek. You mustn't eat cherries. I know they taste nice, but they have nasty stones inside. And the ones on the ground sometimes have maggots in them. You wouldn't like that, my lovely boy. Come here to me."

Tomášek looked puzzled that his great-Děda would deny him these lovely bright-red objects that felt and smelled so nice, but he let it pass. He felt strong hands lift him, and a force, both powerful and wonderfully gentle, raised him high into the air.

Biographies

Eduard Beneš (1884-1948)
Foreign Minister (1918-1935) and President (1935-1938, 1945-1948) of Czechoslovakia.

Leonid Brezhnev (1906-1982)
General Secretary of the Central Committee of the Communist Party of the Soviet Union (1964-1982).

Josef Bühler (1904-1948)
Deputy Governor-General of the Polish occupied territories in World War 2. Tried and executed by the Polish authorities for crimes against humanity.

Winston Churchill (1874-1965)
British Prime Minister (10 May 1940 – 26 July 1945 and 1951 – 1955).

François Darlan (1881-1942)
Admiral of the French navy. Minister of Marine in Vichy France. Prime Minister of Vichy France (1941-1942). Assassinated by anti-Vichy monarchist in French Algeria.

Marcia Davenport (1903 – 1996)
American writer and fiancée of Jan Masaryk. In her 1967 autobiography, *Too Strong for Fantasy*, she wrote of the events leading up to Jan Masaryk's death.

Alexander Dubček (1921-1992)
Slovak politician. First Secretary of the Communist Party of Czechoslovakia (January 1968 - April 1969) during the Prague Spring. Expelled from the Communist Party in 1970. Chairman of the Federal Assembly (1989-1992) after the Velvet Revolution.

Adolf Eichmann (1906-1962)
Lieutenant-Colonel in the SS. A leading organiser of the Holocaust. Kidnapped by Israeli Mossad agents in Argentina in 1960. Tried and executed in Israel for genocide.

Charles de Gaulle (1890-1970)
Brigadier-General in the French Army. Leader of Free French Forces in World War 2 (1940-1944). President of France ((1959-1969).

Reinhard Heydrich (1904-1942)
SS-Obergruppenführer. Deputy Protector of Bohemia and Moravia (1941-1942). One of the main architects of the Holocaust. Assassinated in Prague by Czech agents trained by the British Special Operations Executive. Died of wounds on 4 June 1942.

Friedrich Wilhelm Kritzinger (1890-1947)
German bureaucrat. Reich Chancellery Representative at the Wannsee Conference. Publicly declared his shame at the atrocities committed by the Nazi regime.

Rudolf Lange (1910-1945?)
Colonel in the SS, responsible for extermination of the Jewish population in Latvia. Attendee at the Wannsee Conference. Killed or committed suicide in the battle for Poznań, 23 February 1945.

Martin Luther (1895 – 1945)
Advisor to Foreign Minister von Ribbentrop and attendee at the Wannsee Conference. His copy of the minutes of the conference was discovered in 1947, providing an account of what had been discussed there. Sent to Sachsenhausen concentration camp in 1944 for disloyalty to von Ribbentrop. Liberated in 1945, but died shortly after.

Georges Mandel (1885-1944)
Journalist, politician and resistance leader. Outspoken opponent of Fascism in the 1930s. Government minister from 1936. Minister of Interior under Paul Reynaud (1940). Described by Churchill as 'the first resister'. Arrested by Vichy in 1941 and sent to Buchenwald. Executed by the French Milice on 7 July 1944.

Jan Masaryk ((1886-1948)
Son of Tomáš Masaryk. Czechoslovak Ambassador in London (1925-1938). Foreign Minister (1940-1948). The Czechoslovak Communist government ascribed his death to suicide. A reinvestigation after the Velvet Revolution concluded he was murdered. The highest-ranking, post-war Soviet defector confirmed Masaryk had been on a Kremlin hit list.

Tomáš Masaryk (1850-1937)
Academic, philosopher, teacher, politician. Founder and first President of Czechoslovakia (1918-1935).

Alice Masaryková (1879-1966)
Sociologist and teacher. Daughter of Tomáš Masaryk. Appointed head of the Czechoslovakian Red Cross in 1919. Exiled from Czechoslovakia from 1938 until 1945, and again after the Communist takeover in 1948. Lived the remainder of her life in the United States.

František Moravec (1895-1966)
Czechoslovak army officer, legionnaire and military intelligence officer. Helped plan assassination of Reinhard Heydrich. Left Czechoslovakia after the Communist takeover. Settled in the United States and worked as an intelligence advisor in the US Department of Defence.

Heinrich Müller (1900-1945?)
Chief of Gestapo (1935-1945). Attended the Wannsee Conference. Present in Hitler's bunker at the time of Hitler's suicide. No trace of Müller was ever found.

Jan Palach (1948-1969)
Czech student of history and political economy at Charles University. Died by self-immolation in protest at the Russian invasion during the Prague Spring and the subsequent demoralisation of fellow Czechoslovaks. One month later a lesser-known student, Jan Zajíc, committed suicide on the same spot by the same method.

Philippe Pétain (1856-1951)
Soldier and Marshal of France. Hero of Verdun in World War 1. Chief of State of Vichy France (1940-1944). Tried for treason in 1945 and sentenced to death. Commuted to life imprisonment by order of General de Gaulle. Died in prison on the Ile d'Yeu, an island off the French Atlantic coast.

Paul Reynaud (1878-1966)
Politician and lawyer. Prime Minister of France (21 March - 16 June 1940). Refused to participate in Vichy government. Arrested by Vichy in June 1940 and imprisoned in Germany for the duration of the war. Returned to political life in France after the war and held several ministerial posts.

Augustin Schramm (1907 – 1948)
Sudeten German who became a political commissar (rank of major) and an NKVD agent. Implicated in the murder of Jan Masaryk. Shot dead shortly after in his own flat, probably because of what he knew.

Edward Spears (1886-1974)
Major-General and Member of Parliament. Liaison officer between British and French governments in both world wars. Churchill's personal representative to the French premier. Lost his parliamentary seat in 1945 and became chairman of the Institute of Directors.

Wilhelm Stuckart (1902-1953)
Lawyer and state secretary in the Nazi Interior Ministry. SS-Obergruppenführer. Leading Nazi legal expert who helped frame the anti-Jewish Nuremburg Laws. Attendee at the Wannsee conference. Arrested in 1945 for complicity in the Holocaust and tried in 1948. Sentenced to three years and ten months (time served). On release held posts in local government. Killed in car crash in mysterious circumstances.

Maxime Weygand (1867-1965)
Brigadier-General in World War 1. Appointed Supreme Commander of French forces during the military crisis of May 1940. Served the Vichy government but was against full collaboration. Arrested in 1942 and detained in Germany. Held as collaborator after the war but cleared of all charges in 1948.

Sabine Zlatin (1907-1996)
Polish-born Jewish nurse who took French citizenship and trained with the French Red Cross. Helped to secure release of Jewish children from internment camps at Agde and Rivesaltes. Set up home for Jewish refugee children at Izieu near Lyons. Forty-two of the children and five adults were arrested by Klaus Barbie of Lyons Gestapo in 1944. All were murdered in Auschwitz. Zlatin evaded capture and testified against Barbie at his trial in 1987.

Made in the USA
Lexington, KY
30 July 2017